PRAISE FOR SUSAN STOKER

FOR *JUSTICE FOR MACKENZIE*

"Daxton's desperation to find Mackenzie is rousing and believable, and readers will have a white-knuckle read until the end . . . pure entertainment."

—*Kirkus Reviews*

"Irresistible characters and seat-of-the-pants action will keep you glued to the pages."

—Elle James, *New York Times* bestselling author

"Susan does romantic suspense right! Edge of my seat + smokin' hot = read ALL of her books! Now."

—Carly Phillips, *New York Times* bestselling author

"Susan Stoker writes the perfect book boyfriends!"

—Laurann Dohner, *New York Times* bestselling author

"These books should come with a warning label. Once you start, you can't stop until you've read them all."

—Sharon Hamilton, *New York Times* bestselling author

FOR *RESCUING RAYNE*

"Another winner! Sexy and action-packed—what I've come to expect from Susan Stoker!"

Times bestselling author

"Nobody does intense action better than Susan Stoker."

—Desiree Holt, *USA Today* bestselling author

"Susan Stoker packs one heck of a punch!"

—Lainey Reese, *USA Today* bestselling author

"Susan Stoker gives me everything I need in romance: heat, humor, intensity, and the perfect HEA."

—Carrie Ann Ryan, *New York Times* bestselling author

"Stoker delivers with a masterful, simmering sexual tension that keeps you on the edge of your seat."

—Nana Malone, *USA Today* bestselling author

"Susan Stoker never disappoints. She delivers alpha males with heart and heroines with moxie."

—Jana Aston, *New York Times* bestselling author

"No one does military romance like Susan Stoker!"

—Corinne Michaels, *New York Times* bestselling author

"Susan Stoker knows what women want. A hot hero who needs to save a damsel in distress . . . even if she can save herself!"

—CD Reiss, *New York Times* bestselling author

"When you pick up a Susan Stoker book you know exactly what you're going to get . . . a hot alpha hero and a smart, sassy heroine. I can't get enough!"

—Jessica Hawkins, *USA Today* bestselling author

"I love reading about men in uniform and Susan always delivers . . . the full package!"

—Kayti McGee, *USA Today* bestselling author

"Susan writes the perfect blend of tough, alpha heroes and strong yet vulnerable heroines. I always feel emotionally satisfied at the end of one of her stories!"

—Meghan March, *New York Times* bestselling author

"One thing I love about Susan Stoker's books is that she knows how to deliver a perfect HEA while still making sure the villain gets what he/she deserves!"

—T.M. Frazier, *New York Times* bestselling author

DEFENDING HARLOW

DISCOVER OTHER TITLES BY SUSAN STOKER

Mountain Mercenaries Series

Defending Allye

Defending Chloe

Defending Morgan

Defending Harlow

Defending Everly (TBA)

Defending Zara (TBA)

Defending Raven (TBA)

Ace Security Series

Claiming Grace

Claiming Alexis

Claiming Bailey

Claiming Felicity

Claiming Sarah (Sept. 2019)

Delta Force Heroes Series

Rescuing Rayne

Rescuing Aimee (novella)

Rescuing Emily

Rescuing Harley

Marrying Emily

Rescuing Kassie

Rescuing Bryn

Rescuing Casey

Rescuing Sadie (novella)

Rescuing Wendy

Rescuing Mary

Rescuing Macie (novella, April 2019)

Badge of Honor: Texas Heroes Series

Justice for Mackenzie

Justice for Mickie

Justice for Corrie

Justice for Laine (novella)

Shelter for Elizabeth

Justice for Boone

Shelter for Adeline

Shelter for Sophie

Justice for Erin

Justice for Milena

Shelter for Blythe

Justice for Hope

Shelter for Quinn

Shelter for Koren (July 2019)

Shelter for Penelope (Oct. 2019)

SEAL of Protection Series

Protecting Caroline

Protecting Alabama

Protecting Fiona

Marrying Caroline (novella)

Protecting Summer

Protecting Cheyenne

Protecting Jessyka

Protecting Julie (novella)

Protecting Melody

Protecting the Future

Protecting Kiera (novella)

Protecting Dakota

SEAL of Protection: Legacy Series

Securing Caite

Securing Sidney

Securing Piper (Sept. 2019)

Securing Zoey (TBA)

Securing Avery (TBA)

Securing Kalee (TBA)

Beyond Reality Series

Outback Hearts

Flaming Hearts

Frozen Hearts

Stand-Alone Novels

The Guardian Mist

A Princess for Cale

A Moment in Time (a short story collection)

Lambert's Lady

Writing as Annie George

Stepbrother Virgin (erotic novella)

DEFENDING HARLOW

Mountain Mercenaries, Book 4

Susan Stoker

Published by Montlake Romance, Seattle

www.apub.com

ISBN-13: 9781542042802
ISBN-10: 1542042801

Cover design by Eileen Carey

Cover photography by Wander Aguiar

Printed in the United States of America

DEFENDING HARLOW

Chapter One

Lowell "Black" Lockard was bored.

He leaned back in his office chair, linked his hands behind his head, and stared unseeingly out of his window.

The occasional pop-pop-pop from a weapon penetrated through the insulation in his office. It was a comforting sound, one that Black had gotten used to over the years. Owning a shooting range wasn't exactly what he'd seen himself doing after getting out of the Navy, but here he was.

He enjoyed the work. Enjoyed getting to know the men and women who came to practice their shooting skills. He took pride in the gun and personal-safety classes he taught. But the fact of the matter was that, lately, his life seemed to be missing something.

It wasn't just that the Mountain Mercenaries hadn't been called to go on a mission in a month. It was more. Seeing his friends and teammates falling in love brought attention to the saddest fact of his life—it was routine. Normally he liked that, but with all the stories from his friends about how their women kept them on their toes . . . he couldn't help but wish he had something similar to fill his time.

Black figured a good, hard mission would break him of his ennui. And he knew that made him an asshole. It wasn't that he *wanted* a woman or child to be kidnapped or abused, but anytime someone in need reached out to Rex, their handler, for assistance, Black had a clear purpose. He felt most useful and fulfilled when he was helping others. He'd spent his entire life rushing in when others needed aid—and sitting around an office definitely didn't make him feel needed.

His cell phone rang, tearing Black out of his musings, and he sat forward to look at the screen.

Unknown.

He almost didn't answer it. The last thing he wanted to do was talk to a telemarketer or scammer, but since he was bored, he figured he may as well pick up.

"Hello?"

"Is this Lowell Lockard?"

Black didn't recognize the voice. "Speaking."

"Hi, Lowell. This is Harlow Reese. We spoke a few weeks ago?"

At the sound of her name, Black sat up straight in his chair. Anticipation churned in his gut. Harlow was exactly what he needed . . . in an entirely different way. "Yeah. I expected you to call sooner," he playfully chided.

The woman on the other end of the phone chuckled, and Black smiled at the sound. He liked her voice. It was low and husky. Even her laugh was attractive.

He shook his head at his insane musings. He wasn't looking for what Gray, Ro, and Arrow had. He was perfectly happy simply dating, though he hadn't done even that lately.

He couldn't imagine settling down with one woman for the rest of his life. He wasn't a manwhore, but he enjoyed the dating game. Getting to know someone. Flirting. The anticipation that led up to taking her to bed for the first time.

He tried to concentrate on what Harlow was saying.

"—didn't call. I figured I was overreacting. But . . . the situation has changed, and I was wondering if you might be willing to come back and teach more personal-safety classes for all the women here at the shelter."

The seriousness of Harlow's voice and the implication of her words hit Black hard and fast.

He'd last been to the First Hope Women's Shelter about a month ago on the Mountain Mercenaries' usual rotation. Around once a month, one of them would go to the shelter to interact with the women and children who resided there and make sure all was well. The men also did odd jobs and taught the women personal safety. First Hope was a transition shelter, where women could live until they found affordable housing, got a job, and basically got their feet under them again after whatever life situation had landed them there in the first place. Loretta Royster, the building owner and shelter director, did what she could to keep everyone safe.

Black knew Harlow from high school. It was crazy that they'd both ended up in Colorado Springs after growing up in Kansas. She was a year younger than him, but they'd been in the yearbook club together his senior year. Seeing her at the shelter was a surprise; she'd just been hired on as the chef.

She'd told him a month ago that she was being harassed, and she had inquired about a gun-safety class for herself. Black had mentally vowed to call her if she didn't get in touch with him, but he hadn't.

He regretted that now.

In his defense, he sort of figured that her not calling meant the harassment had stopped. That wasn't a good excuse, however. He should've followed up, and not just because he'd been intrigued by seeing a woman he knew from his past.

"The situation has changed?" he asked. "In what way?"

"Well, when I saw you last, I was the only one the men were harassing. But it's now come to my attention that it's everyone."

"What do the cops say? You *have* been to the cops, right?"

"Of course," Harlow said with a huff. "I'm not an idiot. Loretta has talked to them several times, but since the guys haven't actually *done* anything to us, there's not much they can do."

Black was confused. "Then what are they doing?"

"Stupid stuff. Catcalling when any of the women come and go from the building. They sometimes follow us to the parking lot when we leave. They haven't put their hands on us or come very close, but they're there, watching, mocking us. Things like that. It's freaking out the women and kids, and I hate to see everyone so upset."

"Of course I'll help," Black reassured her. "Do you know the men who're bothering you?"

"No. They're young. Like late teens or early twenties. They hang around the neighborhood. I don't think they care that we see them because technically they're not doing anything illegal. But they hang out in that new park down the street from the building or outside the tattoo shop across the street. The residents don't want to go outside by themselves, and they won't let their kids go play at the park either."

"You working at the shelter this afternoon?"

"Today?" Harlow asked in surprise.

"Yeah, Harl. Today."

"Well, yeah. At least until around four. Zoe comes in then."

"Zoe?"

"The other cook. Loretta hired her about a week after me. When I'm not here, she is, and vice versa. That way all the meals for the residents are covered," Harlow explained.

"She being harassed too?" Black asked.

"Yeah. Everyone is. And it's weird, because Zoe is sixty. She doesn't look it, not with her pink hair and all, but I don't understand why those punks are picking on all of us. Loretta thinks it could be one of the residents' exes who maybe hired them, but since they aren't hurting us or destroying property, the cops won't look into it, and so we have no way of finding out."

Black's heart rate increased. The more she told him about the situation, the more concerned he got.

"Anyway," Harlow went on, "I think maybe meeting with you again and being able to ask more questions and having you show everyone some basic things they can do to protect themselves will give them more confidence."

Black looked at his watch and said, "I'll be there in an hour."

There was silence on the phone for a moment before Harlow asked, "Seriously?"

"Seriously."

"I didn't mean—You don't have to come today. I just . . . you said to call if I felt uneasy."

"Right. And you called me because you aren't comfortable with the situation, and I can do something about it."

Black would do something about it, all right. He would've told Harlow he'd be there in thirty minutes, except he needed to call Rex and inform him of what was going on. He also needed to call Meat, their resident computer expert. Meat could start looking into the ex-husbands and boyfriends of the shelter's residents.

Black knew he was possibly going overboard, that maybe the punks had no connection to anyone and were just getting their kicks scaring the residents at the shelter, but he didn't think so. The building wasn't in the best part of the city, but it wasn't the worst either. Colorado Springs was putting some money into the area, including tax breaks for businesses who opened up there and incentives to developers to try to revitalize the area.

Harlow had been harassed for at least a month now. He doubted the men bothering her would still be doing so just for shits and giggles. Once again, he was pissed at himself for not calling to check on her.

The back of his neck was tingling, a sure sign that more was up with the situation.

Black was happy to have something to do to keep himself busy and satisfy his need to be useful—but more than that, he was looking forward to seeing Harlow. She'd been on his mind over the last month, and he was grateful for any excuse to see her again.

"Go tell Loretta I'll be there in a while. I'll talk to her about what's been going on and what measures are in place to protect the residents. You'll be safe in the meantime?"

He heard the amusement in her voice when she said, "I'm thirty-four years old and have essentially been on my own for sixteen of those years. I think I can manage to survive for the sixty or so minutes it'll take you to get here."

Black smiled. He liked her sass. "Right. Then I'll see you soon."

"Lowell?"

The smile on his face grew at hearing Harlow use his given name again. It had been a long time since anyone had used it, other than his family. Hearing it in Harlow's low, husky voice made his belly churn with anticipation. "Yeah, Harl?"

"Thanks. I know it's been a long time since we've seen each other, or even thought about each other. I just . . . everyone is nervous, and when the cops couldn't do anything, we were kinda at a loss as to what to do. I appreciate you offering to give the classes. I can pay for them. I mean, I was the one who called you."

"We'll talk about it when I get there," Black told her.

There was no way anyone would be paying him for anything. The women's shelter was important to Rex and the rest of the Mountain Mercenaries. Loretta had helped them out time and time again when they'd needed her assistance with a woman or child they'd rescued. Rex would be upset that Loretta herself hadn't called, but Black and the rest of his team would offer whatever help the shelter needed, gratis.

"Okay. Drive safe," Harlow said. "Bye."

She hung up before Black could say a word. He clicked off his phone and stared into space for a long moment. It had been ages since anyone had told him to drive safe, at least someone who wasn't related to him. His parents were great, but they lived on the other side of the country in Orlando. He spoke to them frequently, and while they always told him they loved him, they didn't worry about him, per se.

His brother was a photographer who traveled around the world taking pictures for magazines and organizations. He was five years younger than Black, and always seemed to be getting into questionable situations. Of course, Black was too, but his parents didn't know about that. So Lance was the Lockard their parents worried about.

Harlow probably didn't mean anything by her words. She probably told everyone to be careful. But still, hearing them made something inside Black sit up and take notice.

Deciding right then and there that he was going to ask Harlow Reese out, Black smiled. It had been a long time since he'd really pursued a specific woman, and he was looking forward to getting back in the game.

Still smiling, Black picked up his phone and dialed Rex's number. He needed to tell his handler what was going on. At the moment, he had no information, but Rex didn't like surprises. It was better to talk to him up front and bring him details later than to blindside him with a situation after the fact.

Chapter Two

Harlow rolled and cut the dough, then placed it on the cookie sheet without thought. She could make biscuits in her sleep, which was a good thing, because her attention was definitely not on cooking at the moment.

She had been debating with herself about whether to call Lowell for a week and had finally gotten up the nerve to do it.

When she'd first seen him all those weeks ago, she'd been merely annoyed with the men who yelled things at her when she arrived at the shelter and who liked to hang around the parking lot when she left. She'd thought that learning more self-defense and maybe even a bit about gun safety would be a good thing. She'd thought it was only *her* they were harassing, but when she overheard some of the residents talking about the punks doing the same things to them a week ago, she knew she had to do something.

Because it wasn't only the women who were scared. The kids were too. And that was unacceptable for Harlow. She didn't like it when men used strength or intimidation to abuse women, but when they started in on children, it crossed a line for her. Five kids lived at the shelter at the moment, and it was easy to see they were scared by the harassment.

Jasper Newton was the oldest at thirteen. He was slightly overweight and constantly tripping over his own feet. He was the protector of the group, probably trying to compensate for the fact that his father had abused his mother for years. The abuse had stopped only because Wyatt had up and left his wife and child one day, telling them he didn't want a family anymore, didn't love them, and had found a new girlfriend.

Harlow knew Jasper and his mom were better off, but the young boy had obviously suffered mentally as a result of everything his dad had put him through.

Lacie Bronson was eleven and never really said much. Harlow didn't know her story, but whatever had happened to her and her mom to make them need the services of the shelter had obviously been traumatizing for both.

Milo Hamlin was nine and, while wary, still laughed a lot and made friends easily. Samantha Royal was eight and went to the same school as Milo. They were in the same class as well. Sammie had a crush on Milo and followed him everywhere.

At five, the youngest child in the shelter was Jody Zimmerman. She was an inquisitive girl who spent every moment she could in the kitchen with Harlow. She had beautiful red hair and green eyes. Her mom was young, only twenty-three, as had been her late boyfriend. He'd been killed by a drunk driver days before he was supposed to join the Army, and because of a lack of money and no help from their relatives, Jody and her mom had ended up homeless.

Harlow would do anything to protect the kids who resided in the home. She'd always had a soft spot for children. Their parents' situations were no fault of the kids, and she wanted to do whatever she could to give them some good memories of their childhood. If that was only through food, so be it.

Harlow welcomed the kids into her kitchen with open arms. They often wandered in, carrying books to do homework at the big dinner table or just wanting something to do, and she put them to work assisting with whatever meal she was currently working on. Knowing that most of them had been denied enough food to fill their bellies because of their financial situations, she always had snacks on hand as well.

Every time their mothers had a group meeting, Harlow brought the kids into the kitchen to teach them how to make something new. One day it might be cookies, and another it could be bread. She loved watching them have fun and enjoyed her time with them.

It was mostly because of the kids that she'd called Lowell Lockard.

She'd recognized him the second she'd seen him. They'd gone to the same high school in Topeka, Kansas, and once upon a time she'd had the biggest crush on him. But he was out of her league. Way too popular for the likes of her. She was the girl who liked to hide behind her camera, taking pictures of others rather than being in the spotlight. She'd made a go at being a photographer, but eventually realized she much preferred cooking to being behind a lens.

Lowell had been funny and nice to her when they were teenagers. He hadn't looked down on her, and he'd actually complimented her more than once on the pictures she'd taken. Harlow had known he was going to enlist in the Navy when he graduated, and she'd admired him for wanting to serve his country.

She'd wanted to date him more than she'd wanted her next breath, but even back then she hadn't had the best luck with boys and dating.

After he'd graduated, she hadn't heard anything about him or seen him again—until he'd shown up in the middle of the living room at the women's shelter. It had been a shock, but she hadn't been surprised to learn he owned a local gun range and occasionally volunteered his time at First Hope. She'd heard all about the men who came by every month to help out around the shelter and spend time with the residents. Even back in high school, Lowell had been a champion for those who couldn't defend themselves.

Harlow was a bit chagrined to discover her crush on him was just as strong today as it had been when she was a teenager. He'd grown into one hell of a fine specimen. They were around the same height, but Lowell was all man now. There was no sign of the lanky boy he'd been. His arms were muscular, and his thighs bulged under his jeans. He had a few visible scars, which told her that he'd been through some tough times.

But it was more than his looks. Harlow was well past the age when her head was turned by a good-looking man. She'd met and dated enough men to know that it wasn't what people looked like that made them a good match. It was who they were deep down.

Lowell played with the kids and was a pro at reading the new residents' body language. When Carrie had taken a step backward upon meeting him, he didn't reach out a hand to shake hers, but simply nodded and gave her some space. When Sue refused to meet his eyes, he didn't make her uncomfortable in any way. He just moved on to greet the next woman.

He even had no problem sitting on the floor with Jody and playing dolls with the little girl.

Yes, everything Harlow had seen about Lowell that day a month ago called to her—but she had refused to give in to temptation. She was the poster child for bad dates, and the last thing she wanted was to be disappointed by a horrible date with her high school crush.

She'd decided to admire him from afar and ignore his previous offer of help. But after Sammie had come into the kitchen one recent afternoon, crying because one of the men who hung around the park told her to enjoy sleeping in her bed because she wouldn't have one much longer, Harlow decided enough was enough.

She'd gotten up the courage to call Lowell, and without hesitation, he'd said he'd come right over. That had surprised her. She figured he'd have to fit her and the shelter into his schedule. Never in a million years would she have assumed he'd come over the same day.

"Harlow?"

The feminine voice startled Harlow so badly, she jerked and almost dropped the baking sheet on the floor. Shaking her head at her own clumsiness, she looked up to see Loretta standing in the doorway.

The older woman looked way younger than her sixty-five years. She had embraced her gray hair, and it looked amazing on her. Her blue eyes popped even more with the silver color. She had laugh lines around her eyes and mouth and always had a smile for everyone. Today she was wearing a pair of jeans that molded to her body and a T-shirt that said **SIXTY IS THE NEW TWENTY.**

Harlow quickly turned to the sink to wash her hands. "Hi, Loretta. Can I get you something?"

The other woman shook her head. "Oh no. I'm still stuffed from that delicious breakfast you made. Hiring you and Zoe was the best decision I ever made in regard to this place."

Harlow smiled as she dried her hands. "I'm thrilled you hired us too," she told the older woman. Harlow had been working in a fancy hotel in Seattle and had gotten so burned out, she'd decided to make a change. She'd been looking at restaurants in the Denver area when one of the hotel managers had told her about the job opening here in Colorado Springs. It wasn't something Harlow had considered, but after hearing all about Loretta, how long she'd lived in the area, and how she'd been helping out residents for over thirty years, applying felt like the right thing to do.

Harlow had only been in the Springs for a short while, but she loved it. Enjoyed being able to go hiking, appreciated the fresh air, loved looking out the window of her apartment and seeing Pikes Peak. She felt safe here too, even though the shelter wasn't in the best neighborhood.

The city was trying to revitalize the area, which was code for *cleaning it up*. Most of the storefronts around the shelter were still empty, but a few blocks down, new stores and restaurants were opening almost every week. There were also expensive condos being developed several streets over, which would bring customers to the new businesses.

"Did you get ahold of Black?" Loretta asked.

Harlow nodded. "Yes. I was going to tell you, but I needed to get these biscuits in the oven," she told the older woman. "He's going to come over today to talk to you."

She watched Loretta's shoulders sag in relief.

Feeling guilty that it had taken her so long to call Lowell, Harlow quickly tried to reassure her. "I'm sure he'll figure out what's going on, and if those boys are just punks, he'll set them straight and send them on their way. He also said he was happy to meet with the residents and teach them more self-defense."

"Good . . . that's good," Loretta said. Then she sighed. "Getting old sucks. Once upon a time, I would've gone toe-to-toe with those boys."

Harlow took a longer look at her boss—and didn't like what she saw. There were bags under her eyes, and her brow was furrowed in concern. "Has something else happened?"

"Something else?" Loretta asked tiredly. "You mean other than the fact my residents are being harassed and we can't figure out why, the cops' hands are tied, I have a waiting list twenty names deep with no room for the women who need help, *and* I have a date tomorrow night?"

"You have a date?" Harlow asked, her brows shooting up in surprise, ignoring everything else she'd said. It wasn't that she didn't think Loretta could or should date; the other woman was beautiful and had a heart the size of Texas. But she hadn't heard of any particular man in her life.

Loretta's lips quirked. "I'm too old to date, but yes. Edward wouldn't take no for an answer. He's taking me out for dinner."

Harlow knew who Loretta was talking about. Edward O'Connor. He was an Irishman who owned a bakery on the other end of the street from the shelter. He frequently brought over day-old sweets and bread that would normally be thrown away. Harlow could bake, but having the sweets delivered made her life a lot easier in the mornings. She liked the older man and was tickled pink that he'd asked Loretta out.

"I once went on a date where the guy kept leaning over the table and taking food off my plate. He'd use his fork to spear a piece of shrimp, saying"—Harlow lowered her voice—"'You don't mind if I have a taste, do you?' And without waiting for me to say yes or no, he'd just take my food."

Loretta smiled. "You and your bad luck, child. I can't believe some of the stories you've told me about your dates. Are you sure you aren't stretching the truth a wee bit?"

Harlow returned the smile. "Absolutely not. Every single thing I've told you has happened to me when I've been out with a guy."

"When the right man comes along, you'll change your mind."

"No, I don't think so. Remember Charles?"

Loretta rolled her eyes. "Don't remind me."

"Oh, but I must. He ordered for me, and I thought it was sweet, like he was trying to be gentlemanly. That is, until he ordered me a Diet Coke, quizzed the waitress on how many calories were in the meals, and ultimately chose the baked chicken with a side of vegetables—with no butter—for me."

Loretta groaned and shook her head. "So he was a jerk. Just because you aren't a skinny-mini doesn't mean you're fat or that you have to lose weight."

"I know," Harlow said. And she did. She was happy with her size. She liked to eat—she was a chef, for God's sake. She was never going to be a size two. Or ten, for that matter, but she wasn't obese, liked to go for walks, and did try to watch what she ate. But needless to say, that had been her last date with Charles.

She'd had so many bad dates in the past that she'd made the decision to put off dating for a while, focusing on work instead. She'd stuck to her guns for almost a year now.

"Seriously, when the right man comes along, you'll know it. You'll see," Loretta said.

Harlow shook her head but didn't respond. She'd been around the older woman enough to know that she wasn't going to change her mind. Loretta was stubborn. *Extremely* stubborn. So Harlow did what she knew was the best way to take Loretta's mind off whatever topic she was digging in her heels about—she changed the subject.

"Anyway, Lowell said he'd be here in an hour"—she looked at her watch—"about thirty minutes ago. He'll want to talk to you about everyone's exes, I'm sure. But he said that he'd help us."

"Thank goodness," Loretta said. "You know what Black does, right?"

Harlow knew his nickname was Black, but because she'd known him in high school as Lowell, it was what she called him. She tilted her head at Loretta's question. "You mean about the gun-safety classes at the range he owns?"

"No, dear. I'm going to tell you something that isn't exactly public knowledge. I only know because I've helped them out in the past, and I'm telling *you* because I trust you, and you have a history with Black. He and his friends are a group called the Mountain Mercenaries."

Harlow gasped. "People hire them to kill others?"

Loretta barked out a laugh. "No, child. Lord. They're hired to find and liberate kidnapped women and children. Their services don't come cheap, and those who hire them have connections. It's not like you can just look up Rex, the leader, and his crew on the internet and email them. They take the most desperate cases: women who have disappeared into the sex-trafficking racket, kids who've been taken by noncustodial parents . . . they even assist in abuse cases now and then."

Harlow was confused. "But I thought mercenaries were motivated by money?"

Loretta shrugged. "I don't know or care how they came up with their name, and while I'm sure they have to be bringing in good cash for doing what they do, the main thing Rex and his team are motivated by is justice. They don't like to see women or children abused by others—men *or* women. They're all former Special Forces of one sort or another. They have the training that's needed to slip into foreign countries and rescue people without detection. Or stay right here in our own country to find and rescue a woman or child in need."

"How do you *know* all this?" Harlow asked. On the one hand, she was shocked, but on the other, it made sense. She could tell just by looking at Lowell that he was the kind of man who could be relied on. He was strong and compassionate, but he had a look in his eyes that clearly communicated he wasn't a man to be messed with. That was one of the main reasons she'd finally caved and called him.

"I run a women's shelter." Loretta shrugged, as if it was obvious how she knew about a mysterious group of deadly men. "Rex contacted me a few years ago and asked if I had room for a woman they'd rescued from an abusive situation. I didn't, but after hearing her awful story, I *made* room. Over the years, I've learned more and more about the Mountain Mercenaries. And after meeting all the men—except for Rex, who even the guys haven't met—I can honestly say they are some of the most moral and upstanding men I've ever had the pleasure of working with."

Harlow knew that was high praise coming from Loretta. She had never been married and didn't have any children. When she was in her twenties, she'd joined a cult, though she hadn't known it was a cult at the time. The leader had been abusive and controlling, and ever since she'd escaped, Loretta had kept men at arm's length. For her to praise this Rex character, his organization, and the men who worked for him . . . it was pretty huge.

"It's true I knew Lowell in high school," Harlow agreed. "I mean, we weren't close. And I knew he'd joined the Navy after he graduated."

Loretta nodded. "Navy SEAL, I'd bet," she said. "Anyway, thank you for calling him, child. I should've called Rex, but I thought this would blow over and those boys would get bored."

"I thought so too," Harlow said.

"Anyway, I'm happy to share with Black what I can. He knows there are some things I can't disclose because of privacy laws."

"How will he be able to help us if he doesn't have all the details?" Harlow asked.

Loretta smiled but didn't answer.

"What?" Harlow asked.

"Rex and his team have their ways of finding out everything," Loretta told her. "I'll let him know what's been going on around here, and I'd bet everything I have they'll be able to find out more about the exes than I'd ever be able to tell them. Faster too."

Harlow shivered. She wasn't so sure about this anymore.

As if she could read her mind, Loretta reached over and patted Harlow's hand. "Don't stress," she ordered. "Your Lowell is one of the good guys. He'd never pry into your background without a good reason."

It wasn't as if Harlow was worried about what Lowell might find on *her*. She was as boring as a thirty-four-year-old woman could be. She got along with her parents. Had gone to community college for a year or two before transferring to a culinary school, got good grades, and never been in trouble with the law, aside from a few parking tickets on her record.

But knowing that Lowell *could* find out everything about her if he wanted to was a little daunting. It reminded her of a man she'd gone on a date with who'd pulled out a sheath of papers and presented them to her, explaining he'd gone ahead and done an extensive background check on her to make sure she was good enough to marry.

It was creepy and invasive as hell—and that had been the end of *that* date.

"I hope he won't," Harlow said.

Loretta simply smiled again. "Better finish those biscuits before Black gets here and distracts you." And with that, the older woman turned around and left the kitchen.

Harlow checked the time and realized that she had only about twenty minutes before Lowell would be arriving. She quickly stuffed the cookie sheet into the preheated oven. They should be finished about the time Lowell got there.

Wiping her forehead on her sleeve, Harlow had the brief thought that she wished she had a change of clothes, but then mentally rolled her eyes at herself. Lowell wasn't coming over to pick her up for a date or anything, so she shouldn't be worried about what she was wearing. She had on a pair of jeans, a T-shirt, and flip-flops. The apron she always wore in the kitchen covered most of what she was wearing anyway.

She knew her hair was probably a disaster, as usual. She had it pulled back out of her face into a messy bun on the back of her head so it wouldn't get into the food she was cooking. She wore no jewelry, and her nails weren't painted. Most of the time, she felt like a failure when it came to the "girly arts"—and that thought was further reinforced by her many failed dates.

Harlow truly believed that the dates failed not necessarily because of *her*, but because she seemed to attract men who definitely weren't right for her. Like the time she'd agreed to go out with a guy who was an admitted outdoorsman. She'd thought that sounded great; she liked to be outside too.

Well, he'd picked her up and taken her to the lake. He'd brought two chairs, thank God, but only one fishing rod. He'd then proceeded to drink beer and fish for two hours. He hadn't even realized she was bored, because he was a self-absorbed asshat. She wouldn't have minded so much if he'd actually talked to her while he'd fished, but the one time she'd tried to start a conversation, he'd shushed her and said she was scaring the fish.

Finally, she'd told him she was calling an Uber and leaving. He hadn't been ready to go and told her he'd call her later. She hadn't been surprised or disappointed when he hadn't.

Suffice to say, Harlow was gun-shy when it came to dating. She wasn't opposed to being in a relationship, but in order to *have* a relationship, you had to actually spend time with someone. And in her world, that never ended well.

Sighing, she began to wipe down the counter as she mentally went over the dinner menu. It was Zoe's turn to cook tonight, and she wanted to make sure the other woman had all the ingredients to make lasagna.

Chapter Three

Black leaned against the doorframe and watched Harlow putter around the large kitchen. It was beside the big living room, and one of the double doors stood open. The sound of cars driving up and down the road in front of the building was slight and didn't detract from the hominess of the space. The glow from the window over the sink made her blonde hair seem even lighter.

Loretta had greeted Black when he'd arrived and thanked him for coming. She'd informed him she'd be in her office, ready to answer any questions he had, but first he could go and greet Harlow.

He couldn't help but smile at the thought. He'd always liked Loretta. She wasn't very subtle, but that was part of her charm.

His attention was brought back to Harlow when she accidentally bumped into the corner of a counter, let out a soft *ouch*, and rubbed her hip.

There was something about her that made him feel . . . calm. And that was a big deal, because most of the time Black was anything *but* calm. He was constantly scanning his immediate surroundings for threats, a throwback to his time as a Navy SEAL. But it was more than that. Even when he was alone in his apartment, he had a hard time relaxing. TV bored him. He hardly ever made it all the way through a movie before thinking of something else he should be doing. It took him forever to read a book because he could only get through a chapter or so before getting restless.

But he realized that he could stand there and watch Harlow for hours.

She wasn't doing anything super interesting—cleaning the kitchen, taking a sheet of biscuits out of the oven and muttering at them under her breath—but she fascinated him. She was constantly in motion, and at the moment, he could tell she was nervous about something.

The men harassing her? Whatever she was cooking? Him? He didn't know.

How long he'd been standing there watching her, Black wasn't sure, but it was inevitable that eventually she'd spot him.

But he didn't expect her eyes to widen, a gasp to escape her mouth, and Harlow to stumble backward, tripping over her feet in the process.

She fell to the floor, and Black lost sight of her for a split second.

He immediately strode across the room and around the island and saw her sitting on the floor, wincing. Holding his hand out to her, he said, "I'm so sorry. I didn't mean to startle you."

She shook her head, then reached out and grasped his hand in hers, allowing him to help her stand.

Several impressions hit Black at once.

First was how soft and smooth her hand was. Second was how good she smelled—like vanilla. Third was that, once standing, they were eye to eye.

He was used to being the short one in his group of friends, but the last few women he'd dated had been petite. He'd thought shorter women were his speed, but he liked being able to look into Harlow's dark-blue eyes.

At the moment, it was obvious she was embarrassed. A light-pink hue washed over her cheeks, but she gamely smiled at him. "I'd like to say I'm usually not so clumsy, but I'd be lying."

Black smiled back at her and reluctantly dropped her hand. "I remember that about you."

The pink in her cheeks got darker. "I guess I haven't grown out of it after all these years."

"It's endearing."

Harlow rolled her eyes. "It's endearing in a six-year-old. In a grown woman, it's just embarrassing," she countered.

"I'm sorry I scared you," Black apologized again, fascinated by the play of emotions on her face. He was an expert interrogator, largely because of his skill in reading body language and nonverbal body cues. At the moment, Harlow was an open book.

She waved off his apology. "No, it's my fault. I knew you were on your way. I was distracted, thinking about tonight's dinner. Not to mention I've been a bit jumpy lately."

Black shook his head. "It *was* my fault," he insisted. "I forget to make noise when I'm around civilians sometimes. I learned in the Navy to always walk absolutely silently. It's a hard habit to break."

She looked at him then. Right in the eyes, without trying to hide the fact that she was examining him. What she was looking for, Black had no idea, but he held her gaze steadfastly.

Finally, she said, "I'd suggest that you wear a bell or something when you're out in public, but that would probably be overkill."

Black smiled again. "Yeah. There are times when going unnoticed has its advantages. But today wasn't one of them. Again, I'm sorry for startling you."

Instead of continuing to insist that it was her fault, which was ridiculous, she merely nodded. He liked that.

"Are you hungry?" she asked.

"What?" The question itself wasn't surprising, as she *was* in a kitchen, but he hadn't expected her to offer to feed him.

"Are you hungry?" she repeated. "It's after lunch, and if you didn't have a chance to eat, I can put something together for you real fast before we talk."

"I'm good," Black told her.

"It's no problem," she insisted. "I mean, it's not like I'm going to make you a four-course meal or anything, but I can throw together a sandwich or a salad. It's not a big deal."

Black recognized her attempts at feeding him were just another way she was trying to deal with her nervousness. He didn't like that she was uncomfortable around him, but at the same time, he hoped it meant she felt the same crazy chemistry he did when they were around each other.

"I had something earlier," he reassured her, then gestured toward the table off to the side. "Shall we sit while you tell me about the trouble you and the others have been having?"

Harlow nodded and brushed by him. The tantalizing smell of vanilla teased his nostrils once more as she passed. Black resisted the urge to wrap his arm around her waist and pull her back into his body. Barely.

It was crazy. He hadn't reacted this way toward a woman in years. The last time he'd had chemistry like this with someone, he'd been in his early twenties. He'd dated the woman for a year, but in the end it turned out that their chemistry had been completely sexual. They'd had nothing in common and nothing to talk about when they weren't in bed.

Shaking his head and concentrating on the here and now, Black followed Harlow to the table and held her chair as she sat. He took the chair next to her and pulled it a bit closer than was socially acceptable. He'd learned that making people slightly uncomfortable generally encouraged them to talk more.

He didn't start the conversation, but instead let the silence stand between them. Again, this wasn't an interrogation, but he had a feeling that Harlow would try to downplay what was happening, and he wanted her a little off-kilter so she'd be more apt to tell him the truth.

"I guess you want to know more about why I called you, huh?" Harlow asked after a moment.

Black nodded, still not speaking.

His tactic worked, as Harlow licked her lips and began to babble. "It's not as if anyone has done anything *wrong*. I mean, they're annoying, but isn't everyone? Generally, I get along so much better with kids than I do adults. I like being by myself too because most of the time people are just irritating. Loretta met with the cops—I told you that, I think—and they said until the guys do something illegal, their hands are tied. And aggressively whistling at women and telling them how hot they are isn't against the law. I can't imagine why anyone would think it's a good idea to hang around outside a women's shelter and ask out the residents. I mean, men are dumb, but they can't all be *that* stupid."

"Men are dumb?" Black asked when Harlow stopped speaking.

She nodded. "I can't tell you how many dates I've been on when the guy acted like a dumbass. If there was an award for being on the craziest dates, I would have won the Oscar equivalent by now."

"Really?" Black was intrigued.

"Yes. Men really are ridiculous. And when they think they might get some, they get even dumber. So I'm guessing, since the guys hanging around here are young, maybe they're just horny or something."

Black couldn't stop the smirk from forming.

Harlow shook her head, brought a hand up to her face, and rubbed her forehead. "I'm sorry. I'm going on and on." She dropped her hand, looked him straight in the eyes, and said, "I don't think they're horny. I don't know what their agenda is, but I dread running into them when I get here. Sometimes they're here, and sometimes they aren't. Sometimes there's just one of them, and other times there's a pack. They whistle and jeer, but they haven't touched anyone yet. Though, one afternoon after my shift, I went to my car in the public lot and someone had stuck those plastic googly eyes all over my driver's-side window. It sounds funny, but it wasn't."

"I don't think that sounds funny at all," Black said, all humor gone from his expression now.

"I just . . . I love this job. I love the people who live here. I want them to get back on their feet. I want the kids to gain some confidence. But it's hard to work when I'm wondering what some punk is going to do next. It's hard for the women to move on when they're scared to walk outside this building. It's frustrating, and I just want them to stop."

Black reached out and took one of her hands in both of his. She didn't pull her hand away. In fact, she closed her fingers around his and held on.

"My team and I will figure this out, Harlow. We'll make sure you and the others can come and go without worry. We'll make them stop."

Harlow bit her lip, then nodded.

Black didn't let go of her hand, but tilted his wrist to look at his watch. "What time are you off today?"

"Now. I had breakfast and lunch duty today. Zoe's got dinner and breakfast tomorrow. I just stayed around because you said you were coming over."

Black felt bad that he'd made her stay. "I still need to talk to Loretta," he told her. "How about this: you go home now, and I'll pick you up later and take you to dinner. We can discuss the situation more then. I'm sure I'll have more questions for you after I talk to Loretta."

Harlow eyed him for a long moment before pulling her hand from his grip and sitting back. "I'm not going on a date with you," she said.

"Who said anything about a date?" Black asked gently.

If he was being honest with himself, he *had* been thinking along those lines. The connection between him and Harlow was strong, and he never would've thought she'd turn him down. Except . . . then he remembered what she'd said about her bad dates and wanted to kick himself.

"I don't date," she told him.

"Ever?"

"Well . . . for almost a year," she explained.

Black didn't respond, in the hopes she'd explain to fill the silence. It worked.

"Look. I like you—what I know of you, that is—but dates haven't seemed to work out for me. On one of the last ones, the guy kept using the wrong name when he was talking to me. When I finally called him out on it, he admitted that he was still in love with his ex and he'd asked me out because I looked a lot like her."

"Ouch," Black said.

"Yeah. So anyway, that was around the four hundred and sixty-second bad date that I've had in my life, and I heard the world record for bad dates was four hundred and sixty-three, and that's one record I don't want."

Black grinned. She was funny.

"It's not funny," she griped, but he could see her lips twitching. "It's just that with my track record, I've come to the conclusion that I can't trust myself when it comes to men. So I'm taking a break from the dating scene for a while."

"Did you give yourself a timetable for this no-dating thing?" Black asked, curious now.

"Well, no. I figure I'll know when it's time to get back on the horse, so to speak." She blushed and continued quickly. "I'm not opposed to getting married and having children someday, but with one bad date after another, I just got to the point where I was scared of even *trying* to find a normal man who wouldn't ask me what brand of makeup I use because he wanted to try it himself."

"Fine. So it's not a date," Black told her, resisting the urge to grin at her latest date gone wrong. He was relieved that she hadn't put off dating forever, just for now. He could work with that. "We need to talk about the case and what's going on. I need to lay some ground rules for you—and before you protest, they're the same ones I'll be telling Loretta about this afternoon, and ones all the residents need to follow. And we both need to eat, so we can just kill two birds with one stone."

Black kept his face blank as Harlow scrutinized him.

After a moment, she asked, "What are your thoughts about taking food from my plate while we're eating?"

He blinked. "What?"

Harlow sighed and shook her head. "Never mind. Fine."

"I won't need to eat off your plate because I'll have my own meal," Black told her. "But if you want to try something that I've ordered, I'm more than happy to share. And where do appetizers fall in that question of yours? I mean, they usually come on one plate—we'll have to share."

He was glad to see a slight grin on her face. He definitely didn't like that Harlow had such a low opinion of dating. Especially because he'd decided while he was standing in the doorway watching her that he definitely wanted to take her out.

"Appetizers are meant to be shared," she told him seriously. "But if you even come near my plate with your fork, I'm going to stand up and walk out."

"My fork will stay far away from your plate," Black vowed.

"Good," she mumbled.

"But if you want a taste of something I've got, all you need to do is ask." He couldn't stop the innuendo from slipping out.

Harlow didn't call him on it, but he knew she understood because she blushed. "I won't," she told him firmly.

"I'll pick you up at your apartment at five thirty," Black told her.

"No. I'll meet you at the restaurant. Just tell me where it is," she countered.

Black shook his head. "No. Nonnegotiable."

"This isn't a date," Harlow insisted. "I'm perfectly able to meet you there."

"Why?" Black asked, trying to understand her reasoning. "This is a business meeting. Surely the person who will be teaching you how to keep yourself safe can be trusted to pick you up."

"It isn't that," she said, her gaze lowered.

"Then what is it? Help me understand."

"I need to make sure I have transportation," Harlow said.

Black clenched his teeth together. "I'm not going to do anything that will make you want to leave early," he said.

"You don't know that."

"Look at me," Black ordered.

Harlow sighed, but looked up.

"I'm not going to do anything that will make you want to, or need to, leave early," he repeated. "I'm a gentleman, and I know how to treat a woman." He willed her to believe him.

"This isn't a date," she said, more to herself than him.

"Not a date," he agreed.

She nodded. "Fine. You can pick me up. But I swear to God, if this goes bad, I'm going to move to Alaska and become a nun."

Black chuckled. "You do know that men outnumber the women up there, right? So if you're going to relocate to get away from men, that's not the state to move to."

He was relieved when a smile formed on her lips.

"Do you always get what you want?" she asked.

Black shrugged and decided that maybe not answering was the better move at the moment. He pulled out his cell and asked, "What's your number?" When she hesitated, he clarified quickly, "You know, just in case I'm running late or something comes up."

She rattled it off for him, and Black added it to his contacts. He sent her a quick text and, when the phone in her pocket beeped, said, "I know I gave my number to you a while ago, but now you have it handy."

He hid his grin from her as he stood and pushed his chair back under the table. He sort of understood her aversion to dating, but that wasn't going to stop him from getting to know her better—and from her getting to know him in return. He just wouldn't call it dating. He was determined to show her that not all guys were dicks. He wasn't sure exactly what he was up against, but he'd hopefully learn more tonight.

Black hadn't thought his talent for getting information out of people would ever apply to his personal life, not like this, but he was suddenly very glad he was an interrogation expert. The key was being subtle enough that Harlow wouldn't catch on to what he was doing. He was looking forward to it. Looking forward to spending time with her.

She stood up, and Black gestured to the door of the kitchen. "I'll walk you out." There wasn't a door leading outside from the kitchen. She had to walk through the main living area of the building and either exit out the front door or head to the back of the building and go out that way.

"You don't have to do that," she protested.

"I know. But tell me honestly—would it make you feel better if I did? What if those guys are out there?"

She sighed. "All right, fine. Yes, it would make me feel better."

Black didn't dare smile. "Right." Then he gestured toward the doorway again.

Harlow took the apron off over her head and hung it on a hook on the wall. Then she walked over to a cabinet and pulled out a flowered tote bag and a sweatshirt. She didn't say anything as she preceded him through the doorway.

Black's hand hovered near the small of her back, but he refrained from actually touching her, even though his fingers twitched with the need to do so. Harlow was full figured, and watching her backside sway as she walked was giving Black all sorts of X-rated ideas. He didn't exactly have a type, but he couldn't deny that he badly wanted to see Harlow stretched out on his bed, naked, smiling up at him.

"Lowell?"

His eyes snapped to hers, and he tried to look like he'd been paying attention the entire time instead of lusting after her.

She shook her head and grinned. "You didn't hear me, did you?"

He shrugged. "Sorry, no."

"Some Navy SEAL you are," she joked.

"You been talking to Miss Loretta?" he asked. He didn't care that she knew he'd been a SEAL. He didn't even care if she knew about the Mountain Mercenaries. He hoped both of those would be pluses in her eyes rather than negatives.

"Maybe," she said coyly.

"What did you say while I was so rudely not paying attention?" he asked.

"I just wanted to thank you for coming over today and for doing what you can to help."

"You're welcome," he said easily. Then did what he'd been thinking about. He put his hand on the small of her back and gently guided her toward the door. "Now, let's get you in your car so you can relax before our . . . meeting tonight."

He'd almost slipped and called it a date. He made a mental note to never *ever* call any of their get-togethers "dates."

She nodded and headed for the door. Black noted that she didn't pull away from his touch, and he smiled. This was going to be fun. It had been a long time since he'd been the one to pursue a relationship. In today's culture, women had no problem being up front with what they wanted, be it a date, a kiss, or just sex. It was refreshing to be the pursuer for once.

Harlow was cautious and unsure about being with him, and that made her even more refreshing. He wouldn't push her past what she was comfortable with, but the anticipation of courting her, without her realizing it, was heady. And exciting.

Black turned his attention from the warm body he could feel through the shirt under his fingertips to his surroundings as they exited the building. He looked up and down the street and saw nothing out of the ordinary.

The shelter was located in the middle of several other three-story properties, making up one large block. They looked like they were probably all built around the same time. The two buildings on either side of the shelter were empty, and the one on the end of the block was currently being renovated. Black made a mental note to find out who it belonged to and what they were planning on doing with the space.

On the other side of the street, he spotted an antiques store, a tattoo parlor, and a pawnshop, along with two empty retail spaces with dusty, tinted windows.

An alley ran behind the buildings, allowing for deliveries from trucks. Black knew Loretta lived on the top floor in one of the smaller rooms and used another for an office, leaving the remaining private rooms for mothers to share with their kids. On the second floor, there was a large open room with five beds, where the women without children stayed. It wasn't ideal long term, but it was safe, warm, dry, and free. All things that the women who stayed there needed.

Loretta could've packed more people into the shelter by putting bunk beds in the large shared room, but having eleven adults and anywhere from five to ten children living in the building at one time was hectic enough. Adding more women would stretch the shelter's resources and just make things all the more chaotic, and the last thing everyone needed was more stress.

Black walked Harlow to her car in the parking lot at the opposite end of the street from where the park was located. He remembered her saying the punks liked to hang out at the park, and he turned to look behind him. He didn't see anyone lurking about. A big, white box truck was parked outside the antiques store, and a customer entered the tattoo shop.

"Do you see them?" Harlow asked nervously.

Black turned his attention back to her. "No. I'm just getting the lay of the land."

"Oh. Okay."

He looked up. "Those lights work?" he asked.

"Yeah. Although they aren't super bright," Harlow told him.

He frowned and kept walking. The parking lot was directly across the street from a vacant and crumbling gas station. Black had parked in the lot and hadn't thought too much about it, his attention on getting to the shelter. But now that he imagined Harlow, or Zoe, or any of the other women in the shelter walking to their cars alone, or with their kids, it made the hair on the back of his neck stand up.

On the other side of the alley beyond the parking lot were a row of trees and the backside of a run-down mobile home park. There was so much about the situation that he didn't like, but Black knew he couldn't exactly change the location of the parking lot or the shelter itself, no matter how much he wanted to.

Harlow led him over to a bright-red Ford Mustang convertible. He turned to her and arched an eyebrow.

She smiled and shrugged. "What can I say? I love it."

"It's a sweet ride," he told her honestly. Of course, it also brought attention to her, which he didn't like. She would be better off in a nice sedate black Honda or Toyota. But he had a feeling if he mentioned that to her, she'd roll her eyes and tell him to fuck off. And he wouldn't blame her.

"It is. For years, I had a used Honda Civic. I hated it. It wasn't me. I'm not the most extroverted person in the world, but there's something about the wind in my hair and the sun shining down on me that makes me feel free. I would've gotten a motorcycle, but I knew my parents would have a cow, so this was the next best thing."

The thought of Harlow on a motorcycle made Black's stomach turn. Not so much because he worried about the kind of driver *she* might be, but because he knew most of the time it was the skill, or lack thereof, of *other* drivers that caused accidents. "It suits you," he told her honestly. And it did. He could picture her laughing and smiling as her blonde hair blew in the wind.

He couldn't wait to see it in person.

Strengthening his resolve to know her better, Black merely smiled when she eyed him suspiciously. Finally, she nodded and turned to her car. He watched as she lowered the top and noted how long the process took. If she did that every time she came out here to drive home, it gave the assholes harassing her more time to approach.

Putting it aside for the moment, he waited until she'd gotten inside and sat down. Then he put his hands on the edge of her window and leaned over. "I'll be by to pick you up at five thirty," he reminded her.

"Oh . . . you need my address," she said.

He didn't. He could easily get it from Loretta or Meat, but he nodded anyway. "Text it to me."

"Right. I will."

Black didn't move.

"Lowell?" she asked. "Is there anything else?"

There was. He wanted to tell Harlow how pretty he thought she was. He wanted to tell her that he wasn't sure he ever wanted to get married, but he might want to be her boyfriend. That he wanted the right to sit next to her as she drove home . . . and he couldn't wait to see if she smelled like vanilla all over.

But he didn't. She'd obviously been burned by men often enough in the past that he shouldn't do anything to make her think they were dating.

If anyone could do covert operations, it was Black.

So he simply shook his head and said, "I'll see you later. Drive safe."

"I will. You too."

Then he took a step away from the convertible and waved.

Harlow smiled back at him and slowly pulled out of the parking lot. He watched as she drove cautiously down the street. Yes, the speed limit wasn't exactly fast, but watching the way she looked both ways three times before pulling out and how she slowly accelerated made it clear she didn't drive her car the way it was meant to be driven. Fast and with abandon.

When Black turned to walk back to the shelter, he caught sight of something to his left.

He turned to look and thought he saw someone duck into the pawnshop. No, maybe it was the tattoo parlor. He wasn't sure which business the man had disappeared into. He kept his eyes on the storefronts as he walked toward the shelter. No one else entered or exited any businesses. It could've been a regular customer, or maybe it wasn't. He wasn't sure.

But one thing he *was* sure about was the fact that Loretta's shelter was going to get a brand-spanking-new security system. Complete with exterior cameras. It wouldn't stop the harassment, and it wouldn't make the cops get involved if no one was actually breaking the law, but it would help Meat and Rex identify the perpetrators, and Black would be able to "talk" to them and find out what was going on.

Taking one last look around before he entered the shelter to talk to Loretta, Black felt the hair on the back of his neck stand on end once more. He didn't see anyone suspicious, but he had a feeling whatever was going on was more than just a few bored teenagers.

A man stared through the glass window at the door of the shelter across the street, where the dark-haired guy had disappeared. He'd seen other men come and go from the First Hope Women's Shelter, but it had been on a regular basis, near the beginning of the month. Not in the afternoon—and they never walked anyone to their cars when they left.

He'd seen the old guy come and go more frequently, but this one wasn't old. Not in the least.

He'd watched him park his fancy-ass Mazda6 down the street and seen how the old bitch had greeted him at the door. He hadn't been inside very long when he'd reappeared with one of the cooks. He was looking around, assessing the area, and acting very protective of the woman at his side.

Sighing, the man pressed his lips together. He didn't need this. Things had been going so well. He could almost see the end of his very long mission. But he had a feeling this guy was going to mess up everything.

It was time to step up the pressure. He'd get what he wanted or else.

Chapter Four

Harlow jerked when someone knocked at her door at precisely five thirty. Even though she'd been expecting it, the sound still startled her. Smoothing her hair behind an ear, she went to the door and looked through the peephole.

Swallowing hard, she opened the door and stared at Lowell.

She was in big trouble here.

He looked amazing. He'd changed into a pair of black jeans and a black T-shirt that molded to his body. He looked . . . lickable.

Shaking her head at herself, Harlow forced a smile. "Hey."

"Hey," he returned.

She couldn't help but stand there and stare back as his eyes took her in from head to toe. Because this wasn't a date, Harlow had refused to get dressed up for him. She was wearing a simple pair of jeans and a T-shirt, but she had taken the time to brush her hair out, which now fell around her shoulders. She still had on her flip-flops, but had decided that afternoon to paint her toenails a bright red.

It was a spur-of-the-moment choice, and she couldn't keep her toes from curling as his gaze reached them.

He looked back up at her and smiled. "I like the toes."

Harlow forced herself to roll her eyes instead of simpering like an idiot. "Thanks," she said as curtly as she could. "Let me grab my purse, and I'll be ready to go." She turned, leaving him standing at her apartment door. She picked up her purse, which was sitting on her kitchen counter, and spun back around to leave—but she bounced off Lowell's chest instead.

His hands came up and caught her biceps before she could fall to the ground.

"Easy, Harl."

She knew she was blushing, and she ducked her head to try to hide her reaction to being near him.

"You okay?" he asked, tipping her head up with a finger under her chin and casually tucking her hair behind her ear with the other hand.

The brush of his fingers on the sensitive outer edge of her ear made goose bumps rise up on her arms. She wasn't used to men being this close to her. So close she could smell the soap he'd used to shower and could feel his body heat.

Nodding, Harlow took a step backward. "I'm fine. I didn't realize you'd be right there . . . since I didn't invite you in." She couldn't help tagging on that last part since she was discomfited. She hadn't asked him to step inside while she'd grabbed her purse because she wasn't going to be that long, and honestly, she didn't want him in her space.

Not because she was scared of him or what he might do, but because she had a feeling once he was in, he was *in*.

She'd dated dozens of men in the past. Not that the dates had gone particularly well, but she had a niggling feeling that Lowell was different. He could hurt her. *Really* hurt her. The other men she'd dated were mere blips on her life radar, but Lowell was already different from the other men she'd gone out with. She had a history with him. Once upon a time, she'd had a crush on him, maybe still did, and the more time she spent around him, the more she remembered why she'd liked him so much.

Back then he was a nice boy, but now, all indications were that he was an amazing man.

She was in *so* much trouble.

Lowell smirked at her. "Sorry I came in without permission."

He didn't look sorry. In fact, he looked extremely pleased with himself.

Harlow shrugged the strap of her purse onto her shoulder and took a step toward her door. "I'm ready to go."

Luckily, he didn't insist on getting the grand tour of her place, not that there was much to see—it was a two-bedroom, two-bathroom apartment with a kitchen and living area.

He held out an arm, indicating she should precede him to the door. She did and, when she felt his hand settle on her lower back, sighed internally. He'd done that earlier in the day too, and the second she'd felt the warmth of his palm on her body, she'd relaxed. Just knowing he was there, that he had her back, made her much less afraid of who might be lurking outside the shelter.

The same feeling settled over her now, except it was . . . more. She wasn't afraid of who might be outside her apartment, but his touch made her feel safe all the same.

Not a date, she reminded herself, and she lengthened her stride to step away from his touch. He didn't comment, simply held the door open as she exited the apartment. They made their way downstairs, through the lobby of the complex, and out the front door. Harlow made sure to stay at least three feet ahead of him as they walked toward his Mazda in the parking lot.

He held open the passenger-side door for her as she settled into the seat, and shut the door once she was safely inside. Harlow studied Lowell as he confidently strode around to the driver's side.

She wasn't sure what it was about him that made her feel so comfortable. She wasn't like this with most men, at least she hadn't been in the past. She and Lowell were the same height, but somehow he seemed so much bigger than her. Harlow knew a lot of that was his personality and confidence. He oozed competence and put out a dangerous vibe.

She'd sensed it the first time she'd seen him a month ago. He made her want to spill her guts, tell him everything.

Even that afternoon, as he'd sat next to her in the kitchen and patiently waited for her to tell him what had been going on, she hadn't been able to stop herself from blurting out everything she'd been thinking. It was weird, and even a little scary.

But not scary like when she'd gone out with a man she'd met online and he'd stared at her with big bloodshot eyes all night. She'd had no desire back then to fill the awkward silence as she had with Lowell.

He settled himself into the driver's seat and smiled over at her. "Ready?"

"Ready," she told him.

Still grinning, Lowell backed out of the parking space and headed for the exit. He steered toward the interstate and Harlow asked, "Why are you going this way?"

"I thought I'd show you what this baby can do," Lowell told her, caressing the dashboard.

Harlow rolled her eyes. She knew she'd been doing that a lot around him, but she couldn't help it. "You know, I once let a guy pick me up, and he'd wanted to do the same thing—wanted to show off his car and how fast it could go."

"And?" Lowell asked when she didn't continue with her story.

She turned to him. "Oh, he showed me how fast he could go, all right. I was holding on to the oh-shit handle so tightly, I know I probably left fingernail marks. He gunned it to over a hundred miles an hour and was all proud of himself, but then red and blue lights went off behind us, and he started swearing and panicking. I was crying and pleading with him to pull over, to stop the car, but he only went faster."

Lowell's hand took hold of hers, and instead of pulling her hand away, she held on. Generally, she tried to keep her dating experiences light and often joked about them. But that particular incident still had the power to freak her out. She didn't know why she'd brought it up in the first place—Lowell definitely wasn't like that guy—but now that she had, she couldn't back out. She rushed through the rest of the story.

"He continued to try to evade the cops, and actually got far enough ahead of them that I guess he felt comfortable stopping."

"Thank God," Lowell said, squeezing her hand.

"Yeah. He stopped, then turned to me and said, 'I'm sorry,' and threw open his door and ran into the trees on the side of the road."

"He left you there?" Lowell asked incredulously.

"Yup. And the cops pulled up behind the car and executed a felony stop."

"Oh shit."

"Right? I had to put my hands on my head, walk backward toward them, and lie on the asphalt. They swarmed me and handcuffed me and left me right there on the ground as they searched for my date. Eventually, they helped me up and let me talk. I told them that I was on a first—and last—date with the asshole and knew nothing about him. They caught the guy later that night after using dogs to search for him. He had an outstanding warrant for drugs, and he not only had marijuana on him, but a vial of Rohypnol too."

"Motherfucker," Lowell said under his breath.

"Yeah. So if it's all the same to you, I don't really want to know 'what this baby can do.'"

"Look at me," Lowell ordered.

Taking a deep breath, Harlow did.

He was alternating between looking at the road in front of them and running his eyes over her face in concern. "I was teasing you because I noticed that you don't exactly drive your Mustang like Danica Patrick."

"Who?"

His lips quirked, but then he looked worried again. "No one. I'm not going to put your life in danger. When you're with me, you're safe. I don't do drugs. I'm not wanted by the police for anything, and I'd sooner stab myself in the eye with a rusty fork than do *anything* that will scare you."

His words both reassured and calmed her. "Thank you."

"You really *haven't* had good luck in picking dates, have you?" Lowell asked with a smile.

Harlow tried to relax in the seat and shook her head. "No. But in my defense, before that particular date, my mom had just lectured me about getting older and how she wanted grandbabies. So I was trying to show her that I was trying. I should've just told her to mind her own business."

"I know how that goes. My mom is dying to have grandbabies to spoil as well, but between me and my brother, she's despaired of ever having them."

"You don't want kids?" Harlow asked, trying to ignore the fact that Lowell hadn't let go of her hand.

"It's not that I don't want them," he said. "I just haven't met a woman who I want to spend the rest of my life with, never mind having children with."

Harlow nodded. "I get that. Boy, do I."

They both chuckled.

Neither said anything for a while as they drove toward downtown.

Finally, Harlow asked, "Where are we going?"

"The Pit."

"Where?"

Lowell smiled. "Since this isn't a date, and we're talking about the shelter, I decided I should take you to the place where me and my team conduct business. The Pit."

"It sounds scary. Please tell me there aren't snakes on the floor and Indiana Jones isn't going to pop up and run pell-mell through the place being chased by members of an ancient civilization because they want their artifact back."

Harlow stared at Lowell when he threw his head back and laughed loud and long. She couldn't help but chuckle herself. The man sitting next to her was so different from any man she'd dated in the past—no, wait . . . this wasn't a date. Nope. Not even close.

"I can't wait to tell the others that. No, Harl, The Pit is a combination bar and pool hall. It's pretty much a hole-in-the-wall kind of place."

"Why do you do business in a bar?" Harlow asked.

"To be honest, I'm not sure. The Pit is where we were interviewed when we were first asked to join the Mountain Mercenaries . . . I'm assuming you know about the team?"

She nodded. "A bit. Loretta told me. I'm sorry if she spoke out of turn, but she was trying to reassure me that you knew what you were doing and could help us."

"I can help you," Lowell confirmed. "And in a nutshell, me and my teammates are all former Special Forces soldiers, and we work for Rex, getting women and children out of untenable situations."

"Why 'mercenaries'? I mean, it doesn't sound like that's what you guys really are."

Lowell shook his head, and a small smile formed on his face. "Why do women always concentrate on that word?" he asked, more to himself than her.

Harlow answered him even though he hadn't really asked. "Because. It's weird that you call yourselves something that you technically aren't. I wouldn't start a catering business and call it Harlow Photography."

"Point taken. I don't know why Rex chose that name. Probably because it was catchy and sounded better than Colorado Badasses, or Your Worst Nightmare."

Harlow couldn't stop the bark of laughter that escaped. "True."

"The bottom line is that it doesn't matter what we're called. We're six men who go where we're needed and do what we have to do to rescue those who need a helping hand. I know women are empowered, and there are many who are just as talented at what they do as we are. But the fact remains, there are a lot of men out there who feel the need to subjugate and beat down the women and children in their lives. They take advantage of teenagers who are too young to know better or those who have had horrible lives. They hurt them and force them to do things against their will. It's not right, or fair, and me and my friends are playing a small part in trying to right those wrongs."

Harlow wasn't sure how their light and playful conversation had turned so intense, but she turned slightly in her seat to better look at Lowell. His teeth were clenched, and the hand on the steering wheel was holding on so tightly, she could see his knuckles turning white. He obviously felt deeply about the topic and his job, and Harlow couldn't be prouder of him.

"I'm proud to know you, Lowell Lockard."

He looked at her in surprise. "What?"

"The world needs more men like you and your friends. I don't know why men like the ones harassing the shelter are the way they are. Why they feel the need to exert their power over those they deem weaker than them. But I'm glad you're there to help tip the scales. Other than the high-speed-chase guy, generally I haven't been afraid of my bad dates, I've just been disgusted by or disappointed in them. But I know there are a lot of women out there who're in bad marriages and relationships, and it helps knowing there are people who care. People who will put their own lives on the line to help get others out of those situations, if asked."

Lowell pulled into the parking lot of a dark and seedy-looking building, and Harlow wasn't surprised to see the neon sign above the door that said **The Pit**. This was exactly the kind of place where she imagined Lowell and his fellow badasses would meet.

He stopped the engine, brought the hand he was still holding up to his mouth, and kissed the back of it. "Stay put. I'll come around."

He went to let go of her, but Harlow held on to his hand. "This isn't a date," she said, not sure if she was reminding him or herself. "It's a work meeting. I let you pick me up, but I should've driven myself. And I can open my own door and pay my own way."

Lowell leaned into her, and Harlow forced herself not to pull back. "I know this isn't a date. You don't date. I heard that loud and clear, Harl. But in my world—and make no mistake; when you're with me, you're in my world—a man opens a door for a lady. He walks on the outside of the sidewalk, he picks her up whenever possible, and he pays for drinks and meals. If it makes you feel better, you can think of this as a business expense I can write off on my taxes."

Harlow stared at him for a beat, then nodded. What else could she do? She didn't want to like Lowell's world, but she had to admit it felt good being there. She'd had doors shut in her face when men had entered ahead of her and hadn't held them open. She'd had to pay for her own meals on dates. And she'd even had an experience when she'd literally almost been run over by a bus in Seattle because she'd been forced to walk on the outside of the sidewalk near the curb.

"Okay," she said.

"Okay," Lowell said with a small smile. Then he squeezed her hand once more and climbed out.

"Not a date, not a date," Harlow chanted to herself quietly as Lowell walked around his car to come to her side. He opened her door and held out a hand. Taking a deep breath, Harlow put her hand back in his and allowed him to help her up and out of the low seat.

He didn't let go of her once she was standing next to him, though. He simply shut the car door and led her toward the bar.

Not a date, she told herself once more as Lowell smiled at her and pulled open the heavy wooden door.

Chapter Five

Not a date, Black chanted in his head. With every story that Harlow told him about her past dating experiences, he understood more and more why she was so reluctant to reenter the dating scene. But the more he got to know her, the more he *wanted* to know. He wanted to erase every single one of her bad experiences and replace them with pleasant ones.

But he couldn't label anything they did as a date. No way. No how. Check.

"Black!" He heard someone call out as they entered The Pit.

Smiling, he lifted his chin at Meat. He saw Ball and Ro standing at the bar as well. He held out his arm, letting Harlow walk ahead of him. The second she started toward the bar, he placed his hand on the small of her back once more. It hadn't escaped his notice that she'd kept out of reach back at the parking lot of her apartment. He'd never force himself on her, but he *was* going to do everything he could to show her that he was worthy of dating. That she could break her rule about going out—as long as it was with him.

It also hadn't escaped his notice that when he did touch her, she frequently broke out in goose bumps. He liked that. Liked knowing that he affected her just as much as she did him.

He might not show it outwardly, but he was definitely affected.

Her vanilla scent was stronger tonight, as if she'd reapplied her lotion or perfume before he'd shown up. He loved her hair too. She'd left it down, and it brushed her shoulder blades as she walked, the purple tips enticing him. He wanted to touch it, see if it felt as soft as it looked. Wanted to see those dyed locks resting on his arm, his chest . . . his thighs as she knelt over him.

Taking a deep breath, Black forced his thoughts away from the dangerous route they were taking. Yes, he was attracted to Harlow, but they were nowhere close to being naked together.

"Hey, Black," Meat said as they approached. "Let me guess, this is Harlow."

"Yes. Harlow, I'd like you to meet my friends and teammates, Meat, Ball, and Ro."

"Hi," she said shyly.

"And what am I, chopped liver?" Dave asked from behind the bar.

Black smirked. "Sorry. And this is Dave. He's in charge around here. When he's not here, Noah works behind the bar."

"That's right, and don't you forget it," the gruff bartender said. His voice gentled when he asked, "What can I get you, young lady?"

"Oh, um, a Woodford and Coke?"

"Is that a question, or is that what you want?" Dave asked.

Black was about to lambaste the older man when Harlow laughed. "Sorry. That's what I want. I just wasn't sure you'd have the bourbon."

"Of course I have it. Jeez, you think this is a skank bar or somethin'?"

Harlow smiled but wisely didn't answer. She reached for her purse. "Can I start a tab?"

Dave looked startled for a second, but then grinned at Black. "I don't know, Black. Can she start a tab?"

"Shut it," Black muttered to the bartender, then put his hand over Harlow's. "I got this."

Unsurprisingly, she glared up at him and opened her mouth to protest.

Black placed a finger over her lips and asked, "Remember what I said in the car? This is my world. Deal with it."

She rolled her eyes, and when he dropped his hand, she said, "I guess *your* world is better than the world of the guy who told me he wanted a partner in life. I thought it was actually pretty nice that he wanted a partner—until he pulled out a list of all the bills he needed help paying and handed it to me."

"No shit?" Meat asked.

"No shit," Harlow confirmed. "I haven't had the best luck with men."

Black shook his head behind Harlow to tell his friends not to go there. Luckily, they understood and dropped the subject.

"I've got bills," Black told her, "but I can definitely pay them on my own."

"Me too," she told him with a slight lift of her chin.

Black liked her independence. "Now that *that's* covered, shall we?" he asked, gesturing toward the back room.

"Oh, of course," she said, reaching for the drink Dave had placed on the bar in front of them.

Black grabbed the beer Dave had given him without having to ask what he wanted and followed Harlow toward the back room. As they walked, Black told her, "Dave has been here forever. He works a lot. He was injured a bit ago, and I think that hurt his pride more than anything else. Noah took over while Dave was healing, and while Noah's good, he isn't Dave. The guy makes The Pit what it is. He's got his quirks, but he's the best bartender I've ever known."

"He's too skinny. He needs to eat more," Harlow said.

Black almost choked on the sip of beer he'd just taken.

"I'd like to see you tell *him* that," Ball said.

"I will," Harlow said. "But maybe not today."

She smiled over at his friend, and Black frowned. Maybe having his buddies here wasn't the best idea. Yes, he needed their help with the situation at the women's shelter, but both Meat and Ball were single. The last thing he wanted was for one of them to decide they were interested in Harlow.

"She doesn't date," he blurted—then immediately cringed.

"Yeah?" Meat asked.

"Interesting," Ball added.

"I don't either," Ro threw in.

"You've had some bad experiences too?" Harlow asked him, seemingly oblivious to the undercurrents between Black and the others.

"Of course. But that's not why I don't date," Ro told her.

Black silently steered her to the table on the right in the back room with gentle pressure on her back. There were pool tables all around the room, and this particular table was where they did all their business. It was set off to the side and private.

"It's not?" Harlow asked.

"No. I don't think my wife would approve of me taking out someone else," Ro told her with a straight face.

Harlow grinned. "Probably not."

Black knew he was being irrational, but he didn't like Harlow smiling at Ro . . . even though he also knew without a doubt that his friend would never cheat on Chloe. He tamped down his jealousy as best he could. "Meat, did you find out anything about the exes of the residents at the shelter?"

And just like that, the easygoing feeling among the group disappeared. Black hated seeing worry lines replace the relaxed look on Harlow's face, but the sooner they talked business, the sooner he could get to the "not dating" part of the night.

"I put the names that you gave me through my database," Meat said, "and I have to say, most of those men aren't exactly pillars of society."

"I think we guessed that," Black said dryly.

"Right. So, Nathanial Taylor, otherwise known as Nate, is twenty-four and has been arrested once for domestic battery. His ex-wife, Carrie Taylor, is twenty-seven and moved out while he was incarcerated."

"Any evidence he's been in contact with her?" Ball asked.

"The residents aren't supposed to call or talk to their exes," Harlow threw in. When all four of the men around the table turned to stare at her, she quickly said, "Not everyone has an ex, but it's a general condition of living at First Hope. I know that doesn't mean that they don't, but it's against the rules. The waiting list to get into the shelter is pretty long, and I don't think any of the residents would risk breaking the rules and getting kicked out."

"I agree," Ro said. "I've been there enough to get the vibe that they all know how lucky they are to be there."

"Exactly," Harlow said.

"Right. So if I can continue," Meat said a little impatiently.

Black was ready to tear him a new asshole if he upset Harlow, but her lips twitched as if she was trying not to smile, so he let it go.

"The divorce went through without any issues. Since neither Nate nor Carrie had much money, and they didn't have kids, it was fairly straightforward. Wyatt Newton is currently living with his new girlfriend and her kids. He—"

"Wait—she has kids?" Harlow asked, leaning forward in her chair.

"Yeah," Meat said. "Two. An eleven-year-old boy and a five-year-old girl. Why?"

"What an asshole," Harlow said before taking a long drink from her glass. "He just up and left Julia and Jasper, telling them he didn't want a family anymore, said he'd found a new woman to love. Looks like *that* was a big fat lie. At least the part about not wanting a family."

"Did you expect him to be an upstanding citizen?" Black asked gently.

"Well, no, I guess not," she said, turning to him. "But Jasper isn't doing well. He's only thirteen, and he's upset that his own father threw him away. He doesn't trust anyone anymore, and that's just wrong for someone his age. If you can't count on your father, who *can* you count on?"

"He can count on us," Black said firmly. "And you. And Loretta and his mom. It sucks that had to happen to him, but would it be better for his father to still be living with them and cheating on his mom and treating him like shit?"

"No," Harlow said grudgingly. "But he's struggling. And if he knew his father's new family included a boy around his age, it would devastate him. Heck, maybe that's why he's struggling," she mused. "Maybe he overheard his mom talking about it or something."

"I'll talk to him," Black said.

"Me too," Ball chimed in.

"We could invite him to play football with us . . . er . . . soccer to you Americans," Ro added.

"Um, he's not exactly athletic," Harlow told them. "His dad always wanted him to play football—real football, I mean, *American* football—and Jasper didn't want anything to do with it."

"What does he like to do?" Meat asked.

"Play video games," Harlow said.

"Let me know which ones, and I'll add him to one of my teams," Meat told her.

"Thanks," she said softly. Then she looked each man in the eye and said, "Thank you. I know he'd love that. But if you don't mean it, don't start anything with him. Don't promise to spend time with him, then go back on that promise. He's had enough of that in his life."

Ball frowned at her. "We aren't like his asshole of a father," he scolded Harlow gently. "If we say we're going to do something, we're going to do it."

Black felt Harlow tense beside him and had opened his mouth to soften Ball's words when Harlow nudged him with her elbow and asked, "Is that another rule about your world?"

He huffed out a breath. "Yeah, Harl. It definitely is."

"What rule? What world?" Ro asked.

Black waved his hand. "Nothing. Never mind."

"I'm sorry," Harlow told the group. "I shouldn't have jumped down your throats. Of course you aren't like Wyatt. I appreciate you offering to hang out with Jasper."

Black liked that she had no problem admitting when she'd been wrong. "What else, Meat?"

"Sue Myers, Ann Smith, Lauren French, and Kristen Schaefer don't have any big, bad exes in their pasts that I found on my initial search. They've fallen on hard times, no doubt about that, but their reliance on the shelter doesn't seem to be because of an ex-boyfriend or -girlfriend. Declan Hamlin is a first-rate asshole, beat on his wife and kid, and when she finally stood up to him, kicked them both out. The divorce isn't final, and he's fighting every little thing that Melinda asks for—except custody of their son, Milo. He doesn't want the kid, just doesn't want Melinda to get any money or belongings.

"Zachary Morehouse is deceased, as you know. That's a sad case, as he was about to join the Army. He and Bethany Zimmerman weren't married yet, even though they have a five-year-old daughter. Anyway, then there's Charles Royal, otherwise known as Chuck. He just turned forty and has been fired from at least ten different jobs. He's an alcoholic who prefers to sit around the house and drink rather than work. His wife, Lisa, had two jobs to try to keep a roof over their heads, but it wasn't enough. When they were kicked out, he disappeared. I haven't been able to find him yet.

"And lastly, there's Travis Bronson. If I had to guess, this is the guy we should be looking into the most. He's forty-nine now and ten years older than Violet. They got married when she was only eighteen. She's been in and out of the hospital most of their marriage—with broken bones and stories about being clumsy. Lacie was born after ten years of marriage, and Violet has had several miscarriages since then. From what I can piece together, Violet fled with her daughter after Lacie ended up in the emergency room with a broken arm. There's a note in her file that says the nurse suspected abuse in the home. Travis is one mean son of a bitch, and he's not happy that his wife and daughter disappeared."

Black put his arm around Harlow and squeezed her waist in support. She'd gotten paler and paler as she'd listened to Meat recite the awful things about the residents she cooked for. He and the others were used to hearing about the worst of human nature, but Harlow obviously wasn't.

"So you think Travis has found them?" she asked.

"I didn't say that," Meat corrected.

"But you said—" She didn't get any further before Meat interrupted.

"I said if I had to guess, he was my top suspect. But nothing that you've told Black matches what our experiences are in cases like this."

"What do you mean?"

"I highly doubt the men harassing you and the others are any of the exes of the residents. The youngest is Nate Taylor, but he's African American—and you didn't say anything about any of the men you've seen being black."

"They aren't," Harlow confirmed.

"Right. So it's not him. We have a lot more research to do before we can say who's behind this and why. It could be just as you thought—a bunch of bored punks picking on women and kids because they can. Or it could be someone's ex hired them to make trouble for some reason or another. Or maybe it's someone from *your* past, or Loretta's. Or it's something completely unrelated to any of you.

"The thing you need to understand is that we never jump to conclusions. There are a million reasons why this could be happening, and until we narrow that million down to just one, we'll continue to look at everyone and every situation. Now . . . we need to talk about *your* exes."

With that, Harlow's eyes got wide, and she looked at the men, who were staring at her expectantly, before turning to Black. "I don't have any exes."

"Harl," he said gently. "Since I've seen you today, you've told me at least four stories about dates gone bad—including the asshole who took you on a high-speed chase and was planning on roofie-ing you after or during your date."

She shook her head. "Right, but I wasn't actually *dating* any of them. I mean, I've been *on* dates, but usually it's only one before they show me what douches they are. I wouldn't consider them ex-anythings."

"Someone was going to roofie you?" Ro asked.

At the same time Ball said, "A high-speed chase?"

Harlow glanced at the other men, then dropped her head on her arms on the table. "Shoot me now," she mumbled.

Black brushed her hair out of the way and placed his hand on the back of her neck. He squeezed lightly in support as he said to his friends, "How about you let me get that info from her? I'll pass along anything that might be pertinent."

He felt goose bumps pebble on Harlow's skin and inwardly smiled in satisfaction. No matter what she might say verbally, she enjoyed his touch. He could work with that.

"How long have you known each other?" Meat asked with a tilt of his head.

"Since we were teenagers," Black said immediately.

Harlow sat up at that. "Well, we met in high school, but I didn't see him again until last month when he came by the shelter."

"So you've been seeing each other since then?" Ro asked, obviously trying to figure out the dynamics between them.

"No. But I did give her my number," Black said with a smile.

Harlow rolled her eyes. "I called him because of everything that's been going on. A month ago, he said that he'd help get me enrolled in a beginner's gun-safety class at his range. I called today to ask if he'd be willing to come back to the shelter and teach more self-defense stuff to the women because of the harassment."

"So . . . you knew each other in high school, you saw each other after years and years last month, you called him earlier today, and now you're dating?" Ball asked, trying to sum up the situation.

"No!" Harlow denied.

At the same time, Black said, "Yes, except for the fact we aren't dating."

He smiled at Harlow and reminded his friends, "Harlow doesn't date. As she's said, she hasn't had good luck in that area. So we're just chatting. Talking about the situation at the shelter."

"I think I want to know more about these not-so-great dates of yours," Meat said. "I've never met anyone who's given up on dating altogether before."

Black knew he was teasing *him* more than he was Harlow. It was obvious to his friends that he felt protective of, and was attracted to, the woman next to him. He narrowed his eyes at Meat and shook his head slightly.

Meat either didn't see him or ignored his warning, because he went on. "I mean, Black hasn't dated in forever, but I don't think he can blame that on dates gone wrong. He's just a picky son of a bitch who's like that *Seinfeld* character. He always finds something wrong with the women he's been with. You know . . . too clingy, not clingy enough, too tall, her name is too weird—things like that."

"Jesus, Meat, shut the fuck up," Black growled.

"It's only fair," Harlow said. "If I have to tell you all about *my* messed-up dating history, I should know about yours in return."

"How about this? I don't want to know about *either* of your fucked-up past dates," Ro said dryly. "Chloe is waiting for me at home, and she hasn't been feeling well for the past week, and tonight is the first night she's feeling good enough to do more than sleep in our bed, if you know what I mean. So if we can get on with this so I can go home to my girl, I'd appreciate it."

Black smirked and Harlow blushed.

"Fine," Meat conceded. "But seriously, Harlow, if you have even the slightest bad feeling about any of the douchebags who couldn't see for themselves how awesome you are, you give Black their names, and he'll pass them on to me. I *do* want the name of the roofie guy, though. That's nonnegotiable."

"Okay," she said quietly.

Black hadn't taken his hand from her nape when she'd sat up, and he gave her another squeeze in support.

"Right, so . . . tell us more about the men hanging around the shelter," Ball ordered. "We need to know everything you can remember about them. What they look like, if they have an accent, if you've seen them driving any specific vehicle, tattoos, everything."

For the next twenty minutes, Harlow told the men everything she could. Unfortunately, it wasn't a lot. They knew the men were young looking, liked to wear baggy pants and white shirts. She rarely saw them in cars, and they didn't have any discernible accents. Basically, they had nothing concrete to go on.

"I'm sorry, guys. I usually try not to look directly at them when they're taunting and yelling stuff. I suppose I can try to get closer to them the next time I see them so—"

"No!" all four men exclaimed at once.

Harlow winced and held up her hands. "Okay, okay. It was just a thought."

"If you see them, you walk the other way," Black ordered. "Better yet, if you're close enough, go back inside the shelter and call me or one of the others. I'll make sure you have everyone's phone numbers. And if you're already in the parking lot, you get in your car and leave immediately. Don't stop to put down the top either. You can do that later."

"The top?" Ball asked.

"She's got a Mustang convertible," Black told the others.

Ball whistled. "Sweet ride."

"It is," Harlow agreed with a smile.

"She drives like she's ninety," Black teased.

"I do not!" she argued.

"From what I saw, you do," Black countered.

"So I'm not a speed demon like you," she said. "And I'm a safe driver. There's nothing wrong with that."

"No, there's not," Black agreed.

Harlow looked at the others. "I appreciate you trying to help. I mean, the men make me uncomfortable, but I can't imagine how the others are feeling. Especially with their backgrounds. I hate that Violet and the others have been through what they have. It sucks."

"It does. And we're going to bloody well get to the bottom of it," Ro said firmly. "Now . . . are we done here?" he asked.

Black, Ball, and Meat smiled.

"We're done. Get home to Chloe," Black told his friend. He'd never been jealous of his friends before, but something about the anticipation gleaming in Ro's eyes got to him tonight as it never had in the past.

And it wasn't about the sex. Okay, it wasn't *just* about the sex. It was about having someone in your life who was just as excited to see you as you were them. It was about having someone to share your days and nights with.

"I'm going to talk to Rex about getting some cameras set up outside the shelter," Ball said. "We need to get some eyes and ears on the perimeter."

Black nodded. He'd already thought about that himself, but figured the others would take care of it.

"I'll keep digging," Meat said as he pushed up from the table. "There's got to be something we're missing."

After the other men had left, Black turned to Harlow. "Are you okay?"

She sighed. "Yeah. I just hate this."

"I know." And he did. Black had seen the devastation that abuse and neglect caused women and kids firsthand. Wanting to get her mind off the things she'd heard about the residents' pasts, he asked, "So you aren't working tomorrow morning?"

She shook her head. "No. Zoe took dinner tonight and has breakfast in the morning. We switch off, and if one of us has plans, we'll cover for the other. Sometimes Loretta gives us both a morning off. When she does, we make sure there are muffins and lots of other breakfast foods for everyone to munch on when they get up."

"You sound like you really enjoy it. I take it working there is very different from being a chef in a restaurant?"

"Night and day," she said definitively. "Don't get me wrong, sometimes I miss making fancy meals and making sure the presentation is perfect, but making comfort food and seeing the women and kids eat as if they've never tasted anything better is so much more rewarding. Not once has someone sent their plate back to me because they thought something was under- or overcooked."

"You like the kids," Black said. It wasn't a question.

"No. I love the kids," Harlow said, fiddling with her empty glass. "They're innocent in everything. And they love learning. Even the boys are excited to be in the kitchen. You should've seen the grin on Jasper's face when the homemade bread he made came out perfectly. And the little ones' favorite thing to do is decorate sugar cookies. I only wish I'd made the change sooner."

"Do your parents still live in Topeka?" Black asked.

"Yeah. They're both retired now. Mom volunteers at least thirty hours a week, and my dad works in his woodshop about as much. What about your folks?"

"They moved to Florida not too long after I graduated from college. They love Orlando and the weather down there."

"I bet they're proud of you," Harlow said.

Black shrugged. "I guess. Although there's not much to be proud of as a gun-range owner."

"You haven't told them about the Mountain Mercenaries?"

"No. I know it might not seem like it, with how easily Loretta spoke to you about us, but we don't exactly go out of our way to tell people who we are and what we do. It would make us and our loved ones targets."

"I hadn't thought about it that way," Harlow said. "I'm sorry. I'll keep my mouth shut about it."

Black smiled and nudged her with his shoulder. "It's fine. I trust you."

She frowned at that, but asked, "And your brother? I think you said he was a photographer?"

"Yup. He's usually out of the country on an assignment. He's freelance and goes where the excitement is. He's sold pictures to *National Geographic* and all of the major news outlets."

"Is it dangerous?"

"Yes and no. I mean, obviously being in the middle of an Egyptian coup is dangerous, but so is lying in the middle of the African prairie when there's a stampede of wildebeests."

Her eyes got big. "Did that happen?"

"What? The coup or the stampede?"

"Either."

"Yes."

"Wow."

"Yeah. So Mom and Dad generally worry about Lance more than they do me. For all they know, I'm hanging out here in Colorado Springs with my gun-loving friends," Black said with a smile.

"Thank you, Lowell," Harlow said sincerely.

"For what?"

"Where do I start? Thank you for your service to our country. I know you probably saw and did a lot of shitty stuff. For helping out women and kids who need it. For helping *me*. For not being weird about my quirks. For introducing me to your friends. For trusting me with what you do. Just . . . thank you."

"You don't have to thank me," Black said quietly, wanting more than anything to take her in his arms and kiss the living daylights out of her. Her cheeks were flushed, probably because of the bourbon in her drink. He had a feeling she thought her T-shirt and jeans were a type of armor, that he couldn't possibly be attracted to her in them, but she'd be wrong. She looked comfortable and relaxed—exactly how he liked a woman to be. And he couldn't help but think about the effort she'd gone to with her hair and toenails . . . possibly for him.

Black wasn't ready to get married, wasn't sure he ever wanted to tie himself to a woman that deeply, but he wanted Harlow. Wanted her under him, over him, and any other way he could get her.

"You want to play pool?" he asked, gesturing toward the room with his head.

She looked at the game tables, then back at him. "I probably shouldn't. Since we're done talking about work, I should have you take me home."

"I still need to hear about all of these bad dates of yours," Black reminded her.

Harlow groaned. "Do I have to?"

"Yup." Black kept his tone light and teasing. "You heard Meat. We need to figure out if any of those guys could be involved in what's happening at the shelter."

"Fine. But I'm going to need another drink. And I guess I'd feel more comfortable if I could do something with my hands while I tell you all my secrets."

The image her words brought to Black's head was indecent and carnal. He could give her something to do with her hands . . . but he forced back the thought and stood. "Come on. We'll tell Dave that you're ready for another and then get the table set up. You've played pool before?"

She stood as well and put one hand on her hip. "Oh yeah, Lowell, I've played pool before." Her eyes were gleaming with challenge.

"You brave enough to make a small wager?"

"Bring it," she responded.

Chapter Six

Harlow groaned as she woke. Her head was throbbing, and she felt as if she'd been sucking on cotton balls all night. The second she opened her eyes, she remembered everything about the night before.

Damn it.

She turned over onto her side and stared at the water and bottle of pills on the small table by her bed. Closing her eyes, she replayed the previous evening.

She'd sucked down the Woodford and Cokes as if they were glasses of water instead of booze. She and Lowell had played one game of pool to feel each other out, to see where their strengths and weaknesses lay. Then the competition had been on. They'd planned on playing the best out of three games. That had turned to the best out of five. Then seven. In the end, Lowell had beaten her four games to three.

It was a good thing that she didn't have to go to the shelter to cook this morning, because she hadn't been this hungover in a very long time. If ever.

Lowell had drunk two beers, then switched to water. He'd skillfully gotten her to recount as many of her embarrassing dates as she could remember as they played.

She'd told him about the guy who'd asked if he could have sex with her feet at the end of the night, and when she'd declined, he'd offered to pay for the privilege.

She'd told him about the time her date had taken her to an expensive restaurant, and at the end of the night, he'd put the cloth napkins in his pockets. When she'd asked him what he was doing, instead of just admitting he was stealing, he'd said that his nose was running and he wanted to make sure he had something to wipe it with later.

Harlow told Lowell about the blind date a friend had set her up with. The man had shown up in a car that was barely operational. He smelled like BO and had the worst breath she'd ever had the misfortune of smelling. She'd tried to back out of the date, but he'd started crying, so she'd decided to just go through with it. He'd tried to kiss her the second she'd gotten in his car, and his hands were sweaty as he tried to hold hers. During the drive, he'd told her how much he loved her and how many kids they were going to have when they got married and lived in his mom's garage. They'd gone to a fast-food restaurant for dinner, and he'd proposed when he brought her back to her apartment. Needless to say, when she'd said no, he'd cried again.

Then there was the man who'd taken one look at her when he'd arrived at her door and turned around, walking away and mumbling under his breath that he wouldn't have come if he'd known she was "fat."

And finally, she'd told him about the guy she'd agreed to a second date with—her first second date in a very long time, and she'd worked really hard to make him a nice meal in her apartment. He'd excused himself after eating and was gone for way longer than she'd expected. Harlow had thought maybe he was having gastrointestinal issues and hadn't wanted to embarrass him by asking if he was okay when he finally emerged from the back hallway of her apartment.

It wasn't until she'd gone to bed later that night that she'd found out he hadn't been in her bathroom at all. He'd jacked off all over a stuffed rabbit that had been on her bed at the time.

Lowell hadn't laughed at her bad luck. He hadn't told her she was being silly for taking a break from dating. In fact, he'd been pissed on her behalf, especially about the guy who had ejaculated on her bed. He'd demanded to know if she'd pressed charges, and when she admitted she hadn't, had just told the guy off in no uncertain terms the next time he'd called, Lowell still hadn't been happy. He'd mumbled something about looking up that man first to make sure he wasn't in the area, harassing her and the residents at the shelter.

And, as if telling Lowell all her deep, dark horror stories about dating wasn't embarrassing enough, she'd gotten so drunk, she hadn't been able to walk to the car on her own. He'd had to put his arm around her to keep her upright. She remembered their conversation on the way to his car in the parking lot with complete clarity.

"I'm sorry I got so drunk."

"It's fine, Harl."

"I never do this. Ever. Especially around a guy."

"I'm glad you trust me enough to let go."

"I do, you know."

"Do what?"

"Trust you."

"Good. Because I won't hurt you, Harlow. I'm not like those douchebags you've dated."

"I know you aren't. I feel like I've known you forever, even though I haven't seen you in years. This is the best nondate I've ever had."

"Me too."

"And I would've won if we played best out of nine."

He turned her then so they were face to face and belly to belly. "I have no doubt you would've."

Harlow thought he was going to kiss her, but instead, he turned her and helped her into his car, even leaned over and buckled her seat belt before shutting her door and walking around to the driver's side.

When he sat down, Harlow said, "You have a nice ass."

"Thanks. Yours isn't so bad either."

She smiled at him, then closed her eyes as he started the car. The world spun drunkenly as he drove her home, but Harlow didn't care. She felt protected and had no doubts whatsoever that Lowell would get her home safe and sound.

Wincing at how much she'd told him, Harlow opened her eyes and saw the pills and water once more. She remembered Lowell helping her into her apartment and helping her take off her jeans.

"Take off your jeans, Harl."

"Are we having nondate sex?"

"No, baby. You're drunk as hell, and I'd never take advantage of you like that. I'm trying to make sure you're comfortable so you can sleep."

"Oh. Okay."

Her hands fumbled so much he finally brushed them away and eased her onto the bed. He then unbuttoned her pants himself. He drew down the zipper before going to stand at the end of the mattress.

"Raise your hips, baby."

She did, and he pulled her jeans down her legs. "Take your bra off now, Harlow."

Without thought, she sat up and reached behind her to unhook the clasp. It took a few tries, but she finally managed to undo it. She reached into one sleeve of her T-shirt and pulled the strap down, then did the same on the other side. She pulled the bra out of her shirt through the armhole.

"I'll never get tired of seeing you do that. Now lie back."

Harlow did as ordered, feeling the room spinning crazily around her.

"Here, take these and drink this."

She opened her eyes to see Lowell sitting on the edge of her mattress holding a bottle of water and two small white pills in his hand. Without thinking about what he was giving her, she sat back up and took the pills. Lowell put a hand behind her back to support and hold her steady as she finished the entire bottle he'd brought for her.

He eased her back to the bed, leaned down, and kissed her forehead.

"I put another bottle of water by your bed. Drink it when you get up in the morning . . . or later this morning, I guess is more appropriate. Take the pills when you get up too."

"Mmm, 'kay."

That was the last thing Harlow remembered. She must've fallen asleep. She looked down at herself and saw that she was still wearing the T-shirt she'd put on before Lowell had shown up at her apartment the night before. She could see her bra on the floor by the bed, and her jeans were lying at the end of the mattress.

She was as embarrassed as could be about getting drunk in the first place, but for some reason, she wasn't mortified about Lowell helping her in her apartment. He'd been so matter-of-fact about it. He hadn't made her feel bad about being drunk, and he didn't seem put out by having to help her.

Harlow had a momentary pang of regret about giving up on dating. If she was ever tempted to break her self-imposed ban, it would be with Lowell Lockard. But the second she decided to go out with him, he'd likely do something that would make her regret it.

So no. No matter how nice he'd been last night—er, this morning—she'd just have to settle for being friends.

Sitting up and groaning at the pain that flashed through her head, Harlow picked up the pills and uncapped the bottle of water. She swallowed the painkillers and shuffled to the bathroom, sipping at the water the entire way.

Her phone was sitting on the edge of the counter. Harlow didn't remember how it had gotten there, but she picked it up—and the first thing she saw was a text from Lowell.

Lowell: Call me when you get up so I know you're okay.

She stared at the note for a long moment before closing her eyes and leaning over the counter. "You are not dating Lowell Lockard," Harlow muttered before reaching for her toothbrush. *No matter how much you might want to.*

Harlow: I'm up and alive. :)

Black stared at Harlow's text in relief. He was sitting in his office at the range and had been debating with himself on whether or not to call her. He didn't want to seem too eager, but on the other hand, he was truly worried about her. She'd had way too much to drink the night before, and it was mostly his fault. He'd thought about staying the night to make sure she didn't get sick and choke, but in the end decided that might be pushing his luck.

He'd thought that having a few drinks would loosen her up and make it easier for her to tell him about the dates in her past. He'd been right, it *had* made it easier, but he'd let it go on too long. He should've cut off their games at five. But she'd convinced him she was fine, and he'd believed her.

She hadn't been fine. She'd been trashed and just good at hiding it. He appreciated the fact that she didn't get mean or emotional when she drank, but he regretted not making sure she'd eaten before taking her to The Pit. That had been a mistake, and one he wouldn't make again.

Shaking his head, Black huffed out a long breath. He understood Harlow a lot better now. He couldn't blame her for swearing off dating. If he'd had the kind of luck she'd had, he would've done the same. The way her dates had treated her infuriated him. Jacking off in her house? Carrying around date-rape drugs? Proposing on the first night they'd met? Man, she'd certainly come into contact with some real losers. He'd made a mental note of the men's names and had already passed them to Meat for investigation. He almost hoped one of her past dates was behind everything that was going on; it would give him an excuse to beat the shit out of him.

Interestingly enough, nothing that happened the night before had turned Black off from wanting to get to know her better. It was exactly the opposite. He liked that she wasn't willing to settle. That she knew her own worth. It made being with her a challenge, but Black was up for it.

The phone on his desk rang, and he leaned over to answer it. "Black's Gun Range."

"It's Rex," the digitally altered voice on the other end of the phone said.

Black was well used to the fact that Rex disguised his voice. When Black had first started working for the Mountain Mercenaries, he'd been beyond curious about their elusive boss, but now he took the man's eccentricities in stride. "Rex," he replied in greeting.

"Heard you had an interesting night," Rex said.

Black smiled. Rex didn't miss much. Especially when the events took place in The Pit. Black assumed he had the place wired, but it didn't bother him in the least. "Meat talk to you?" he asked his boss.

"Yeah. His research's underway. And you should also know there's nothing else in the wings at the moment."

Black understood and appreciated what Rex meant. He was informing him there weren't any cases looming for the Mountain Mercenaries. That didn't mean one couldn't pop up without warning, but at the moment, he was free to concentrate on Harlow and the women's shelter.

"Good. Do you have any new information for me?"

"Not yet. But I don't like what I've heard from Meat."

"Me either. Especially now that I've gotten to know Harlow a little more."

"You've known her for one day," Rex said dryly.

"It's been more than a day, but in that time, I've gotten to know her fairly well," Black insisted.

Rex chuckled. "Right, I've forgotten how you boys operate."

"It isn't like that," Black said irritably.

"Uh-huh."

"It's not," he insisted. "Look, I know the others are happy being tied down, but that's not me. I'm not necessarily looking for a wife right now."

"What *are* you looking for?" Rex asked perceptively. A little *too* perceptively.

"I wouldn't mind dating Harlow. She's funny, interesting, and smart," Black said. "I'm not opposed to being in a relationship."

"Hmmm."

"You don't believe me?" Black asked.

"It's not that. But I know you, Black. I know you've been restless lately. I get wanting to show Harlow that not all men are douchebags, and I agree that maybe at this point, you haven't thought past dating her. But you're not normally as protective of anyone as you seem to be with Miss Reese. I'm not judging you. If all you want is to get your rocks off, have at it. But don't talk yourself out of something else you might *really* want. If you do, you'll regret it for the rest of your life."

There was more meaning behind Rex's words, but Black was too annoyed by his insightfulness to think about it. "She's not interested in dating right now."

"And yet the two of you stayed at The Pit until two in the morning, laughing, talking, and playing pool. She got drunk, and you stayed sober to make sure she was safe. Then you took her home and, I'm assuming, got her settled and left her safe and sound in her bed. Don't bullshit me, Black. I wasn't born yesterday. Call it what you want, but last night was a date. Harlow was as into you as you were her."

"So I have to get your permission to date now?" Black asked flippantly.

"No." Rex's voice quieted. "All I'm saying is to let yourself be happy. You deserve it as much as she does."

Black wasn't sure what to say about that. Rex was right, he *did* deserve to be happy, just as Harlow did, but one day in, and he was already confused about his feelings for her. He hadn't lied: he wasn't opposed to being in a long-term relationship with someone, but things seemed extraordinarily complicated at the moment with Harlow.

"The day I met my wife, I knew she was it for me," Rex continued. "Sometimes you just know."

"I'm not ready to get married," Black told his handler.

"Just be open to the relationship," Rex said. "Don't talk yourself out of it before you see where it can go. You can be friends and still hang out with her. You don't have to call what you do with her dates."

Shit, now Rex was reading his mind.

Black was done. He wasn't going to talk about his love life with his boss. "You call for a reason, Rex?"

"You mean other than to tell you I approve?" Rex asked with a chuckle.

"Yeah, other than that."

"Actually, yes. Meat ordered cameras. They'll be in sometime tomorrow. You and Arrow can install them at the shelter the day after."

Black sat up straighter in anticipation. He was going to check on the ladies at the shelter anyway. He tried to remember when Harlow said she was working but couldn't. He knew Zoe was taking breakfast today, but wasn't sure what the chefs' schedules were for the rest of the week. "Ten-four," he told Rex. "I'll get with Arrow and see what he needs from me."

"Later," Rex said.

Black hung up when he heard the dial tone in his ear. He sat at his desk for a long while, thinking about everything Rex had said, and about what *he* wanted. It was obvious Harlow was uneasy about relationships, but the two of them had definitely clicked regardless of her feelings on dating.

He liked hanging out with her. She was exactly how he remembered her being in high school. Funny, considerate, and honest.

Three traits he needed in a girlfriend.

Shaking his head, Black huffed out a breath. "Not a girlfriend," he mumbled. He closed his eyes, still going over the call, and eventually decided Rex had just confirmed what he himself had already decided.

Not about marrying Harlow, but taking things one day at a time. He might find out she secretly liked to kick puppies or had some other unforgivable trait.

Then his mind wandered to the way she'd felt tucked against his side, and he smiled. She fit against him perfectly. Since they were the same height, their bodies aligned as if they were made for each other.

Black opened his eyes and reached for the keyboard to his laptop. Harlow had enough shitty dates under her belt to last a lifetime. He couldn't wait to show her there were some good men still out there, himself first and foremost. He'd plan the most amazing dates for the two of them to erase the memories of all the bad ones—without calling them dates, of course.

He'd have to be sneaky, but he was a former Navy SEAL. He could do sneaky.

Turning his attention to the computer, Black got busy researching the best places to take a woman in Colorado Springs. Their outings had to be different and unconventional so Harlow didn't suspect they were dates.

Feeling more anticipation than he had in years about spending time with a woman, Black scrolled through the suggestions on a website he found, and grinned. This was going to be fun.

Chapter Seven

Harlow puttered around the kitchen getting the evening meal ready. Normally cooking soothed her, quieted her mind, but this afternoon her mind was anything but quiet. She hadn't heard from Lowell after she'd sent him the text the day before yesterday, letting him know she was all right. She'd tried not to be disappointed about that, but failed.

Which was silly. She and Lowell weren't dating. She'd told herself that a million times . . . but something inside refused to think of him as just a friend.

It was Loretta who'd informed her when she'd shown up for lunch duty—the schedule had changed, as it frequently did—that Rex had requested they put up cameras on the outside of the property, and two of the Mountain Mercenaries would be coming over to install them today.

Harlow had tried not to get her hopes up that Lowell would be one of the men to arrive, but it was impossible. She felt the same way she had back in high school right before the yearbook club meetings. Anticipation and nervousness.

"Stupid," she muttered to herself as she chopped the fresh vegetables for the salad she was making.

"What's stupid?"

Harlow almost chopped the tip of her finger off when she heard his voice.

Looking up, she saw Lowell standing in the doorway of the kitchen, much like he had the last time he'd been there.

"You really need to stop scaring me," she scolded.

He merely smirked and retorted, "I actually purposely made noise this time. *You* really should be more aware of your surroundings." Then he strolled over to her and kissed her on the cheek in greeting as if it were nothing out of the ordinary.

Harlow's heart was beating double time, and she hadn't done anything more strenuous than stand completely still as he'd kissed her.

"How are you?" he asked.

"Good."

He nodded and smiled at her, and Harlow almost melted into a puddle right there in the kitchen.

"You look good. Me and Arrow will be here for a while putting up external cameras. Would you be willing to be our guinea pig once they're up? Help us make sure they're all aimed in the right directions and stuff?"

"Of course."

"Great. I'll be back later then."

Then he reached up and fingered a lock of her hair that had come down from the bun she'd thrown it in before starting the dinner prep. Without another word, he smiled even wider, then left.

After he was gone, Harlow couldn't stop thinking about his actions. About how he'd so nonchalantly kissed her. Fingered her hair as if he did it every day. She went over it again and again in her head, until she finally had to scold herself for analyzing it to death.

Lowell knew where she stood about dating. In her experience, men didn't go out of their way to be just friends with women. Especially men who looked like Lowell.

She'd stalked him on the internet the night before. She hadn't been able to find much, but what she did find impressed her. Lowell was a highly decorated Navy veteran, and she understood that what little she could find online was probably only the tip of the iceberg when it came to his accolades. Navy SEALs did a lot of top-secret operations, so it was likely he had a lot of medals and commendations under his bed, so to speak.

There were several articles in the local paper about him and the others volunteering time and money for charities that helped at-risk women, sick children, and those generally down on their luck. He occasionally went to the high school and offered free self-defense classes for the girls, and was even named Volunteer of the Year at the local Boys & Girls Club one year.

Yes, Lowell Lockard was a good man. And there was no reason for him to expend energy on her when she'd flat-out told him she wouldn't date. She was a chef, for God's sake. She spent her days in the kitchen, and enjoyed it. She pictured him with someone who could go hiking for hours and days, who loved camping, kayaking, white-water rafting, and other outdoor sports. She didn't mind being outside and enjoying the fresh air and views, but she hated bugs and sweating. Two things she had a feeling didn't faze Lowell in the least.

Not only that, but he was one hundred percent different from the men she'd attempted to date in the past. He was simply out of her league. Harlow knew it, and she had a feeling he knew it too.

Taking a deep breath and putting him out of her mind, she turned her attention back to the meal she was making. Roasted chicken with asiago polenta and truffled mushrooms. Most of the kids wouldn't eat the mushrooms, but she included them for variety anyway. Not to mention they perfectly complemented the simply flavored chicken. She was going to add a salad and, to top it off, chocolate brownies with butterscotch drizzle for dessert.

She could hear Lowell and his friend talking outside as they installed the cameras. Hearing them, knowing they were close, soothed her. For the first time in at least a month at the shelter, Harlow relaxed completely. No one would dare harass any of the residents, or her, when the men were outside working.

Harlow knew she'd been tense over the last few weeks. Cooking and baking usually relaxed her, but lately, every time she got near the shelter, her entire body tensed up.

She'd actually been very close to quitting when she'd decided to call Lowell instead. She didn't want to leave, but the harassment was stressing her out and making her extremely jumpy. She hadn't said anything to Loretta and felt horrible about even thinking about leaving. The older woman had taken a chance on hiring her, since the job was way different from the usual restaurant jobs she'd had in the past, and Harlow appreciated it more than she could say.

She also hated the idea of leaving the kids. They touched her in a way no one else could. She'd always wanted a family. But with the way her life was going, it looked like that would probably never happen. Especially since she'd put the moratorium on dating.

"It smells good in here."

The deep male voice once again scared the shit out of her. Harlow jerked, then cried out in pain when the knife she'd been rinsing sliced her finger.

"Damn it, Arrow! I told you to make some noise before you came in here," Lowell bit out as he pushed his friend aside and strode toward her.

Harlow could only stare at Lowell as he approached. He looked amazing. Physical labor agreed with him. A sheen of sweat covered his forehead and neck, and the white T-shirt he was wearing was streaked with dirt. His black hair was mussed, and even the five o'clock shadow on his jaw already seemed darker.

"Let me see, Harl," he said in a calm voice, taking hold of her hand and shutting off the water in the sink.

Harlow let him examine her hand, and she swallowed hard as his brow furrowed when he saw the cut.

"Sorry," Arrow said as he came closer and stood on her other side. "I thought you heard me clear my throat."

Harlow shook her head. "I wasn't paying attention."

"This doesn't look too bad," Lowell told her. "It doesn't look like you'll need stitches. Do you have a first-aid kit around here?"

"Of course," Harlow told him. She gestured to a cabinet on the other side of the room. "Over there."

Arrow immediately headed in that direction.

Harlow remained in front of the sink with Lowell. She faced him, their bodies extremely close together.

"Being near you makes me realize how badly I must stink," he said softly. He had grabbed a paper towel and wrapped it around her finger and was now putting pressure on the cut, holding her finger captive in his strong grasp.

She shook her head in denial. "You're fine."

He chuckled. "I'm not, and I know that because your vanilla scent and the smell of butterscotch and chocolate is almost overpowering."

"I'm sorry," she whispered.

"Don't ever be sorry for smelling like dessert," he said huskily.

"This thing is awesome," Arrow said as he came toward them, making Harlow jerk away from Lowell in embarrassment. But Lowell reached down and put his free hand on her hip, keeping her close.

"It's got just about everything a professional medic would have," Arrow continued, riffling through the medical paraphernalia in the first-aid kit.

"Your idea?" Lowell asked, scarily accurately.

Harlow shrugged. "You already know I tend to be clumsy, and with kids around here, I figured it couldn't hurt to be prepared."

She couldn't interpret the look on Lowell's face, so she turned her attention to Arrow. He was a bit taller than she and Lowell. His hair was very short, almost buzzed, and he was just as muscular as all the men on his team she'd met so far. He was handsome, but she didn't feel the sparks she felt when she looked at Lowell.

"It looks like the bleeding has almost stopped."

Harlow looked down at her finger and saw that Lowell had taken the pressure off and was examining the cut closely. His neck was bent as he was looking at her finger, and Harlow's hand actually twitched with the intention of brushing a lock of hair off his forehead, but she caught herself before she did something super embarrassing.

"I'm fine," she said. "You have no idea how many times I've cut myself. It's a job hazard. Just throw a Band-Aid on there."

Without a reply, Lowell looked at Arrow. "I'll need some Steri-Strips, hydrogen peroxide, a regular Band-Aid, and some antibiotic cream."

"Coming right up," Arrow said, digging around in the first-aid kit.

"Seriously, Lowell, all I need—" She didn't finish her sentence because Lowell wrapped his arm around her waist and steered her over to a section of counter that she'd already cleaned after making the brownies.

"On the count of three, hop up," he told her.

"What? *No*, Lowell."

"One. Two. *Three.*"

With no choice, Harlow did as he ordered and gave a little hop to help him boost her up on the counter. He held her waist firmly until she had her balance, then moved one hand to her knee. He gently pushed it outward until he was standing between her legs.

Harlow knew she was blushing, but she couldn't control it no matter how hard she tried. Her legs were spread, and if the counter were just a bit shorter, she would have been crotch to crotch with Lowell.

He took her hand in his once more and busied himself doctoring the slight cut. After he dabbed the hydrogen peroxide on her skin, he gently blew on her finger, trying to soothe the slight sting. Then he used the Steri-Strips to hold the cut together, slathered the antibiotic goo on it, and covered everything with a Band-Aid. The entire process took only a minute or two, but Harlow had never felt so cared for as she did right at that moment.

"Okay?" he asked, resting his hands on either side of her hips on the granite countertop and leaning closer.

Harlow nodded.

"Good. I'd like you to meet another teammate of mine. This is Arrow. Arrow, this is Harlow Reese. One of two cooks for the shelter and one hell of a pool player."

Harlow managed to take her eyes off Lowell's to look over at his friend. "Hi." She ignored the heat coming from Lowell's forearms as they touched her outer thighs.

"Whatever you're making smells delicious. Chocolate?" Arrow asked. "Morgan would love it."

"Morgan?"

"My girlfriend. Morgan Byrd."

Harlow stared at him in surprise, but was too polite to ask the question on the tip of her tongue.

But her curiosity was obviously plain to see on her face, because he said, "Yes, *that* Morgan Byrd. She's doing wonderfully."

"Oh my. I admire her so much!" Harlow gushed. "I mean, I don't know everything she went through, but I saw the interview she did with Barbara Walters, and I cried for her. I can't imagine being kidnapped and held for a year." Then something occurred to her. She whipped her head back around and stared at Lowell. "That was you guys? *You* found her?"

"That was us," Lowell said quietly.

Harlow gripped his wrists tightly. "Oh my God! That must've been so scary."

"I'm not sure I would say *scary*, but it was definitely a surprise," he said with a small smile.

She turned back to Arrow. "I can get you the recipe. No! I'll make another batch, and you can bring them to her." She pushed at the man standing in front of her. "Move, Lowell. I need to get the flour back out. Oh crap, I might not have enough butterscotch! I need to go to the store—"

"Calm down, Harl," Lowell said, moving his hands back to her hips and holding her still on the counter.

"No! I need to make brownies for Morgan. It's the least I can do after what she's been through. Oh, I know—maybe I can make you and her dinner one night?" she asked Arrow. "I mean, if you tell me what she likes, I'm happy to make it."

Arrow chuckled. "You don't need to cook anything fancy. Morgan isn't picky. Food is food for her at the moment. It doesn't matter what it is as long as she gets to eat a full meal whenever she wants."

At his words, Harlow closed her eyes and willed the tears that had formed not to fall. Her lips quivered, and she pressed them together, trying to stop herself from crying.

"What's wrong?" Lowell asked gently. "Talk to me, baby."

Inhaling deeply through her nose but keeping her eyes shut, Harlow croaked, "I just feel so bad for her. And all the women here. They've been through so much, and the hardest thing I've had to go through in my life is being burned out at my job and moving here without knowing anyone. I just wish I could do more to help. Like you guys do."

She felt Lowell's hands move up her sides until they were resting on her neck. His thumbs brushed lightly back and forth along her jaw. "You help more than you know, Harl."

She shook her head in denial.

"Look at me."

Sighing, Harlow took a deep breath, then opened her eyes.

Lowell's face was right in front of hers, the look in his brown eyes intense. She didn't understand what it meant. "What you do here is huge. You provide a healthy meal three times a day for everyone who lives here. You think most of them had that where they came from? Probably not. And Loretta tells me that you frequently stay past your scheduled hours to play with the kids. To teach them how to make sweets. To spend time with them. Time is precious, Harlow. Anyone can give twenty bucks to a charity organization, but very few give up their time to sit with a child and ask how their day at school was. Very few will spend their evenings off teaching a mother how to make meals so when she gets a place of her own, she can feed her kids. You're helping, Harlow. No doubt about it."

Harlow sniffed and, as a tear fell from her eye, blinked hard. Lowell was there to wipe it away.

"These women and kids will remember you long after the women I've rescued will remember me. They'll remember your smiles and how good the food you made for them was. They'll remember how you spent time with their kids without asking for anything in return. They'll remember you as a light in a very hard time in their life. That's gold, Harl. Pure fucking gold."

She could read the sincerity in his eyes. Lowell believed every word that came out of his mouth. "If you think the women you rescue don't remember you, you're delusional."

He merely shook his head.

"They do," Harlow insisted. She turned her head to look at Arrow. Lowell dropped one of his hands, but kept the other on the side of her neck. It felt good there. Too good.

"I'd still like to make dinner for you and Morgan sometime . . . if she'd be okay with that."

"She'd love it," Arrow reassured her. "But I have to warn you, if you make dinner for *us*, you're gonna have to make Gray and Allye and Ro and Chloe dinner too. And if you make *them* dinner, then you'll probably have to make something for Ball and Meat as well."

"Don't leave *me* out of the dinner party!" Lowell complained.

Arrow smirked. "One thing you'll learn about us is that we all love a good meal. Too many times we have to eat protein bars while on a mission. We'll never turn down home-cooked food."

"Deal," Harlow said.

"Do you want to help us with the cameras, or would you rather stay here and make brownies?" Lowell asked.

Turning back to him, Harlow paused. She had a deep desire to do something for Morgan, but she also wanted to spend as much time with Lowell as possible.

He grinned and rubbed his thumb along her jaw once more. Harlow hoped that he didn't notice the goose bumps that rose on her arms as a result of his caress.

"How about this? You come help us with the preliminary settings. We have to send the feeds back to Meat to make sure everything is where he wants it. While we're doing that, you can come back in and make your brownies."

"Are you sure?" Harlow asked. "I can help you guys with whatever you need."

"I'm sure."

"Okay."

"Okay."

Harlow stared at Lowell, waiting for him to pull away or say something else. When he did neither, she furrowed her brows and said, "Lowell?"

"Yeah, Harlow?"

"Um . . . are we going to go test your camera thingies?"

He sighed. Then brushed his thumb once more over her jaw and finally took a step back.

Harlow missed the feel of him against her inner thighs immediately, but she managed to hide her reaction. At least she thought she did.

Lowell held out a hand. Without thought, Harlow took it in her injured one, and he helped her hop down from the counter. Then he led her through the kitchen without letting go. She didn't miss the smirk that Arrow shot his friend's way, but she ignored it, too busy enjoying the feel of Lowell's calloused hand in hers.

Chapter Eight

"So . . . you and Harlow, huh?" Arrow asked Black as they pulled away from the shelter. They'd gotten the cameras installed with help from both Harlow and Loretta. They now had a clear view of the front and back doors, the sidewalk in front of the shelter, and part of the alley behind the building. Meat had wanted to set up cameras on the front corners of the building, but they had to get permission from the owners before they could install them. At the moment they could only put cameras on the shelter property itself.

A container of brownies drizzled with butterscotch sat on the seat between the two men, the scent of the still-warm treat permeating the air.

"No," Black said.

"Are you seriously going to sit there and pretend that you aren't into her?" Arrow asked in disbelief.

"No. I'm into her, all right, but we aren't dating. And if any of you assholes even *hints* that we are within earshot of her, I'll kick your asses," Black said.

"Okay, what am I missing?" Arrow asked. "You're into her, she's obviously into you, but you aren't dating and don't *want* to date?"

"I want to date her," Black clarified for his friend. "But she has a hang-up with the word. So I'm going to be her friend. Her *very* good friend."

Arrow grinned. "Yeah?"

"Yeah."

"Good luck with that."

Black looked over at him. "What does that mean?"

"Nothing."

"Spit it out, fucker," Black said in exasperation.

"She's different," Arrow said. "She's not like a lot of the women we've been with during our careers. From what I've observed so far, she doesn't give a shit that you were a big bad SEAL. When she looks at you, she sees Lowell, the boy she knew in high school. Not the hardened asshole you are now."

"And?" Black asked.

"She seems like a forever kind of chick. The way she talks about those kids at the shelter makes it obvious she wants kids of her own. She'll make a wonderful mother. And it's easy to see that she's got a crush on you. But . . . you could destroy that woman, Black. You might lust after her, and I can't blame you because she's got some bangin' curves. Just tread carefully. You could play her like a fiddle, take her out without calling it a date, fuck her until you've got her out of your system, then simply stop calling her. Hell, if you aren't dating, you don't even have to break up with her. But it would still fuck her up."

Black didn't like what his friend was saying, but it wasn't anything he didn't already know.

"I haven't seen you act like this around a woman since we've met. You're usually more reserved. You let them come to you, and you take what they offer. You're definitely pursuing Harlow. You're like a wolf on the prowl. But any woman who cries just thinking about what another has been through, what Morgan went through, isn't someone you should fuck with. Mentally or physically."

"I got it, asshole."

"Do you?"

"Yes," Black bit out. "I'm not fucking with her."

"So, you're okay with seeing where things go, and if they end up with you and her standing in a church saying vows, you're good? If you knock her up, you won't freak out?"

"Fuck, Arrow, I've only known her again for three days. I'm not like you and the others. I'm not ready to fucking marry her and watch her pop out my kids. Jesus."

"That's exactly what *I* said before I met Morgan," Arrow replied, not perturbed in the least by his friend's tone. "And what Gray said. And Ro. When you meet the woman you want to spend the rest of your life with, you just know."

"Well, I *don't* know. I'm just having fun. So is she. You think I don't realize she has a crush on me? I'm not an idiot. She wants me as much as I want her. I'll let her pretend we aren't dating, and things will work out fine in the end. If we get tired of each other, we'll go our separate ways, and she won't have anything to worry about."

Arrow shook his head but didn't say anything.

Black pressed his lips together in frustration. He was happy for his friends who'd found women, but he wasn't ready to settle down . . . was he?

Two days later, Black was in his office at the gun range catching up on paperwork when his phone rang.

"Black's Gun Range," he answered.

"I just sent you a video," Meat said instead of greeting him.

Black immediately wiggled his mouse to turn on the screen of his computer and clicked on his email account. He opened the message from Meat and saw the attached video. He clicked on it even as Meat began to speak.

"It looks like the harassment is still going on. This is a compilation of the last two days since we installed the cameras."

Black watched and listened as voices off camera called out to the women who entered and exited the building. It didn't matter if the residents were by themselves or in a group. It didn't matter if they had their children with them. The punks didn't discriminate, and verbally harassed them all. Saying they looked hot, wanting to know how much they charged. When the women didn't rise to the bait, they continued their harangue. They stayed on the other side of the street from the shelter, but that obviously didn't make the women feel any safer.

It wasn't until Harlow appeared on the video that Black felt his heart rate increase. He watched as she walked out the back door into the alley carrying a bag of trash.

A voice offscreen immediately rang out.

"Hey, baby. Hey, I'm talkin' to you."

"Go away."

"Awwww, don't be like that. I can make you feel good. Don't you like to feel good?"

"I have a boyfriend."

"So?"

"So?" Harlow threw the bag of trash into the garbage bin and turned to face the man who was speaking to her. He was obviously standing at the end of the alley because she stared in that direction with her hands on her hips.

"Why can't you leave us alone? Why are you harassing us?"

"Because I can. Because this is my part of town. You do-gooders don't belong here."

"The shelter has been here longer than you have. It was here way before you grew into your dick. If anything, this is our part of town, and you don't belong here."

As proud as Black was of Harlow for sticking up for herself, he was also pissed. She should know better than to egg on a punk.

"You don't know shit! You better watch your back, bitch."

Black saw the moment when Harlow realized she probably shouldn't be standing in an alley provoking a man who could easily hurt her with no remorse. She shook her head and backed up toward the door to the shelter. She was smart not to turn her back on the man, but Black still worried about who might be sneaking up at her backside.

Luckily, she reached the door without incident. The man was still offscreen, but Black heard him call out right before Harlow slipped inside.

"We're watching you, bitch. Your cameras can't keep you or any of the other bitches inside safe. Remember that! It's in your best interest to move on."

Then the door shut, and the alley was quiet again. Black realized that he was clenching his fists together tightly, and his nose was almost touching the computer screen. "Damn it," he swore.

"Harlow call to inform you what's been going on?" Meat asked.

"No." And that bothered Black more than he wanted to admit. He'd spent the last two days after Arrow's lecture telling himself that he wasn't doing anything wrong by flirting with Harlow. That they could have a fling, then go their separate ways. He'd forced himself to not text, call, or stop by the shelter to check on her and the others.

But it had sucked. He'd missed her. Which was crazy. It had been less than a week since they'd reconnected. And it was obvious the harassment had been amped up. He didn't like the threat for Harlow to watch her back.

He was done trying to keep his distance. One, he didn't like that she was keeping things from him. And two, he liked hanging out with her. He liked her sunny disposition. Liked her enthusiasm when she talked about what was on the menu for the day. He just plain liked *her*.

He'd pretty much decided to put his plan to date her—without calling the outings "dates"—on the back burner, but no longer. They needed to talk. And there obviously needed to be a more visible presence of men at the shelter. The women there needed protection against the assholes who had decided it was fun to harass them.

"Any luck on the background checks?" Black asked Meat.

"Nothing yet. But there are a lot of people to look at. You know how it is, it's like going down a rabbit hole. You look into one person, and that leads you to someone else, and to someone else. But so far, while there's no doubt the residents in the shelter have been with some extreme douchebags, I haven't uncovered a reason for anyone to have hired the punks to harass them."

"Could it just be a local gang who's bored and fixating on the shelter?" Black asked.

"Yeah, it's possible."

"Then we should pay them a visit," Black said. "Stop with the investigating and just grab their asses, scare the shit out of them, and warn them to stay the fuck away from the women." He was frustrated that things were moving so slowly. When they went on a mission, they made decisions on the fly. They didn't have to necessarily follow all the rigid rules and laws the various branches of the military had to. But this kind of thing was different. It was not only in their backyard, so to speak, but so far there hadn't been any evidence that anyone had broken any laws.

"You know we can't do that," Meat said, frustration easy to hear in his tone. "Rex wants to make sure we play this by the book so we don't piss off the police chief. You know he works closely with him, and Rex doesn't want to do anything to damage that relationship."

"Fine," Black said. "I scheduled a personal-safety class for this weekend, but we need to move it up. You can tell by the body language of the women that they're frightened. And I can't blame them."

"Good idea."

"Can you call Ball, Gray, and Ro, and see if they can join me?"

"Why can't you call them?" Meat asked. He didn't sound pissed, just curious.

"I've got a chef I need to talk to," Black said.

Meat chuckled. "Go easy on her. She might've sounded tough on the tape, but she was scared out of her mind."

Black nodded. He knew she was. That's part of why he was so upset with her. If she'd been so scared, she should've called him. Texted him. Something. But she hadn't reached out at all.

He knew she was probably confused about where they stood. Hell, *he* was confused. But not anymore. He made a vow to spend as much time with Harlow Reese as possible. He'd escort her to work, then back to her car when she was done for the day or night. He'd bring her to the range and teach her how to shoot. He'd spend as much time with her outside of the shelter as his job allowed. Harlow might not want to date, but he didn't have the same reservations.

"Have you gotten permission to put up the other cameras yet?" Black asked Meat.

"No. And it's pissing me off. The buildings on either side of the shelter are vacant, but I haven't been able to find out who owns them yet. And that's suspicious in itself. The stores across the street have denied us access as well."

"Fuck. Why?"

"They wouldn't say. But I have a feeling it's because of the clientele. They aren't the kind of people who like being on camera."

"Damn it. You told Rex?"

"Yup. He's pissed."

Black whistled. When Rex got angry, heads usually rolled.

"Right. When I call the others, I'll see if they'd be willing to set up rotating watches on the shelter. At least for the short term. We can't keep it up forever, but maybe at least until we have some sort of clue as to who's behind all the harassment."

"Sounds good," Black said. And it did. He planned to watch over Harlow, but that left the residents, Zoe, and Loretta vulnerable. "Let me know if you get any more interesting videos."

"You know I will," Meat reassured him. "Later."

"Bye."

Black hung up and clicked on the video to start it from the beginning. As he watched Harlow face off against the unseen man, his blood boiled all over again.

No. Just *no*.

He'd told her what being a part of his world meant, but he'd neglected to inform her that it included fucking *telling him* when she was scared and worried about something. Hearing the punk threaten her definitely counted.

Shutting down his computer, Black pushed back his chair and grabbed his leather jacket and helmet on the way out the door. He'd ridden his Harley to the office today, and while he knew it was safer to go home and get his Mazda before going to see Harlow, he didn't want to take the time.

He needed to let her know once and for all how things were going to be from here on out.

Chapter Nine

Harlow rubbed her eyes as she sat in her car. It was a little after three, and Zoe had probably left the shelter an hour or so earlier. Harlow had dinner duty tonight, then breakfast tomorrow.

She hadn't slept well last night, every little noise making her sit up in bed in fear that someone had broken into her apartment.

The men had stepped up their harassment. The not-so-veiled threats the guy in the alley had spat at her had also affected her more than she wanted to admit. Now she dreaded coming to work—and she hated that. She loved *being* at work, but not the actual getting-inside part. The harassment both pissed her off and scared her at the same time.

Taking a deep breath and deciding to just get it over with, Harlow grabbed her purse and pushed open her door. She'd started leaving the convertible roof up when she came to work because of the time it took to raise and lower it.

Keeping her head down so as not to make eye contact and encourage any of the punks if they were hanging around, she slammed her car door, beeped the locks, and headed for the shelter.

She'd taken several steps before slamming into a hard body. She would've bounced back and fallen on her ass if the person hadn't grabbed hold of her arms.

Looking up in alarm, Harlow was ready to knee in the nuts whoever had hold of her, but she froze when she looked into Lowell's pissed-off brown eyes.

"In a hurry, Harl?"

Looking around, Harlow didn't see any of the punks who'd been hanging out, and she sighed in relief. Then she met Lowell's eyes and decided to be honest. "Yes. I wasn't sure if any of those guys were around, and I just wanted to get inside as soon as possible."

"They were around," Lowell told her. "But when they saw me, they scattered."

"Oh . . . that's good," she said lamely.

"Come on," Lowell said, turning toward the shelter. He put his arm around her and rested his hand on her waist. Her hip brushed against his as they walked, but she didn't try to pull away. Having him close felt good. Her nervousness disappeared like a puff of smoke with him by her side. It was as if, with Lowell there, she could do anything. Say anything.

They walked in silence down the street, past the vacant building next to the shelter, and up to the front door. Lowell held the door open for her after she unlocked it and was right on her heels as she entered. He relocked the door and followed her into the kitchen. Harlow put her purse in the cabinet and picked up her apron. She pulled it over her head and finally turned to face him.

As usual, he didn't say anything. He simply stood there with his arms crossed, staring at her. She hated when he did that. Even though she understood it was a tactic he used to make her uncomfortable and get her to talk, she wasn't able to withstand it.

"Hey, Lowell," she said nervously, at a loss as to what else to say.

"You didn't call me," he said.

"What?"

"You didn't call me," he repeated.

"Oh, um . . . I didn't know I was supposed to?"

He moved then. Pushed off the wall he was leaning against and crowded into her personal space. Harlow backed up, but the counter prevented her from getting away from him altogether. He put his hands on the granite behind her and leaned in.

He smelled good. Really good. She resisted the urge to bury her nose in the space between his neck and shoulder and looked at him. The second she met his gaze, he spoke.

"I saw the video."

"Video?"

"Of that asshole harassing you in the alley."

Oh shit. "Oh."

"Yeah. You didn't call me, Harlow."

"I know."

"Why?"

"Fine. I should've called you. But, Lowell, we just met. Well . . . met *again*. I wasn't aware that I had to call you every time something happens in my life. I didn't call you when I was in the grocery store and someone bumped my cart with theirs and didn't apologize. I didn't call you when I smashed my finger in my closet door and it started bleeding again. I didn't call you when I dropped a packet of rice at home and had to spend twenty minutes making sure I got every grain so I didn't step on any with my bare feet later. I'm an adult, and I've been on my own a long time."

He shook his head and picked up her hand. The one she'd cut earlier in the week. He slowly started to peel off the bandage as he spoke. "You called me a week ago because you were scared of these punks. You needed help, and you called *me*. You knew I'd help you, and it had nothing to do with the fact that we knew each other when we were teenagers. There was something between us when we saw each other a month ago, and there's something between us *now*.

"I told you before that you're in my world now, and a part of that includes you *calling* me when shit happens that freaks you out. And don't deny you were freaked out. I saw you, baby. You were scared, even though you did a good job of hiding it from that asshole. You're an adult. I know you can handle all that other shit, but if someone threatens you, I want you to *call me*."

Harlow blinked as he inspected her finger. He brought it up to his mouth and kissed it gently. Then interlaced his fingers with hers on both hands and shifted until her arms were behind her back and her spine arched.

"Here's what's going to happen from here on out. You text me when you're ready to leave to come to work. I'll meet you in the parking lot, like I did today, and escort you inside. When you're ready to go home again, text me, and I'll make sure no one fucks with you on your way back to your car. Got it?"

Harlow shook her head. "No, that's too much."

"It's not. Give me your schedule, and if you forget to text me, I'll still be here waiting for you."

"Lowell, *no*. Seriously, that's too much. I can handle it."

"What happens when they cross the line from verbal harassment to assault? What if they come after little Sammie? Or if Jasper thinks he can take them on?"

Shit. He didn't play fair. "But you escorting me to and from work won't stop them from turning on the others," she said as reasonably as possible.

"True. But if they see me hanging around more often, and the rest of the team as well, then maybe they'll think twice about picking on people weaker than them."

Harlow wanted to protest the weaker thing, but she knew he was right. Lowell still had her hands in his own behind her back. She gazed into his eyes. "I don't want to be a burden."

He snorted. "You are absolutely not a burden," he told her.

She quickly tried to think of another excuse and came up blank.

"We're friends," Lowell pressed. "We might've just reconnected after all these years, but seeing you on that video today sucked. I may not have been able to do anything about what happened, but I would've liked to have known about it. You called me for help, Harl. Let me help you."

"Okay."

"You'll let me know when you're coming and going?"

"Yes."

"You'll call me if something happens that I need to know about?"

"Yes."

"Good. You're working tonight and breakfast tomorrow, right?"

"Yeah. And lunch too. Zoe needed to do something tomorrow, so I'm working three meals in a row, and then she'll do the same."

"I'll be picking you up at your apartment the morning after tomorrow then."

"What? Why?"

"You'll see."

Harlow narrowed her eyes at the man standing in front of her. Most of the time she liked when he was being all bossy and protective, but he had a weird gleam in his eye that she couldn't interpret. "I don't like surprises."

"You'll like this one."

"Lowell," she protested.

"Harlow," he singsonged right back at her.

She rolled her eyes. "Let me go, I have to start dinner. The kids will be here soon, and they'll be hungry. I need to get their snacks ready."

"Are you really okay, Harl?" Lowell asked.

She melted. How could she stay irritated with him when he looked so concerned? "I'm okay. I admit that going to and from my car isn't my favorite part of this job, but I love it when I'm actually inside. Thank you for escorting me."

"You're welcome. Text me when you're ready to go tonight. No matter what time. I'll be pissed if you don't."

"Fine."

"Good."

He leaned down, still holding her hands hostage, and kissed her forehead. She closed her eyes and inhaled deeply, taking his essence into her lungs as if she could keep him there forever.

All too soon, he let go of her and stepped back. He walked to the big table where the kids would soon be eating their snacks, and picked up a helmet and leather jacket that had been sitting there. She hadn't even noticed them earlier.

"You have a motorcycle?"

He obviously heard the excitement in her voice, because he smiled. "Yeah. You like that?"

"Well, yeah. What's *not* to like?"

"You wanna go for a ride sometime?"

Harlow couldn't figure out if there was a sexual innuendo in his words somewhere, but his face was emotionless, so she decided she was just projecting what she wanted to hear. "I'd love to."

Lowell winked. "Then I'll make it happen. Text me later, Harl."

She nodded, and then she was alone in the kitchen.

Letting out a breath, Harlow shook her head and tried to clear it. Every time she was around Lowell, she felt off-kilter. He was different than anyone she'd ever hung out with before . . . in a good way. He was bossy, though only because he was trying to make sure she was all right. But it wasn't like they were boyfriend-girlfriend. He was just being a good friend.

Ignoring the voice in her head that was practically screaming she was lying to herself, Harlow headed to the fridge to check out what Zoe had prepped. They sat down at the beginning of each week and planned out every meal, so they could help each other with preparing. Sighing in relief when she saw everything was ready for her to start dinner, Harlow put the encounter with Lowell out of her head and got to work.

Harlow: Hey.

Lowell: Hey. You ready?

Harlow: I will be in ten minutes or so. But you really don't need to come by. It only takes me a minute to get to my car.

Lowell: I'll come in and get you.

Harlow: *eye roll*

Lowell: Ten minutes. Don't step foot outside the building, Harl. Or I'll be upset.

Harlow: Fine.

Lowell: See you soon.

Harlow wanted to be annoyed, but she couldn't be. Not when Lowell was looking out for her safety.

When the kids had gotten home from school, they'd told her that Gray, "the really tall guy," had been leaning against the front of the building next to theirs and had greeted them as they'd filed inside.

Julia had pulled her aside while the kids were eating their snack, and said Gray had told her and the other mothers that someone would be there every day when the kids got off the school bus to make sure no one made them uncomfortable. It was easy to see the relief in Julia's face, and in the other moms as well. With their backgrounds, the harassment could be the final straw for them.

Harlow had offered to entertain the kids while dinner was cooking by teaching them how to break eggs one-handed without getting any shell in the bowl. It would kill two birds with one stone, as she could prep the scrambled eggs for the morning. It had been hilariously fun, and everyone had cheered on each child when their turn arrived.

Making dinner for sixteen people—seventeen if Harlow ate with them, eighteen if Edward came over, which was more and more often—was never an easy task. Breakfast and lunch seemed easier, because the residents came in at different times and ate off the buffet they prepared. But dinner was the one time they did their best to have everyone eat together. It was a noisy affair and mostly joyous. For the last week or so, it had been more somber as the harassment from the men increased and everyone was more on edge.

But tonight, everyone had been happy and relaxed, and Harlow knew it was because of Lowell and his fellow Mountain Mercenaries. She just hoped they could figure out the reason behind the harassment.

She grumbled about having to text Lowell to escort her to her car, but if she was being honest with herself, she was relieved. Edward had offered to walk her to the parking lot, but the thought of someone deciding he was an easy target didn't sit well with her. She'd never forgive herself if someone hurt the seventy-year-old.

It had been close to nine when she'd finally texted Lowell. The kids had decided they wanted to help clean up, and then she stayed late to help Jasper with his homework. The eighth grader was having trouble with his English assignment. He had to answer questions about the book *Lord of the Flies*. It had fascinated Harlow when she was his age, so she had no problem talking with him at length about the psychological aspects of the story.

Exactly twelve minutes after she'd texted him, Lowell strode into the kitchen of the shelter. Harlow felt a blush bloom on her cheeks and sternly told herself to get it together.

"Hey."

"Hi," she responded. "I'm almost ready. I just need to grab my stuff."

Lowell stood in the doorway as she grabbed her purse and shrugged on her sweatshirt.

He walked behind her through the main living area at the shelter, nodding to Carrie and Ann. Bethany and Kristen were sitting on the couch reading, and Violet and Lisa were playing checkers. Harlow felt their eyes on her as she crossed the room. In the last week or so, pretty much all of the residents had commented on her luck and how handsome they thought Lowell was. She'd told them over and over that they were just friends, but not one of them believed her.

But walking by his side, knowing the others thought he was a catch, made her feel . . . good. He wasn't even *with* her, and she was proud to be near him. It was crazy.

Despite knowing if she continued to spend time with him, she'd get in deeper and deeper over her head, Harlow wasn't sure what to do about it. She liked being with Lowell. He was funny and caring, and he made her feel as if she were the only person in the world when he was talking to her. She'd never felt that way with a man before. Ever.

Deciding to just go with the flow—he knew she didn't want to date, so she didn't have to worry about that—Harlow nodded at the women as she passed. She'd just have to control her crush on the man. Nothing would come of it because they weren't dating, so her heart would be safe. She'd just be his friend, and when whatever was happening between them was over, he'd move on and find someone he could spend the rest of his life with.

Lowell put his hand on her lower back as she unlocked the dead bolt of the door. She loved when he did that. The weight of his hand never failed to make her feel safe. They walked out, and she relocked the door. Then they walked side by side, with Lowell by the curb, to the parking lot.

Looking around, Harlow didn't see anyone. The street was deserted. The shops across from the shelter were closed and dark. There were lights in the parking lot, but they weren't all that bright, and she'd always felt vulnerable there, especially at night or early in the morning before the sun came up. The abandoned gas station across the street also creeped her out. It was dark, and she always imagined it would be easy for someone to lie in wait to attack an unsuspecting person, like her.

"Thanks for walking me to my car," she told Lowell when she clicked her door locks.

"You're welcome. What time are you getting here in the morning?"

Harlow bit her lip. "Well, I usually try to get here around five. That gives me time to prepare breakfast and get some fresh bread or biscuits baking before everyone gets up and going. Edward's been bringing doughnuts and stuff, but I like to offer a variety of things for everyone to choose from."

"Then I'll see you here around five."

"That's early," she told him.

He grinned. "Yeah, but it's fine. I usually get up around four thirty to work out. I'll just sleep in a bit, meet you here, then go home and start my run."

"Really? You get up at four thirty every morning?" she asked.

"Yup. Guess all those morning workouts in the Navy stuck with me. I usually can't sleep past six, even when I go to bed late. You?"

"Me what?" she asked.

"Are you a morning person?"

"Well, yeah. But I'm not getting up to work out . . . obviously." Harlow gestured at herself as she said the last part.

"Why obviously?"

"Duh, Lowell. Look at me. Do I look like I work out?"

He moved so fast, she didn't see him coming until he was right in front of her, his hips against her own, pressing her back against her Mustang. "You look like warm nights and beautiful sunrises."

Harlow stared up at him. "I don't know what that means," she whispered.

"It means whatever you're doing, just keep on doing it," he said in a low, husky voice.

Harlow didn't know where to put her hands, so she rested them lightly on his chest. "Oh. Okay."

"And you should know—not tomorrow, but the day after—I'm picking you up at your apartment at four in the morning. Is that going to be an issue?"

Harlow widened her eyes in shock. "Four? Why so early?"

"It's a surprise, remember?" he said.

"I'm not sure about this. Nothing's open that early."

"Trust me."

"I do, it's just . . ." She stopped herself from saying anything else and shook her head. "Fine. At least I know it's not a date, because *no one* goes on a date at four in the freaking morning."

He grinned at her and, ignoring her commentary, said, "Text me when you get home." Then he reached around her for the handle of the car door.

"Why?"

"So I can make sure you got there all right."

She wrinkled her nose and asked, "You aren't going to follow me home? I mean, you're being all protective and stuff, so I just assumed."

Lowell stared down at her for a long moment before grinning again. "Oh, I'm following you home. I just wasn't going to tell you."

Harlow rolled her eyes, not sure if he was kidding or not. "Whatever. Go home, Lowell. You've done your bodyguard duty for the night."

"I'll see you in the morning. Drive safe," he said softly. He closed the door behind her and headed for his Mazda.

Don't read anything into his behavior, Harlow warned herself. *He was a SEAL. He rescues women for a living. Just because he's going to ignore your demand and follow you home anyway doesn't mean he wants anything more. Besides, you don't date . . . remember?*

Knowing she was losing the battle to keep herself emotionally separated from Lowell, Harlow drove home, watching his headlights in her rearview mirror . . . and feeling comforted and safe the entire way.

~

Nolan Woolf glared at the two cars as they pulled out of the parking lot and headed down the dark, empty street. "Damn meat-headed bodyguard," he mumbled under his breath. He was standing out of range of the stupid cameras the man and his friend had put up earlier that week. The conveniently busted lights on the far side of the building he owned kept him in the shadows, hidden.

He was so close to getting what he wanted, but the stupid bitch who owned the shelter was standing in his way. He'd hoped the men he'd hired to harass everyone going in and out of the building would be enough to scare her off. But so far it hadn't worked.

And, in fact, it seemed to make things worse. Now he had to deal with the cameras *and* the assholes who'd begun to hang around, watching over the women. That hadn't been in his plans at all.

He looked down at the can of gasoline in his hand and clenched his teeth.

This would work. It had to.

He wasn't going to hurt anyone—he just needed to scare them. That would set his plan in motion again.

Nolan hadn't trusted anyone else to do this for him. The punks he'd hired were good for intimidation, but he didn't think they could keep their big mouths shut when it came to this. Besides, there was something thrilling about watching fire consume everything in its path.

Keeping to the shadows, Nolan walked away from the shelter. Then he quickly and quietly crossed the street and headed back the way he'd come, behind the tattoo parlor and the pawnshop. There were no cameras on this side of the street. He went down to the end of the block before arriving at his destination.

He pushed open the back door of the deserted gas station, which he'd left unlocked the night before, and entered the dark building. It smelled funky, like rotting milk, but he ignored the stench. It wouldn't matter much longer anyway. He stacked a few boxes together and crumpled some random newspapers that were lying around. He doused the entire pile with gasoline, then placed the empty gas can outside the back door.

He wasn't dumb enough to leave it at the scene of the crime. He had no doubt the cops and fire investigators would figure out the fire was deliberately set, but he wasn't about to leave any evidence behind that might lead back to him.

Then, with an evil grin, Nolan struck a match.

He dropped it on the pile he'd made and sighed in satisfaction when the debris went up with a whoosh. Moving quickly, he eased out the back door, making sure to keep it cracked open to allow air to get inside to feed the fire. A lot of people who set fires made the mistake of not feeding them—of closing all the doors, maybe thinking that would keep the fire from being discovered too soon. But Nolan knew flames needed oxygen to flourish.

And flourish was exactly what his fire was doing. He backed away from the gas station, once more careful to keep to the shadows and away from the fucking cameras the assholes had put up. He had no idea how much of an area they covered.

He watched for as long as he could, until he heard sirens in the distance. By then, it was too late. The entire building was engulfed in flames, and the pumps were about to be overtaken. Nolan hoped there might be some gasoline left in the tanks underground. It would be awesome if those went up too.

Maybe the explosion would wake up the bitches inside the shelter. Maybe the kids would cry. They would definitely be scared. He was counting on it.

Chapter Ten

Black wasn't happy. He'd spent most of the day at the women's shelter answering questions and trying to keep everyone calm. Harlow had been amazing. She'd cooked nonstop, making sure the coffee was always fresh and keeping everyone's bellies full as they fretted and worried.

The fire at the gas station had been exciting and scary for everyone. The kids had watched the fire trucks and emergency vehicles arrive from the shelter's third-floor windows.

Black hadn't learned about the explosion until after he'd arrived home the evening before. He'd felt his phone vibrating with messages, but didn't want to answer since he was driving. The only reason he hadn't lost his shit when he'd finally learned what was going on was because he'd just come from Harlow's apartment complex, and knew she was safe and sound inside.

Rex and Meat were doing what they could to find answers as to how and why someone had set the gas station ablaze. The investigator hadn't determined the origin yet, although he did confirm it was arson. His only other comment was that it was a good thing the gasoline tanks had been empty, because otherwise there would've been a possibility the fire could've spread across the street to the vacant building near the parking lot. And if the vacant building had gone up in flames, it was likely those would've spread to the occupied women's shelter.

All of the residents at the shelter had been on edge, and Black had volunteered to hang around to reassure everyone they were safe. Of course, the main reason he'd chosen to take the first shift was currently fussing over the children, who'd just gotten home from school. The kids were still hyped up from the excitement the night before.

"Tell me the truth," Loretta said quietly. "Are we in danger?"

Black and the owner of the shelter were standing off to the side in the common room. Most of the mothers were in the kitchen with their kids and Harlow, and the remaining residents were either still at their day jobs or somewhere else in the building.

"Honestly? I can't really say one way or another," Black told her. "Meat is still looking into the people who we think might have a beef with someone living here, but he hasn't found anything that would point to one person definitively."

"Do you think the gas station was set on fire deliberately?"

Black looked the older woman in the eyes and nodded. "It's not a coincidence."

Loretta sighed and sat down on the edge of a beat-up old sofa behind her.

"Are you okay?" Black asked, concerned at the look on her face.

"No. I'm tired. And I feel like a sitting duck."

"You aren't alone in this," Black told her. "The Mountain Mercenaries are committed to making sure you and your ladies are safe. We won't let anything happen to you. You're too important to us. You've helped us out over the years, and it's our turn to help you."

She smiled up at him weakly. "I appreciate it."

It seemed she was going to say something else, but they were interrupted by Harlow's soft voice. "You look like you need a cup of tea."

Black looked up and saw her standing near them with a steaming cup and a small smile. She looked just as tired as Loretta. She'd texted him early that morning, letting him know she was leaving her apartment, and she'd been working nonstop ever since. Black had left for a few hours to get some work done at the gun range, but when he'd gotten back to the shelter, she'd seemed just as energetic and peppy as she'd been at five in the morning.

But it was obvious that she needed a break.

He watched as she leaned over and handed Loretta the cup, then sat down next to her and patted her leg. "Are you okay?"

"I'm fine, child."

"Is Edward coming over for dinner?"

"Yes. He would've been here already, but he was up in Denver visiting his grandbabies."

"Zoe should be here any minute. She'll take good care of everyone," Harlow told her boss.

"Thank you," Loretta said. "I appreciate everything you've done. The children love you, and it's obvious that you care about them right back."

"I do. They're amazing."

Just then, Zoe opened the front door and breezed in. She was followed by Ball, who was taking a turn at keeping watch over the shelter for the next few hours. "Whew! Looks like I missed a lot while I was gone, huh?" she asked.

Black lifted his chin in greeting to Ball.

"Is someone going to fill me in?" Zoe asked.

Harlow opened her mouth, but Black stepped forward and pulled her to her feet instead. She let out a slight *umph* as she stumbled, her hands landing on his chest to steady herself.

Black saw her inhale deeply before she took a step back. He inwardly smiled, but didn't dare let one ounce of his pleasure or amusement show.

"I'm sure the second you go into the kitchen, the kids'll tell you all about it," Loretta told Zoe dryly. "But there will be a shelter meeting tonight when the kids go to bed, and we'll discuss everything that's been going on. Ball, I'm hoping you can help me answer questions."

"Of course," Ball told her with a nod of his head.

"Everything's prepped for tonight's meal," Harlow told Zoe.

"Thanks for taking an extra shift," Zoe said.

Harlow waved off her words. "It's no problem. I probably would've stayed anyway after what happened last night."

"You go home and relax," Zoe told her. "I'll put the chicken for tomorrow night in the fridge to thaw so you'll be good to go when you get here to start dinner. I do still owe you a shift, though."

"Thanks. We'll figure it out. Lowell, let me grab my purse, then I'll be ready to go." Zoe followed her to the kitchen.

When it was just him, Loretta, and Ball, Black turned to the older woman and said, "You need anything, don't hesitate to call Rex. Got it? He'll get in touch with us, and someone will be here as soon as humanly possible."

She smiled into her cup and nodded after she took a sip. "I know how you guys work," she said. "I'll call."

"Good."

Then Harlow was back. She'd taken off her apron, and Black decided there wasn't anything sexier than the jeans and tank top she was wearing. She shrugged on a long-sleeve shirt, and he was almost disappointed. Harlow might think she was overweight, but she was wrong. She was perfect. His fingers itched to tug down one of the straps of her tank top so he could lick her skin. He already knew she smelled like vanilla, but he wanted to see if she tasted like it as well.

Telling himself to chill, he still couldn't stop himself from reaching out and putting his hand on the small of her back as she passed. He needed to touch her. When she didn't pull away, his lips twitched. He loved knowing Harlow liked his hands on her.

They walked out the door and toward the parking lot, the blackened shell of the gas station across the street a reminder of what had happened the night before. For the hundredth time, Black was glad the damn thing hadn't exploded—especially when they were leaving. They'd been lucky.

"It feels like we've done this before," Harlow said when she reached her car.

He grinned at her. "So we have."

"Are you really picking me up at four tomorrow morning?"

"Yes."

"What should I wear?"

He looked her up and down and said, "What you have on now is perfect."

She nodded. "So jeans are okay? And sneakers? Should I bring a jacket?"

"Yes to all three. Maybe layers on top. It can be chilly in the morning, but it warms up fast once the sun rises."

"Can't you give me a clue? It doesn't make sense that we'd go anywhere at that hour. Especially if we're going to talk business or whatever."

Black shook his head. "You're just going to have to trust me."

She let out a huge sigh, then shrugged. "Fine. But I hope it's okay if I bring my jumbo travel cup of coffee with me."

"Of course."

"Lowell?"

"Yeah, Harl?"

She bit her lip, then asked, "Do you think everyone is safe?"

He knew exactly what she was talking about. "For now, yes. Until we know who torched the gas station and why, we won't know what we're up against. All we can do is keep an eye on the cameras, and if someone gets too close to the shelter, we'll be there to check it out. Don't worry about it."

"I can't help it. Those kids are precious. And their moms have already been through hell. Who's doing this?"

"I don't know," Black admitted; then he took a risk by leaning into her and resting his forehead against hers. They stayed that way for a minute or two before he felt her hands hesitantly touch his sides. Then she moved her head so it rested on his shoulder and gave him her weight.

Knowing this moment was a turning point of some kind, Black didn't say anything, simply wrapped his arms around her waist and returned her hug. He buried his nose into her hair, loving the scent of vanilla on her skin. When she finally pulled back, Black couldn't help but notice how some strands of her hair stubbornly stuck to the stubble on his jaw. As if they were as reluctant to let go of him as he was of her.

He ran the back of his fingers down her cheek. "You okay?" he asked softly.

She nodded. "Yeah. I'm tired."

It was the second time he'd heard those words come from a woman's mouth tonight. "Then let's get you home so you can get some shut-eye before our . . . outing tomorrow."

Again, he'd almost screwed up and said *date*. Thank God he'd managed to choke the word down before it escaped.

Black opened her car door and waited until she was settled in the seat before closing it behind her. Looking around, he saw nothing out of the ordinary, but that didn't mean he was satisfied. Something evil was lurking. He could feel it in the air. Whatever was going on wasn't over. Meat and Rex needed to work faster to uncover whatever it was.

He didn't know the women who lived at the shelter all that well, but he'd gotten to know the kids. They were more open than their mothers. Jasper was the hardest nut to crack. He had his shields up and wasn't about to let them down for Black, or any male.

The girls—Lacie, Sammie, and Jody—were mostly happy children who, after a bit of shyness, had accepted him. Black knew it was mostly because Harlow had made it clear that he was *her* friend, but he'd take it.

Milo was torn between wanting to trust him and wanting to be like his idol, Jasper. Black had a feeling with a few more visits, the little boy would come around.

Yeah, the last thing he wanted was for any of the families in the shelter to be caught up in whatever was going on. If someone had a beef with one of the women, Rex should be able to ferret that out. If it was something more, they needed a clue, a scrap of information, *something*. As of now, they were shooting in the dark. And he hated that. They *all* hated that.

Harlow gave him a little wave as Black got into his vehicle. He quickly started it up and gave her a chin lift to let her know it was okay for her to pull out. Even though he kept his eyes peeled for anyone or anything out of place, Black saw nothing suspicious as they drove away toward Harlow's apartment.

Chapter Eleven

Harlow took a sip of her coffee and stared out the windshield of Lowell's Mazda. It was still dark outside, and she was too tired to think about where he was taking her.

She hadn't slept well the night before. She kept having nightmares about the shelter blowing up and watching from the outside as everyone burned to death inside. So when her alarm went off at three thirty, she was tempted to roll over and ignore it, but had a feeling that Lowell would drag her out of bed if he had to. She could tell he was excited about wherever they were going.

Besides . . . she was curious.

And she was looking forward to whatever he had planned.

It had been a long time since anyone had surprised her with anything. Generally, she didn't like surprises, but she had a feeling whatever Lowell had up his sleeve would be epic.

She'd told him she trusted him, and she hadn't lied.

So here she was. Four in the morning, tired as hell, but game for whatever Lowell wanted to do.

Harlow hadn't had much time to explore the area, so when she finally thought about paying attention to where they were going, she was already lost. The darkness didn't help her orientation either.

"Can you tell me where we're going yet?" It was the first thing she'd said other than a mumbled "Good morning" when he'd knocked on her door.

"You'll see."

Too tired to complain, Harlow put her drink in the cup holder and her head back on the seat and closed her eyes.

"Sleep, Harl," Black said quietly.

She felt his hand on her thigh and looked at him. "I didn't sleep well last night," she apologized.

He looked upset at her words, but merely said, "I'll wake you when we get there."

She wanted to tease him by saying of course he'd wake her when they got to the mystery destination they were headed toward. It wasn't like he was going to drive her somewhere, then let her sleep in the car while he got out and did whatever. But instead she said, "I'm just going to rest my eyeballs for a bit. I'm not going to sleep."

He grinned at her. "Okay, baby. You rest your eyeballs."

She shut her eyes again, and the last thought she had was how nice his hand felt on her leg and how glad she was that he hadn't removed it.

What could've been seconds or hours later, Harlow felt a hand on her shoulder and heard Lowell's low voice. "Wake up, baby. We're here."

Sighing, Harlow sat up and opened her eyes. If possible, she was even more tired than she'd been earlier. She looked out the windshield and blinked in confusion. They were sitting in front of a fairly large building. She didn't recognize it and had no idea where they were, but a sign over the door said **Challenge Unlimited**.

Running a hand over her face, she said the first thing that came to mind. "Um . . . I don't like challenges. This isn't one of those superhuman workout things, is it? Because I'm telling you right now that I've never done a burpee in my life, and I'm not about to start now."

Lowell let out a loud guffaw, and she turned to look at him in surprise. She'd seen him laugh before, but it was a rare thing.

"I thought you trusted me," he said when he had himself under control again.

"I do. But you also told me that you worked out every morning, and since we're up at the crack of dawn parked in front of a business with the word *challenge* in the name, what else am I supposed to think?"

"I'm coming around," he told her instead of answering the question. Harlow picked up her now-lukewarm coffee—they must've been driving for more than a couple minutes—and took a large sip. She figured that she would definitely need the caffeine for whatever Lowell had planned.

He opened her door and held out a hand. "You don't have to chug that. Bring it with you."

"You mean they allow coffee in hell?" she quipped.

He chuckled, and once again, the sound went straight to her belly. She accepted his hand to help her out of the low car, then clutched her travel mug in her other hand as he shut and locked the car door before they headed for the entrance to the building.

They walked hand in hand, and he opened the door for her. They entered a brightly lit retail space with everything from bicycles to clothing for sale. She looked at Lowell in confusion, but he simply strode to the back of the room, where a desk of sorts was set up.

"Lowell Lockard and Harlow Reese, checking in," he told the teenage girl behind the large wooden kiosk.

The teenager greeted them with a smile and said, "Hi! Welcome to Challenge Unlimited. We've got a continental breakfast set up in the back room. There are waivers you'll need to sign, and once everyone checks in, we'll play the safety video. We should be ready to go in about thirty minutes. If you need to use the restroom, make sure you do so before we leave. You won't have another chance once we get to the top."

Harlow blinked. Top? Top of what? She opened her mouth to ask the girl in front of them, but Lowell spoke before she could.

"Thank you. We'll be ready." Then he pulled her in the direction the teenager had pointed.

They were almost through the door to the back room when Harlow tugged hard on Lowell's hand, bringing him to a stop.

He turned to look at her, and she almost melted at the concern in his eyes. "What's wrong?" he asked.

"Nothing's wrong. I just want to know right this second what we're doing here and what's going on. Why can't I pee later? And what are we going to the top of?"

Lowell looked at her for a beat, then said, "I'm a little stunned that you don't like surprises."

"I just never have. Especially not when it comes to doing something with someone of the opposite sex. It's never turned out well for me, which you're very aware of. I'm two seconds away from sitting on that bench over there"—she pointed at an uncomfortable-looking wooden bench along one wall—"and just waiting for you to be done with whatever it is you came here to do."

"We're going to be driven up to the top of Pikes Peak, and then we'll come down on bikes," Lowell told her without hesitation.

"Um . . . you do remember that I'm, like, the most uncoordinated person ever, right?"

"You don't actually have to do much other than steer," he tried to reassure her.

"Lowell, the last time I got on a bike, I was ten," she told him.

He frowned. "You're really worried about this, aren't you?"

"Yes!" she practically shouted. Then took a deep breath. "Pikes Peak is, like, really high. I look at it outside my window at home. I'm going to fly head over heels over the handlebars or something. How fast are we going to be driving—er, biking? I'll kill myself if I crash at high speed."

Lowell took her head in his hands. "Breathe, Harl."

"I told you once that I'm not an outdoorsy girl. I thought you understood. I just . . ." Her words trailed away.

"What?" he urged.

She'd never admit what she was about to say if they were on an actual date. The last thing she wanted to do was admit to something that would turn him off. But since things between them weren't like *that,* she threw caution to the wind.

"I don't want to embarrass you. I saw a few of the others who've already checked in milling about. They're all . . . athletic looking. Like you. My butt probably won't even fit on the seat. I won't be able to keep up with everyone, and then you'll feel like you have to hang back with me, and you'll be miserable."

"Harlow, you could never embarrass me. I'm proud to hang out with you. You're an amazing person and beautiful to boot. Even half-asleep, you're exquisite. I thought you would enjoy this. There's really no athleticism involved. I swear. I saw the bikes we'll be using, and they aren't anything professional. They have big, cushiony seats. Hell, you think I like sitting on bicycle seats? That shit hurts a man's junk. Our balls get all squished and shit. And as far as keeping up, we'll get on the bicycles at the top of the hill and coast all the way down. It's not a race, just a nice, easy ride downhill. We'll be wearing safety gear, and you only have to go as fast as you're comfortable with. I just figured you might like to do something fun. To get your mind off what's been going on. But if you really want to leave, we will. I'd never force you to do something you don't want to."

Harlow stared into his eyes and could see the sincerity in them. He had a point about the small seats and his manly parts. Thinking about his dick made her feel all squirmy inside, so she tried to distract herself. She licked her lips, and saw his eyes dart down to her mouth before meeting hers once more. She liked the look in his eyes, but she still wasn't sure about this.

"I'll make you a deal," Lowell said. "We'll watch their safety video, and if you still have doubts, we'll bail. We can go out to breakfast instead. Then I'll take you home."

"But you already paid," she protested.

He shrugged. "It's not a big deal."

Hating that she was being a chicken, Harlow took a deep breath and nodded. "I can do this. I'm not going to wuss out. I just had a momentary freak-out. But if something happens, I get to say I told you so."

Lowell leaned in close and rested his forehead against hers. It was the second time he'd done that in as many days. Harlow didn't know what to think about that.

"I've got your back, baby. I know you can do this. But more than that, I think you'll have fun. You won't have to pedal, all you have to do is steer. I've heard the views are amazing from up there, and we'll get to see the sun rise as we're coming down the mountain."

"You haven't done this before?" she asked.

He pulled back. "No."

That made up her mind once and for all. For some reason, she'd imagined him bringing other women here to do the same thing. This seemed an awful lot like a date to her, but he hadn't *asked* her to come. He'd simply told her he was picking her up, and he'd brought her here. He wasn't acting very datelike . . . except for picking her up, paying for the bike ride, and holding her hand.

Okay, all those things were very datelike. Although he *had* told her those things, other than the hand holding, came with being in "his world."

"Fine. I'll do this. But if I end up in the hospital with a busted head, you have to call and explain to my mother what happened and whose idea it was."

"Deal," Lowell said with a huge smile. "I have no problem talking with your mom. I bet she's just as funny as you are."

Wait, what? What just happened? He didn't have a problem talking with her mother? No one liked to talk to someone else's parents. It was like . . . a thing. A rule. Something.

Harlow followed behind Lowell as he led her back toward the room with the continental breakfast and scary legal forms they had to sign.

"I went on this date once, and when I got to the restaurant, there was a woman sitting with the guy I was meeting. She was older, and he introduced her as his mother." Harlow knew she was babbling, but she had a point. "I knew right then and there this wasn't going to end well, but I stayed anyway. Throughout dinner, she asked me weird questions, like when my birthday was. I swear to God she was trying to get enough information on me to do some kind of background check. But that wasn't the weirdest thing. No, after our food came, she pulled her son's plate over to her and cut up his steak for him! She offered to cut *mine* too. And if that wasn't bad enough, after we'd finished eating, she told us that we should continue our date at the bowling alley, and she'd already reserved a lane."

Harlow was practically panting when she got done with her story. Lowell had led them into the room and off to the side, away from the half dozen or so people who were already there.

"You can't be okay with talking to my mom," Harlow continued. "She's my *mom*. It's not normal."

"Do you love her?" Lowell asked.

She blinked. "Of course."

"Does she worry about you?"

"Lowell, yes. She's my mother."

"Then I have no problem talking to her. You're her daughter. She loves you and wants the best for you. If you get hurt, I'll take complete responsibility, and I'll explain to your mother *and* your father what happened, and what I'm doing to make sure you get better. They're a part of your life, and will always *be* a part of your life. I'd be a dick to not want to get to know them. And just to reassure you, I love my parents too. But I'd never take them on a date with me, and I'd never let my mother cut my food. So you don't have to worry about that."

Harlow's mind spun. Finally, she just shook her head and asked, "Why are we talking about this?"

"You started it."

She huffed out a laugh. "You sound like a ten-year-old." She raised the pitch of her voice to sound like a child. "You started it!"

He smiled—then reached for her sides and began to tickle her.

"Lowell . . . stop it! No! I'm ticklish!" She giggled and writhed, trying to dislodge his fingers from her sides. Eventually he stopped, and Harlow realized he had his arms around her, and her hands were resting on his chest.

"Less nervous now?" he asked quietly.

"Yeah. I am. Thanks," she responded just as quietly. And she was. She couldn't believe she'd just told him about *another* horrible date she'd had, but he hadn't laughed. He'd simply reassured her and moved on.

It was getting harder and harder to tell herself that she didn't want to date this man.

"Come on. Let's get you something to nibble on. I'm sure it's not as good as your homemade biscuits and such that you make for the kids at the shelter, but it'll fill your belly. We can go out for brunch when we get back." And with that, he squeezed her waist, then took her hand in his once more and headed for the table laden with store-bought goodies.

An hour later they were at the top of the road that led up to Pikes Peak. The weather was chilly, but it was absolutely clear outside. A few stars were still twinkling above their heads, and the lights of Colorado Springs far below them were breathtaking.

Harlow took a deep breath and turned to grin at Lowell. It was hard to breathe since they were fourteen thousand feet above sea level, and she had goose bumps from being cold, but this was an amazing experience.

She was still nervous about being flung over the handlebars of her bike, but she'd actually felt better after watching the video. It explained that they wouldn't be flying pell-mell down the mountain. They'd take frequent breaks, and if anyone got scared or nervous, they could call it quits and ride the rest of the way down in the van that was following behind the bikes for safety reasons.

"If I forget to tell you later, I had a good time this morning," Harlow told Lowell.

In response, he leaned over, picked up her gloved hand, and kissed the back of it. She couldn't feel his lips against her skin because of the leather glove, but the gesture touched her all the same.

"Glad I could make you smile, Harl. It looks good on you."

She was going to respond, but their group leader chose that moment to ask, "Everyone ready?"

The others around her cheered their agreement, and then they were off.

Harlow was very careful for the first five minutes or so, then she let herself go. She didn't worry so much about how fast she was going or if some wild animal was going to leap out in front of her. She simply enjoyed the experience.

The best part was when they all stopped at an overlook and watched the sun rise over the eastern plains of Colorado. One minute the sky was all pink and hazy, and the next, the bright yellow light of the sun was in her eyes. It was probably one of the most beautiful sights she'd ever seen.

To top it off, Lowell had pulled his bike up right next to hers and held her hand throughout the entire thing. Harlow turned to tell him how much the moment meant to her, but he took the words right out of her mouth when he leaned close and gently kissed her cheek.

He didn't say anything, but Harlow knew the moment would forever be etched in her brain.

"Having fun?"

She nodded, knowing her voice wouldn't work.

"Good."

"Okay, folks, we've still got about half this mountain to conquer. Time to get moving!" their leader exclaimed once the sun had risen all the way above the horizon.

The rest of the trip down the mountain was uneventful, but Harlow couldn't remember when she'd had as much fun. Looking at her watch, she was amazed it was only nine thirty. It seemed like an entire day had passed. As the guides were putting the bikes back into the trailer, Harlow yawned.

Lowell put his arm around her, and it felt like the most natural thing in the world to rest her head on his shoulder. "You look beat."

She shrugged. "I told you I didn't sleep well last night. I kept having nightmares about the shelter blowing up."

His body tensed. "I think I'm just going to take you home," he said. "You can get a nap in before you have to go back and work this afternoon. It's a bit early for brunch anyway."

Harlow really didn't want to go back to her empty apartment, but there was no reason for Lowell to spend any more time with her.

Come to think of it, there'd been no reason for him to bring her to do the bike ride this morning either.

"I can come by the shelter later and talk about the things I was going to discuss with you this morning."

And just like that, the excitement of the morning crashed and burned.

This wasn't a date.

It had been way too easy to fall into the mind-set that it *had* been. But Lowell wanted to talk about the situation at the shelter with her, and she'd gone and made more out of the outing than there was.

"Right," she said after the silence had gotten too weird between them. "That sounds good."

Lowell didn't say anything, but Harlow could feel his eyes on her. She watched with way more interest than the situation warranted as the last of the bicycles were loaded up. When they all climbed back into the fifteen-passenger van, she maneuvered herself so she was sitting on the end of one row of seats, and he had to sit in another row behind her.

She knew he wasn't pleased, but he didn't say a word. Once they arrived back at the Challenge Unlimited building, she waited patiently by his car while Lowell tipped their guides and said his goodbyes.

Feeling let down was stupid. He hadn't said it was a date, and she'd told him over and over that she wasn't interested in dating. She felt like a petulant six-year-old but couldn't shake her funk.

As usual, Lowell opened her car door and waited until she was settled in the seat before closing the door behind her. He came around and climbed in on his side. He started the car and headed down the road without a word.

The silence was excruciatingly awkward, but Harlow didn't know what to say to break it. It took about forty-five minutes because of traffic to get back to her apartment. Forty-five minutes where she wanted to cry every second.

She held herself together long enough for Lowell to walk around and open her door. "I guess I'll see you later," she said breezily, ignoring the frown on his face. "Thanks for the new experience this morning. I never would've done something like that on my own."

"Harlow—" he started, but she interrupted him.

"I had fun. Thanks." And with that, she turned to flee.

But Lowell caught her by the elbow. "Text me before you head out. I'll meet you at the shelter and walk you in."

Keeping the tears from falling by sheer will, Harlow nodded. She would've done anything at that moment to get away from him before she embarrassed himself. He'd want to know why she was crying. And there was no way she could explain the riot of emotions swirling inside her. Disappointment. Embarrassment. Sadness.

Luckily, he dropped his hand, and she immediately turned and walked blindly toward the apartment complex. She opened the door and went inside the lobby without looking back.

If she had, she might've felt a little better at seeing the equally unhappy look on Lowell's face.

Black was in a piss-poor mood. His morning had been amazing. One of the best dates he'd ever been on. Harlow had been nervous at first, but once she'd decided to embrace the experience, she'd gone all out. He'd loved seeing the smile and pleasure on her face. None of the stress he'd gotten way too familiar with seeing had been in evidence.

They'd watched the sun come up, and he'd felt a true connection to her. He hadn't been able to stop himself from kissing her. Of course, he'd wanted to feel her mouth under his, to taste her, but he'd controlled himself and only given her a peck on the cheek. The vanilla scent that he so associated with her drifted up, and it was all he could do not to lay her down on the ground and take her right there.

Black couldn't remember a time he'd been this worked up over a woman. Couldn't remember because he'd never *been* this interested in someone. The thought had startled him, and he'd screwed up. He'd tried to make their outing seem less like a date and more like a break from business, and the second he'd mentioned the shelter, she'd clammed up.

All the enjoyment had leached out of her face, and she'd closed herself off from him. He'd given her room in the van to hopefully get over it, but it had just increased the awkwardness between them.

He'd hurt her. And that thought killed him. He hated that his off-the-cuff remark had done the opposite of what he'd wanted it to. He'd thought reminding her that it wasn't a date would make her feel more comfortable.

The tears in her eyes when she'd turned to walk into her apartment had slain him. He wanted to kick his own ass. He should've just kept his mouth shut. No woman wanted to be told that a man was only spending time with her because of work, no matter how much they protested dating. Especially after the kind of morning they'd had. He was an idiot.

The only thing that made him feel better was the fact that she'd felt *anything* about what he'd said. She might not be ready to admit she wanted to date him, but her actions spoke louder than words.

Making a vow right then and there to not bring up work when they were together, except when they were at the shelter, Black mentally planned his next steps. He'd have to be careful; she was extra wary now. Any trust she'd had in him had taken a hit, and he needed that back. Needed it more than he'd ever thought he'd ever need a woman's trust.

They weren't knee deep in a jungle rescue or in the middle of a shoot-out in some pissant country. He wasn't rescuing her from a drugged-out sex trafficker and wasn't trying to smuggle her across the border to reunite her with her family. But the need for her trust was still there. Was just as important as if they were in the middle of the ocean awaiting rescue.

Deciding reinforcements were needed, Black smiled. He had just the thing to get on Harlow's good side again. He wanted to see her smiling and happy, not upset. It might take a few days to coordinate, but he knew his friends would be up for it.

Chapter Twelve

A week had passed since Lowell had taken her for the ride down Pikes Peak, and Harlow had gotten her head back on straight. She and Lowell were *friends*. That was it. She might wonder what it would be like to kiss him, to have him throw her down on a bed and ravish her, but that was her old high school crush talking.

She was an adult. An adult who was perfectly happy living by herself and being single. She didn't *want* Lowell for a boyfriend. He'd eventually let her down, and that would suck. So they were friends. She texted him each day before she left home, and he met her in the parking lot near the shelter. Then he escorted her to her car when she was done working. It was fine. Perfect.

Even the harassment had calmed down. The men were still lurking about, but with the addition of the cameras and the noticeable presence of the Mountain Mercenaries, they'd toned down their antics.

Of course, there was still odd stuff happening now and then. Cars drove by very slowly, the occupants staring at whoever happened to be walking in or out of the shelter. The driver and passenger never said anything, but it was still creepy.

When Lowell's friend checked out the license plates, they always came back as having been stolen or from cars that hadn't been licensed in years. He said the plates were probably stolen from a junkyard—the owners just hadn't thought twice about leaving them on their wrecked or old cars.

Loretta seemed as tired and stressed as ever, but Edward was spending the night at the shelter almost every evening now. It was actually against the rules to have a man sleeping there, but Loretta had asked each of the residents if they minded, and no one did.

This morning, Harlow was going shopping with Zoe to stock up on what they needed for the next month. Zoe was about to leave for a couple of weeks. Her daughter-in-law was scheduled for a C-section tomorrow and there was no way Zoe was going to miss her second grandbaby being born.

Loretta had altered the schedule so Harlow didn't have to be at the shelter in the mornings. The residents could grab cereal or muffins that Harlow would make the night before. Even so, the schedule would be tough, but she didn't mind. It would take her thoughts off Lowell.

The two women headed out of the shelter at ten that morning to drive to Costco. They were taking Loretta's minivan so there'd be room for all the food.

"Hey, girls. Lookin' good this morning!" a voice called out as soon as they exited the shelter.

Harlow rolled her eyes.

"Why don't you come over here and get a tattoo?" a second man yelled from across the street.

"No thanks!" Harlow told him and kept walking toward the parking lot.

"Don't be a bitch!" the first man yelled.

"Why am I a bitch?" Harlow mumbled to Zoe. "I answered him politely."

The other woman chuckled.

"You think you're too good for us?" the first man demanded, crossing the street.

Harlow was immediately alarmed; he was coming straight for them. In the past, they'd always kept their distance.

She put her arm up, trying to push Zoe behind her, but ended up tripping over her feet, and her back smacked the brick wall of the vacant building next to the shelter.

The man came right up to her, ignoring Zoe. The second guy did the same, crowding in on Harlow's side.

"We're sick of you and your kind being in our hood," the first man hissed.

Harlow turned her head to try to get some space, but looked right into the eyes of the other man. They were both tan from hanging out in the sun all day, and their teeth were brown from chewing tobacco. They wore dirty T-shirts and long, baggy shorts that rode low on their waists and hit below their knees.

Harlow tried not to be intimidated by anyone, but these two men were definitely scaring the shit out of her.

"The shelter has been here for a long time," she said quietly, trying to keep the tremor from her voice. She knew better than to show fear to the enemy. They'd use it against her.

"Can't you bitches see this is *our* turf now?"

"The city is trying to revitalize the area," Zoe said from nearby. Harlow could see she was wringing her hands and trying to figure out what to do to help. But the last thing Harlow wanted was for the older woman to be hurt. And she had no doubt these men could hurt both of them. They were bigger, stronger, and definitely meaner.

"What a fucking joke," the first man spat. "Revitalization don't mean shit. When the apartments go up here, who do you think is gonna be living in 'em? Me and my friends, that's who. We're taking over this area for ourselves."

Harlow's mind spun with questions. Apartments? She didn't know anything about any apartments being built. She hadn't even known the vacant buildings on either side of the shelter had been sold. The guy was probably just talking out his ass. Trying to be tough.

As if he could read her mind, the second man said, "Low-income housing, bitch. That's what these buildings are gonna be. And you and the other bitches living all safe and cozy are gonna find yourselves smack dab in the middle of *our* world. Day in and day out. We've seen that fat boy who lives there. He looks lonely. He needs some real men to hang out with, don't he, Bear?" The man nudged his friend with an elbow.

Harlow glared at them. "Leave him alone. The last thing he needs is getting in with the likes of you."

"The likes of us?" the man named Bear asked between clenched teeth.

Harlow swallowed heavily. Whoops. She shouldn't have said that.

"You think you're so much better than me?" Bear asked.

Harlow figured it was a rhetorical question and kept her mouth shut. But he didn't give her a chance to answer anyway before he continued.

"News flash, bitch. The only thing that's kept you safe from me and my homies is a couple hundred bucks a week. But I'm starting to think that's not enough. No bitch disrespects me and gets away with it. Obviously, you and the others aren't getting the point. No one wants you here," he hissed, leaning in close.

He and his friend hadn't touched her, but Harlow shivered anyway. She could practically feel his hand closing around her throat, threatening.

"Fucking leave already so the new apartments can be built and we can all move on with our lives."

Harlow didn't respond, just stared at the cold, dead blue eyes boring into hers. She wished Zoe would do something, like go back to the shelter to call for help. Instead, she was just hovering next to her, as if she didn't want to leave her alone with the gangbangers.

The spiderweb tattoo on the man's neck was creepy looking, and she knew what the two teardrops by his eye meant. This wasn't a good guy. Not in the least.

She stood stock-still, afraid to move the slightest inch and set him off. She didn't even dare to breathe.

"What the fuck?" a deep voice shouted from nearby.

"Get. The. Fuck. Out!" Bear growled, before turning and sprinting across the street with his buddy. They ran by the tattoo parlor and the pawnshop and disappeared around the back of the building.

"Damn it! Are you okay?" Lowell asked.

Instead of answering him, Harlow leaned over, braced her hands on her knees, and tried to get her breath back. She was breathing in and out as if she'd just run for miles. She felt Lowell's hand rest on her lower back as he stopped next to her.

"You want me to go kick their arses?" Ro asked from next to Lowell.

"No. Not without backup, and I'm not leaving Harlow," Lowell said.

Harlow wanted to smile but couldn't find it in her yet.

"Harlow? Are you okay?" Zoe asked.

Closing her eyes, Harlow knew she had to get herself together. Bear and his friend hadn't touched her. Hadn't done anything, really. Just spouted off more shit like they'd been doing for weeks.

"She's okay," Lowell answered for her. She felt his fingers slip under the hem of her T-shirt, and she shivered in a different kind of reaction as his calloused fingers caressed the sensitive skin of her lower back.

As usual, goose bumps broke out when he touched her.

Slowly, she stood and took a step away from Lowell. She couldn't think when he touched her. And she couldn't afford to read anything into that touch. He was off-limits. So off-limits it wasn't even funny. *Friends. Just friends,* she chanted to herself.

"I'm good," she tried to reassure Zoe and the two men, who were currently frowning at her.

Ro looked toward one of the cameras and said to Lowell, "Should've been caught on tape."

"What'd he say to you?" Lowell asked, not looking away from her face.

Harlow pressed her lips together, not ready to relive the experience just yet.

"He said that he and his buddies would be moving into apartments that would be built here. Said they would be low-income housing, and there was no way the area would be revitalized," Zoe blurted.

"What else?" Ro asked in a deadly tone that startled Harlow.

She knew Lowell and his friends had to be good at what they did. They were former Special Forces soldiers, after all. But she'd never seen that part of them. All she'd seen were men trying to help abused women feel safe, who sat on the floor and played games and dolls with the kids.

But Ro sounded so unlike the man she'd gotten to know, it was scary.

"Something about a couple hundred dollars keeping us safe. I didn't understand that part," Zoe volunteered.

"I'm calling Meat," Ro stated, pulling out his phone. "We need the audio files from the cameras."

Harlow startled badly when she felt a hand on her face. "Easy, baby, it's just me."

Nodding, she felt stupid. Of course it was Lowell touching her. He brushed her hair over her shoulder. "Where were you guys headed?"

"The store," she told him. "We need to do some grocery shopping. Zoe's going out of town for a couple of weeks."

Something flashed in Lowell's eyes, but Harlow couldn't read it. He turned to Ro. "I'm going with them," he told his friend.

Ro nodded. He had his phone up to his ear. "I got this. I'll stay until you get back."

"If you can just walk us to the van, we'll be fine," Harlow tried to assure him, but Lowell wasn't listening. He reached out and took

Zoe's hand in his and steered Harlow toward the parking lot. "Come on, ladies. The sooner we get this done, the sooner we can get back for lunch."

Knowing there was no changing his mind, Harlow let Lowell escort them to the minivan in the parking lot. She looked around as they walked and didn't see any sign of either Bear or his friend. Thank goodness. She unlocked Loretta's van and looked at Lowell.

"I'll follow you," he said, reading her mind. Then he leaned forward and kissed her on the cheek before turning and heading for his Mazda.

Harlow climbed into the van in a daze. That was the fifth time Lowell had kissed her, and each time was more confusing than the last. She tried to tell herself that it was just how Lowell was, that he kissed others in that respectful, almost brotherly way, but in all honesty, she didn't see him kissing *anyone* else. Not Loretta, or any of the residents.

When they were on their way, Zoe said, "Maybe I shouldn't leave."

"No, absolutely not. You're going," Harlow told her in no uncertain terms.

"But—"

"No. You're going to go to Pueblo to relax and meet your grandbaby."

Zoe smiled. "Well, all right then."

Harlow returned the grin. Then said, "Well, that was fun. Not. Why didn't you go back to the shelter? Or call for help?"

"I wasn't going to leave you," Zoe said in an offended tone.

"We couldn't have taken them on," Harlow said. "There's nothing you could've done if they'd wanted to beat the crap out of us. I would've preferred you be safe and sound inside."

"Dear," Zoe said in a soft voice, "if I fled, one of them would've probably chased me down. I wouldn't have made it inside. We were too far away. And once their adrenaline got going by chasing me, it's more likely they would've wanted to release that energy. Get my meaning?"

Unfortunately, Harlow did.

"So I stood still, hoping not to agitate them further. I figured they would say what they needed to say and then they'd leave. Besides . . . I saw your man's Mazda pull into the parking lot and knew he'd be there way before I could get help."

"He's not my man," Harlow protested.

Zoe's eyebrows raised in disbelief.

"Seriously. I knew him in high school, but that was forever ago. I've told you about my horrific dating life. I'm not going to do anything that might mean losing his friendship or finding out he's secretly a freak who wants to lick my toes."

"*I'd* let that man lick my toes," Zoe said with a smirk.

"Zoe!" Harlow exclaimed.

"What? He's one fine specimen of a man. As are his friends." She shook her head at Harlow's continued look of surprise. "Loosen up, Harl. Of course the man isn't perfect. No one is. I think that's your problem. You're looking for someone who doesn't exist. Every man has faults. Some are more apparent than others, but if you hold out for someone who never makes a mistake, never says the wrong thing, and who treats you as if you're made out of pure gold, you're setting yourself up for disappointment. Besides, that would be boring. *You* make mistakes, so why can't the man you're dating?"

"Zoe, I don't expect a guy to be perfect. But it might be nice if he didn't bring his mother along on a first date, or if he didn't burst into tears when I turn down his marriage proposal the first time I meet him, or if he didn't secretly jack off on one of my stuffed animals when he was invited into my apartment—"

"Okay, okay, those are bad, but honey, I truly think when you let down your guard, when you stop trying so hard and take a look around, you'll find love where you least expect it."

"I've tried," Harlow protested. "I've accepted dates from men I've met in the grocery store, I've smiled at them in the library, I've been receptive to going out with guys I've worked with in the restaurant industry . . . but nothing happened. I've also dated guys I met online, and a lot of those dates were horrible, but I just don't know where to meet men anymore if it's not on those dating websites."

"Have faith, my dear," Zoe said, and reached over and patted her hand. "I have a good feeling about you. You took a chance and moved to Colorado without knowing anyone, and I think things happen for a reason. You just have to be patient and let things work out the way they're supposed to."

Harlow smirked as she turned into the Costco parking lot. "Right. Do you have the list?"

"Of course," Zoe responded.

Harlow turned to open her door—and screeched in surprise when she saw someone standing by her window.

She put her hand on her chest and scowled at Lowell. She heard Zoe chuckle next to her, but was too busy opening her door to yell at Lowell to deal with her friend.

"You scared me!" she scolded.

"Sorry," he said, but smiled when he did so.

"No, you're not," she grumbled.

Lowell reached out, grabbed her hand, and led her around the front of the van to where Zoe was standing. "You ladies ready to do this?"

"Absolutely!" Zoe said perkily, as if she hadn't just been in a standoff with two punks twenty minutes ago.

Lowell squeezed Harlow's hand, and she sighed. "Ready," she parroted.

They pushed two carts around the giant store, stocking up on food and snacks. The kids ate a lot, and the women wanted to make sure what they put in their mouths was good for them rather than empty calories. It took an hour and a half for them to collect everything on the list and make their way to the checkout counter with the overflowing carts.

Lowell had followed along beside them without complaint, reaching items on the upper shelves and picking up the heavier jars and boxes. He even pushed Zoe's cart when it got too full to maneuver easily.

All the food had been scanned and placed back into the carts when Harlow swiped the credit card Loretta had given her to use for supplies.

"I'm sorry, ma'am, your card was declined. Do you want to try again?" the cashier asked.

"Of course. It should be fine," Harlow said, and swiped the card once more.

"Sorry," the cashier said with a pained look. "Declined again."

"What the heck?" Harlow asked under her breath.

Then Lowell's hand appeared in front of her, and he swiped his own card through the slot. "We'll just use this one," he told the stressed-out cashier.

"Cool. Looks like that one went through." He waited for the long receipt to print and held it out to Lowell. "Here you go, sir. Have a nice day."

Harlow snatched the receipt from the teenager before Lowell could take it. "I'll talk to Loretta and see what's wrong," she told him. "She'll make sure you get paid."

"I'm not worried about it," he told her.

"Lowell, you just bought over seven hundred dollars' worth of groceries!" she told him, though he was more than aware.

"And?"

"And you can't just do that."

"Harl, it's fine. I'm sure Loretta will figure out what happened and reimburse me."

She sighed and turned to push the cart out of the store.

"Why are you so upset about this?" he asked, pushing the other cart next to her. Zoe walked in front of them toward the van.

"I just . . . I don't want you to think I'm taking advantage of you," she blurted.

"Why would you think that? You didn't ask me to buy the groceries. You didn't ask me to come with you today. In fact, you have yet to ask me for much of *anything*. Why in the world would I think you're taking advantage of me in any way?"

When he put it that way, she sounded stupid.

"Remember when I told you that you were living in my world, baby?" Lowell asked.

Harlow nodded.

"That means that you never have to feel guilty about anything I do for you. You're my friend, and friends do stuff for each other. When I'm with Allye, and Gray isn't around, I won't let her pay for anything either. If I went shopping with Chloe, and her card was declined, I'd absolutely cover it for her. The same goes for Morgan. Or Zoe. Or Loretta. You're thinking too hard about this, Harlow. Let me do something nice."

He was right. She was making this about her, when it wasn't. "Okay. Thank you, Lowell."

"You're welcome. Now, come on, we need to get this stuff in the car and back to the shelter before it thaws. You sure the pantry will hold all this?"

She smiled. "I'm sure." Harlow forced herself to keep her voice light, just as his was. Being friends with Lowell was good. Maybe not as good as being under him in bed as he thrust inside her and made her orgasm . . . but still good.

Yeah. She was an idiot.

Chapter Thirteen

"Let me have a shot at him," Black begged Rex.

He and the other Mountain Mercenaries were sitting at The Pit talking about what had happened earlier that day. It was late because they'd waited for Gray, who'd been watching over the shelter that evening. He had stayed to make sure no one was lurking about, then came straight to the bar for the meeting.

"No," the altered voice on the phone said. "He hasn't touched anyone and hasn't broken any laws."

"He threatened Harlow," Ro pointed out. "She was completely freaked."

"It's not time yet," Rex insisted. "Look, I'm not saying those assholes don't need taking down a peg. They do. But until we have more information we can hold over their heads, they aren't going to talk."

"I can make them talk," Black insisted.

He was pissed. And frustrated. The more time he spent with Harlow, the more he liked her, and he hated what was happening to her and the other women.

"What have we found out about what that asshole Bear said to Harlow?" Arrow asked. "What did he mean about that money? A couple hundred bucks a week from who?"

"We don't know much," Meat said. "Whatever money Brian Pierce, or Bear, or whatever name he's going by, is being paid is probably in cash, because his bank accounts aren't showing any deposits."

"What about his friends? Do we have their names?" Ro asked.

"Of course. The teenager with him today was Malcolm Sullivan, nineteen years old and a high school dropout," Meat said, reading from the tablet in front of him. "The others who've been in the area and have been caught on tape harassing the women are Elliott Chapman, twenty-three, and Brody Garvey, twenty-five."

"How old is Pierce?" Black asked.

"He's the oldest of the bunch," Meat told him. "Twenty-nine."

"So they're all old enough to be in serious shit if they're charged with anything," Ball commented.

"Well, so far they haven't *done* anything," Gray commented.

"The hell they haven't. You didn't see Harlow today before I could get to her. That asshole was all up in her face, and he was threatening her," Black growled.

"But he didn't touch her," Rex said from the phone.

"It doesn't fucking matter!" Black exploded. "Do we have to wait for him to beat the shit out of someone before we do anything? That's not how we operate, and you know it, Rex. What the fuck are we waiting for?"

The room was silent after Black's outburst. He knew he was treading on thin ice, barking at Rex like he had, but he was pissed at their handler for not doing more. They were sitting around watching cameras like a bunch of pussies. He wanted to get Bear—sorry, Brian fucking Pierce—in a room and *make* him give them the answers they were seeking. It would take one night, that's it, and all of the shelter's worries would be done. But for some reason, Rex wouldn't allow it.

"Are you done?" Rex asked calmly.

Was he done? No. But Black bit out, "Yes."

"Good. Look, three out of four of these punks have felonies already on their records. They're being extremely careful to not cross any lines of doing anything illegal. They all have airtight alibis from the night the gas station was torched. Those assholes aren't the ones we want here. We're searching for a ghost, and the only way to find him is through those punks. The second we snatch one and work him over, the puppet master will disappear in a puff of smoke."

"So . . . what? In the meantime, they get to scare the shit out of vulnerable women and kids?" Gray asked, taking up the protest on Black's behalf.

"That's why you're all taking turns being there," Rex said calmly. "You're putting pressure on the guy pulling the strings. They're fraying, if today was any indication. We just need to keep the pressure on him, and he'll break."

"And who will be caught in the cross fire?" Meat asked rhetorically.

"I've got this," Rex said, his voice showing his impatience for the first time. "We'll find out who's behind it."

Black stared at his hands on the table. He didn't like the feeling coursing through him.

Doubt.

Since the day Rex had hired him and the others, they'd done everything the mysterious man had asked without question. They trusted him wholeheartedly, and Rex had never let them down. Yet he couldn't help but think that Rex was wrong about this situation.

Yes, this case was personal for him, but Rex's attitude about the case—and lack of action in general—was rubbing him the wrong way.

"Work out a schedule to keep the shelter covered," Rex ordered. "We can't watch over all the women every hour of the day, so they also need to work together to keep an eye out for each other. Travel in pairs. Keep their phones handy so they can call 911 if they have to."

Again, the feeling of wrongness almost suffocated Black. There were ten women living in the shelter. Almost all of them had jobs. Then there were Loretta, Zoe, and Harlow. Not to mention the five children. There was no way the six Mountain Mercenaries could keep them safe, with all the women coming and going, when they didn't even know where the threat was coming from. It was maddening and frustrating.

"I'll be in touch. Keep me up to date if anything else important happens." And with that, Rex disconnected the call.

The six men were silent for a beat before Ro said, "I bloody well don't like this."

No one else said anything, but Black knew they were all in agreement.

Something was up with their handler. It wasn't like him to ignore threats against women and kids. There was no way they could protect everyone. Someone was going to get hurt. And Black was afraid that someone was Harlow.

She was scared, but she'd never been in the situations most of the residents had been in. Hadn't learned when to back down or how to protect herself. Yes, he'd taken the time to teach Harlow and the residents some simple self-defense moves, but that wasn't going to protect them if someone really decided to ramp up the harassment.

"I think it's a mistake to concentrate on just the residents," Meat said after a moment. "I've looked into all the names I've got, and nothing is making my ass pucker. I'm either missing someone, or we're on the wrong track."

"Edward?" Gray asked.

"What about the douchebags Harlow has dated?" Black asked.

"Zoe? She's divorced, right?" Arrow threw out.

"Widowed," Meat corrected.

"Then there's Loretta," Ball said. "What about *her* exes?"

"What about that other thing Bear said?" Black asked after a moment.

"Which part, specifically?" Meat asked.

"That asshole said something about apartments being built."

"Yeah . . ." Meat began clicking on his tablet. "Shit. I've been so busy looking up everything I could find about the exes, and doing other shit that Rex hasn't had time to do for whatever reason, I didn't even think about looking at the developers in the area."

"Right. If it turns out someone has bought the other buildings, why wouldn't they want the shelter too?" Ball asked.

"We need to talk to Loretta to see if she's received any offers, and from whom. Then we need to figure out who already owns the other buildings and track down what plans they've made for them, if any. Talk to the city and see if any permits have been applied for yet," Ro said, warming to the topic.

"I have a feeling we've wasted a shitload of time on the exes," Black said in frustration.

"Yeah, well, I've been doing the best I can," Meat said a little belligerently. "Rex has basically checked out and hasn't been much help. Meanwhile, I've been trying to dig as deep as I can into everyone."

"No one is blaming you," Arrow told him. "If anything, we should've thought about the building being the reason behind all the harassments way before now."

"This is gonna take a while," Meat muttered as he began clicking on his tablet. "And I'm going to need my computer. I can't do shit on this thing."

Sensing the meeting was about to break up, Black said, "I have a question for you guys."

When everyone gave him their attention, he asked, "I thought it might be a good distraction for Harlow, and anyone else from the shelter who wants to come, if we did one of those breakout-room things. You know, where you have to solve puzzles to get the combination to get out of the room? I was wondering if you guys would come too. And Gray, Ro, and Arrow, maybe see if your women wanted to join us?"

"Sounds fun," Ball said.

"I'm in," Arrow said.

"Breakout rooms?" Ro asked.

"We'll explain them to you later," Gray told their British-born friend. "When were you thinking, Black?"

"Soon. I think everyone could use the break," Black said.

"How about a few days from now? Maybe Thursday night?" Meat asked as he looked at his tablet. "Since it's not a weekend, there are spaces left for the one downtown."

"What time?"

"Seven," Meat said.

"Good, that'll give Harlow time to feed everyone before we have to leave. Make the reservation for twenty. I know some of the women work, so they won't be able to come, and some just won't want to, but that will cover us. Someone will need to stay back at the shelter, though."

"I'll stay," Meat volunteered. "Those rooms are too easy for me."

Black rolled his eyes, but it was Gray who said, "Whatever, dude. You just can't go an hour without your electronics."

"True," Meat agreed easily. "Done. Reservation made. Black, I charged your credit card."

Black didn't even blink. He didn't give a shit about the money. He had plenty. Between being single, a Navy SEAL, what he earned at his gun range, and what Rex paid him, he was set for life.

"You want to work out a schedule for watching the shelter?" Ro asked.

"I'll put together a preliminary one, and you guys can let me know what works and what doesn't. Gray, I know you need to work around Allye's dance schedule, and Ro, you and Arrow can let me know if Chloe or Morgan have anything going on that you can't miss."

"Damn, you're like a regular mommy, putting together our weekly extracurricular calendar," Ball teased.

"Fuck yeah, I am," Meat said, not perturbed in the least.

Black pushed back his chair. "Harlow has mornings off since Zoe will be gone for almost two weeks. I'll be at the range early if you need me."

"You want one of us to escort her inside when she gets there tomorrow?" Gray asked, knowing that Black had been watching over the pretty chef.

"Thanks, but no. I got it." Black knew his friends were curious as to what was going on between him and Harlow, but he didn't want to deal with their shit. Gray, Ro, and Arrow would get all mushy and tell him that love conquered all, and Ball and Meat would simply be glad he was getting some.

Whatever was going on with Harlow was between the two of them, and no one else. "Later," he said as he pushed to his feet and headed for the exit.

He gave a chin lift to Noah, who was working behind the bar, and shot off a text to Harlow as he made his way to his car.

Lowell: Just checking in.

It took only seconds for the three little dots on the bottom of the screen to show up, indicating she was responding. He liked that she didn't make him wait to hear from her. The only time he never got an immediate response was when she was cooking.

Harlow: All's good here. You?

Lowell: Same. Text me when you leave your place tomorrow, and I'll meet you. Do NOT leave your car before I get there.

Harlow: Has anyone told you that you're bossy?

Lowell: Yes.

Harlow: I see it had no effect.

He couldn't help but smile at that.

Lowell: See you tomorrow. Try to get some sleep.

Harlow: Easier said than done.

Lowell: You still having nightmares?

Harlow: Not so much.

He knew she was lying, and frustration hit that he couldn't do anything about it. Of course, a nice, long orgasm would do wonders for helping her body shut down, but he didn't think she'd appreciate him suggesting that. God, he had to pull himself together and stop thinking about getting Harlow into bed. As if *that* was possible.

Lowell: I'm sorry. We're trying to figure this out.

Harlow: I know you are. And I'm grateful.

He didn't want her to be fucking grateful, damn it.

Lowell: Night.

He didn't wait for her to respond, simply clicked off his phone and threw it on the dashboard of his car before turning on the engine and gunning it out of the parking lot. He knew he should've said something else. Ended their conversation differently, but he was so fucking frustrated, he was on the edge of losing it.

He was pissed at Rex. Pissed at Brian "Bear" Pierce for fucking with Harlow. Upset that they'd spent so much time concentrating on the exes when the most likely reason behind the harassment—interest in the building itself—had been right in front of them the entire time. And he was frustrated over his relationship with Harlow.

He scoffed. What relationship? It had only been two weeks since they'd reconnected, he realized. They were no closer now than they'd been when he'd first seen her almost two months ago.

No, that wasn't exactly true. He felt as if he was starting to know her fairly well. They'd spent a lot of time together simply talking and having a good time.

He smacked his palm on the steering wheel.

He liked Harlow Reese. She was compassionate and funny and a damn good chef. He'd eaten enough of her meals to know that much about her. But he wanted more. He wanted the right to put his arm around her shoulders just because he liked being near her. He wanted to be able to pop over to her apartment, simply because he missed being around her.

The bottom line was, he didn't want to hide behind the charade of talking to her because of the shelter or harassment anymore.

He wanted a relationship with Harlow. He wanted to make love with her. Wanted to know what kinds of noises she made when she came. Wanted to know which side of the bed she liked to sleep on. Wanted to know if she snored or if she hogged the covers.

Tomorrow night, he needed to step up his game. He still needed to stick close for her safety. He'd use that as an excuse to spend as much time with her as possible, and eventually, he hoped, he'd break down her walls.

Satisfied with his reasoning, Black gunned the engine and took his frustrations out the way he usually did. By driving fast.

Later that night, he did the other thing that always reduced the tension inside him. He jacked off. Picturing Harlow's face the entire time.

Nolan Woolf was getting impatient. He was ready to start applying for permits and putting his plans into motion, but the small fact that he still didn't own the women's shelter was fucking everything up. It was smack-dab in the middle of the other buildings he'd acquired, and he couldn't continue with his plan without that property in his pocket.

He'd had the forethought to purchase the other buildings under different company names. He'd used one of his cousin's friends, a somewhat shady lawyer, to assist him in filing the paperwork as anonymously as possible by creating bogus limited liability companies. That way, if someone was checking up on him or the properties in the area, they'd hopefully never realize one person actually owned them all.

What more did that old broad want? He'd offered a very competitive price for the building, but hadn't heard one word from her. He knew she'd received a few other offers for the property recently, but he was sure his was the strongest.

Nolan knew the city wanted developers to remodel the existing buildings to keep their "historical charm," but fuck that. He was going to raze the motherfucking things. His plans included building cheap-ass apartment buildings in their place and raking in Section 8 money from assholes living off the government, like the four chumps he'd hired to harass Loretta Royster and her tenants. He'd already had blueprints drawn up, making the apartments as small as he could get away with. Building apartments rather than condos would earn him ten times the rent money. It was the perfect plan.

Except for that fucking old woman standing in his way.

He didn't give a damn about the women who'd lose their home once she sold the building. They probably deserved to be beaten and homeless.

He needed to up his game. The fire at the gas station hadn't done the trick. Hadn't scared Loretta into accepting his offer.

He needed to give the old bitch a reason to sell. He'd already intercepted her mail and reported her credit cards stolen so they'd be canceled, but that obviously wasn't enough. She could easily get that straightened out. He needed to do something more drastic.

A smile formed on his face. He couldn't believe he hadn't thought about this before now.

First Hope Women's Shelter was a nonprofit. Loretta probably relied on funds from the government to keep it up and running.

What if that money stopped coming in? Perhaps his offer would look a lot more attractive then.

Nolan rubbed his hands together as he planned. He'd call the same shady lawyer who'd helped him before and see what he could come up with. Loretta would regret not accepting his offer.

Chapter Fourteen

"I'm not sure about this," Harlow whispered to Black as they stood in the lobby of the Great Escape.

"Why?" Black asked.

He looked around at the crowd waiting to be shown into the three rooms they'd been assigned. There were eighteen of them who'd decided to come to the impromptu night out.

They'd split up into three teams of six. Gray, Allye, Carrie, Violet, Lacie, and Ball were on one team. Ro, Chloe, Julia, Jasper, Harlow, and Black were on another. And Arrow, Morgan, Loretta, Edward, Ann, and Sue were on the last.

Black knew that his friends would let the others on their teams do most of the work, as they were all very good at this sort of thing. They'd only step in if their teams got stuck.

When Harlow didn't answer his question, Black nudged her and asked again, "Why aren't you sure about this?"

She shrugged. "I don't know."

He stepped behind her and put his hands on her hips. Then he leaned in and said in her ear, "Just relax and have fun. This *is* supposed to be fun, you know."

"Why do I feel so nervous then?" she asked, looking over her shoulder at him.

Black was having a very hard time keeping his feelings for Harlow to himself. He'd gone over to the shelter that afternoon and walked into the middle of controlled chaos. The kids were in the kitchen "helping" her make dinner, but causing more work for Harlow than anything else. Loretta had been assisting Bethany and Carrie with job applications; they were trying to find something more lucrative than the fast-food restaurants they were currently working at. Sue and Lisa were on their phones, and the others were all hanging around, talking and laughing.

Instead of looking frazzled, Harlow had taken everything in stride, as usual, stopping to compliment the children on something they'd done well, and even giving Kristen a hug as she passed.

The woman was always "on." Always helping someone else. Black felt tired simply watching her. But he loved that about her. Loved that she was so friendly and open. He liked her sunny disposition.

He'd never met anyone who could just keep going and going and going . . . and be super friendly the entire time.

"There's no need to be nervous. We can't actually be trapped in the room because someone is watching through cameras the entire time. Even though there's an hour time limit, I have no doubt we'll figure out the clues and get out of there before then."

"It's not that. It's just . . ."

"What, Harl?"

Her vanilla scent was making him think about other things, intimate things, and Black struggled to pay attention to what she was saying.

"I just want Jasper to have a good time. I want him to feel successful at this. He's had such a hard time with his dad leaving and living in the shelter. He still hasn't opened up very much."

Black's heart melted. She was always thinking about others.

"I promise he'll love this. I have no doubt he'll get into it and be a pro at finding the clues. But if for some reason he isn't, I'll help steer him in the right direction."

"Have you done this before?"

Black nodded. "Yeah. Not this exact room, but ones like it."

She turned to face him, either not realizing that his hands were still on her hips or not caring. She grabbed hold of his sleeves and said, "I bet these are boring for you and your friends, huh? You guys do this sort of thing for a living. Or you did when you were in the military."

He smirked. "Not boring. I could never be bored when I'm around you, Harlow."

She blushed, and he liked seeing how easily he could affect her. Her blue eyes sparkled with an emotion he couldn't read. She licked her lips, and Black had to force himself to not lean into her and take them with his own.

It was official. He was obsessed.

"I like your friends' girlfriends," Harlow said, breaking the eye contact and looking across the room where they were standing.

"They're likable people," Black told her.

"I mean, it's not like I thought I *wouldn't* like them, but I wasn't sure what to say to Morgan. I'm so glad she's okay, and she looks great. Don't you think she looks great? I have no idea how she got through what she did. And Allye is beautiful. I hadn't heard about what happened to her, I don't watch a lot of national news, but I love her hair. That white streak is so unique. Her eyes are super cool too. I can't believe that guy targeted her because of such simple things. That's crazy! And I think Chloe and I seem a lot alike. We're the same age and height and even have the same body type. Oh, I wanted to ask her if she might give Loretta some advice. You said she works with money, right?"

Harlow's comment reminded him that he needed to talk to Rex and have him look into Loretta's money situation. Meat had taken a cursory look into her accounts early on and found nothing amiss. But it couldn't hurt to check again, and Meat had more than enough on his plate at the moment. It was possible the credit card she'd given Harlow and Zoe hadn't worked for some clerical reason, but he needed to make sure.

"She doesn't officially counsel people on investments and stuff anymore, but I'm sure she'd be willing to help," he told Harlow.

"Oh, then maybe I shouldn't bother her. I don't want to bring back any bad memories or anything."

Black had told Harlow the basics about the three women she'd met tonight. She'd already known about Morgan; everyone knew that the woman had been kidnapped and held against her will in the Caribbean for a year. Her father had made sure that no one forgot his child was missing.

"It's fine," he told her.

"Is everyone ready?" the perky staff member asked from the doorway.

Everyone nodded, and she led them down a hallway to an open area with three doors. She gave them the speech about how they were completely safe and someone would be watching over the rooms to make sure no one panicked, and to help if they got stuck on a clue. Then she wished them good luck, and the three groups split up.

"This is exciting and scary at the same time," Chloe said.

"That's what I told Lowell," Harlow agreed.

"It's stupid," Jasper mumbled.

"Behave, Jas," Julia scolded her son.

The door behind them shut, and they found themselves in a small room, almost too small to fit them all. There was a briefcase on the floor by another door and nothing else. Chloe tried the doorknob, and of course, it was locked.

And thus started the night. Eventually, they figured out that the flashlight in the briefcase was also a black light, and they used it to find a code written on the wall that would unlock a secret compartment in the briefcase. Inside was a key that opened the door, and that led into a larger room filled with boxes and other miscellaneous stuff.

Black and Ro stood back and let the ladies and Jasper do most of the work. They found blocks of wood seemingly with gibberish on them, holes to look through to find more clues, and eventually three more keys, which were needed to unlock a large box at the back of the room.

There was one point when the ladies were stumped and getting frustrated. Black caught Jasper's eye and gestured to a toolbox on the floor. The kid looked confused for a moment, but quickly knelt down and inspected the toolbox, and it only took him a moment to find the small map tucked away under the various wrenches and screwdrivers.

His mom, Chloe, and Harlow were ecstatic that he'd found the clue they needed to proceed, and it was easy to see how proud Jasper was of himself.

In the end, it took them forty-nine and a half minutes to find all the clues and solve the mystery. Jasper was the one who input the code into the combination lock that opened the heavy door and let them out.

It turned out they were the second group to exit. Arrow, Morgan, Loretta, Edward, Ann, and Sue had beaten them by a full five minutes. They took great glee in pretending they were bored out of their minds and had been waiting on them forever.

Gray, Allye, Carrie, Violet, Lacie, and Ball weren't far behind Black and the others, escaping in fifty-two minutes.

They took a huge group picture together, and then each team used the props the business provided to take silly pictures relating to the mysteries they'd each solved.

Overall, the outing was a huge hit, and Black was relieved to see Harlow relaxed and happy. "You ready to go?" he asked softly after she'd said her goodbyes.

She bit her lip and watched the others head back to their cars. "You think they'll be safe going back to the shelter?"

"Of course. Ball is headed over to escort them all inside, and you know Meat is already there. Edward is staying the night with Loretta as well. They'll be fine."

She looked at him then. "Thank you for being so awesome with Jasper. Don't think I didn't see you giving him a few clues. He loved being able to solve some of the things we couldn't."

"He's a good kid," Black said with a shrug.

"You weren't too bored tonight, were you?"

"Bored? No way, baby. Watching you do that little victory dance when you figured out that if you shone the black light into that one box, you could read the clue was worth just about any amount of money."

She blushed and lightheartedly punched him on the arm. "Shut up."

In retaliation, Black spun her and wrapped an arm around her chest. He used his free hand to tickle her side. "Did you just tell me to shut up?"

"Stop! Oh my God, let me go, Lowell!"

He continued tickling her for a beat, but quickly realized he was only torturing himself, not her. Her ass bucked against his dick, and he could feel her tits brushing his arm as she writhed in his grasp. Praying he could keep himself in check, he let go and stepped back.

She turned to him—and Black almost lost his breath. She was absolutely breathtaking. Her blonde hair was in disarray around her head, the purple ends brushing against her breasts. The cotton blouse she was wearing wasn't fancy, but he could see her nipples were hard under the material. She was smiling huge, and it lit up her face.

"You don't fight fair," she complained.

Somehow, Black managed to speak normally. "No one ever does," he said seriously.

She sobered at his words. "That stinks."

Sorry he'd ruined her good mood, Black tried to salvage it. "You hit like a girl," he teased.

"That's because I am one."

"Yeah, I noticed." The words popped out before he could stop them.

Harlow stared at him for a long moment, the air electric with the chemistry arcing between them. Finally, she said, "I never pictured you like this."

"Like what?"

She waved her hand toward him. "Relaxed. Chilled. All smiley. Even in high school, you were pretty intense."

"I'm *not* usually like this," he told her honestly. "I think you bring it out in me."

It took a second for his words to register, but when they did, she grinned. "Go me."

"Yeah. You ready to head home?"

She nodded. "Thanks for organizing this, Lowell. I wish all the women could have come, but I know that Carrie, Violet, and the others had fun. Even Loretta did, I think. She's been super stressed lately with everything that's been happening, so it was good for her to get away."

"You're welcome," Black told Harlow. He reached out, took her hand in his, and started for his car in the lot. He'd followed her back to her apartment earlier so she could drop off her car, then he'd driven them both to the strip mall where the escape room was located.

He got her situated in his car, and they drove in silence for a while as he headed back to her apartment. "Zoe will be back in about a week and a half," Harlow said after a few minutes. "Give or take a day or two, depending on how things go with her daughter."

"Yeah. I'm sure you'll be more than ready for a break."

"No. I mean, yeah, but it'll be weird because I'll miss seeing everyone more often too."

Black knew she meant that. She loved being at the shelter. Loved cooking for everyone.

"I . . . uh . . . was wondering if you wanted to come over to my place for dinner when she's back?"

Black blinked in surprise and turned to look at her. He could see the blush on her cheeks in the passing streetlights.

"Not a date." She chuckled nervously. "Because, you know . . . but I thought the least I could do was make you a nice dinner for all you've done to help me out. Escorting me to and from the building and stuff."

When he still didn't answer right away, she babbled on. "It's not a huge deal, I mean, you're probably busy anyway, but I just thought I should offer."

"How about you come to *my* place?" he asked. Black wanted to throw his head back and yell out his excitement that she'd offered to cook for him. She might not want to call it a date, but it *so* was. The first time they ate together, though, he wanted it to be on his turf. He wanted to spoil her. To show her that he wasn't like those assholes she'd been with in the past.

"Oh, um . . . yeah, I could do that. I can go shopping and bring over what I need."

"No. Send me a shopping list, and I'll pick up everything beforehand."

"That's not right. I can—"

"Harlow," he interrupted. "Send me a list. It's the least I can do if you're willing to cook for me on one of your nights off."

"Well, okay. A week from Wednesday?"

"Sounds perfect." It was too far away, but if she thought that was going to be the next time they did something together, she was mistaken. "I have something I need to do Saturday morning in Manitou Springs. I don't know how long it will take, and I don't want to miss you texting when you leave for the shelter. How about I pick you up around eight in the morning, we can go to the Manitou Springs Incline, then I'll take you to work?"

"Oh, you don't have to babysit me. I'm sure I'll be okay for a day, walking from the parking lot to the shelter by myself."

"Harlow . . . do you want to come with me or not? If not, I'll just do it another time."

"No, no, that's fine. I'll come with you."

It was almost scary how well Black knew her. He knew she wouldn't want to put him out in any way. "Great. Oh, and wear sneakers and comfortable clothes."

"I always wear comfortable clothes," she quipped. "But wait . . . what is this incline thing? You do remember what I told you before the bike ride, right? That I'm not coordinated, and exercise isn't my thing?"

"I remember," Black said, having a hard time keeping a straight face.

"Why do I have a feeling I'm going to regret this?" she mumbled.

Black chuckled and reached out to brush a lock of her hair behind her ear before returning his hand to the steering wheel. He was also having a hard time keeping his hands to himself. He always wanted to touch her, and not just in a sexual way. He was comfortable around her, liked having her near.

"You won't regret anything," he swore. He wouldn't let her. No matter how long their relationship lasted, he'd make sure they parted on good terms. He didn't want her to hate him. The thought was abhorrent.

They were silent for the rest of the trip to her apartment complex. The parking lot was well lit and she lived in a safe part of the city. He'd never felt uneasy about her living here, thank God.

"I guess I'll see you tomorrow," she said.

"Yup."

"Thanks again for organizing tonight. Do I owe you anything?"

He raised his eyebrows and simply stared at her.

Harlow rolled her eyes. "Sorry, stupid question. I forgot that I was in Lowell Land tonight and not the real world."

"I'm glad you had fun," he said, ignoring her sass.

"I did. It was nice that Jasper got to see not all men are assholes."

"I'm hoping maybe *you'll* realize that sooner or later as well," Black told her.

Harlow brought surprised eyes up to his, then bit her lip. "Drive safe. See you tomorrow."

"I will. Bye, baby."

He watched until she'd entered the lobby of the apartment building before pulling away. He'd pushed her a bit harder than he probably should've, but he wanted so badly for her to realize what they could have together.

They'd be combustible if she'd only open her eyes and realize that he wasn't like the jerks she'd dated in the past. He'd treat her like the amazing woman she was.

"Another day, another brick busted in her wall," he said to himself as he drove home.

Chapter Fifteen

Harlow looked at the stairs in front of her and crossed her arms. "No," she said emphatically.

Lowell had picked her up right at eight, and they'd driven west of the city to Manitou Springs. It was an adorable little tourist town with cute, kitschy stores and a chocolate shop that made her mouth water . . . even at eight thirty in the morning.

But Lowell had turned, bypassing the shops and heading south for a bit before pulling into a crowded parking area. She couldn't believe how many cars there were this early in the morning.

When she got out and saw exactly what the Manitou Incline was, she refused to take another step.

"It'll be fun," Lowell cajoled.

"Seriously?" she asked, glaring at him. "What part of 'I'm not athletic' did you not understand?"

"We don't have to go fast. Look, there are kids and dogs doing it."

Harlow kept her arms crossed and scowled. Then she shook her head and said under her breath, "I could be sitting in my apartment in my fat pants or pajamas, drinking coffee. Instead, I thought I was doing you a favor. And I didn't bother to look up what this incline thing was." She sighed, then looked at Lowell and said louder, "I'll stay in the car. You go on and"—she waved her hand at the steps—"do your thing."

"It's only a mile, Harl. You can do that."

"How many steps?" she snapped, knowing better than to trust him.

"Two thousand, seven hundred and forty-four."

"Jeez," she muttered. "Lowell, I get winded going up two flights to get to my apartment."

"But they're made out of railroad ties. And the view from the top is so cool."

Harlow looked up. And up and up and up.

"There's a two-thousand-foot elevation gain. It averages a forty-one percent incline, with the steepest part being sixty-eight percent. It's so neat. You're going to love it."

She looked from the excitement on Lowell's face back to the stairs. They looked like they were literally going straight up. She didn't really understand the percentages that he'd given her, but she wasn't an idiot. She could see that at certain places, the stairs were almost vertical.

Without a word, she turned away from the stairs and headed back to his Mazda in the parking lot.

"Harl . . ." he said, jogging to catch up to her.

"Go for it, Lowell. I'll hang out down here. I'm sure you can run up and down that thing in, like, twenty minutes."

"Harl," he said again, grabbing her elbow and forcing her to stop.

She turned to him. "This was a joke, right?"

He stared at her for a second, and her stomach got tight. She'd been *so* sure he was pulling her leg. After their conversation before biking down Pikes Peak, he couldn't actually think this was a good idea . . . could he?

Then his lips twitched—and she breathed a sigh of relief.

"You jerk!" she said, laughing as she punched him in the arm.

"Ow!" he said as he feigned an injury, holding his biceps. "You should've seen your face," he said with a grin.

"Please tell me you actually have something planned for this morning other than giving me a hard time," she said, more relieved than she could express that he hadn't really expected her to climb all those stairs.

He winked. "Of course I do. There's an artist co-op that has some amazing stuff in Manitou Springs. There's also a chocolate shop that has the best sweets. I thought we could walk around and chill out before I had to get you back to work."

"That really was mean, Lowell. What if I'd believed you?"

"I know," he said. "But I knew you wouldn't."

There *had* been a moment when she honestly hadn't been sure if he was messing with her, but she decided not to go there. "I'll forgive you on one condition," Harlow said.

"Anything," he said.

"Our first stop is for some of that chocolate."

"You got it, baby." Then he reached out and pulled her toward him. Her arms automatically went around his waist, and one of his hands flattened against her spine, the other resting on her lower back. He didn't say anything, just stared down at her with a look in his eyes she couldn't interpret.

Inhaling, Harlow was once again struck by how good Lowell smelled. She wished she could bottle it up and save it to take out and sniff when she was having a crap day. Pulling back, she said matter-of-factly, "I'll never be as athletic as you, Lowell. I wasn't kidding when I said I don't even like to work out. I'll try a lot of things. Skydiving, going up in a hot-air balloon, biking down Pikes Peak—but voluntarily climbing thousands of steps won't ever be my idea of a good time. I mean, look at me. This is as good as I get."

His eyes were heavy lidded when he did as she ordered, dropping his gaze from her face to her chest, down to where their hips were mushed together, then back up to her face. "You couldn't get any more beautiful, Harlow. I like you exactly how you are. Come on, let's go get you some chocolate. There's a coffee shop down there too. I have a feeling a nice big cup of joe wouldn't be amiss right about now."

Harlow looked back as Lowell took her hand and led her to his car. "You've really done it? Climbed all the way to the top?" she asked.

"Yup. It sucked. Won't do it again unless I have to."

All Harlow could do was laugh. Thank God he hadn't really expected her to climb all those stairs. If he had, this morning probably would've made it right up there with one of her bad dates.

Black smiled at something Harlow said, but inside he was questioning himself.

He'd seen the look on her face when she'd asked if he was joking. He'd thought she'd laugh when they arrived at the incline and tell him to fuck off. But instead, she'd seriously thought for a moment that he'd planned an outing that included climbing a shit-ton of stairs.

It had been a miscalculation on his part, and even though he'd done it as a joke, he could've ruined everything he was trying to build between them if she'd thought he was serious. He'd been smiling and saying the right things as they walked around the town, but he couldn't let it go.

"Lowell," she said.

"Yeah?"

"You haven't heard a word I've said, have you?"

Oh shit. "Sorry, Harl. Honestly . . . I can't stop thinking about what a bad idea it was to tease you about the incline."

She grinned.

Black frowned at her.

"Lowell, you'd be a dick if you *actually* expected me to climb all those stairs. You'd be a dick if you didn't apologize. You'd be a dick if you didn't feel maybe a *little* bad about it. But you're obviously not a dick." She held up her large coffee and gestured to the bag he was carrying with all the chocolate she'd let him buy her. "You've more than made up for the minute or two that I felt uncomfortable."

He stopped walking and turned to face her. "Does this . . . is this going to change things between us?"

"What? No."

"Good."

"Lowell, I like you. You're funny, you're selfless, and you make me feel safe. I know that when I'm with you, I don't have to worry about anyone messing with me. Or even bumping into me. I like being around you. You're smart, and I love watching you interact with the kids. I'd hate for my lack of athleticism to change anything."

"Just like I'd hate for my bad attempt at a joke to change anything," he returned.

"Great. Now, come on. I saw some beautiful stained-glass pieces in the artist co-op that I want to check out."

This time, when Black smiled, it was genuine. He didn't know what it was about women and shopping, but he was very glad he'd made time to do this with Harlow today.

The other good thing that had come out of the morning was that he now had another idea for a "nondate." She'd given it to him herself. He wasn't sure if he'd be able to pull it off before their dinner, but he was going to try.

That night, after work and after Lowell had followed her home, Harlow sat on her couch, staring into space for a long while. The morning had started off on slightly shaky ground, but Lowell had quickly turned it around.

But thinking about how easily she'd forgiven Lowell for his joke made her rethink all the other bad dates she'd been on.

Had she been overly critical of them? She didn't think so.

Deciding she needed some advice, Harlow picked up her phone and dialed. It was late back home, but she knew her mom wouldn't care.

The phone rang twice before she heard her mom's voice. "Hey, sweetie."

"Hi, Mom."

"Is everything all right? It's late."

"I know. I'm fine. I just hadn't talked to you in a while and thought I'd call to see how you and Daddy were."

They chatted for twenty minutes about nothing in particular. Harlow got caught up on her mom's volunteering job at the local theater and about the good, and bad, shows she'd seen for free. She learned her dad had started selling online some of the stuff he made in his woodshop.

Eventually, her mom said, "So why don't you tell me why you're really calling? Everything okay with your new job?"

Harlow sighed. Figured her mom knew she wasn't calling just to shoot the shit. "The job is fine. Mom . . . how did you know Dad was the man for you?"

"Wow, that was kind of out of left field," her mom said.

Harlow laughed. "I know. Sorry."

"Are you dating someone?"

"No!" Harlow said immediately. Then gentled her tone. "I mean, not really. You know how I feel about that. I've had my fill of bad dates to last me a lifetime."

"*Not really*, huh?" her mom asked, picking up on her words.

"I've been hanging out with someone . . . I went to high school with him. Lowell Lockard. Remember him?"

"Hmmmm, I can't say that I do."

"He was a year older than me, and we didn't run in the same circles. He was in that yearbook club with me my junior year, and I had a crush on him. He joined the Navy and went off to save the world right after high school."

"And he's in Colorado Springs now?" her mom asked.

"Yeah. It's a long story, but he got out of the Navy and owns a gun range." Harlow figured it wasn't her place to tell her mom about his other job. "Anyway, there's been some weird stuff happening at the shelter, and I called him to see if he would help out with some self-defense classes for the residents. One thing led to another, and we've been sort of hanging out."

"I see."

Harlow had no idea what her mom "saw," but ignored that for now. "Anyway, I started thinking about you and Daddy, and how you always said that you knew he was the man for you after only a few dates. *How* did you know? Was it something he said? Did?"

"I'm not sure I can explain it," her mom said gently. "It was more a feeling than anything else. When we weren't together, I'd think about him constantly. When I thought of something funny, I wanted to share it with him. When something interesting happened in my life, I wanted to call him over all my friends. I felt comfortable with him. After a while, I didn't care so much about making sure I looked perfect when I saw him. I could wear my old ratty pants and didn't worry about what he might think. I could tell him anything and knew he wouldn't think I was being silly."

"But how did you know he returned your feelings? That he wanted to be with you as well?"

"We just clicked, honey. It was an unspoken thing. We had crazy chemistry, and I know all my friends thought I was going to hell for fornicating before I was married, but the best day in my life was when we slept together for the first time."

"Ewwww, Mom, I don't want to know that!" Harlow said, wrinkling her nose.

Her mom chuckled. "You asked. But seriously. I knew no matter what I did or where I went that I could rely on him to be there for me if I needed him. Have I ever told you the story about when the house I lived in with three other girlfriends was robbed?"

Harlow drew in a harsh breath. "No, Mom. Shit! What happened? I can't believe you haven't told me this before."

"Calm down. I'm fine, as you know. Anyway, it was around dinnertime, and I was supposed to meet your dad at the mall for a date. He had to work that night and offered to come pick me up, but my house was out of his way, so I told him I'd meet him there. Anyway, I was getting ready, and a man broke into the house. He had a gun, and he made my roommates and me all hunker down with him in a bedroom upstairs. We were so scared he was going to either shoot or rape us. We had no idea what to do. The man paced back and forth, obviously out of his head, either on drugs or just mentally ill, muttering and smacking himself in the head with the pistol every now and then.

"Anyway, I think we were huddled together in that room for about an hour, when the next thing I knew, your father was there. He burst into the room and tackled the intruder. He beat him so badly, I was afraid he was going to kill him. It took me and both my roommates to pull him off the man. I asked your dad how he knew I was in trouble, and he told me that he knew something was wrong the second he realized I wasn't at the mall to meet him."

"Wow," Harlow said. "That's crazy."

"Yeah. The man went to jail, and your father asked me to marry him the next day. He said he almost lost his mind when he realized what was happening. The point I'm trying to make is, being with your dad makes me feel safe. It's not that he's the best athlete or even all that handy with weapons. But when push comes to shove, I know he'll do whatever it takes to protect me. If that means tackling an armed man and beating the hell out of him, he'll do it. If it means dropping me off at the entrance to the grocery store so I don't have to walk in the rain from the car to the door, he'll do it. That feeling of having a partner who truly wants what's best for me—that's what made me realize I wanted to spend the rest of my life with him."

Harlow wanted to cry. She loved her dad, of course she did, but she'd never really seen him in the same light her mom obviously did. It was almost impossible to think about the balding man with the potbelly tackling a man with a gun.

But then . . . hadn't she felt that way about him when she was little? He could kiss a boo-boo and make it feel better. He could buy her an ice cream and make a bad day go away. And him reading her a story was the highlight of her night.

Her mom hadn't made Harlow's feelings about Lowell any clearer, however. She'd actually just confused her more.

"I knew he loved me as much as I loved him when he didn't hesitate to track me down when I was one minute late," her mom said, finally answering Harlow's earlier question. "People are late all the time. If I was just another date, he wouldn't have worried. He might've just assumed I canceled on him. Back then, we didn't have cell phones we could whip out and text someone to find out what was up. He cared about me enough to come find me and see what was wrong. That's how I knew he was it for me."

Harlow sighed. God, she loved her parents. "You're lucky," she said.

"Yes, I am. Now tell me about Lowell."

"There's not much to tell," Harlow waffled.

"Harlow," her mom chided. "This is the first time in years you've actually told me the name of one of your male friends. In fact, I think it's the first time you've ever *had* a male friend. I've heard all about your awful first dates, and you told me you've sworn off men for the near future. Now you're calling, telling me that you've been hanging out with a former classmate who you just happened to have a crush on, *and* you're asking me how I knew your dad was it for me? Spill."

"I just . . . I'm scared."

"Of what?"

"That he doesn't like me as much as I like him. That I'll lose my heart to him, and he'll tell me he's sorry but he only wants to be friends. He told me that he isn't looking for a relationship. What if I get in too deep, and he hurts me?"

"There's no guarantee of anything in life, Harlow," her mom replied. "That man could've killed me and my friends. If that happened, you wouldn't be here. You just have to take what life throws at you one day at a time."

"But I've told him over and over that I don't date."

"And?"

"And he's okay with that. We hang out, but I don't know how to change things, or if I should even try."

"You hang out?"

"Yeah. Today we went to the cutest little tourist town and shopped. The other day, he took me on this bike ride down the road that leads to the top of Pikes Peak. He hangs out with me at the shelter when I'm working, and I'm going to his place soon to make him dinner, to thank him for helping out with the residents and the self-defense class he gave to everyone for free."

"Honey," her mom said gently, then paused.

"What?"

"I don't think you have to worry about trying to change the status quo between you and this young man."

"Why?"

"You aren't stupid. I don't know why you can't see this," her mom said with a laugh. "Honey, you're *already* dating him."

Harlow shook her head in denial. "No we aren't. He agreed to no dating." But the second the words left her mouth, she realized how stupid they sounded. She smacked herself in the forehead.

"I hope that sound was you realizing what's going on," her mom said dryly.

"Oh my God. I've been dating him without realizing it," she said.

"Ding ding ding!" her mom sang. "Sounds to me like you've got a real gentleman on your hands. It's about time. I didn't like hearing about those other losers you went out with."

Harlow almost choked on her laughter. "Should I say something? Should I let him know I know?"

"Just let things happen," her mom instructed. "You don't need to put a label on everything. You've always been like that, honey. Just enjoy spending time with him. Okay?"

"I'll try." Harlow's mind was still whirling with the realization that she and Lowell Lockard were dating.

"Now, want to tell me why you think the residents need self-defense lessons? Are you safe?"

Harlow spent the next ten minutes or so telling her mom about what was going on with the shelter, at least as much as she knew, which wasn't much. She reassured her that Lowell and his friends were looking into it and she was in good hands. She finished by saying, "You know how you said that you felt safe with Daddy? That's how I feel when I'm with Lowell."

"Good. I have a feeling when you really need him, he'll be there for you. Unlike those other asshats you went out with."

"Mom!" Harlow scolded.

She just laughed. "I love you, honey. I'm glad this job is working out for you. I know you weren't happy at the hotel in Seattle."

"I love working there," Harlow reassured her mom. "The kids really tug at my heartstrings. Will you say hi to Daddy for me?"

"Of course. I expect you to call me more often to tell me about your young man."

"He's not mine, Mom."

"Hmmm."

Harlow knew better than to continue to argue with her mom. Once her mind was made up about something, it was made up. "I'll talk to you soon. I love you."

"Love you too, baby. Be safe."

"I will. Bye."

"Bye."

Harlow hung up the phone and sighed. She wasn't sure whether she should feel better after talking to her mom or freaked out by the revelations she'd had.

Not giving herself time to think about it, she picked up her phone again, surfed the web for the perfect picture, then edited it. The picture was taken from the top of the Manitou Incline, looking down the steep steps. She drew a stick figure at the top with its arms in the air, à la Rocky Balboa. She clicked on Lowell's name and attached the picture with a smiley face emoji. She typed out the words, *Look! I made it to the top!* Then she sent it with only a small twinge of doubt.

Biting her lip, she waited for a moment and then saw the three dots letting her know he was typing out a response. Within seconds, her phone vibrated.

Lowell: For the record, I have no doubt you would've kicked those stairs' ass if you had to.

The tears in her eyes surprised her. Harlow blinked them back, smiled, and quickly typed out a reply.

Harlow: Damn straight.

Lowell: I had a good time this morning . . . you know, after I stopped being a dick.

Harlow: Me too.

Lowell: I'll see you tomorrow. Text me before you leave home.

Harlow: I will. Sleep well.

Lowell: You too.

Smiling bigger now, Harlow fell over sideways on her couch, brought a pillow up to her face, and screamed into it. Then she dropped the pillow and said softly, "I'm dating Lowell Lockard. Holy shit."

Chapter Sixteen

The next few days went by relatively smoothly—and that made Black nervous. He hadn't seen Brian Pierce or his cronies, which set off his internal alarm. He escorted Harlow to and from the shelter every day. He'd had a few days to put into motion his next surprise for her, and he hoped like hell he didn't screw this one up, as he almost had their last morning outing.

She'd be coming over to his apartment next Wednesday for dinner, and he couldn't wait. Harlow hadn't been to his place yet, and he couldn't get over the idea that seeing her in his space would somehow be soul satisfying. His apartment wasn't anything fancy. Unlike Gray and Ro, he didn't have a huge-ass house overlooking acres of trees, but he did have a nice patio that he used as much as possible.

Before then—his next surprise. He just had to convince her to let him pick her up at the ass-crack of dawn once more.

He was leaning against the counter in the kitchen at the shelter, with Harlow at his side, watching Sammie and Milo take care of the dishes from dinner. They were rinsing them in the sink and putting them into the dishwasher.

"So . . . I was thinking I'd pick you up in the morning, and we could go do something," he told Harlow as nonchalantly as he could. He wasn't sure how much longer he could get away with setting up dates for the two of them without her realizing what was going on.

She chuckled. "How early this time?"

Black winced. "Four thirty."

"Does it involve exercise in any way, shape, or form?"

He smiled. "No."

"Are you sure? You're not just saying that?"

"After what happened last time, you think I'd lie about it?"

She tilted her head and looked at him. "When you put it that way, probably not. Okay, I'll bite. Sure."

"You won't regret it."

Harlow looked at him with eyes so filled with emotion, Black wasn't even sure where to start to try to decipher her thoughts.

"I know I won't," she said after a beat. "I have no doubt that you won't let me down. You've proved that time and time again."

Her words echoed in Black's brain. She was right. He *wouldn't* let her down.

A loud crash sounded in front of them, and Black immediately took a step forward, blocking Harlow from whatever was happening and keeping her behind him.

Sammie and Milo looked at him with huge eyes. A broken bowl lay on the floor at their feet. The little boy quickly looked from Black's face to his hands—which were still in fists at his sides—and burst into tears. Sammie, not knowing what her idol was crying about, immediately joined in.

The next thing Black knew, Jasper had run over from the table and was standing between him and the crying kids at the sink.

"Easy," Black said, taking a step away from the teenager.

"They didn't mean it," Jasper growled. "Don't hurt them."

Black was pissed off at Wyatt Newton, the man who had obviously taught Jasper to think a beating was an appropriate response for a broken dish.

He opened his hands and spread his fingers apart, then slowly held them out from his sides. "Nobody is going to hurt anyone," Black said softly, in what he hoped was a conciliatory tone. "It was an accident. Accidents happen."

"You stepped toward them with your fists clenched," Jasper accused, not standing down.

"I was thinking about something else when I closed my fists," Black told the teenager. "When I heard the crash, I stepped forward to protect Harlow from whatever was happening. It took me a second to figure out what it was. That's all. I would never raise a hand to anyone here. *Ever.*"

Jasper looked from Black to Harlow. "Are you all right, Harlow?"

"Of course, Jasper," she said quietly, and Black felt her hand rest on his upper back as she peered around him, but she didn't push him out of the way. "Lowell and I were talking, and I wasn't paying attention to what the kids were doing."

"What in the world is going on?" Loretta asked as she came into the room, followed by Lisa and Melinda.

"Sammie, are you hurt?" Lisa asked her daughter.

"Milo? What's wrong?" Melinda chimed in.

"A dish was dropped. That's all," Black informed the newcomers. "I think they're crying because they were startled by it. And because they thought I might punish them. But Jasper came to their defense, and now everyone knows that I'm not mad. Harlow isn't mad. Stuff happens. Dishes get broken. It's not a big deal." He kept his arms out to his sides and looked at the sniffling little girl and boy. "Do you guys think you can help your moms clean up the broken bowl so no one steps on it and gets cut?"

Milo nodded, but Sammie simply continued to stare at him with big eyes.

"You were protecting Harlow?" Jasper asked, his confusion easy to see.

"Yes," Black told him. "I know it's hard to trust anyone, but you can absolutely trust me and Gray and the others. We spend our lives trying to help kids like you, and people like your mom and the other women here at the shelter. As big men, we know we could easily hurt those who're smaller and not as strong as us, but that's not right. I heard the crash and didn't know what was going on, so my first instinct was to get in front of Harlow and protect her."

"I don't need protecting," was Harlow's muttered response behind him.

Black didn't take his eyes off Jasper. He could see his words were penetrating. It would take a while, as he'd been through a lot in his young life, but Black hoped Jasper would realize that not all men were like his father.

"I trust him," Harlow said as she finally moved around to Black's side. "He was protecting me, just as you were protecting Milo and Sammie."

Jasper's body finally relaxed. He nodded and slowly walked back to the kitchen table, where he'd been doing homework.

After a few minutes, the mess had been cleaned up, and Milo and Sammie had gone upstairs to get ready for bed. Loretta had fussed over them both, and Black saw her sneak the youngsters a small piece of chocolate to boot.

"Well, that was exciting," Harlow said dryly after the kitchen cleared out.

"I hate that Jasper felt the need to protect those kids from me," Black said.

Harlow put her hand on his arm. "Don't take it personally. It takes time for them to overcome hard-learned lessons."

"I know. I still hate it."

"You're a good man," Harlow told him, looking at him with admiration in her eyes.

Now Black *really* wanted to kiss her . . . but she still thought they were friends. Didn't want to date.

Consciously relaxing his hands so they didn't clench into fists again, Black decided tomorrow he was going to let Harlow know that not only were they dating, but they would be doing so for the foreseeable future.

They just clicked. They got along better than Black got along with most people in his life.

"You about ready to go?" he asked. Meat would be driving by the shelter in a bit to make sure all was well and to scope out the area. There hadn't been any more fires or incidents, but because the arson investigators didn't have any leads on who might've set the gas-station fire, no one wanted to leave anything to chance.

"Yeah. I just need to get the cereal bowls down so the kids don't have to climb on any furniture to get them out of the cabinet in the morning, and put out the fruit, and make sure there's enough milk and juice."

Black smiled at Harlow as she flitted around the kitchen, making sure everything was ready for breakfast in the morning since she wouldn't be there. "When does Zoe get back?"

"She's supposed to be back this Sunday. I heard Loretta on the phone with her earlier tonight. I didn't get a chance to ask her if everything was going okay."

"I'm sure it's fine. Zoe would call you if something was wrong."

"True. Okay. I think I'm ready," Harlow told him.

Black reached out without thought and caught her hand in his. He twined their fingers together, loving how right it felt. She didn't protest or pull away, so she must feel it too.

He opened the front door and looked around, making sure things looked safe. He was about to step onto the sidewalk—when he stopped and stared at the side of the building.

Written in large, red block letters were the words **GET OUT**.

He heard Harlow draw in a deep breath as she saw the vandalism.

Black pulled out his phone without a word and dialed Meat's number.

"I'm on my way," Meat said.

"Good, because someone spray-painted shit on the wall of the shelter," Black said.

"What? Motherfuckers. Okay, okay, I've got my laptop with me. Instead of just driving by, I'll go in and see what I can find out. Is Loretta still up? I'm going to need to talk to her, maybe show her the tapes and see if she can recognize whoever did it."

Black immediately felt better. He hated that someone had gotten this close to Harlow and the others, though. While they were eating dinner, someone had stood right outside and defaced the building.

Even worse, they still didn't know who wanted the women and the shelter gone, or why. The "who" was probably someone who wanted the building, but Meat hadn't been able to narrow that down yet. He also admitted he hadn't had a chance to dig too deeply into the owners of the surrounding buildings, but on the surface, those properties all seemed to have been purchased by different developers or companies.

Seeing the fear on Harlow's face, which she was trying so hard to hide, Black made a decision.

Fuck what Rex wanted.

Black was going to make it his top priority to have a nice one-on-one chat with Brian "Bear" Pierce. This harassment was going to end once and for all.

He knew going behind Rex's back was risky. In fact, if Black made even one mistake, it could jeopardize the entire Mountain Mercenaries operation, and could possibly get him kicked off the team altogether. But it was something that had to be done.

Black knew the others had been getting equally frustrated with Rex and the way he'd seemed more and more distracted lately. But this time it was affecting a case, something that hadn't ever happened before.

Arrow had sat the team down and told them the little he knew about Rex and his wife. It hadn't really been a shock to discover their handler was directly affected by the human-trafficking trade, considering how passionate he was about tracking down missing women and children. But it possibly explained his recent distraction.

Black couldn't help but wonder if half the team finding women to spend their lives with had brought back the agony of Rex losing his own wife. Arrow had gotten the idea they were deeply in love. Just as Black had already seen the differences in the way Gray, Ro, and Arrow did their jobs now that they had someone else to consider, he was starting to see a difference in Rex as well.

Considering the way Black was feeling so helpless about Harlow's situation, hating not having all the information they needed to stop the harassment and keep her safe, he could only imagine how *Rex* must feel, not knowing if his wife was dead or alive.

All that aside, it didn't excuse their handler's lack of attention on this case. Even if it meant going rogue, Black couldn't sit back and ignore Bear's role in the entire situation anymore.

"I appreciate it," Black told Meat. "And I'm sure Loretta is still awake. She said she had some paperwork to take care of. Just shoot her a text and let her know you're on the way and that you'd like to come inside for a while. But everything looks calm for now. No sign of anyone lurking about. I'll hang out with Harlow in the parking lot until you get here. Just to be sure all is well."

"Right. I'll be there in ten." Then Meat disconnected the call.

"Lowell?" Harlow asked tentatively when he'd put his own phone away.

He didn't answer, but pulled her gently out of the doorway and shut and locked the door behind him. When he'd started escorting Harlow to and from work and spending so much time at the shelter, she'd given him a key. Looking to his right, then left, Black saw nothing out of the ordinary. It was dark, and the streetlights made the shadows seem even darker. He turned and headed for the parking lot at a fast clip.

Harlow didn't say a word, simply tightened her grip on his hand and followed along behind him. He pulled her to her Mustang and waited for her to open the door. He got her seated behind the wheel, then went around to the passenger side and climbed in.

"Why is this happening?" she whispered as they sat in the dark in her car.

"I don't know," Black said, and he hated that he had no answers for her.

"Should I call Loretta and tell her what happened? We need to get that cleaned up so the kids don't see it. Maybe I—"

"Shhhh," Black interrupted her. "Meat will have already called and filled her in, and I have no doubt he'll pull strings to get someone out here tonight to take care of the wall."

"Really?"

"Really. So . . . four thirty tomorrow?" he asked, desperate to take the worry out of her tone.

She looked at him for a long moment. It was no wonder making out in cars was popular. There was something about sitting there with Harlow that felt especially intimate.

"What *is* it with you and getting up butt-early in the morning?"

"So that's a yes?" he pushed.

She huffed out a breath. "Of course it's a yes. And you promise there won't be any exercising involved?"

She'd already asked him that, but he'd repeat his answer as many times as she needed to hear it. "Promise."

She turned her head, looked out the front windshield, and bit her lip.

"What is it? I swear not to play another joke on you."

"It's not that. I just . . ." Her voice faded.

He could see the second she decided against saying whatever it was that was on the tip of her tongue. "You can tell or ask me anything, Harl," Black reassured her.

"Thanks for being so cool with Jasper tonight."

Black wanted to know what it was she'd *really* wanted to say, but he let her change the subject. "Of course. The kid's been dealt a shit hand. If you can't trust your father, who *can* you trust?"

"You get along with your family, right?" she asked.

"Yes. My pop is awesome. He works too hard, though."

"Kinda like someone else I know," Harlow said with a smile.

"I don't work too hard," Black denied.

"Lowell, you own your own business, you go out of the country on a moment's notice, you came to my aid when you barely knew me, and now you spend most of your days watching over me and the others at the shelter. I'm sure there's stuff going on behind the scenes that I don't know about in the investigation, *and* you're spending time with me some mornings. You definitely work too hard."

"*You* are not work," Black said without dissembling. "If anything, you make my days go by faster, and there's no place I'd rather be than hanging out with you."

His words hung in the air, and the chemistry that was ever present sparked to life between them once more.

Black didn't know if he leaned forward or if Harlow did, but the next thing he knew, they were inches from each other. He couldn't take his eyes off her lips. She licked them and left behind a sheen of moisture that he ached to taste.

Just as he was about to close those remaining inches, a knock sounded on his window.

Harlow shrieked in fright, and even he startled badly.

Turning, Black saw Meat standing there and smirking at him. He gave a little wave.

With a regretful look at Harlow, Black said, "Sit tight for a sec." Then he turned and climbed out of the car. "I haven't informed Loretta of the damage yet," he told Meat as they walked in front of the Mustang, keeping Harlow in sight while they talked.

"I'll take care of it. She's expecting me. I'll get pictures of the wall and call in some people I know who will at least cover it up for tonight. They'll get to work scrubbing the wall tomorrow after the kids head off to school."

"And the video surveillance?"

"I'll download it tonight, send it to Rex, and see what Loretta can tell me."

"You think Rex is going to do more than he's done so far?" Black asked. He knew Meat felt the same way he did about their handler's lack of action on this case.

"I don't know. But I'm not liking the way this case is escalating, even if no laws, other than this latest stunt, have been broken yet. I called Gray on my way over here, and if you're up to having a 'chat' with this Bear character, you've got our support."

Black nodded. Fuck yeah, he was up for that. "I'd already decided I couldn't wait for Rex's permission to make that happen. Tomorrow's not good, but maybe in a few days?"

"Big plans?" Meat teased.

"Yeah. If you must know, Harlow and I are hanging out in the morning. There are some things we need to discuss."

"About the shelter, of course," Meat said with a chuckle.

"Of course."

Still grinning, Meat said, "Right. Well, I'll get with the others and see what we can do to invite Bear for a chat."

"Thanks, Meat," Black told him.

"Of course. Get her home," he said with a nod to Harlow.

Black nodded and walked to the driver's side of Harlow's Mustang as Meat headed off toward the shelter. "You okay?" he asked.

"Yeah. Why wouldn't I be?"

"No reason. I'm going to follow you home."

She rolled her eyes. "I figured, since you've trailed me every time I leave here."

"Drive safe, and I'll see you in the morning."

"Okay. Lowell?"

"Yeah, Harl?"

She bit her lip, then gave him a sheepish smile. "See you tomorrow."

Black headed for his Mazda. He really wanted to know what it was she wouldn't say, but a dark parking lot wasn't the place or time for long conversations or kissing . . . even though both were something he craved.

"Down, boy," he muttered to himself as he climbed into his car and started the engine.

Tomorrow was a new day.

Chapter Seventeen

Harlow rested her head on the seat in Lowell's car and stared at him. This was beginning to be a habit . . . one she liked. He'd been at her apartment promptly at four thirty this morning. She had her travel cup of coffee and was wearing jeans, a long-sleeve T-shirt, and a pair of sneakers. Lowell had on black jeans and a white T-shirt with a button-up shirt thrown over it. His black hair looked like he'd just run his hand through instead of combing it, and he had a sexy five o'clock shadow.

He looked delicious.

Harlow couldn't get the conversation she'd had with her mom out of her head. And last night, she'd almost kissed Lowell. She would've been embarrassed about it, except for the fact that he'd leaned into her as well.

The thought that Lowell Lockard wanted to kiss her was almost enough to make her pull out a notebook and start drawing hearts and scrawling *Harlow + Lowell* all over it.

But she settled for knowing that she definitely saw interest in his eyes when he looked at her. And that he was picking her up, again, for something that he was very carefully not calling a date.

Come to think of it, all of her *bad* dates had happened in the afternoon or evening. There might be something to be said for having early-morning dates instead.

"Did you sleep okay?" he asked quietly as they drove.

"Yeah, not bad. You?"

He shrugged. "Meat called about thirty minutes after I got home to talk about some stuff."

When he didn't elaborate, Harlow asked, "What stuff?"

Lowell looked uncomfortable, which made Harlow nervous.

"Nothing that I want to get into this morning. I want you to relax and have fun. There will be time enough for other stuff later."

Okay, *that* didn't bode well for whatever it was Meat had told him, but Harlow didn't have a chance to protest, to tell Lowell that she was a big girl and could take whatever it was he needed to say, because they pulled into a parking lot.

"Why are we here?"

"Here" was the Colorado Springs Hotel Elegantè Conference and Event Center. Harlow had never heard of it and was completely confused as to why they would be at a hotel.

"You'll see," Lowell said with a grin and shut off the car.

Shaking her head at his grin and the way he loved being all secretive and stuff, Harlow decided to trust him as she watched Lowell walk around the front of the car. She had to admit, though she'd never really liked surprises in the past, probably because they'd always sucked, with him, she was starting to be a fan. A big fan.

He opened her door, helped her stand, and then laced their hands together as he walked her toward the front doors of the hotel. Harlow loved how easily he intertwined his fingers with hers. As if he didn't even think about it.

They entered the lobby—and she stopped dead in her tracks, gaping at the sign in front of the small table off to the side, then at Lowell. "You didn't."

He grinned. "I did. You said you had no problem with this, so I thought, what the hell?"

The sign said, **RAINBOW RYDERS HOT AIR BALLOON RIDES.**

"We're going up in a hot-air balloon?" she asked.

"If that's okay with you."

She beamed. "Yes! It's more than okay! I've always wanted to do this. I can't believe it!"

"Come on then. Let's get checked in and get on with it," Lowell said.

Harlow tugged on his hand, and he stopped, looking back at her in concern. "Is everything all right?"

Without thinking, Harlow stepped close and kissed him.

She had surprised him enough with the brief peck that she'd pulled back before he even had a chance to move. But as soon as her lips left his, Black wrapped an arm around her waist and tugged until she fell against him.

Then he tilted his head and kissed her back. Hard.

Harlow wasn't inexperienced when it came to kisses. She'd had her share of good kisses, great kisses, and some pretty disgusting ones as well. But *nothing* compared to the feel of Lowell's lips against her own. She felt the stubble on his cheeks against her face as he kissed her. Goose bumps immediately raced down her arms and the back of her neck, and she closed her eyes to fully experience the first taste of his lips on hers.

He swept his tongue along the seam of her mouth, and she eagerly opened for him. Instead of plunging inside and mauling, his tongue played with hers, licking and retreating, coaxing her to loosen up and let him in deeper.

When she moaned low in her throat and relaxed fully against him, he moved a hand to the back of her neck and kissed her as if there were no tomorrow. He wasn't teasing anymore. He devoured her mouth, and she loved every second of him taking control.

It wasn't until she heard someone whispering about them getting a room that she remembered where they were.

Lowell obviously heard the comment too, because he immediately lifted his lips from hers, but he didn't move his hand from her neck or his arm from around her waist. He simply stared at her as if he were seeing her for the first time.

Feeling a little uncomfortable, and needing to fill the silence, Harlow blurted, “I hope my breath isn’t awful from the coffee.”

He grinned and shook his head. “No, baby. You’re perfect. If I could bottle up the way I felt while kissing you, no one would ever need to drink coffee to get going in the mornings again.”

She blushed.

His grin widened. “You ready?”

“As I’ll ever be, I guess.” She thought she’d be embarrassed, but Lowell made it impossible. He didn’t leer at her or make any sexual innuendos, simply grabbed hold of her hand again and made his way over to the desk to check in.

Within fifteen minutes, they were climbing into a van to be taken to the launch site. Once they arrived, she saw three balloons were lying on the ground, ready to be inflated. Harlow watched in fascination as Lowell helped with the process, and soon they were being escorted into a large wicker basket with two other couples.

Harlow looked up into the gaping hole of the balloon and couldn’t control the goofy smile on her face. The balloon they were riding in was yellow with stripes of different colors and the Rainbow Ryders logo in the middle. The whoosh of the burners being turned on to lift the balloon was loud in the morning stillness.

She turned to Lowell, grinning wider. “Holy crap, this is so awesome!”

He smiled at her and kissed her forehead. “Yup.”

Then she turned back around and held on to the edge of the basket as the pilot made last-minute adjustments. Before she knew it, they were ever so slowly lifting off the ground. Harlow felt Lowell step up behind her. His hands rested next to hers on the edge, and she felt completely surrounded by him.

She vaguely heard the pilot talking to them about what he was doing and where they would be floating that morning, but she could only stare at the sight of Pikes Peak bathed in the morning light as they slowly rose into the air.

Sighing in contentment, she allowed herself to lean against Lowell. One of his hands moved from the basket to rest against her lower belly. Harlow had never been more satisfied in her life as she was at that moment.

The ride seemed to last forever, but at the same time, it was all too soon before the pilot was steering them toward a large open field. Throwing caution to the wind, Harlow turned in Lowell's arms.

He was looking at her instead of the impressive view in front of him. "Was it everything you hoped it would be?"

"You need to stop arranging for me to do things when I mention them offhandedly," she said in reply. "Please tell me that you haven't set up a skydive."

"Do you want to go skydiving?" Lowell asked.

She wrinkled her nose and shook her head.

He chuckled. "Then, no, I haven't set that up."

"Good. Although I have no idea how I'll top this."

Lowell immediately shook his head and frowned at her. "You don't have to top anything, Harl. It's not a contest."

Deciding she was going to clear the air—even though this wasn't exactly the best place, not with the other couples around and with the whoosh of the burner going off intermittently—Harlow took a deep breath. She licked her lips, then blurted, "This has been one of the best dates I've ever been on."

Then she held her breath to wait for his reaction.

She was fairly certain he wasn't going to be shocked at her words. For as slow as she'd been on the uptake, it was more than obvious that they were dating, even if their courtship had been unconventional.

"Me too," he said simply.

Letting out the air she'd been holding, Harlow smiled at him.

"So you finally clued in, huh?" he asked. His thumb rubbed up and down her side, making sure to press just hard enough so he wasn't tickling her.

She shrugged. "It took my mom to point it out."

"You aren't freaked?" he asked.

"Not really. I mean, I get it. I'd flat-out told you that I didn't want to date. You slid under my radar so smoothly, I didn't even realize what was going on."

"It's what I'm good at," he said without conceit.

"I see that," she told him. "But for the record, you can rub my feet, but I'm not sure about you wanting to have sex with them; stealing napkins from restaurants is out of the question; and if you need to masturbate, my stuffed animals are off-limits."

He threw his head back and laughed, and Harlow found the arch of his neck extremely fascinating. She didn't get nearly enough time to satisfy her curiosity before he lowered his head and kissed her. It was a short and fast kiss, unlike earlier that morning, but no less exciting. "Got it," he said.

"Okay, folks, we're getting ready for touchdown. Brace yourself and hold on," the pilot announced.

Lowell turned her around and once again stepped up behind her. Harlow could feel him flush against her back, hips, thighs. He stood against her, bracing her—and she knew at that moment that she was in way over her head. She could easily fall in love with him . . . if she wasn't already. Which was crazy, because he'd come right out and said he wasn't looking for a long-term relationship, and even just a few days ago, she would've said the same thing.

But standing there, safe in Lowell's arms, she knew without a doubt that he'd never let anything happen to her if he could help it. Just like her dad felt about her mom.

Harlow had a feeling that she'd managed to find the man she was meant to spend the rest of her life with. The problem was, she wasn't sure he felt the same.

Shaking her head and telling herself to take things one day at a time, Harlow vowed to enjoy her time with Lowell, no matter how long it lasted.

She was a realist. She knew he liked her now, but if things got even more serious, would he back away? Would he decide that he didn't want to continue with a relationship because of the expectation of marriage? She had no idea, but she was willing to take that chance.

The thought of having to reenter the dating game had been abhorrent. Lowell had managed to slip in stealthily and make it extremely painless, and that was all right with her.

Black crossed his arms over his chest and forced himself to stay where he was. He was once again at the shelter, watching Harlow finish up in the kitchen before she left with him.

The last several days had been amazing. The morning of the balloon ride, he'd finally gotten to taste Harlow, and it was everything he'd dreamed of and more. She'd lit up in his arms. And every time he'd seen her since, he'd stolen a few more kisses.

He was hungrier for her than ever.

This afternoon, he'd escorted her inside the shelter, then left to talk to Meat and the others while she was busy in the kitchen. Tomorrow, Arrow and Ball were going to hunt down Brian Pierce and "invite" him to come speak to them. Black would meet up with them and the rest of the team and see what they could find out from him. Black had no worries about roughing him up. It wouldn't be the first time they hadn't played fair to get information, and it wasn't as if Black was going to kill the man—he just wanted all the facts of the case, and the quicker Bear gave up what he knew, the faster he'd be returned to his street corner.

With that set, Black felt a little calmer. The last thing he wanted was something happening to Harlow or any of the residents at the women's shelter. He'd hung around enough lately to have gotten to know everyone fairly well. The kids were adorable, and a great reminder why he and the Mountain Mercenaries did what they did.

He'd put in hours at the gun range now and then, and things were running smoothly there as well. He had great employees and managers, and they didn't need him around to keep the place operating efficiently.

And since Rex seemed distracted lately, there weren't any other cases on the horizon either. So Black was free to concentrate on Harlow and whatever was going on at the shelter. Maybe it was nothing. Maybe Rex was right to not seem overly concerned. But Black didn't think so. He had an itchy feeling on the back of his neck, and that never boded well.

But he had to set it aside for the moment. Tonight, Black was going to take Harlow to his apartment, let her feed him, then hopefully get some more kisses from her. He wasn't worried about rushing them into bed. He was enjoying the chase. Now that she was aware of the fact they were dating and was okay with it, they could see where things took them. Black had a feeling things would move fairly fast if the chemistry between them, and how hot their first kiss had been, was any indication.

He had no idea how long he'd been waiting for Harlow to finish up the preparations for dinner, but it didn't matter. He could stand there and watch her forever. He'd been chatting with a few of the residents, Kristen, Melinda, and Sue. Kristen told him she and Sue had found an apartment they could afford if they split the rent. He was happy they'd been able to get back on their feet enough to get a place of their own.

Melinda wasn't quite there yet, but she was satisfied at the moment that Milo seemed to be doing much better in school. Before the pair moved into the shelter, his grades had been steadily going downhill because of the abuse at home with her ex. But they'd been slowly getting better, now that he had more stability in his life and his father was out of the picture.

Loretta came into the kitchen then—and Black immediately stiffened.

He could tell by looking at her face that something was wrong. She was trying to hide it, but it was obvious—at least to him.

"It smells delicious in here," she said in a fake chipper tone.

Harlow obviously noticed something was wrong too, because she put down the dish towel she was holding and came over to the older woman. "Is everything all right?"

"Of course," Loretta said.

Harlow frowned and looked over at Milo and Sammie, who were sitting at the table nearby, then at little Jody, who was playing with some hand-me-down Barbie dolls in a corner. "Are you sure?" she asked quietly.

"I'm sure," Loretta said. "We'll talk tomorrow. I gave you the night off, and you need to get started on that. You did way more than your share by getting the lasagna in the oven—I think we can manage to remove it before it's burned." She smiled to let Harlow know she was teasing.

"I'm going, I'm going," Harlow said, returning the smile. Then she lowered her voice. "But you know if you need anything, all you have to do is call."

"I know, child. Thank you. Don't you worry about us. Edward should be here in about thirty minutes, and I've got Black's number, as well as his friends', all saved in my cell just in case."

Black wanted to talk to Loretta privately to find out what was bothering her, but when he saw how stressed she looked at the thought of Harlow pressing the issue, he relented. Hopefully he'd get the information they needed out of Brian Pierce, and he'd have something positive to tell Loretta. It had to be stressful being responsible for all the women and children living in the shelter.

"The lasagna should have another forty minutes or so. I baked some fresh bread today, so when there's ten minutes to go, slather some of the garlic butter I've already prepared over the top and inside, then pop it in with the lasagna for about five minutes. If you want, you can sprinkle some cheese over the top. There's a salad in the fridge, and I made chocolate pudding for dessert."

Black's mouth was watering. He wasn't the best cook, but he got by. Generally, he ate when he was hungry and didn't care much about what he put in his mouth. But being around Harlow was making him change his thoughts on food. The things she made were absolutely delicious. Make-his-mouth-water good. He made a mental note to add thirty minutes to his workout schedule, because with Harlow cooking for him, he had a feeling he'd need it.

"We got it," Loretta told Harlow again. "Shoo, girl. Get."

She laughed, then hugged Loretta. "Thanks for giving me the night off. I know I worked alone when I first started, but I'd forgotten how much of a help Zoe is."

Black would've missed the expression on Loretta's face if he hadn't been looking right at her. She looked like Harlow had just told her someone had died.

But by the time Harlow pulled back from the hug, the smile was back on Loretta's face.

"Call if you have any questions," Harlow said again. "I'll be back tomorrow, probably around ten thirty or so."

"Have a good time tonight. We'll talk tomorrow," Loretta told her.

Harlow nodded and turned to Black. "Ready?"

He nodded. He was super curious about what Loretta wanted to say to Harlow, but now wasn't the time to press. As Harlow went to collect her purse, he approached Loretta and said softly, "Meat will be coming over after dinner. If you need something—*anything*—before then, don't hesitate to call."

"Thank you," Loretta said. "It's been nice having you boys around. Not only does it make this big ol' place seem safer, it's good for the kids and women to see how men *should* act."

Black nodded, then spontaneously leaned down and kissed her cheek. He smiled when she blushed.

When Harlow came back over to them, Loretta said, "You better watch out, I might steal your man out from under your nose if you're not careful."

Harlow linked her arm with his and said breezily, "It would never work out between the two of you. He's a morning person like me."

Loretta laughed and mock frowned. "Darn."

Black simply shook his head. "Ready?" he asked Harlow.

"Yeah." Then she turned and called out, "I'll see everyone tomorrow!"

Everyone waved and said their goodbyes. As Black walked her through the shelter, he had to laugh because it took her forever to get out the door. She had to make sure everyone around her had whatever they needed, and she talked to each resident before they left.

Black locked the front door behind them, and she said, "This is new."

"What?"

"Leaving when it's still light outside," she said.

"Doesn't mean it's safe," Black warned her.

As he expected, Harlow rolled her eyes. "I know. But it's definitely not as spooky out here in the daytime."

"Hey!" a voice called out, and Black stiffened. He turned, keeping Harlow behind him, to stare across the street.

All four of the men they were investigating were hanging out on benches outside the tattoo parlor. Elliott, Malcolm, Brody, and Brian were lounging there as if they didn't have any other place to be, which they probably didn't.

Black didn't respond, simply stood there and stared at the foursome.

"Just saying a friendly neighborhood hello," Elliott yelled.

"Yeah . . . because we're all about making sure this neighborhood doesn't have any outsiders," Malcolm chimed in.

Black frowned, knowing they were trying to make a point, but not sure what it was.

"Come on," Harlow urged, pulling on his shirt. "Let's just go."

He glared at the men for another heartbeat before putting an arm around Harlow's waist and turning his back on the punks. He had no doubt that he'd hear it if they decided to try to ambush them. Besides, he didn't think they had the balls to attack him. Not in broad daylight, at least.

Brian, otherwise known as Bear, yelled out a final parting shot. "Hey, bitch, if you want to fuck a real man, just let me know!"

Black clenched his teeth and debated grabbing the punk right then and there. He knew he could subdue all four of the men, even if they didn't fight fair. He'd been a Navy SEAL and had learned a thing or two from his friends as well.

But crossing the street to deal with them meant leaving Harlow vulnerable. And he wouldn't do that.

"Ignore him," Harlow said softly, grabbing hold of the belt loop on the back of his jeans. "Please?"

"It's okay," he told her, refusing to turn around and give Brian what he wanted: attention. "I'm not going to kick his ass."

"But you want to," she joked.

"You have no idea. But you know what I want more?"

"What?" she asked, glancing at him as they walked briskly to the parking lot and his car.

"You in my apartment. In my kitchen. Smiling and happy. Relaxed."

She smiled. "That sounds good."

He clicked the locks on his car and held open the door for her. He made sure she was settled before shutting it and heading to his side.

After he was seated, with the doors locked once more, he casually told her, "You should know that you aren't cooking for me tonight."

"What? Lowell, that was the deal!" she huffed.

He shrugged, not at all repentant. "If you think I'm going to invite you to my place, and then watch as you slave over my stove cooking dinner, you're insane."

"I was going to make beef bourguignon. It's easy to set up, and I wouldn't be slaving over anything."

"Don't care. The first time you're in my space, you aren't cooking for me. I bought some steaks and chicken, whichever you prefer. I'll grill them up, then we can settle down and watch a movie or something. I want you relaxed, Harl."

"Cooking *is* relaxing for me," she insisted.

Black brought his hand up and smoothed a lock of hair out of her face. Then he fingered the purple end for a beat before meeting her eyes. "I know. But I'm being selfish. I know how you get when you cook. Everyone disappears, and you can't concentrate on anything else. It's adorable. But for tonight, I want you to concentrate on me. On *us*."

"Oh," she said. It was more breath of air than word. "Okay."

"Okay," Black echoed, then turned his attention to the road.

It took about fifteen minutes for him to drive to his apartment complex. He'd looked into buying a house recently, but he hated thinking about the upkeep that would take. He didn't like lawn work and didn't want to have to worry about the place being empty when he went on missions.

He pulled into the parking lot and heard Harlow suck in a breath. "Wow. This complex is gorgeous."

She wasn't wrong. There was a large pool in the middle of the buildings, which were strategically placed around the rolling hills of the area. "Wait until you see the view from my balcony," Black told her. "It definitely doesn't look anything like where we grew up."

She giggled. "That's for sure."

"I had to wait an extra three months for the perfect unit to become available, but when I get to wake up to the sun shining on Pikes Peak, it makes it worthwhile." Black pulled into his assigned parking space and made a mental note to contact the front office about getting a visitor pass for Harlow. He helped her out of his car and led the way toward the door to his building.

Just when they were about to enter, he heard another car pull in.

Looking in that direction out of habit, Black stopped in his tracks.

He would know that black Audi anywhere. Following it was a beat-up old pickup truck.

"Fuck," Black swore under his breath.

"What? What's wrong?" Harlow asked, looking at him in confusion.

"Looks like our nice, relaxing evening for two just got shot to hell."

"Why?"

He gestured to the parking lot with his head. "Because we have company."

Harlow turned to look where he was gesturing. Gray, Allye, Ro, Chloe, Arrow, and Morgan were climbing out of the two cars. The men had shit-eating grins on their faces, and the women were smiling happily.

Gray walked up to them and held out a hand. Black shook it, but also shook his head at the same time. "Heard you were grilling out," his friend said. "Figured we'd stop by and chill with you."

"We brought food," Allye offered, somewhat apologetically.

"I made brownies," Morgan said with a smile. Arrow put his arm around the much smaller woman. She was holding a glass pan with her brownies, and Arrow had a grocery bag in his free hand.

"I brought the alcohol," Chloe said triumphantly. She held up a bottle of tequila and margarita mix.

"Hey, Black," Ro said with a grin. He was also carrying a grocery bag filled to the brim with enough food to feed everyone.

Knowing his plans for the night had changed, Black rolled with it. "Well, let's not stand out here all afternoon, we've got steaks and chicken to grill."

"Hi," Harlow said. "It's good to see everyone again."

"And just so you know, just because we brought food doesn't mean we expect you to cook it for us," Allye said. "Black's talked about what an amazing chef you are, and I looked you up online. I'm impressed."

As they headed inside, Harlow waved off Allye's praise. "I wouldn't mind. I love cooking. Obviously, since I've made it my life's work."

"Nope. They invited themselves over, so they can cook their own damn meal," Black said, knowing he sounded grumpier than he'd intended.

Ro chuckled. "If you'd have let us invite you over to *our* place, we wouldn't have had to show up out of the blue," he scolded.

Black didn't want to get into it at the moment. He'd turned his friends down repeatedly, telling them he and Harlow weren't dating. That they were simply discussing what was happening at the shelter. They'd obviously called bullshit and taken matters into their own hands.

Black paused at the doorway, holding Harlow back after everyone else had entered. "Now's our chance to escape," he said, only semijokingly. She turned to face him, and he was struck anew at how pretty she was. It wasn't what she was wearing; it wasn't makeup or lack of it. It was simply her. Her eclectic hair, her blue eyes, her personality.

"If you bailed, they'd never let you forget it," she chided. "Besides, I wouldn't mind getting to know them better. I haven't met too many people here in the Springs yet."

Suddenly feeling like a heel, he pulled her close and kissed the side of her head. "They already like you, Harl. Don't feel as if you need to be anyone you aren't around them."

"I like them too . . . at least the little I saw of them the other night at that escape-room thingie."

"You guys comin'?" Arrow called out.

"You ready for this?" Black asked Harlow, ignoring his friend.

"Bring it," Harlow said with a small smile.

Grabbing her hand, Black followed his friends to the elevators. He didn't know what the night would bring, but it probably wouldn't be making out on his couch, as he'd planned.

But he'd get to spend time with Harlow, so it would be a good night no matter how it turned out.

Chapter Eighteen

"Have you been able to see Nina much since you moved here permanently?" Harlow asked Morgan.

It was late. Dinner had been cooked and consumed. The girls had been steadily drinking margaritas, except for Allye, who had passed.

They were currently sprawled on his oversize couch, the one Black had visualized lying on with Harlow, making out and getting to know each other better. Morgan had just finished telling Harlow and the others about the little girl, Nina, who'd been rescued from Santo Domingo with her.

There weren't many places to sit in the apartment, which was generally why Black didn't have a lot of get-togethers. He and the other guys were currently standing in the kitchen, letting the women have some girl time.

"So . . . want to deny that you're dating Harlow some more?" Gray asked with a smirk.

Black took his eyes off Harlow and looked at his friend. He shook his head. "I knew that's why you assholes came over tonight. To harass me."

Ro smiled and sipped his beer. "Nah, not completely."

"But seriously, it looks like things are going well between you two," Arrow observed. "I thought you said that she was gun-shy about dating and refused to enter the fray again."

"She was. Is. But I kinda snuck under her radar."

"Knew you would," Arrow said. "In fact, I had fifty bucks on you."

Black glared at his friends. "You bet on whether or not she'd go out with me?"

Gray and Ro looked only slightly chagrined. "Have to admit that it's unusual for a chick to not want anything to do with you," Gray said.

"If you'd had dates like she's had, you wouldn't think so. One asshole came to her place for dinner and actually jacked off on one of her stuffed animals." He shivered. "God, I can't imagine how close she may have come to being hurt by him. Because we all know he might not have stopped there."

The amusement on the other men's faces disappeared.

"Are you bloody kidding?" Ro asked with a scowl.

"And that's just the tip of the iceberg. I told you a little about Roofie-and-High-Speed-Chase Guy. Once she explained why she wasn't dating anymore, I understood. And honestly, I was okay with that for a while. But the more I got to know her, the more I liked her. And you know the rest. I started being sneaky and taking her out on dates without actually calling them that. She finally realized what was going on."

"And she wasn't mad?" Arrow asked.

"No. More embarrassed that she hadn't realized it sooner. I guess she had a talk with her mom, and it clicked."

"You know you're fucked, right?" Gray asked.

"Well, I hope so," Black joked.

"I'm serious. You can kid about this if you want, but she's not like the other women you've dated. She's marriage material."

Black rolled his eyes and took a large swallow of his beer. "Whatever. Just because you and Allye are on the verge of tying the knot doesn't mean the rest of us are champing at the bit to do the same."

"I was," Ro said.

"I'd marry Morgan tomorrow if she asked," Arrow added.

"And I've got the ring burning a hole in my pocket, so to speak," Gray added. "I'm just waiting for the right moment to ask Allye to marry me . . . you know, since she's carrying my kid and all, I figured we should make it legal and shit."

Black's mouth fell open at Gray's announcement. "No shit?"

"No shit," Gray confirmed. "Why do you think she's not out there guzzling down those margaritas with the others?"

"Fuck!" Arrow exclaimed. "Congratulations, man!"

"Seriously, that's bloody awesome!" Ro added.

Black put down his beer and gave Gray a heartfelt hug. "Congrats," he said after he'd pulled away. "You guys have to be over the moon."

"We are. She doesn't have any parents to share the news with, so I'm hoping to go visit my mom soon, and we'll officially break the news to her. Allye's only around two months along right now, so we want to wait for another month to let my mom know she's going to be a grandmother. I'll find a time to ask her to marry me sometime between now and then."

"Get on that," Arrow advised. "If you want to be married before that kid arrives, you'll need to plan things fast. No woman wants to look pregnant in her wedding pictures."

"Oh, we've talked about what kind of ceremony we want," Gray assured his friends. "We want something low key, at the house, with just our very close friends in attendance."

"Still, there's a lot to plan," Arrow insisted. "Cake, invitations, music . . . it's endless."

"Sounds like you know what you're talking about," Ro said. "Something you want to tell us?"

They all chuckled, but Arrow merely shrugged. "Told you I'd marry Morgan tomorrow if I could."

Black said, "Well, I just started dating Harlow. We aren't planning weddings and deciding how many babies we want."

"Uh-huh," Gray said skeptically.

"We aren't," Black repeated.

"Look, all I'm saying is that I haven't seen you act this way around any other women. Not that you've even dated anyone recently. She's different. *You're* different with her. If I had to guess, I'd say she's it for you."

Black shook his head. "Don't go getting all fucking mushy on me. Just because *you* guys have all met women you want to propose to after a week doesn't mean I have. We're dating. I enjoy spending time with her, but if she told me tomorrow she was done, then that would be that."

"Really?" Arrow asked. "Because *you've* been the one all up in Rex's face because he hasn't been doing as much as you think he should for this case."

"And you've refused to let any of *us* escort Harlow to work," Gray added.

"Not to mention the fact that you're itching to get your hands on this Brian guy because he said some shit to her," Ro reasoned.

"I'm protecting *everyone* in that shelter," Black protested. "You heard what he said. He threatened her and everyone else who lives there. We protect women and kids. It's what the Mountain Mercenaries do."

"Fine. Let me put it a different way," Gray said. "You were worried about Allye when you picked us up in the ocean, right?"

"Of course," Black said.

"You joked with her and helped keep her occupied while we brought her to shore."

"And?" Black didn't know what point his friend was trying to make, but he wished he'd hurry up and make it.

"When we got there, we didn't have time to make sure she was safe. We had to leave her with some man Rex was working with, and just hope he was on the up-and-up, and that he'd get her back to San Francisco safely."

"Fuck, spit it out already," Black growled.

"What if that was Harlow?" Gray's eyes were knowing as he looked at Black. "What if the roles were reversed, and it was *Harlow* who was in the middle of the ocean, and you rescued her and then had to leave her behind?"

"It wasn't," Black said, a sick feeling in his gut.

"But it could've been. What if it was *Harlow* we found in that hut in Santo Domingo? What if *her* brother was trying to kill her? Would you be as blasé about her as you are right now? Would she be just another woman we've rescued?" Gray asked.

"I've known Harlow a long time," Black countered. "She's not a stranger. It's different."

"Is it? You're normally a protective man, Black," Gray continued. "We've all seen it. But not like this. Not like you are with her. Hell, you can't even walk by her without touching her. On the shoulder, on the hand, something. Can you honestly stand here and tell us that you'd be okay with dating her for a while, then letting her go her own way?"

"I can't answer that because we've only just begun seeing each other. That's like me asking if you think you'll ever break up with Allye. It's not a fair question," Black protested.

"You can make up whatever excuse you want, but that's all they are. Excuses. Look, what's wrong with wanting more? Why are you going *into* a relationship thinking it'll end? Why don't you just see where things might go?"

Black took another sip of his beer and thought about Gray's question. It wasn't as if he wanted things to end with Harlow. It was just . . . they *always* ended. He got bored. The woman got clingy. Something about her got on his nerves. It was just a fact that he'd rarely lasted longer than a few months in a relationship. There was a reason his friends compared him to the iconic *Seinfeld* character.

But . . . it had already been almost a month and a half with Harlow. Granted, their relationship hadn't exactly been "normal," but he'd spent a lot of time with her, and his interest had only increased. He'd gone out of his way to plan things for them to do together that he knew she'd enjoy. While he wanted her, all of her, most of the time that wasn't his end goal when he spent time with her. He liked being around her. Liked watching her interact with the others at the shelter. Liked making her laugh.

"I see it's sinking in," Ro said cheekily.

"Fuck off," Black mumbled.

The other men smirked.

"And if you ever ask me to picture Harlow in any other fucked-up situation we've been in, or suggest that she'll ever *be* in a situation like the ones we rescue women from on a regular basis, I'll kick your ass. All of you," Black warned.

"Told you," Gray said, speaking to Ro and Arrow. "He's over-the-top protective . . . just like I was with Allye, like you were with Morgan, and you with Chloe."

"Fine. Thinking about Harlow being in danger makes me want to hurt somebody. Which is why we need to get this Brian guy and shut this shit down now," Black said. Then he proceeded to tell them about what Brian and his friends had said as he and Harlow were leaving the shelter that afternoon.

"Rex still doesn't see any reason for us to pick up Brian," Arrow said.

"He's wrong," Black said flatly. "I don't know what's going on with him, but he's distracted. Meat said he had to ask him twice for the additional information he'd gathered about Wyatt Newton. And that's not like Rex."

"Has he gotten back to Meat with the background check on Edward? Or Loretta?" Ro asked.

"Not that I know of. I don't like this," Gray said. "I'm with Black. I know he's anxious because he wants to protect Harlow, but we've got a bunch of nothing as far as this case is concerned. So we'll pick up Brian and see what we can find out. And we'll tell Rex what we did after it's done, and after we have the information we need. But Black, you have to stay in control," Gray warned. "I know you want to kick this guy's ass, and you can do your thing and threaten him and make him think he's never gonna see the light of day again . . . but you know you can't kill him, right?"

Black sighed as he walked over to the sink and poured out the rest of his beer. "I know," he said grudgingly. "I'm pissed at him, but I'm not an idiot. The last thing we need is our shit blowing back onto the ladies at the shelter. But if he starts spouting off about Harlow, you guys need to make sure I don't go too far."

"You know we will," Arrow said.

"Of course," Ro agreed.

"We've got your back," Gray said. "No one disses one of our women and gets away with it unscathed."

Black wanted to protest the "our women" thing in regard to Harlow, but since he was trying to be honest with himself . . . he admitted that it felt right.

Harlow *was* his. Maybe not forever. Maybe just until she came to her senses and figured out he was far from perfect.

But he silently hoped that she'd be his for a hell of a long time.

"So . . . you and Black, huh?" Morgan asked.

Harlow smiled shyly at her new friends. She'd been nervous to hang out with them because they all seemed way more put together and sophisticated than she was. Allye was a beautiful dancer, Chloe was a gazillionaire, and Morgan was . . . well, she was the strongest woman Harlow had ever met. Chloe and Allye had been through some tough shit, but knowing what Morgan had survived amazed her.

Harlow wasn't that strong. There was no way she would have been brave enough to endure what the other women had and still be as funny, outgoing, and friendly. It was safe to say these women intimidated the hell out of her. She wasn't anyone special. She had loving parents; had grown up in Topeka, for God's sake; and made food for a living. She didn't want to be famous, didn't want to be rich, only wanted to be able to make people happy by cooking them good meals.

"I knew Lowell in high school," Harlow said, answering Morgan's question. "He was a year older than me, and we were in a yearbook club together. He was only there because he was trying to have something on his résumé that would look good for recruiters."

"I can't picture Black as a high schooler at all," Allye said. "I mean, the first time I met him, he plucked my freezing ass from the Pacific Ocean. He was wearing all black and was super polite. I bet he was popular, wasn't he?"

Harlow nodded. "Extremely. I was surprised he even talked to me in that class. But he did. He was nice."

"You liked him!" Chloe exclaimed a little too loudly.

"Shhhh!" Harlow scolded her, looking nervously toward the kitchen, where the men were having what looked like an intense conversation.

"You did!" the other woman said a bit softer.

"Well, duh," Harlow drawled. "Who wouldn't?"

Everyone giggled.

"But I knew he'd never look twice at me. Besides, he was graduating and heading off to save the world. I can't tell you how surprised I was when I saw him in the shelter the first time. And he actually remembered me! I was shocked. Seriously. I look nothing like I did in high school."

"You have a distinctive name," Allye informed her. "Of course he remembered you."

Harlow shook her head. She wasn't going to argue about it, but she knew that probably wasn't the case. "Anyway, then he gave me his number, and I about died. I wanted to call him practically every day, but I couldn't think of a good reason. I mean, I asked him about beginner gun-safety classes, but it's not like I was in a hurry to actually shoot a weapon. But then when the other women started getting harassed, and no one knew what to do about it, I figured I should call. For their sakes."

"And now you're dating," Chloe said. When Morgan shook her head in exasperation, she defended herself. "Hey, I want to get to the good stuff. We don't know how long our men will be in there chitchatting, and I want to know about these nondates they've been on."

"You know about that?" Harlow asked, surprised.

"Just what Ro's told me. That Black told them you've had some bad experiences with dating, so he was taking you on sneak dates."

Harlow giggled again. Yeah, that was exactly what they were. "So you all knew I was dating Lowell before me, huh?"

Morgan smiled and shrugged.

Allye nodded.

And Chloe said, "Yup. That's how being with one of the Mountain Mercenaries works. Nothing's a secret, and we all know everything about everyone. For instance, did you know Black got his nickname when he ran into a door the first day of boot camp and got a huge black eye? The other recruits started calling him Blackie, and it eventually got shortened to Black and stuck."

Harlow hadn't known that. She shook her head, enthralled.

"And Ball's last name is Black, so you'd think that's what people would call *him*, but when he was in the Coast Guard, he had a reputation for always knowing when the shit was about to hit the fan, and everyone always said he was 'on the ball.' That apparently just became Ball."

It was fascinating to learn these little things about the very macho men in the other room. Harlow listened, riveted, soaking up every scrap of information she could.

"Did you guys hear about why Ball quit the Coast Guard?" Morgan whispered.

Harlow was tempted to say something about how it wasn't nice to talk about the men like they were, but on the other hand, she really wanted to know. She kept quiet as Morgan continued.

"I heard Arrow talking to him one night on the phone. I only heard Arrow's side of the conversation, but he was commiserating with Ball about a woman messing up some mission he'd been on. I guess they'd chased down a boat in the Gulf of Mexico, and she didn't do something properly. When they went to handcuff the bad guys, one pulled out a gun the woman hadn't noticed and shot Ball."

"Holy crap, really?" Allye asked. "I didn't know that."

Morgan nodded. "Ball's arm was never the same, and he was honorably discharged from the Coast Guard as a result. And then he joined the Mountain Mercenaries."

Harlow felt sorry for Ball. He seemed like a really nice guy, and it sucked that he'd been shot. It sucked that it had happened because someone else didn't do something properly, and it sucked even more that he'd been discharged as a result of someone else's actions. She'd met some pretty kick-ass women in her life. Police officers who could take down a man three times their size. Firefighters who didn't hesitate to run into a burning building. Soldiers who fought just as hard for their country as their male counterparts.

She looked over to Lowell's kitchen, where he and his friends were still talking.

Seeing where she was looking, Allye said, "Don't feel bad. I swear sometimes our men gossip more than we do. Look at them in there, chatting it up." She gestured toward the kitchen with her head.

"They're probably talking about Meat, and the fact that he spends more time on his computer than talking to real, live people," Morgan said.

"Maybe he's got a secret lover who he's never met, and the only way they've communicated is via the internet," Chloe said with a smile.

The women giggled.

Then Allye took a deep breath and said, "Or they're talking about me being pregnant, and Gray is probably trying to get ideas on how to propose to me in some super-huge and grand way."

Everyone went silent at Allye's announcement—then Chloe and Morgan screeched in excitement and practically leaped on the other woman in their hurry to congratulate her.

Harlow didn't exactly screech, but she did hurry over to the woman to add her hugs.

"You're *pregnant*?" Chloe asked, once she had herself under control.

Allye nodded. "About two months along. We haven't said anything before now because, you know . . . we wanted to be sure. But you guys are my friends, and like you said, nothing's a secret with the Mountain Mercenaries."

"That's so amazing," Morgan said with a huge smile on her face. "Congrats!"

"I guess that's why you aren't drinking with us," Harlow said.

"Yup. Although I'm super jealous of you guys."

"Why?" Morgan asked.

"Because I know how Gray gets when I get drunk. He can't keep his hands off me," Allye said with a satisfied smile.

"Him too?" Chloe asked.

"Isn't it awesome?" Morgan asked.

"I wouldn't know," Harlow said.

The other three women stared at her with speculative glances. "Guess that answers the question of how Black is in bed," Allye said dryly. "Taking things slow, huh?"

Harlow nodded.

"I don't think there's any question about how he'll be in bed," Chloe said. "Not with the way he's been looking at her all night."

"How's he been looking at me?" Harlow asked. She knew she was blushing, but needed to hear the answer.

"As if he's been in the desert for weeks, and you're a tall glass of water," Morgan told her.

Feeling the heat in her cheeks deepen, Harlow couldn't stop the "Really?" that popped out.

"Really," Allye confirmed. "I guess we decided to crash your little dinner party prematurely."

"Well, uh . . . I don't think tonight was going to be the night we got down and dirty," Harlow said honestly. "I mean, don't get me wrong, I'm looking forward to it, but we've only kissed. I don't think we'd go from a few kisses straight into sex."

"Don't hold your breath," Chloe said not so innocently, looking up at the ceiling.

Everyone laughed once more. They all settled back into their seats, and Chloe and Morgan started grilling Allye about her pregnancy, and why she thought Gray might be talking to the others about ways to propose.

Harlow let her mind wander. She was happy to have been welcomed into the group, but a part of her already missed hanging out with Lowell. She'd been looking forward to cooking with him and snuggling on the couch. She was being honest with the others when she'd said she didn't think tonight was the night they would make love for the first time, but that didn't mean she wasn't disappointed they didn't get to spend any time alone together.

"Are these seats taken?" Arrow asked from behind the couch.

"What seats?" Allye asked. "There isn't enough room for all of us in this apartment."

"No one asked you to come over," Black teased as he came around the couch. Without pause, he leaned over and grabbed Harlow's hand. He pulled her to her feet, sat, then pulled her down to sit on his lap. He braced her back with one hand and rested his other arm over her thighs.

Harlow blinked in surprise. It had taken him but ten seconds to completely rearrange her on the couch. He hadn't even spilled her drink while moving her. She wanted to be irritated, but how could she? She was just lamenting that she'd missed out on cuddle time with the man, and now here she was . . . cuddling.

"We'll host the next one," Ro said immediately. "And we'll make sure Ball and Meat are there too."

"Feels weird without them," Morgan agreed.

"We should get going," Gray said softly to Allye. "You feeling okay?"

"I'm fine. I'm pregnant, not sick," she reprimanded.

She stood, and Gray was immediately at her side. His hand palmed her belly, and he pulled her back against his front. "Right."

Harlow loved the banter not only between the couples themselves, but between the friends. It was what had always been missing in her life. Friends. True friends to hang out with, get tipsy with, and to girl talk with. Without thought, she leaned a bit and rested her head on Lowell's shoulder. His arm tightened around her, and she knew without doubt that he'd make sure she didn't lose her balance and topple off his lap. Which was, of course, a possibility, and not just because she'd been drinking.

The others agreed that it was time to go, and Harlow noticed that Lowell didn't protest. She wondered if he'd missed the cuddle time as much as she did.

"We'll just let ourselves out," Gray said dryly when Black didn't stand up to see them to the door.

"You do that," he said.

Everyone laughed and said their goodbyes. The women promised to be in touch soon, as they'd exchanged numbers.

"I'll lock the door behind me," Ro said.

"'Preciate it," Black told him.

Then it was just the two of them. Harlow didn't move from her spot on top of Lowell. If anything, she melted into him further.

"Have fun tonight?"

She nodded. "Yeah."

"You sound surprised," Lowell observed.

"It's just . . . they're all so down-to-earth. I never in a million years thought I would be drinking with Morgan Byrd. I mean, I watched that show where she was interviewed, and if that happened to me, I'd probably still be in a mental hospital trying to deal with the shit she went through."

"No, you wouldn't," Lowell said.

"You don't know that," Harlow protested.

"I do. You've got an amazing core of strength inside you. It doesn't come to the surface very often, because you don't need it, but every time one of those assholes around the shelter says shit to you, or does something, your first thought is for others. You want to know how Loretta's dealing with it. If the kids heard. If the women saw. I have no doubt whatsoever that you can more than deal with whatever comes your way."

"Thanks," Harlow whispered.

"You sound tired."

"For some reason, I got up at five thirty this morning. Maybe from my phone alerting me to a good-morning text," Harlow quipped, then yawned.

He immediately followed suit and yawned as well.

She giggled. "I guess yawns really are contagious."

"Yup. Why don't you close your eyes for a while?" he asked.

"I should be going. I know you have stuff to do tomorrow."

"Just for a while," he cajoled. "I'll wake you up in a bit and take you home. I just don't feel like I've gotten to spend any time with you tonight."

"We've been together practically all day," she told him.

"But I've had to share you."

"Wow. That was a really nice thing to say."

"Hmmm," he muttered. "I love my friends, but I was looking forward to hanging out with you all night. Instead, I got the third degree and had to share the steaks I bought with them."

"But we got brownies in return," Harlow teased.

"So you'd take brownies over my exclusive company?" he asked.

"No." Harlow sat up and looked him in the eye. "I've had a wonderful time with you the last several days. From the hot-air balloon to watching you play Barbie dolls with Jody, to seeing you laugh and joke with your friends, to getting to know the other women. But sitting here like this, with just you, is the icing on the cake."

He brought a hand up to her neck and urged her to rest on his shoulder once more. "Close your eyes. What'd you call it? Rest your eyeballs? We'll get up in a bit."

"Okay." There was literally no other response she could give.

Nolan Woolf watched the man leave the shelter and sneered. Over the last week, he'd started sitting up on the third floor of the building next to the shelter, watching who came and went. He'd learned the men's routines easily. They weren't trying to conceal themselves or what they were doing.

If Loretta Royster thought hiring bodyguards would keep her precious building safe, she was mistaken.

Wiping a bead of sweat from his forehead, Nolan scowled as the man walked down the sidewalk toward the parking lot. He had a computer bag over his shoulder and looked like he was on a mission to get somewhere. To do something. To look up something.

Nolan felt his chance was slipping away. Loretta still hadn't responded to *any* offers to buy the building. Why she was stalling, considering the harassment, he didn't know. But it didn't matter . . .

He'd put his other plan in motion. And he'd been reassured that action had already been taken. That the accusations had been taken seriously and were being investigated.

The government didn't take kindly to people misappropriating funds earmarked for community services.

Why he hadn't made the anonymous complaint earlier, he didn't know.

Without money, Loretta Royster wouldn't be able to stay in business. She'd *have* to take the offers to buy her property seriously. And when the time was right, Nolan would make one last bid, just a little higher than the rest, just to make sure she chose him. He could offer more than the building was worth, but that would just make him look suspicious. Especially if the bodyguards who'd been lurking around managed to look too deeply.

She should've just accepted *his* bid for the building; then he wouldn't have had to resort to all the subterfuge, and her reputation wouldn't be on the cusp of ruin.

Chapter Nineteen

After lunch the next day, Harlow stepped into Loretta's third-floor office and shut the door behind her. It was a cozy space with a window that overlooked the alley on the back side of the building. There were bookshelves on one wall, full of books and odds and ends, a window seat beneath the window, and a large, wooden desk along another wall.

Loretta was sitting behind it, looking very somber.

Instantly uneasy, Harlow sat in one of the two chairs in front of the desk. She'd never seen Loretta look so serious.

"First of all," Loretta began immediately, "I want to apologize for what happened at the store, about the credit card I gave you not working. Somehow it got canceled. When I called to inquire about it, the bank was very apologetic, but they said someone had disputed a charge, so they canceled it."

"It's okay," Harlow said. "Lowell said he was happy to help."

Loretta nodded. "As you know, First Hope is a nonprofit. I receive money from the state to keep this place up and running." She ran a shaking hand through her hair and went on. "I got word yesterday that there was an anonymous accusation that I've been misappropriating the funds I've been receiving."

Harlow sat up straight. "But that's a lie!" she exclaimed.

"Thank you, child." Loretta sighed. "Of course it's not true, but the state takes accusations like that seriously. They've frozen the shelter accounts while they investigate. The grants I've been receiving have also been stopped until everything is figured out."

"That's not fair!" Harlow said, feeling heartsick. "Can they really do that? Just take some random anonymous complaint and make you and everyone who lives here suffer while they look into it? What happened to innocent until proven guilty?"

Loretta looked saddened. "They can really do that. And the investigation could take months, even if I completely cooperate with them and let them see all of the accounting records."

"What about a lawyer? Would having one speed things up?" Harlow asked.

"Maybe."

"What can I do to help?"

Loretta gave her a sad smile. "Bless you, Harlow. Instead of worrying about yourself, of course the first thing you want to do is help. I'm not sure there's much to help with at this point."

"We can do fund-raisers. Get the community involved," Harlow insisted.

"You're so sweet. But . . . here's the thing . . . I'm not sure I *want* to fight."

"What? Why not? You haven't done anything wrong!"

"I know, and the auditors will eventually see that. But the truth is, I'm tired. I'm sixty-five years old. I can't remember the last time I've been on vacation. I've given so much of my life to this place, and frankly, thinking about retiring is a small relief. I won't have to worry myself sick when a new resident shows up, wondering how I can make her feel safe, and I won't have to take up any more of the Mountain Mercenaries' time. I know deciding to let this place go might make me selfish, but I can't help but feel as if this is a sign."

Harlow couldn't begrudge Loretta living her retirement years in relative peace. Running the shelter was tough—even she could see that. And Loretta had been doing it for years on her own.

"I've actually been thinking about retiring for a while now, even before I got word that I was under investigation. I just thought I'd wait a couple more years. I've gotten several offers on the building. The money I'd make would be enough to allow me to buy a condo, or maybe move out to Florida and into one of those retirement communities."

"You've gotten offers to sell?" Harlow asked. "I didn't know that."

"I haven't really been trying to keep it a secret. I just wasn't seriously considering selling, so I didn't talk about the offers. But now I'm thinking maybe it's time."

Harlow wanted to be happy for Loretta, but she couldn't help but think of herself. She loved working here. Loved feeling as if she was making a difference in the lives of the women and kids. Now she'd have to find a new job. "Does Zoe know?" Harlow asked.

"She does. I talked to her this morning before you came in. She quit. After spending time with her son and her new grandbaby, she's decided to move down to Pueblo to be closer to them. She'll get to spoil her grandkids by cooking for *them* now."

Harlow's stomach clenched. "And me?" she asked quietly. Harlow couldn't say more. She knew if she did, she'd probably break down.

"I'm so sorry, Harlow. I didn't hire you thinking this would happen. I'd never do that to anyone. I'm going to do everything in my power to help you find another position. I still have a lot of connections in Colorado Springs. As far as working here, I can pay for part-time hours out of pocket in the short term. I think dinner is the most important meal. Everyone seemed to manage pretty well with getting breakfast on their own while Zoe was gone. If you can make sure there are easy things to make for lunch, and maybe even continue to pack the kids' lunches, that would be great. I think it's important to continue to have our group dinners during the week, but you'd have the weekends off."

Harlow couldn't stop the tears from overflowing and falling down her cheeks.

"Oh Lord, please don't cry! You're going to make me start up again," Loretta choked out.

Not able to withstand seeing the older woman crying, Harlow got up and walked behind the desk to comfort Loretta. She got down on her knees and hugged her around the waist. It was several moments before either woman could speak.

"Of course I'll stay to help," Harlow told her. "I'm so sorry. What's going to happen to everyone who lives here?"

Loretta patted her cheek. "I knew from the second I met you that you would be good for this place. The kitchen is the heart and soul of any home, and you've made this a *true* home for everyone who's been here. I'm working with some of my connections to make sure everyone has someplace to go. Unfortunately, some of the kids will have to change school districts, but at least I think I can find homes for everyone."

"Do they know yet?"

"Most do. Not the kids yet, though. We're holding off on telling them until we have a move-out date. There's no use letting them stress about the situation for longer than necessary."

"Are *you* okay?" Harlow asked, getting up and going to sit in the chair she'd vacated.

"I've lived in this place for what seems like forever. Did you know this used to be a hotel?"

Harlow had heard the story before, when she'd interviewed for the chef position, but she shook her head, encouraging Loretta to keep talking.

"I spent time in the very kitchen you work in today. I helped my grandmother get breakfasts ready for the guests. I love this old, crumbling building. It holds as many good memories as bad. I love what I've done here, helping women and children who need a safe place to stay for a while, but thinking about how scared they are when they first arrive, and how terrified the kids are, breaks my heart even today."

Harlow's heart bled for her boss. Loretta was one of the most giving people she'd ever met in her life, but even selfless people needed time for themselves. It sucked that someone had sullied her reputation and gotten the shelter's funding frozen. She was disappointed that Loretta wasn't going to try to fight the accusations, but she did understand how the older woman felt.

That didn't mean she wasn't stressed, though. Harlow had moved to Colorado Springs to do something different. The last thing she wanted was to go back to the rat race that was being a chef in a busy restaurant.

For a heartbeat, she thought about buying the building from Loretta herself, but immediately dismissed the idea. She didn't have the money, and it obviously took a lot of capital to keep the place running smoothly. Who knew if she'd be able to get the same grants and support from the state as Loretta had, especially considering the misappropriation-of-funds accusation?

She'd have to start looking for another job, maybe one that involved working with children and women, like she did now. She didn't want to go back to the restaurant life, but she would if she had to.

"I'd appreciate it if you kept this to yourself for now," Loretta said. "Most of the residents know, but the last thing I'd want is for one of the kids to overhear someone talking about it. Especially Jasper. He's just beginning to settle in. To trust. And this is going to knock him for a loop."

"Can I tell Lowell?" Harlow asked.

Loretta sighed. "I had hoped to keep this quiet a bit longer, but it's not fair to keep it from them. Not after the way they've stepped up to try to figure out who's behind the harassment we've been experiencing.

Yes, you can tell him. He and Rex might have connections you can use to find a new job as well."

"Thanks," Harlow said. She stood and said, "I should probably go down and start getting dinner ready so you guys will be good to go when I head out tonight."

"What are we having?" Loretta asked, obviously trying to get things back on an even keel between them.

"Veal marsala, green-bean casserole, and angel food cake with strawberries for dessert."

"Maybe I should hire you as my personal chef when I retire," Loretta joked.

Harlow gave her a small smile and turned to head for the door.

"I'm really sorry," Loretta said softly as Harlow was about to exit.

Not sure what else to say, Harlow merely nodded and headed down to the kitchen.

Black cracked his knuckles and looked down at Brian "Bear" Pierce.

He wasn't so arrogant now. He was sitting in a wooden chair with his arms zip-tied behind his back and his legs tied securely to the chair as well.

Black had been working him over for at least an hour. He could go for hours more. He didn't even feel tired, but he knew continuing to torture the man would be for naught. It was obvious that they'd gotten everything they were going to get out of him.

Becoming an interrogator hadn't been on the short list of things Black wanted to do with his life. While in the Navy, he'd gone through training on how to withstand common torture techniques the enemy might use to get him to talk. He'd only been captured once, but that had been enough. Black hadn't cracked, but he'd gained a new appreciation for the techniques that could be used to break a man.

He'd used them more than once during his job with the Mercenaries. He wasn't proud of it, but when push came to shove, information was the most important thing, and he had a knack for being able to get it.

Gray, Ball, Arrow, and Ro stood behind Black, showing a united front to Brian. Meat was currently at the shelter. He was pissed he was "missing out on the fun," but was mollified a bit by the fact that he was on the cusp of finding out some new information he'd been researching.

Brian had admitted he didn't know the name of the man who'd hired him and his friends, but he'd described him down to the mole on the side of his neck. Of course, knowing the man had brown hair, brown eyes, was "middle age," and had a beer belly wasn't exactly the kind of information that would help to find him.

"I'm sick of this," Gray said. "He's not telling us anything useful."

Black knew his teammate was trying to scare Brian, so he went along with it. "So what should I do?"

"Cut off his ear," Ro said matter-of-factly.

"What? No! Don't come near me!" Brian said in a high-pitched, panicked tone.

"Not his ear," Arrow chimed in. "Take one of his thumbs."

"*Shit!* No!" Brian cried as a large stain spread across his lap.

"Did you just piss your pants?" Ball asked.

"Look, I'm telling you what I know! I swear! The mole dude met with me a couple of times and told me to have my buds harass everyone who lived in the building."

Black leaned over Brian, trying not to inhale too deeply, as the man seriously stank of fear, piss, and body odor. "Why?" Black asked in a low, harsh tone.

"He wants the building!" Brian shouted. "He gave me a couple hundred bucks and promised me and my friends free apartments when they were built. But he couldn't start building the damn things until he owned the building."

Black stood up and held out a hand to Ro. "Hand me your knife."

"No!" Brian screeched. "I'm telling the truth!"

"We already know about the apartments," Black told the quivering man. "You aren't telling us anything we didn't already know."

"He owns them all!" Brian blurted desperately. "All but the shelter! He made some offers when he heard some other investors in the area were sending her unsolicited offers for the building, but the old broad hasn't responded to any of them. He can't get the permits to build and start making money off the state until he owns all the buildings on the block. He said something about doing something to make sure she'd have no choice *but* to sell, and sell to him."

Now *that* was news to Black. As far as they knew, the buildings had all been bought by different companies. Not to mention whatever the mysterious contact was going to do, or had already done, to make Loretta sell.

He saw Gray slip out of the room, presumably to call Meat with the new information.

Black cracked his knuckles and stood up straight. "Now, how about we discuss your attitude toward the women and kids who live in the building?" Black asked.

"I was just doing what I was told to do," Brian retorted. "Besides, they're just chicks."

"Just chicks?" Black asked. "And that means what?"

"Come on, you know. They flirt and act all coy and shit, then when it comes time to put out, they're all like, 'I said no.'"

Black didn't like what he was hearing, or the fact that Brian seemed to have gotten a second wind and a bit of his courage back. "So you're saying it's okay to take what you think they're offering even if they say no?"

"Well, yeah. They want it. They always do."

Enough was enough. Black nodded at Ball and Ro, and they moved behind Brian and pulled his head up so he had no choice but to look at the man in front of him.

"What gives you the right to force a woman to have sex? I don't care if she's *begging* you to make love to her—the second she says no, you stop. Period," Black said, despite knowing Brian wouldn't change his thinking just because he told him to. "And what gives you the right to terrorize other people? I'll tell you what—*nothing*. You think because you're bigger and badder than them, you can do whatever you want? You think it's fun to make someone cry? You like having people be scared of you?"

Black leaned in, placing his hands on Brian's thighs and putting all his weight on them. Brian cried out in pain as pressure was put on the small cuts Black had made on his legs earlier, but Ro and Ball held him still as Black made his point.

"I've got news for you, *Bear*. There's always someone bigger and badder. In your case, that's me and my friends. You think we're pretty boys who don't know the rules of your world, but you're wrong. We don't need rules, because we can *go* anywhere and *do* anything we want. You're nothing but a low-down piece of scum on the bottom of our shoes. So here's a tip—we don't see you again. If we do, this little interlude will seem like a day at the spa. And if you think I'm kidding, know that I could absolutely kill you right here, right now."

Black moved his hand to Brian's throat and squeezed. He watched as his face began to turn red and his eyes bugged out.

"No one would know where you went. No one would ever find your body. Your family would always wonder what happened. Your kid—yes, we know about your son—would never know what a scumbag his father was, which would probably be a gift for him. No one would miss you. If you want to continue breathing, you'll find another place to hang out. You won't meet with your contact anymore. You'll forget the shelter exists. You hear me?"

Satisfied when Brian nodded as best he could with a hand around his throat, Black abruptly let him go. Brian gasped for air, and when

Ball and Ro let go of his head, it immediately fell to his chest, as if it was too heavy for him to hold up any longer.

Black was keyed up. Frustrated that they didn't get more out of the asshole tied to the chair, but satisfied he'd scared the man enough that he wouldn't be an issue for the women at the shelter anymore. That he wouldn't be bothering Harlow.

Black wrinkled his nose at the stench of piss coming from Brian. It really was amazing how the biggest bully turned to mush the second someone stronger and meaner got their hands on him. He nodded at his friends, and they took out their knives and cut Brian loose. He immediately fell sideways to the concrete floor, moaning.

Everyone took a few steps away from the pathetic man lying on the floor to have a conversation without him overhearing.

"You are one scary motherfucker," Ball said. "I swear, I could beat on someone all day, and they still wouldn't break, but one look at you with a knife in your hand, and the perp always starts singing like a canary. It's spooky."

Ignoring his friend, Black said, "We need to talk to Loretta. Find out the details about the offers she's had."

"I'll call Rex," Ball said.

"He's not going to be happy," Ro warned.

"Tough. We got more info, and hopefully Meat can do something with it once he talks to Gray. Rex should've paid more attention and done more digging, then maybe we wouldn't have had to resort to finding the information *our* way," Ball said.

"Go," Arrow ordered. "We'll clean things up here."

Black nodded and turned to leave. He'd have to change clothes and shower before heading to the shelter.

He needed to see Harlow. Needed her light to combat the darkness stirring in his soul. He was good at what he did, but it took a toll. Normally, it would take days for him to feel normal again. But he had a feeling just being around Harlow would ground him. Would make him remember why he did what he did. To protect her and others like her. Innocents. People who didn't have the skills to protect themselves. And he'd use every one of those skills to make sure Brian and his cronies didn't put a single finger on her. It was bad enough they used words to scare her. But the thought of them actually touching her was abhorrent.

Black exited the warehouse and didn't look back. He knew his teammates would get rid of any evidence that might've been left behind. The owner of the building was the father of a teenage runaway they'd found after she'd been missing for three months. She'd been in New York City with a man thirty years older than her, completely strung out on drugs. They'd brought her home, and the last they'd heard, she was taking a few classes at the local community college and slowly acclimating to her new life.

Her father had offered the use of several of his warehouses, no questions asked, whenever the Mountain Mercenaries needed them. The team didn't take advantage of the offer very often, but today, having that connection definitely came in handy.

As it turned out, Black wasn't able to get to the shelter until much later than he'd planned. Rex called the moment he got out of the shower, and stupidly, Black answered. "Black."

"What the fuck is your problem?"

"I did what needed to be done."

"Bullshit. You jeopardized my entire organization!"

"The hell I did. You know I'm discreet. You know I'd never do anything to hurt the Mountain Mercenaries."

"You kidnapped an innocent civilian, beat the shit out of him, and threatened him. What part of *any* of that do you think is okay?"

Black was done. He was always respectful with Rex, but today, he'd reached his breaking point. "Maybe if you'd been doing your job, I wouldn't have had to do it for you. Maybe if you had researched Brian Pierce like you said you were going to, you would've found out who was paying him and his asshole friends to harass Harlow and everyone else at the shelter. I wouldn't've had to call in that favor."

"Don't tell me how to do my job," Rex hissed.

"I wouldn't if you were actually *doing* it!" Black insisted. "Look, I respect the fuck out of you, Rex. But you haven't been present in this case—and you know it. Something is going on with you, fine, but that shouldn't mean you leave me and the others in the lurch. We need you. We need your expertise. We can be the muscle all day long and go into whatever godforsaken country you send us into and retrieve women and children, but we can't do it without you having our backs. And right now, it feels a hell of a lot like you've deserted us."

"You know that's not true."

"Do I? Tell me about Brian Pierce, Rex. Does he have a family? Sisters? Where do his parents live? Where did he go to high school? Who are his best friends? Does he have a job? How much money does he have in his bank account? These are all things *you* should've found out by now. All it would've taken is a few clicks on your computer. But you didn't. We've been waiting for you to tell us what we need to know, but we had to find out the intel on our own."

"Fuck," Rex swore.

"There's a lot that we still don't know about what's going on," Black told his mentor and friend. He'd never met the man in person, had only talked to him on the phone. Hell, he didn't even know what Rex's true voice sounded like, as he'd only heard it mechanized. But he still considered him a friend and trusted him with his life.

"We need you dialed in, Rex. There's something big in the works, and we're close to figuring it out, but we need your help. I know you, man. If something happens to any of the women in that shelter, or the kids, you'll never forgive yourself. I'm not saying whatever's going on with you isn't important. I'm sure it's as important as anything else you've ever done. All I'm asking is that you give this situation your attention at the moment. Once we figure it out, you can do whatever it is you need to do. Hell, ask us to help you. All of us will drop *everything* if you need assistance—but don't leave us hanging here."

Black stood in the middle of his bedroom with only a towel around his waist and waited for his handler to say something.

"I hear you," Rex said in a subdued tone. "And you're right. I've been preoccupied . . . and I'm sorry. It's a long story, one I'll share with you at some point, but not now. And it doesn't matter now anyway, because the lead I thought I had on a cold case went nowhere. What do you need?"

Black sighed. It felt weird to have to tell his handler what was going on in the case. Usually, Rex passed intel to *them*. For him to ask what they needed was akin to him admitting that he'd checked out. "Whoever the contact is has done something, or is going to do something, to try to force Loretta to sell the building. We need to know what that is."

"What about the other stuff Pierce told you?" Rex asked.

"Gray gave that info to Meat. We've got a description of a middle-aged man who hired him and his friends to harass the residents. I did everything I could think of to get him to tell us the man's name, but in the end, I believe Brian doesn't actually know it. Meat will use his facial-recognition software to see what he can find. And he'll dig deeper than he's already done to find out who owns all the corporations that bought the surrounding buildings. Apparently, the same person is behind all of them—we assume the mystery contact who hired Brian and his friends. If Meat needs help, I'll have him call you."

"Good. And, Black?"

"Yeah?"

"You're right. I'll never forgive myself if something happens to those women and kids. Thank you for doing what needed to be done."

"Yeah."

"One more thing," Rex said.

Black held back the sigh of frustration. Barely. "What?"

"I may not have been dialed in, but I wasn't so disconnected that I haven't taken it upon myself to look into Harlow Reese."

Black ground his teeth together so hard, he immediately began to get a headache. "I didn't ask you to do that. And I don't appreciate it."

"Be that as it may, I did it anyway. Just like I did with Allye, Chloe, and Morgan. No one fucks with my men, and I know you all don't see it this way, but I'm protecting you as much as I am the women and children we hunt down."

Black didn't respond.

"For the record, I like her. She's as clean as a whistle. There are absolutely no ghosts lurking in her past. She hasn't dated anyone long enough for them to be a problem. She isn't buried in debt. She goes home to Topeka for Christmas every year, and she's one hell of a chef, if the reviews from the restaurants she worked at are any indication. If you let her get away, I'm going to seriously wonder about your sanity."

"Fuck you," Black said without heat. He was pissed that Rex had checked out Harlow, but at the same time, he was relieved to hear she hadn't had some awful childhood or wouldn't have any of the crazies she'd dated looking for her. He already knew she was an amazing chef, and he didn't give a shit about how much money she had. But . . . he knew Rex had done what was necessary to prove he had his Mercenaries' backs.

"I'll see what I can find out about this mystery contact."

"'Preciate it," Black said.

"Later."

Black clicked off the phone without saying goodbye to his handler. He didn't know what was up with Rex, but at least he seemed to be re-engaged now.

He still felt keyed up from his session with Brian and needed to see Harlow more than ever, especially after the intense conversation with Rex.

Quickly getting dressed, he took the time to give Gray a call to update him on the situation with Rex. He then called Meat to give him a heads-up that he was on his way to the shelter. It was five thirty, and Harlow should be getting dinner ready for the residents.

He answered on the first ring. "Meat."

"Hey. It's Black. Just letting you know I'm on my way."

"Great. After talking with Gray, I met with Loretta and got copies of all the offers she's received on the building. She apologized for not telling us about the offers sooner, but since she wasn't thinking of selling, she didn't think it was relevant."

"She's considering selling now?" Black asked.

"Shit, I forgot . . . you don't know. Apparently she was accused of stealing money from the shelter. Someone anonymously reported her. All her funds have been frozen while the state looks into the allegations. She doesn't have the funds to run First Hope anymore. The place was mostly surviving on grants, and now that the money from the government has stopped, she doesn't have enough capital to tide her over during a lengthy investigation."

"Fuck! That must be what Brian was talking about. He said his contact was going to do something to make Loretta want to sell." Black was surprised at how fast everything was happening. Harlow had to be devastated.

"Yup," Meat said. "Obviously, she knows she should've told us she'd been receiving offers before now. I could've already researched the potential buyers and possibly nipped all of this in the bud. Anyway, none of the offers really stand out at first glance. They're all in the same ballpark and from known developers in the area. At this point, none seem to be from anyone who owns the buildings around her—which is weird when you consider someone wants to build apartments. But I'm looking deeper into that too. Because I have a feeling whoever's been behind everything is right here in the palm of my hand. I just have to find him."

"Good."

"Oh—and she's not here."

"What? Who?"

"Harlow. She's not here," Meat said. "She met with Loretta for a while after lunch, then came downstairs looking as if the world was ending. I'm assuming she found out that Loretta is going to close the shelter."

"Where is she?" Black barked, feeling sick. He couldn't believe she'd left without texting him. He knew Bear wouldn't be an issue, since he currently wasn't in any shape to do much of *anything*, but he could've gotten ahold of his buddies.

"After she prepped dinner, she went home," Meat said. "And yes, I escorted her to her car. There was no sign of those punks, not that I'm surprised. They're probably too scared out of their skulls to even look at the shelter again."

"Did you even *try* to get her to stay?" Black asked.

"No. Why would I? Is there something I need to know?"

Rather than getting into it with Meat—because the longer he stayed on the phone asking questions, the longer it would take to get to Harlow—he asked, "When did she leave?"

"About twenty minutes ago. She said she had a headache, and Loretta told her to go home, that she'd see her tomorrow."

"I thought she had tomorrow off. Zoe is supposed to be back."

"I don't know, man. I'm just telling you what was said," Meat informed him. "Loretta didn't tell me anything about Zoe or Harlow, and I've had my head stuck in my laptop since I found out about her financial situation."

"Damn. I'm going over there," he said, worry swimming in his gut. "I need to talk to you again, though."

"Go to Harlow," Meat ordered.

He was already headed toward the kitchen for his keys. "I am. But you should know that I talked to Rex today too. He should be pulling his head out of his ass. He's back on board."

"Fucking fantastic," Meat replied. "It's about time. I've been buried, doing all the research shit for both of us."

"Exactly. He's supposed to be seeing if he can't track down the identity of the mysterious contact. I'm not convinced he'll find anything, but I'm guessing you'll hear from him, so you can catch him up."

"Will do," Meat said. "We'll touch base tomorrow. Watch your six."

Black stopped in his tracks. If Meat was warning him to watch his ass, something was up. "Why? What aren't you telling me?"

"It's just a feeling. The air feels heavy with anticipation. Something's coming. And it ain't good."

Black nodded. He felt it too. He'd thought it was just because of what he'd done earlier that day. A part of coming down from the adrenaline rush that came with an interrogation. "You too," Black told his friend.

"Of course. Ball's coming over to relieve me later and will be staying the night."

"Good. I'll be in touch."

"Ditto."

Black clicked off the phone, grabbed his keys, and stuffed his wallet in his jeans pocket. Something was up with Harlow; she never left work early. He didn't like being in the dark.

He also wished she hadn't left the shelter without texting. He couldn't get the idea out of his mind that Bear might've instructed his buddies to get some payback. He needed to see for himself that she was all right. If anything happened to her, he'd never forgive himself.

Yes, he needed her positivity and happiness to chase away the shadows within him, but he had a greater need to make sure she was safe.

He dialed her number while heading to his car, waiting impatiently for her to answer, but it just rang and rang, then went to voice mail.

Even more worried now, Black jumped into his car. He was almost frantic to get to her place and see for himself that she was safe.

Not questioning his feelings anymore, and suspecting more and more that Gray was right, that Harlow was the woman he wanted to spend the rest of his life with, Black drove as fast as he dared to her apartment. It was time she knew exactly how he felt about her.

Chapter Twenty

Harlow had just sat down on her couch with a cup of tea when someone knocked on her door. She was tempted to ignore whoever it was, but the politeness her mom had taught her was too ingrained.

Sighing, she put her tea on the table next to the couch and stood.

Her visitor knocked again, and this time she heard, "Harlow? Are you in there? Open the door."

Lowell.

Hurrying now, she headed for the door. "Coming!" she called out. She was thrilled he was there. Lowell was just what she needed right now. She'd been depressed all afternoon and worried about not only Loretta, but all "her" kids and the women who lived in the shelter. She had no idea where they'd go or what they'd do. She had no doubt Loretta would do what she could to make sure they were in a safe place, but she hated the thought of not seeing them every day.

Unlocking the dead bolt and the knob, Harlow quickly swung the door open.

"Hi!" she said brightly.

Without a word, Lowell pushed past her, leaving her staring at his back as he stalked into her apartment.

Closing the door slowly, Harlow relocked it and followed Lowell. When she caught up with him, he was standing in her kitchen, his palms resting on the countertop, his head lowered.

She could see his knuckles were bruised, but otherwise he looked okay. "Lowell?" she asked. "Are you all right?"

He looked up then. His dark eyes pinning her in place. "Why did you leave the shelter early?" he asked. No, he didn't ask—he demanded.

Feeling her hackles rise, Harlow crossed her arms over her chest. She'd had a terrible day, and him bursting into her apartment and being rude wasn't exactly how she wanted it to continue.

"Am I not allowed to do anything without your permission?" she asked.

Instead of making him realize that he was being somewhat of an ass, her words seemed to rile him up even more. "No. Not when Brian Pierce and his cronies are out there determined to harass you simply because you work at the shelter."

"Who?" Harlow asked, confused.

But he either didn't hear her question or decided to ignore it, because he went on. "From now on, until I tell you differently, you will text me anytime you go anywhere. I want to know where you are at all times."

"I don't think so," Harlow enunciated carefully.

"That's how it's going to be, Harlow, and you just need to deal with it."

She shook her head. "Get out."

"No," Lowell said, standing up straight and mimicking her stance, crossing his arms over his chest.

"I mean it, Lowell. You can't come in here being all weird and then act like you own me. No one owns me. I'm thirty-four years old, and I've lived on my own for a really long time. I'm not a child, and you can't tell me what to do."

He dropped his hands and took a step toward her.

Instinctively, Harlow backed away, immediately tripping over her own feet in the process. She yelped and fell, landing on her ass and the hand she'd put back to break her fall.

One second she was on the floor, cradling her sore wrist, and the next she was in Lowell's arms, and he was carrying her to the couch.

"Put me down!" she demanded. On one hand, she loved having Lowell's arms around her. It wasn't often that she'd been carried in her life. But on the other hand, she was mad at him. She had no idea what happened to the man she was falling for, but the angry, demanding asshole standing in her kitchen had knocked her for a loop. The last thing she wanted was a man telling her what she could and couldn't do. Especially when she'd had a horrible day.

Instead of putting her down, he sat on the couch with her on his lap. The second he sat, she struggled to get up, but he wrapped an arm around her waist and held her still even as he reached for her wrist with his free hand. "How bad is it?" he asked.

"It's fine."

"Let me see," he demanded.

Sighing, knowing he wasn't going to let her go until she let him examine her wrist, she held it out. He gently manipulated the joint, watching her face as he did, trying to make sure she wasn't in pain as he moved her wrist back and forth.

"I'm clumsy," she said after a while. "It's fine."

"You didn't fall because you're clumsy," Lowell said softly. "You fell because I scared you, and you were trying to get away from me. I'm sorry, Harlow."

She didn't respond, because he was right. She *had* been frightened of him. Between the look on his face and the hard tone of his voice, she'd immediately second-guessed everything she knew about him, and that sucked.

"I would never hurt you," he said. "Ever. I came over tonight because I needed to see you. And I scared you. I'm sorry, baby. So fucking sorry." His voice cracked on the last word, and that was all it took for Harlow to forgive him.

He hadn't touched her. Hadn't lifted his hands to her. He hadn't even raised his voice. Yes, he'd been overbearing and bossy, but in hindsight, she wasn't actually surprised by that. He'd been that way ever since she'd called him to ask for help. But something was different tonight. That was obviously what she'd been reacting to.

"What happened?" she asked, wrapping an arm around his shoulders and leaning into him. He kept her sore wrist in his hand, his thumb absently caressing her.

"I was a SEAL," he said.

Harlow's brow furrowed. "Yeah."

"I've done a lot of things I'm not proud of. But I'd do them again and again to keep my buddies safe. My friends. My country."

"I know," Harlow soothed, not sure where he was going with this.

"One of the things I excel at is interrogations. I seem to have a knack for making people tell me things they wouldn't normally tell another living soul."

The words seemed to hang in the air around them—and suddenly his bruised knuckles made sense. She had no idea who he'd been interrogating today, but it was affecting him.

Harlow thought maybe she should be appalled. Should be disgusted that he'd resort to violence in order to get information. But she wasn't.

"That's why you want me to tell you where I am at all times, isn't it? Because you found something out today?"

He nodded.

"Okay."

"Okay?"

"Yeah. I have no idea what happened or who you talked to, but it's obvious that you heard something you didn't like. I don't want to get hurt, so I'll try to remember to text you to let you know my plans."

"Thank you, baby," he murmured, kissing her gently on the forehead.

"But . . . I'm not sure how much longer I'll be here."

Lowell pulled back and narrowed his eyes at her. "Explain."

"Well . . . like you, I didn't have the best day. Loretta's closing the shelter. She's having money issues. I'm going to have to find a new job. I've found I really like working in a group-home situation, but if I can't find anything else like that here, I might go home to Topeka. I can be closer to my parents and hopefully find a job there."

"No. You can't leave."

Harlow stared at Lowell and struggled to keep her temper in check. "It's not your decision, Lowell," she said with only a hint of her aggravation showing.

He obviously heard it, because he shook his head. "I know. I didn't mean that the way it came out. I mean . . . I don't *want* you to go. I feel as if we haven't even begun to scratch the surface of what we could have together."

"But wouldn't it be better to end it now before we get in too deep? It'll hurt less."

"I have a feeling it isn't going to matter if you break up with me now, or a month from now, or a year," Lowell said honestly.

Harlow's heart skipped a beat. "What are you saying?" she asked.

Lowell shifted her on his lap until she was straddling him. He took her face in his hands and looked into her eyes as he said, "After I did what I did today, my one thought was to get to you. That only *you* could take away the blackness I felt in my soul. A part of me enjoyed terrorizing Brian today, Harlow. I *liked* seeing him flinch from me. I was sorry he cracked so easily. I wanted to spend more time hurting him, scaring him—just as he'd done to you. When everything was over and done, and the shame creeped in about the way I'd enjoyed interrogating him, the only thing I could think about was getting to you. I knew that seeing your smile, seeing you go about your business in the kitchen, would ground me," he explained. "I need your goodness to balance out the badness inside me. It's there. But I'll never hurt you, Harl. Ever. Your good cancels out my bad."

"You aren't bad," she protested, grabbing hold of his wrists and holding on for dear life.

He pressed his lips together, then said, "I am. Sometimes. But I fucking love that you don't see it. No man does what I've done and doesn't have some of the evil in the world soak into his soul. I've never wanted a relationship because . . . I think I didn't want to taint a woman. But I don't feel that with you."

"You don't?" His words confused her.

"No. Don't you see? Somehow, you've got the ability, just by being yourself, to make that shit disappear inside me. One look at you and I feel calm. Centered. I need you, Harlow."

She swallowed hard. She could tell he meant every word. He wasn't just blowing smoke up her ass. She brought a hand up to the side of his face and palmed his cheek. When he closed his eyes and pressed his head into her hand, she was lost.

"You've got me," she told him softly.

His eyes immediately opened. "Do I?"

She nodded.

"We need to talk about Loretta and your job . . . but right now, I can't think about anything other than getting you naked and being inside you."

She squirmed on his lap, his carnal words making her instantly wet. She'd dreamed about being with Lowell for a very long time. First it was the schoolgirl dreams of a teenager, but over the last month, they had grown into the needs of a mature woman. "Yes," she said simply.

To his credit, he didn't ask if she was sure. Didn't shove his hand up her shirt. Instead, he kissed her solemnly, then helped her stand. When he was upright next to her, he took hold of her uninjured hand and twined their fingers. "Where's your room?" he asked.

Without speaking, Harlow headed for the hallway off the main living area. She passed a half bath and a guest room and went straight for the door at the end. She opened it and waited for him to comment on her bedroom.

It was quintessential her. Messy, but comfortable. A bookcase was against one wall, full of books. Romances, recipe books, magazines, and the odd picture here and there. A dresser was next to it, a couple drawers half-open. Her bed wasn't made, the dark-purple comforter hanging half-off the mattress and a slew of pillows stacked up at the head. She knew if he looked in her bathroom, he'd see her lotion bottles strewn all over the counter.

But after one cursory glance around, Lowell only had eyes for her. He turned her back to the bed and put his hands on her biceps. He backed her up, slowly, without a word. She should've felt awkward, but the intensity in his eyes calmed her.

It was obvious he wanted her. He wasn't playing a game. Wasn't being coy. His need was right there for her to see. It was heady, making her feel as if she were a beautiful siren rather than the plain woman she considered herself to be most of the time.

When the backs of her knees hit the mattress, he stopped but still didn't say anything. His hands eased down her sides and grabbed the hem of her shirt. He paused as if to ask permission, and following his lead, Harlow didn't say anything, simply raised her arms over her head and met his eyes without embarrassment.

Black wanted to rip her clothes off and shove himself inside her body so deep, she'd never be able to forget him. But he forced himself to go slow. To show her how much she meant to him.

Gray had been right again; Harlow was different from any other woman he'd ever met. He couldn't stand the thought of her being in danger. If she was taken from him, as Allye had been taken from Gray, he literally wouldn't be able to handle it.

He'd marched into her apartment tonight a total asshole. He could've been gentler. Told her that she was in danger and he worried about her safety. Instead, he'd demanded she tell him where she was at all hours of the day, like a total creeper. Then he'd scared her so badly she'd backed away from him . . . and hurt herself in the process. That had snapped him out of the haze he'd been in faster than anything else could've.

The fact that she was in her bedroom with him right now was a total miracle. One he wouldn't ever take for granted.

He slowly peeled her shirt up and over her head, keeping eye contact with her. It wasn't until he dropped the material behind him that he also dropped his gaze. Her tits were perfect. Plump and full, almost spilling over the pink lace encasing them.

Black could feel the darkness pushing him. Telling him to grab hold of the delicious mounds and squeeze until she cried out. But he forced himself to wait. To simply take her in with his eyes.

As if she could see the barely leashed need inside him, she smiled and reached down for his hands. She placed them on her chest and held them there. "Touch me, Lowell," she said softly. "I want this. I need you."

Taking a deep breath, Black kept hold of his control with an iron fist. He gently kneaded her tits, loving how her nipples hardened under the lace with his touch. Then she reached behind her and unhooked her bra. The cups immediately fell, and suddenly his hands were full of nothing but warm, willing flesh.

He groaned.

The monster inside him was done waiting. Didn't want to be noble any longer.

With the last bit of sanity he had, Black took a step away from Harlow and whipped his shirt over his head. "Take it all off," he bit out, even as his hands went to the fastening of his own jeans.

He was more than relieved when she did as he asked, reaching for the button of her pants. Within seconds, Black was naked. He grabbed his wallet and pulled out a condom. Without a word, he tore it open and rolled it down his rock-hard cock. He couldn't ever remember being this needy. This desperate for a woman.

Harlow stood before him completely naked, and he immediately fell to his knees in front of her. Looking up her curvy body, he couldn't say a word. He'd never felt this off-kilter. Even in the middle of battle, he'd always kept his head. But he'd never seen anything as beautiful as Harlow without a stitch of clothing on.

His hands slowly reached for her and grabbed hold of her hips. He pulled her to him and reveled in the small moan that escaped her mouth as she stepped closer. He held her safe, shivering when her hands landed on his shoulders. It was his turn to break out in goose bumps.

He could smell her arousal. Her blonde pubic hair was trimmed neatly around her pussy, and he couldn't stop himself from leaning forward and nuzzling her there. Black heard another gasp leave her mouth, but it was the hand that moved from his shoulder to his head that told him what she wanted.

"Yes. God, please, Lowell."

His real name on her lips was the tipping point. He'd always been Black. Since boot camp, everyone had called him that. Everyone except Harlow. To her, he was Lowell. Not a soldier. Not a man who had saved her from some horrible fate. Just Lowell.

His hands moved to her inner thighs, not so gently pushing them apart. She giggled and acquiesced to his unspoken command. Her scent intensified. Black leaned forward and, without any preliminaries, ran his tongue between her folds.

She shuddered, and he felt the muscles in her thighs tense. At the first taste of her musk, he was gone.

Black ate her out in earnest, almost desperately, closing his eyes to fully experience the ecstasy that was the woman in his arms. He barely heard her moans, barely felt the way her fingernails dug into his shoulder and her hand pressed against the back of his head, urging him on. All of his focus was on licking the juices that dripped from between her legs.

When he turned his attention from her slit to the sensitive little bundle of nerves, she jerked against him, almost making him lose his grip on her. Not wanting to take the time to ease her to the bed, needing her to give herself to him completely, Black lifted one of her thighs and rested it on his shoulder. She gasped in surprise.

"I won't let you fall," he murmured before moving a hand to her ass to hold her steady. He eased a finger on his other hand inside her, marveling at how tight she was, even as he locked his mouth over her clit.

"Oh, fuck . . . Lowell," she cried as he sucked on her.

He felt her inner muscles tightening around his finger, and he almost came right then and there, thinking about how she'd feel around his dick. He slowly pumped in and out of her as she quivered in his grasp.

She began to thrust against him, and it took everything he had to keep his mouth around her as she gyrated at his ministrations.

Black doubled his efforts to make her come. He wanted to see her face when she went over the edge, though. He lifted his head and raised his eyes to her face. She was staring down at him, and the second their eyes met, he swore something clicked between them. It was a fanciful thought, but he didn't even care.

He pulled his finger out of her body and used it to manipulate her clit. He quickly learned that direct stimulation on her bundle of nerves was more effective than rubbing around it. He pressed hard on her clit as he moved the hand on her ass lower. He fingered her slit with his pinkie, and was rewarded by her thrusting harder, pressing against the finger on her clit.

"Right there! Oh God, yes. Lowell, I'm going to . . . Shit, I'm coming!"

Black was practically holding her up as she hovered over him, but he'd never seen anything more erotic and beautiful in his life. He kept up the pressure on her clit as she flew over the edge. Her nipples were hard buds on her chest, and her face was flushed. She gripped his head and shoulder as if they were the only things keeping her from flying into a million pieces.

She was still shaking when he lowered her leg, stood, and lifted her onto the bed. He didn't wait until she was settled, but climbed up with her and shoved her thighs apart with his knees. He used the head of his cock to caress her still-sensitive clit and waited for her to look at him.

When her ocean-blue eyes met his, he notched his cock to her opening. Her legs opened farther in welcome. "Fuck me, Lowell," she said. "I need you inside me."

That was all the permission he needed. Black sank inside her in one thrust. He didn't stop until he felt his balls press up against her ass. He groaned low in his throat and buried his face in her neck, trying to gain control over his overwhelmed senses.

He felt her squeeze him from inside, and he pressed his lips together. She smelled like vanilla and lust, a scent that he'd forever associate with this first time they made love. He could feel her slick skin against his own, and the sounds she was making in the back of her throat excited him all the more.

Licking his lips, Black could still taste her on them.

She pressed her hips up as much as possible with him pinning her down. "Move," she ordered.

"I'm holding on by a thread here, baby," he muttered into her neck. "Give me a second."

"No," she said. "Use me to get the darkness out. Give it to me."

Black stilled. She didn't know what she was asking.

"Cleanse your soul," she whispered, caressing his face. "Take me hard and get it out."

He couldn't have held back if his life depended on it. He lifted up on his hands and knees over her and said in a low rasp, "Tell me if I hurt you."

"You could never hurt me."

"I mean it, Harl. If I'm too rough, stop me. I'll never forgive myself if I hurt you."

"Shut up and fuck me, Lowell."

And he did.

He'd warned her.

Told her that he had blackness in his soul.

But she hadn't listened, or hadn't believed him.

And it was too late now.

Rearing back, Black pulled all the way out so the only thing inside her was the very tip of his cock.

Then he rammed back inside her. He did it again. And again. He could barely handle the pleasure coursing through his body. She felt so good around him, clutching his dick as he pulled back, as if she didn't ever want him to leave.

When it wasn't enough, when he wasn't deep enough, Black put a hand under her knee and shoved her leg up until her ankle rested on his shoulder. *There.* When he pressed inside her this time, he could feel himself go even deeper.

She groaned under him, pressed up when he thrust forward.

Shoving his hand under her ass, Black held her still as he hammered into her body. When he felt his balls tightening, readying themselves to shoot their load, he moved his hand from her ass to where they were joined. Scooping up some of her copious juices that had been dripping down his shaft to coat his balls, he began stroking her clit. *Hard.*

She shrieked and jerked under his touch, but he didn't stop. Didn't let go of her. Her head flew back, and her torso arched as she came.

Black held on as long as he could, loving the feel of her spasming around his hard-as-nails cock, but it was inevitable that her orgasm would trigger his own. He braced himself over her with both hands, shoved inside her body as far as he could go, and bellowed as he came.

It felt like he would never stop, but eventually he felt himself soften inside her. Not wanting to pull out yet, not even caring that the condom could break, he lifted her leg from his shoulder and collapsed on top of her. He felt her hands grip his back, and they lay like that for several moments. Both lost in sensation.

Finally, Black took a deep breath and felt himself slip from inside her body. It wasn't a surprise since she was extremely wet.

He couldn't wait until he could come inside her and feel their combined juices as he recovered.

The thought should've freaked him out. He'd never come inside a woman without a condom. Ever. But the thought of seeing his come mixed with Harlow's, leaking out of her, was exciting enough to make his cock begin to harden once more.

Moving off Harlow quickly, Black exited the bed and went into the bathroom to take care of the condom. He was back within seconds, relieved to see that Harlow hadn't moved. She lay where he'd left her, sideways on the bed, on top of the covers, completely naked. Her legs were semi-splayed, and her eyes were shut.

If he could've taken a picture of her at that moment and not been a complete perv, he would've. But he didn't need to. He'd never forget how she looked right then. Satisfied, happy, relaxed.

"Come on, baby," he said as he joined her. "Move up here."

She grunted, but allowed him to move her so her head was facing the right way. He straightened the sheet and comforter and climbed under both with her. He pulled her into his arms, and she snuggled right in. Her head rested on his chest, over his heart, and her hand landed on his belly. One of her legs hitched up and over his. He felt surrounded by her, and nothing had ever been better.

"Are the demons gone?" she asked after a moment as they lay in each other's arms.

"Yeah, baby. They're gone."

"Good," she muttered.

He knew they needed to talk about the shelter and Loretta's plans. But Black didn't want to break the intimate moment. He was being selfish for once in his life. He liked having Harlow in his arms like this. Liked knowing he'd satisfied her so thoroughly that she was almost boneless on top of him.

He'd fucked up tonight. *Again.* He'd almost pushed her away with his demanding words. But the thought of something happening to her, of how Brian had been harassing her, of what *he'd* done to Brian, had hit him hard.

Lesson learned. Harlow was a grown woman. A grown, competent woman. She wasn't a teenager or a kid who needed to be told how to live her life. He'd have to be careful in the future to remember that. He'd just wanted to keep her safe.

Chuckling silently to himself, he finally understood what Gray had been telling him all along. That when he found the woman meant to be his, he'd know. He wanted to spend every night just like this. Holding Harlow against him, feeling her breath against his chest. He couldn't imagine being with anyone else. Ever. He was protective as hell of Harlow and would do whatever it took to keep her safe, happy, and healthy.

Nothing else mattered. Not his business, not the Mountain Mercenaries.

Thankful he'd gotten to Brian before the man or his friends could do anything more than verbally harass Harlow, Black relaxed. For now, he was going to enjoy every second of holding his naked, satisfied woman in his arms.

~

On the other side of the city, Nolan Woolf sat in his office and glared at the email he'd just received from one of his real-estate friends.

Loretta Royster was negotiating with someone else for *his* building.

No. Fucking no! That was unacceptable. He'd meant to push her into accepting *his* offer, not someone else's. He knew for a fact that what the other prick offered was below what he'd presented to the old bitch. How *dare* she go behind his back and try to negotiate with someone else!

If he didn't get that building, all his plans would go down the drain. All the money he'd spent forming corporations to hide behind would be for naught.

He *needed* that building.

And he'd have it. One way or another.

Nolan Woolf always won in the end. Always.

Chapter Twenty-One

Harlow had lain awake next to Lowell for at least an hour. She'd awoken early and been unable to get back to sleep. She was tired, but when she realized she was still cuddled up against Lowell, any hope of her falling asleep again disappeared in a puff of smoke.

He was breathing deeply, his mouth slightly open. The scruff on his face only made him look more intense.

Once that word entered her brain, she couldn't stop thinking about it. *Intense.* It fit him. He'd taken her hard the night before, but she'd loved every second of it. Had begged him for it, in fact.

He'd been afraid of hurting her, but Harlow had known she could take him. He'd needed it. Needed *her*. She'd never been needed like that before in her life, and it was a heady feeling. She'd seen the darkness he referred to lurking in his eyes, but the second he'd put his mouth on her—she blushed just thinking about it—the darkness had receded.

When he'd taken her, all she'd seen in his face was desire and . . . dare she say it?

Love.

It was too soon for that, of course, but she knew what she'd seen.

She'd been adamant about not dating, but somehow Lowell had slipped under her shields and burrowed his way in. He'd said if she left him, he'd never recover. The crazy thing was, she already felt exactly the same way about him.

She didn't want to leave Colorado Springs. She told herself she loved the area, wanted to explore the hiking trails more, loved how nice and open most of the people she'd met were. But the truth was, *Lowell* was the real reason she wanted to stay.

Sighing, Harlow knew she should get up. She had a million things to do—looking for another job was at the forefront—but she couldn't make herself move.

Eventually, Lowell stirred. She watched as he went from being asleep to being completely awake and aware of his surroundings in a heartbeat. She supposed it came from being a SEAL and from working with the Mountain Mercenaries.

"Hey," she said, feeling shy for some reason.

"Hey," he returned. "Everything okay?"

She smiled and nodded. "Yeah, everything's good."

"I didn't . . ." He stumbled over his words, and it made her fall for him all the more. "I didn't hurt you last night, did I?"

Harlow lifted a hand and placed it against his cheek, giving in to her need to touch his scruff. "No, Lowell. You didn't hurt me."

"Good. I probably should've run you a hot bath last night, but you knocked me for too much of a loop, and I couldn't think straight."

She smiled. "Ditto. Hungry?"

Right after she asked, she heard his stomach growl.

He chuckled. "Guess so."

"I'll get up and make you something before you have to go."

He stopped her from leaving the bed with a hand on her arm. "We need to talk."

Oh shit. Harlow hated when men said that. It never ended well for her. "Okay."

He must've seen something on her face, because his tone gentled, and he said, "About the shelter and your job, Harl."

"Oh. Yeah."

"As far as I'm concerned, you're officially my girlfriend, and I'm officially your boyfriend," he went on. "We can work on the details of what that means, but in a nutshell, I want to spend as much time with you as I can. Here at your place, and with you at mine. I'll let you know as much as I can what my plans are during the day, and I hope you'll do the same. I'm not saying that to be an asshole, but because I'm worried about you and your safety. I'm not an easy man to be with," he warned. "I'm going to be too protective. I'm going to piss you off, but it's because of the things I've seen and done. I have a feeling I'll worry about you every second that we aren't together. I'll try to curb it, but again, know that it's not me being controlling, it's because I want you to be safe. I don't know what I'd do if something happened to you."

"Nothing's going to happen to me," Harlow soothed. "I've got a badass former-SEAL boyfriend who has some equally badass friends."

"That doesn't mean nothing can happen to you," he warned. "Look at what happened to Allye and the others. Anything can happen. Come to think of it, I never did get around to giving you that gun-safety class you originally asked me about. We'll do that soon."

"Lowell—" Harlow protested, but he went on as if she hadn't spoken.

"And then I'll get you into a self-defense class too. The things I've shown the residents at the shelter are good, but nothing is as effective as actually using the pads and practicing the kicks and moves on an actual human."

"Lowell!" she tried again.

"What?" he asked.

"How about I get up and get breakfast started before you start planning the week and turning me into a ninja?"

"We should shower together," he said, raising his eyebrows suggestively.

Blushing, Harlow shook her head.

"Are you seriously blushing after last night?" he asked.

"Yes," she said, answering him even though she figured it was a rhetorical question. "It's different in the light of day."

"It's not, but I'll give you some time to get used to me. To this," Lowell said, gesturing to where they were still snuggled up together under the sheet. "But you should know, I've never seen anything as beautiful in my life as you last night, when you came apart in my arms . . . twice. Thank you for that gift, baby. I'll treasure it for the rest of my life."

Harlow knew she was blushing even harder, but she managed a small smile. "Thank you for showing me the real you. I'm not scared of you, Lowell. I know you've been through some shit in your life, but don't hide that from me. I don't like that you have to do things that put you in that headspace, but I'd be a hypocrite if I told you to stop. The world needs more men like you. But if I can help you deal with how you feel when stuff gets too intense, great. If you need space or time with your buddies to talk about it, fine—but please don't shut me out."

"I won't. Promise."

"Good. Now, let me go so I can get dressed and make us something to eat before we get on with our day."

He leaned down to kiss her, and Harlow turned her head to the side. "No! Morning breath, Lowell!"

He chuckled and kissed her on the cheek instead. His hand came up and caressed her naked breast, rolling her nipple between his fingers.

Moaning, Harlow said, "That isn't fair."

Shrugging, Lowell didn't say a word, but instead threw back the covers and slid down. He took her nipple into his mouth and sucked. After a while, he switched sides and gave her other nipple the same attention. Eventually, he lifted his mouth and smirked at her. "I don't mind not being able to kiss your lips in the morning, Harl. I can find other things to kiss." And with that, he eased down her body, and she eagerly spread her legs for him as he settled between her thighs.

She didn't have a verbal response, too breathless as he started to lick her pussy once more.

It was almost thirty minutes later when he finally let her out of bed. Harlow was shaking on her feet, but smiling from ear to ear. They hadn't kissed on the mouth—morning breath, of course—but he'd made her come twice with his lips and tongue before taking her from behind. She'd take that over a good-morning kiss any day.

After breakfast, she told Lowell everything Loretta had said about the shelter the day before. About her credit card being mysteriously canceled and the accusations against her. She explained how Loretta felt relieved at the idea of retiring, yet guilty about it at the same time. She told him about Zoe not coming back, her reduced hours, and that Loretta was going to be accepting one of the offers she'd had on the building.

"Loretta said she was pretty sure she could find placements for everyone in the shelter, though, so that's good. I'll only be working dinners Monday through Friday, and not on the weekends."

"I'll see what I can do to help you find another job," Lowell said.

Harlow wanted to turn down his offer, but knew she'd be an idiot if she did. "I'd appreciate that. Loretta said she'd help too. I could probably get a job at one of the high-end restaurants downtown, but I love working with the women and kids. I feel needed. I like the connections I've made with them. Does that make sense?"

"Sure it does," he reassured her. "I know there are a few other shelters in the area. I'll put out some feelers. There's a homeless shelter downtown as well, but I don't see you enjoying that as much."

Harlow shook her head. "No, and it's not because I don't feel for the people who go there, but it's not as personal as sitting down at a dinner table night after night with a group of people who are trying to get back on their feet. Does that make me an asshole?"

"Of course not," Lowell said. "There aren't as many options available for what you want to do, like there are if you went back to being a hotel chef, but we'll figure something out. Maybe we can find a group home for mentally disabled adults or assisted living–type places that need a chef."

It felt good to hear him talk about her as part of a "we" instead of a "you."

"Thanks, Lowell."

"Anytime," he said. "Now, I hate to do it, but I need to get going. I need to meet with the others and find out what information everyone found out overnight. You'll be okay here until it's time to go to work?"

"Of course," she said, waving him off. "I'm a big girl. I think I can handle not being around you for a few hours."

He growled and brought his hands to her sides to tickle her. "You can, huh?"

Shrieking, Harlow tried to wiggle out of his grasp, but he was too strong. "Stop! Okay, okay, I'm going to pine away when you leave my side, and I won't be complete until we're back together," she said sarcastically.

His fingers stopped digging into her sides, and he held her to him instead. "Good. That's what I want to hear."

Harlow could feel his hard cock against her, and she wiggled, wanting to give him a little payback. "Is that a wrench in your pocket, or are you just happy to see me?" she quipped.

"Minx," he mock complained. "Come here." Then he kissed her.

A long, slow kiss that made her miss him before he'd even stepped one foot out the door.

"Text me when you're ready to go to the shelter."

"It'll probably be around three or so. I think Loretta has some money person coming by to talk with the women this afternoon before dinner. Last week, it was an attorney who discussed why having a will was important, and this week it's an investor or something."

"You think she'll continue those educational classes, now that she'll be selling?" Lowell asked.

Harlow nodded. "I don't know why she wouldn't. She didn't say anything about it one way or the other, though. I forgot to ask. Anyway, I'll have the kids help me make their lunches for tomorrow or something while their moms are listening to the speaker." The thought that she wouldn't be around to make their lunches much longer made her sad all over again.

Putting his finger under her chin, Lowell said, "You're amazing, Harl. And I'm a lucky bastard to be the one sharing your life and your bed."

Harlow shook her head. "You're such a guy."

"What?" he asked, pretending to be confused. "What'd I say?"

"Right. Anyway, so my plans are to do a preliminary search online and see what jobs are available around here this morning, plan the meals at the shelter for the next week, and make up a shopping list. I'll leave here around two thirty. I need to go to the store in the next day or so, but I'll have to talk to Loretta first and see if she's got cash for me to use or what."

"I'll be ready and will meet you there," Lowell said. "Be safe."

Harlow rolled her eyes. "Of course. Nothing's going to happen in the next"—she glanced down at her watch—"five hours until I see you again."

Lowell grimaced. "One thing you learn in my line of business is never to tempt fate by saying something like that. I'll talk to you soon."

"Bye."

He kissed her one more time before heading for her door. He was wearing the same clothes he'd had on the night before, but she knew he'd make a stop at his apartment before meeting with the rest of his friends at The Pit.

After learning about what he'd done to Brian the day before, she felt safer than she had in a long time. She doubted he or his friends would be harassing her anymore. But if Lowell wanted to escort her from the parking lot to the door, she wasn't going to stop him. She wanted to soak up every second of time with him that she could.

"Who the fuck canceled her credit cards?" Ball asked.

The entire team was gathered at their usual table at The Pit, although they were drinking coffee instead of beers.

"It had to be this mysterious contact," Black said. "Harlow told me that when Loretta called the bank to inquire what was going on, they told her someone had called and used their automated system to dispute a charge on the card."

"Right," Ball said. "Many banks automatically shut down the card and issue a new one."

"The card wasn't connected to the anonymous report to the state about the funds the nonprofit has been receiving?" Ro asked.

"I wouldn't say that," Meat replied. "I've been up most of the night, and from what I've been able to find out, I'd say the same person did both."

"Explain," Arrow ordered.

"Right. So now we know Loretta has received several offers for the building. She didn't tell us because she didn't feel they were relevant, since she wasn't selling. The building wasn't even on the market."

"Then how could people send her offers?" Black interrupted.

"Just because a house isn't on the market doesn't mean someone can't offer to buy it," Meat said patiently. "Someone could walk up to Gray's house, knock on the door, and tell him they'll give him a million dollars for the place."

"True," Black said. "Go on."

"Since we didn't know about the offers, we didn't make the connection between the harassment and the building. But then we found out from watching that video of Brian threatening Harlow that someone planned to build low-income housing in the area. When I checked the records, all of the buildings seemed to have been bought by different people and companies. It wasn't until after hearing about Loretta's money issues that I really started digging. I would've done it earlier, but with Rex being no help, I was swamped trying to finish looking at all the exes and everything else."

"No one's blaming you," Arrow said quietly.

"I know. Anyway, so I used some of my more creative techniques to find out who owned the various businesses—and every company was handled by the *same* lawyer. When I dug into *his* financial records, I found several deposits over the last couple months from the same person." Meat paused dramatically.

"Who?" Black growled impatiently.

"A Nolan Woolf."

"Who?" Gray asked.

"Do we know him?" Arrow questioned.

"Nolan Woolf is a developer who's known for building crappy properties and not giving one little shit when things go wrong with them."

"So he owns all of the other buildings on the block?" Ball asked.

"Yup. Including the gas station that went up in flames," Meat told them.

"Why would he burn down his own building?" Gray asked. "For the insurance?"

"As of today, he hasn't claimed the insurance money yet," Meat said.

"Which is suspicious in and of itself," Arrow commented.

"Yup. But I'm thinking the fire was all a part of the intimidation factor," Meat said. "Hear me out. He hired Brian and his friends to start harassing the residents, to try to get them so scared they wanted to move out. They were instructed not to hurt the women or touch them, simply to harass them. The harassment morphed into threats, probably more because Brian is an asshole than because Nolan told him to do anything. He put in another offer for the building right after he torched the gas station, probably thinking Loretta would be ready to accept it. But either he didn't realize she was getting other offers, or Loretta was more stubborn than he realized. Anyway, so he somehow got ahold of her credit-card statement and canceled the card. Again, simple harassment."

"Then he got the idea to cut off her money flow," Black interrupted, taking up the scenario. "He called in the anonymous report, and when the government froze all her funds, he figured she'd have to accept his offer."

"Exactly," Meat said, leaning back in his seat with a huge smile on his face.

"What a clusterfuck this investigation has been," Gray said with a sigh. "We've been on a wild-goose chase tracking down all the exes."

"We need to call Rex," Black said. "He was supposed to be figuring out who Brian's contact was. We need to give him Woolf's name if he doesn't have it already."

The others groaned.

"He's checked out," Ball said.

"Call him," Black repeated. "I talked to him yesterday. We had it out. He's back in."

"You had it out?" Gray asked.

They all knew "having it out" with their handler wasn't exactly smart.

Black nodded. "I was sick of him slacking off. He said he'd been working on something, but it didn't pan out."

"About his wife?" Arrow asked.

Everyone looked at him.

"I told you he started Mountain Mercenaries because his wife disappeared," Arrow said quietly. "One day she was there, and the next she was gone without a trace. The cops had no leads, and even with a huge reward, they didn't get any tips that panned out. He hired a private detective, who found what he thought was her trail but lost it when the perps left the United States. Her body was never found, and Rex is convinced she's still out there somewhere. I'm sure he's never stopped looking for her.

"Half of the cases we go on are for people hiring us to find their loved ones—but the other half are from Rex's research into looking for *his* own wife. He follows leads and inevitably finds other missing children and women. From what I understand, Rex and his wife were madly in love, but when the cops didn't find any trace of her, they thought *he* might've killed her at one point."

"So, Black, you think he wasn't helping on this case because he was looking for his wife?" Meat asked.

Black shook his head. "Maybe. He didn't say. All he told me was that the lead he had didn't pan out."

"Well, shit. That sucks," Ro said.

"Maybe when this is over, we can get him to let us work on his wife's case," Ball said.

"The man hasn't told us anything about it," Gray replied with a shake of his head. "What makes you think he'll be okay with us sitting down and dissecting his personal life the way we do when we investigate a case?"

"Because after all these years, and with all his expertise and connections, he still hasn't found her," Arrow said succinctly. "I'm not saying we'll have any luck, but what can it hurt? The man is obviously messed up inside as a result of not having any information about his wife. If we can give him some closure, don't you think we owe it to him to try?"

"Absolutely," Gray said. "But *I'm* not going to be the one to bring it up."

Everyone chuckled and agreed.

"Fine. I'll do it," Arrow said. "He told me about her after that mission in Venezuela. Remember? I told him we'd heard about an American being with the other kidnapped women, and he asked all sorts of questions about her. I know he thought it might've been her. He hasn't given up trying to find her."

"What's her name?" Black asked.

Arrow pressed his lips together and squinted, obviously trying to remember. "Raven," he finally said.

No one said a word for a long moment. Finally, Black said, "Call Rex, Meat. We need him in the know on this one. We need to find Nolan Woolf. Pronto."

Meat nodded and reached for his phone even as Black stood.

"Where are you going?" Ball asked, gathering up his stuff.

"There are some things I need to deal with at the range before I head over to the shelter to meet Harlow. I'll talk with Loretta and see if she knows this Nolan guy."

"Things with you and Harlow are going well, I take it?" Gray asked with a smirk as he stood to leave.

The five of them left Meat to his research and the call with their handler as they headed out of the bar.

"Yeah, you could say that," Black told his friend.

Gray pounded him on the back. "Good to hear it."

"Still doesn't mean I'm getting married," Black mumbled, not wanting Gray to get too big of a head, even though he couldn't deny he wouldn't mind tying Harlow to him all legal like.

"Didn't say you were," Gray said with a smile.

"Speaking of which, you asked Allye yet?" Ro asked.

"Ticktock," Arrow quipped. "Every day you wait is another day your little peanut grows bigger inside her. And the bigger she gets, the more likely she'll want to wait."

"Fuck off," Gray said, glaring at his friend.

Arrow held up his hands conciliatorily. "Just sayin'."

"As a matter of fact, if you have to know, I'm taking her up to Denver this weekend. I made reservations at a fancy restaurant and reserved the honeymoon suite at Hotel Teatro. It's near the Denver Center for the Performing Arts, where we're seeing a show."

"Awesome," Arrow said. "Maybe I'll see if I can get tickets. I'll take Morgan to the same show, and we can spy on you guys."

"Asshole," Gray told his friend and grabbed him around the neck in a headlock.

The two men tussled as the others laughed at their antics. It took another thirty minutes for Black and the others to leave The Pit.

Black was genuinely happy for his friends. He loved Allye, Chloe, and Morgan. Before he'd met Harlow, however, he knew he would've been more cynical about all his friends getting hitched. He hadn't ever felt that bone-deep need to tie himself to anyone. Hell, he was impressed with himself if he stayed with a woman for longer than a few months. But Harlow had already changed him.

Yes, he hadn't been with her very long, but the thought of anything happening to her made him crazy, and that was a feeling he'd never had before. He'd gone off on missions and hadn't thought twice about the women he'd been dating until he'd returned home and realized that he probably should call and touch base.

If a day passed without him talking to Harlow—hell, if a few hours passed—Black got antsy. Wanted to know where she was, what she was doing, and if she was okay. A part of him worried that he was being over the top, but until Harlow balked, he wasn't going to be nervous about it.

Now that he was thinking about Harlow, Black needed to hear her voice. He picked up the phone and dialed her number before he left the bar.

She answered on the second ring. "Hi, Lowell."

Once again, hearing her say his name made something inside him settle. "Hey, baby."

"What's up? Everything okay?"

"Everything's fine. I just wanted to hear your voice."

She sighed. "That's sweet."

It wasn't sweet. It was as necessary to him as breathing. "You still planning on heading to the shelter around two thirty?"

"Yeah. Now that I know what's going on with Loretta and the shelter, it's a lot harder to plan the meals. I want to be sensitive to how much she can afford to pay, but at the same time try to continue buying food that's good for everyone. It frustrates me that the healthiest food is the most expensive. No wonder ramen noodles are so cheap—they're full of sodium and other stuff that isn't healthy for a kid to eat—never mind full-grown adults."

"Mm-hm," Black muttered, letting her know he was listening.

"Did you know you're supposed to do the majority of your shopping from the outside aisles of the stores? The cookies and crackers and most of the cheapest junk are usually in the middle, and the healthy vegetables and other stuff are on the outer aisles. I understand why Jasper weighs what he does. Because cheap food is full of crap. Julia did her best with him, but it takes time, energy, and money to make good meals every day."

When Black didn't answer right away, she asked, "Lowell? Are you still there?"

"I'm here," he reassured her.

"Oh. Right, sorry." She chuckled self-consciously. "I was going on and on. Anyway, yeah, the menu planning isn't going so well. But I'll just have to be more creative, I guess."

"If anyone can figure it out, it's you, baby," Black told her.

"Thanks."

"I'm on my way to the range, I just wanted you to know."

"Okay. How'd your meeting with the guys go? Did you find out anything?"

Black wanted to tell her about Nolan Woolf and everything they'd figured out, but he also didn't want to worry her. He wasn't as concerned about Brian and his buddies anymore, figuring after his "chat" with Brian, he'd be lying low. "We're working on it," he said. "We might have some leads. I'll tell you about them when I see you later."

"Okay," Harlow said.

Black loved how she didn't demand he tell her everything right that second. He knew she was curious, but it felt good that she trusted him to tell her what he could, when he could. That was important to him, considering his job with the Mountain Mercenaries. It wasn't like when he was a SEAL, and he literally wasn't allowed to tell anyone anything because most of the missions were top secret, but Rex still preferred that they not talk about their missions until after they were over. So there would be times in the future when he couldn't talk about where he was going or for how long, but when he got home, it would be nice to have someone to talk to, to decompress with.

"I'll see you later. Text me when you leave for the shelter," he told her.

"I will. Be safe at the range."

"You know it. Bye, baby."

"Bye."

Black smiled all the way to the range. He couldn't remember ever feeling as grounded as he was with Harlow. No woman had made him feel so calm. That was just her personality. He couldn't wait to see her later.

Nolan Woolf stared at the building across the street from his hiding spot, on the second floor of the pawnshop he owned. He'd heard from Elliott, one of the punks he'd hired to harass the residents at the shelter, that Brian, the so-called leader of the group, had been beaten up. Actually, he'd had his ass kicked. And it wasn't by a rival gang or some other punks who thought they were hot shit.

No, he'd been worked over by a professional—and Nolan knew just who'd done it. One of the assholes who had started hanging out at the shelter.

His time was running out, and he knew it.

Wiping a bead of sweat from his forehead, he mentally went through his plan once more.

It would work. It had to work.

A burned-out shell of a building wouldn't be worth much of anything, and the man Loretta was currently negotiating with would surely withdraw his offer. Then Nolan could swoop in and send another offer. She'd have no choice but to accept. No one else would give her anything for the worthless pile of bricks after today.

Nodding to himself, Nolan knew he was doing the right thing. He'd wait until the bitches were in their weekly meeting before acting. They'd all be gathered on the first floor and could easily get out of the building.

He wasn't a bad person. He didn't want to kill anyone. If the bitches lost their possessions—not that they had much to start with—those could be replaced. Nolan only wanted the building. Money was what motivated him. And this way, he could get both. He'd have the building and save hundreds of thousands of dollars at the same time.

He should've done this before now.

Smiling, Nolan wiped the sweat out of his eyes once more. He looked down at the items at his feet. A brick, a couple of bottles filled with gasoline with cloth wicks sticking out of the tops. He'd learned how to make the simple Molotov cocktails from the internet. No one would trace them back to him. He'd been very careful.

Looking out the window once more, he watched as the fat chick, the cook, walked toward the shelter with one of the damn bodyguards at her side. He narrowed his eyes and held his breath, hoping like hell the man wouldn't be staying. Women tended to panic when faced with fire, but he had a feeling the man wouldn't. Therefore, he needed him to *go*.

Chapter Twenty-Two

Harlow stopped at the doorway of the shelter and looked around. The afternoon was warm, and all was quiet. There were a few people inside the tattoo parlor, but they didn't seem to be paying attention to anyone outside the shop.

"I'm sorry I can't stay," Lowell told her. "I have interviews today that I forgot about. I need to hire a couple new managers at the gun range. I'd have one of the other guys stop in, but they're all busy too, following up on leads."

"It's fine, Lowell. I think we can manage without one of you guys hovering for an afternoon. Especially now that you took care of those punks."

"It was only one," Lowell warned. "Not all of them. And while we have the name of the person who we think hired them, we won't know for sure until we find him."

"You will," Harlow told him, waving off his concerns. "I'm impressed that you guys seem to solve all the cases you investigate. You don't stop until everyone is safe. I love that about you."

The second the words came out of her mouth, Harlow panicked. She hadn't meant to insinuate that she loved him . . . had she? People said things like that all the time, right? She loved Brad Pitt, but that didn't mean she *loved* him.

Luckily, Lowell didn't seem fazed by her words, which was good.

Wasn't it?

"I'll stop by after dinner," he said. "That way Loretta doesn't have to pay to feed me."

Harlow wanted to protest, but she was the one who'd been complaining about how expensive food was. "Okay. I'll see you later then."

"Call if you need anything."

"I will."

Then he leaned forward and kissed her. A deep kiss that made Harlow's heart beat faster, and she shifted in his grasp, wanting more. He slowly pulled back, brought a hand up to her face, and ran a finger down her cheek. "Love seeing you blush, baby." Then he kissed her once more, a chaste kiss that still somehow made her long for another. "Be safe."

Before she could respond—her brain felt like it had been short-circuited by his kiss—he was walking back down the sidewalk toward his car.

She quickly slipped inside the shelter and locked the door behind her. She turned to see Julia and Melinda standing there, smirking at her.

"Uh . . . hi," Harlow stuttered.

"Hey."

"Yo. Looks like someone is gettin' lucky," Melinda quipped.

"Shut up," Harlow said with no heat and a small smile.

"Happy for you," Julia said. "He seems like he's one of the good guys."

"He totally is," Harlow said. "How are you guys?"

They shrugged. "We're okay," Melinda told her. "Stressed, but Loretta says she's going to do what she can to help us figure out a place to live."

"She will," Harlow reassured them. "I know this is really hard on her."

Both women nodded. "We just appreciate everything she's done for us so far," Julia said. "Jasper was really struggling, but ever since we've been here, he's gotten better. He's not as cynical, which was really starting to worry me."

"He's a good kid. Him and Milo both," Harlow said. She looked at her watch. "I really need to go get started on dinner. Is the meeting with the investor still on for today?"

Melinda nodded. "Yeah. She's supposed to be here in half an hour."

Harlow knew that wouldn't give her a lot of time to get dinner prepped. She always entertained the kids when their moms were in a meeting. Deciding today they'd get to help her make dinner, Harlow asked, "Is everyone going to be here tonight to eat? Do you know?"

Melinda shrugged. Julia said, "I think Sue and Kristen are working, and Lauren might be out too, but the rest of us are all here."

"Okay, so nine adults, five kids, and Edward, if he shows up. No problem."

Julia shook her head. "I have a hard time cooking for two. I don't know how you do it."

An idea came to Harlow then, and she said, "I've shown you guys a thing or two while you've been here, but maybe I need to start giving more in-depth cooking lessons to everyone. Would you like that?"

Julia's face lit up. "I'd love it! As long as whatever you teach us is easy and fast. I know once I get into a place of my own, I'll be working a lot and won't have much time to spend in the kitchen."

The ideas were flowing fast and furious in Harlow's head. She could totally start up a sort of cooking school for working women. Teach them how to make healthy, fast, affordable meals. Just because someone didn't have a ton of time or money didn't mean that they couldn't make nutritious meals.

"Trust me," she told the women.

They smiled.

"And now I really need to get going," Harlow said apologetically. "When the kids get home, send 'em in. I'll be ready."

"Thank you for being so great with them," Melinda said.

"No need to thank me," Harlow said honestly. "I'd do anything for those rug rats." And with that, she headed through the living area and the door that led to the kitchen.

As she prepared the space for the arrival of the kids and built a timetable in her head of what needed to be prepped and when, in order to be ready to serve at six o'clock, Harlow only let her mind wander to Lowell once. She pulled out her cell phone and shot off a quick text.

Harlow: Just wanted you to know how much last night meant to me. Thank you for being you, and not someone you thought I wanted or needed.

It was a ballsy text, and something she'd probably never be able to tell him face to face. Their lovemaking had been perfect. She'd loved being able to be there for him. He'd taken her hard, and she'd adored every second. That wasn't to say she'd enjoy being taken like that every time, but when it was obvious he was fighting inner demons, it felt good to help him.

His return text was immediate.

Lowell: It was a night I'll never forget as long as I live. Thank you, baby.

She smiled and put her cell into her pocket, then got back to work.

It was time.

It wasn't dark outside, but Nolan couldn't wait any longer. He'd seen a fancy Mercedes park in the lot and a woman wearing a dark-blue suit enter the building. He'd given them ten minutes to get settled, knowing everyone in the place was now sitting in the main area on the first floor. He couldn't do anything about the damn cameras on the building, but he'd dressed for the occasion.

Pulling the baseball cap he was wearing farther down over his forehead, Nolan took a deep breath. He slipped out the back of the pawnshop and clutched the brick. The bag on his shoulder was heavy, and he could hear the gasoline sloshing as he walked briskly around the back of the buildings. He paused at the end of the street.

The tattoo parlor was still open, but because it was almost dinnertime, it was mostly empty. The pawnshop was closed, and he didn't see anyone loitering on the street. Holding his breath, he put his head down and started walking briskly toward the shelter.

There was a large window in the front of the building. The curtains were usually drawn shut, but Nolan knew the layout of the shelter because he'd seen the blueprints. Besides, the buildings he owned on either side of it were almost identical.

He held on to the brick tightly and then without pause drew back his arm and threw it through the window.

The glass shattered, and he heard startled screams from inside the room.

Nolan reached into his bag and pulled out the first of his homemade bombs. He lit the cloth with the lighter he had in his other hand and let it fly through the window.

More screams erupted, and he quickly lit the second Molotov cocktail.

"Hey!" he heard from across the street, and, knowing his time was running out, he threw the second bomb through the window, putting more strength into the throw.

Then he spun and ran as fast as he could down the street to his planned getaway route. He had a moped stashed the next block over, but he had to get to it before anyone could catch him. Nolan wasn't exactly in the best shape. He'd somehow managed to get himself one hell of a beer belly over the years.

He huffed and puffed as he ran and looked back only once. Satisfied to see women streaming out of the building, screaming at the top of their lungs, he disappeared around the corner.

If the fright in their screams was any indication, he'd have a signed contract from Loretta by the end of the day tomorrow.

The building would be his.

The block would be his.

And he'd make money hand over fist.

The end justified the means.

He smiled as he ran.

Black was leaving the gun range for the day . . . finally. He hated interviewing people. He knew it needed to be done, but trying to figure out if someone was being honest and how they'd click with the staff already on hand was draining.

His interrogation experience was helpful, but Black didn't think the people being interviewed appreciated it. He was a fan of long silences and making people uncomfortable so they'd blurt out honest responses instead of the canned ones they'd memorized.

If he heard one more person tell him their biggest "weakness" was being a "perfectionist," he was going to puke. Just once he wanted to hear someone be honest and tell him they didn't like people, or that they couldn't add two plus two. Neither of those things would necessarily keep him from hiring someone; he'd simply have to make sure they were put in the job appropriate for their skills.

His phone rang, and he saw it was Rex. "Hey," he said after answering.

"I've talked to a few of Nolan Woolf's competitors, and not one had anything good to say about the man. And I wasn't getting the vibe that it was simply because he was in the same line of work. They hate him. Said he gives them the creeps. I don't have a good feeling about this," Rex said without easing into the conversation.

"Yeah, me either," Black said. "So where is he?"

"Right now he's in the wind. I've sent his picture to the cops and told them a bit about why they should be on the lookout for him. He's a dead ringer for the description Brian gave, right down to the mole on the side of his neck. If I was him, I would've had that thing removed by now. You know, threat of cancer and all."

Black didn't even laugh. All he could think of was how he'd been doing mundane shit all day and he'd left Harlow vulnerable. If Woolf was desperate to own the building the shelter operated out of, there was no telling what he'd do to obtain it. "Shit. Okay. I'm on my way over to First Hope," Black told Rex. "I was going to wait until after dinner, but after hearing this, I think it's better if I go over now."

"I agree. I'll call the others and update them that Woolf is our guy. I've given his home address to the cops as well, but I'm thinking maybe our guys might have better luck finding him."

Black would feel much better having Gray and the others on the lookout for Woolf, as well as the cops. The sooner they found him, the better. "Okay, I'll be in touch."

"Ditto." And with that, Rex hung up.

Black threw his phone on the seat next to him and started his car. He wanted to call Harlow, to hear her voice and to reassure himself that she was all right, but decided to save time by getting to her as soon as possible instead.

Trying not to worry, he hit the gas a little harder than necessary and started the journey from the gun range to the shelter.

"Good work, Milo," Harlow said as she watched the nine-year-old carefully scoop the spaghetti noodles out of the pan and into the strainer. He wasn't big enough to pick up a pan of boiling water, so she'd given him a spaghetti spoon instead.

"And you're doing such a wonderful job stirring, Sammie," she praised the little girl, who beamed at her.

"How's the bread coming, Lacie?" Harlow asked, turning to watch as the eleven-year-old brushed garlic butter over the top of the bread she'd just taken out of the oven.

"Good!" Lacie said enthusiastically.

"And you guys?" Harlow asked Jasper and Jody. They were setting the large kitchen table. Jasper was doing an amazing job looking after Jody and making sure she didn't drop any of the plates.

"We're good," Jasper said.

At the same time, little Jody said, "Great!"

Harlow took a moment to drink in the scene. She was really going to miss these kids. They were somewhat on the shy side, but they'd come so far in the short time she'd known them.

When she heard the first crash, she thought that Jody had dropped a plate after all, and she turned quickly to make sure no one had gotten hurt by flying ceramic pieces. She was confused when she saw both Jody and Jasper staring toward the door that led to the living area.

It wasn't until she heard some of the women in the other room shouting that she realized whatever happened had been out there, not in the kitchen. She hurried over to Jody and steered her and Jasper behind the counter where she had been standing.

"Put down the spoon, Milo. You too, Lacie. Come over here, all of you." She gathered the children together. She didn't hear another crash, but when the women in the living room started screaming, Harlow knew something major was happening.

Trying not to panic, she quickly looked around the kitchen. The last thing she wanted to do was have the kids go into the other room, where something was making their mothers panic. She rushed to the window over the sink. It was the only window in the room. Because the shelter was located in the middle of a row of buildings, there were only windows on the front and back. There weren't any doors in the kitchen, except the one that led out into the living area.

She looked out the window and didn't immediately see anything. It faced the street, and Harlow could just barely see the lights from the tattoo parlor.

More screams were coming from the other room now—and then Harlow heard someone shout something about a fire.

Knowing she didn't have any time to waste now, she shoved the curtains out of the way and unlocked the window. She pushed upward with all her strength, but the window wouldn't budge. It was probably painted shut or something. Harlow turned, and her eyes swept the kitchen for something she could use to break the window.

She saw the five kids huddled together, their eyes huge in their faces, staring at her as she did her best to stay calm. Eyeing the small cast-iron pan she used to make omelets in the mornings, Harlow picked it up.

"Turn around and cover your faces," she ordered the kids. "I have to use this to break the window, and I don't want you to be hit by glass if it goes flying."

She was relieved to see Jasper taking charge of the kids and turning Milo and Sammie around when they continued to stare at her instead of doing as she asked.

Nodding at Jasper, Harlow turned back to the window. She could smell smoke now. Whatever had happened was serious, and she had to get the kids out. She reared back and hit the window as hard as she could.

The window cracked, but because there was wire mesh in the middle of the glass, the pan didn't do nearly the amount of damage she'd hoped. Harlow stumbled and dropped the pan in the sink. Her palm stung from the force of the hit, but she didn't stop. She picked the pan back up and aimed at the crack she'd put in the pane.

It took a few more hits, but finally the window broke. Using the pan to get as many of the shards of glass out of the way as possible, she then turned back to the children. "Come here, Lacie. You first." Harlow figured she could use Jasper's help on this side of the window, and putting the next oldest kid out first to help from the other side would make things easier on them all.

Smoke was coming in under the door to the kitchen now, and everyone began to cough. Trying not to panic at how fast it seemed the fire was growing—and because no one had come to check on them—Harlow held out her hand to Lacie. "Come on, sweetie. Out you go."

"Are you coming too?" Lacie asked, allowing Harlow to lift her up onto the counter. She stood up and bent over, looking out the window.

"We'll be right behind you. I need you to wait outside and help the others out, okay?"

She saw the women huddled together off to the side, and she called out to them. As they came running toward her, she turned back to Lacie. "Look! Your mom is out there to help you. Okay?"

"Okay."

Sammie and Jody were sobbing now, but Harlow blocked them out. She climbed into the sink herself, bracing Lacie. She put her hands around her waist and looked out the window. The sidewalk was only about five feet down, but now several women from the shelter were there to help. Thank God. "Okay, you got this, Lacie. Grab hold of their hands, and they'll help you down."

Lacie was crying now, but she bravely nodded.

"I know you're scared, but you can do this. You'll be outside and safe in just a second. Ready?"

The little girl nodded once more, and Harlow counted down. "Okay. Out you go."

Within seconds, Lacie was being hugged by her mom and hustled away from the window.

"Where's Jody?" Bethany asked hysterically.

"Milo!" Melinda yelled. "Mommy's here!"

"Get the rest of the kids!" Ann called out.

Harlow nodded and turned to look at the other children behind her.

But they weren't there.

Her heart started racing. Where were they? Holy shit, where'd they go?

"Harlow!"

She spun toward the voice and saw Sammie standing at the bottom of the stairs that led up to the third floor. They weren't very wide, and had been used in the past as a way for employees of the hotel to get to the quarters on the third floor from the kitchen.

"Where'd they go?" she blurted as she hopped down from the sink and headed for Sammie.

The little girl pointed up the stairs. "Jody got scared and wanted to get her teddy bear. Jasper ran after her, and Milo said he was going too. They told me to stay here, but I'm scared!"

Swearing under her breath and berating herself for not watching the kids more carefully, Harlow coughed. She glanced toward the door and saw not only black smoke rolling under the door, but a flicker of orange flames as well.

She turned back to Sammie, to tow her to the window and pass her to the waiting women—but she was no longer there.

She'd run up the stairs after the others.

"No! Sammie! Come back!" she screamed, but the little girl had already disappeared, scared out of her mind and too young to understand that, even with the smoke filling the kitchen, it was safer than heading up.

Harlow couldn't even take the time to be glad that at least one of the kids was safe. She yelled toward the window, "Call 911! The kids got scared and ran upstairs! I'm going after them. I'll be right back!"

Then she immediately turned and headed up the stairs after them. She had no idea if she'd really be right back or not, as the fire seemed about ready to break through the kitchen doors. But she couldn't crawl out the window herself and leave the kids to fend for themselves.

She was breathing heavily by the time she made it to the third floor. The rooms up here were small. Loretta hadn't bothered to remodel them, taking one for herself, one as an office, and using the others as rooms for the women with children.

"Jasper! Milo! Jody! Where are you?" she called out as she rushed down the hallway looking for the kids. She had no idea if they'd gone back into their rooms to grab something, or to hide, but she hoped like hell she'd be able to find them all in time.

She glanced down the stairwell that led into the main room, where the women had been having their meeting—and stopped to stare in horror at what she saw.

A wall of flame. The entire bottom floor seemed to be engulfed, and smoke was rolling up the stairs like something out of a scary movie she'd seen once. Except in the movie, it was a freezing-cold mist that could eat people alive instead of extremely hot smoke that threatened to choke her.

"Harlow!"

She startled badly and turned to see Jasper standing there holding Jody. Sammie was on one side of him and Milo on the other. Both girls were holding on to his shirt and crying, as was Jasper.

Looking around, Harlow made a split-second decision. She couldn't go down the main staircase. Not with the way the fire was eating everything in its path. She ran to the kids and pushed them toward the stairs that led to the kitchen, intending on rushing down the stairs back to the open window, where the other women were waiting for them. But the second she saw the stairs, she knew it was too late. Black smoke was rolling up the kitchen stairway, and the heat wafting from below was super intense.

Choking back a cry, Harlow knew their only choice was barricading themselves inside one of the rooms and trying to get the attention of someone below so they could make sure the firefighters knew where they were.

"Follow me," she ordered, and headed for Loretta's office. It wasn't ideal, as it was at the back of the building, facing the alley, but Harlow was afraid to go into the rooms above the living area. She didn't know exactly how fire worked, but she figured those rooms would be overcome with smoke and flames faster than ones on the other side.

She slammed the door once everyone was inside and said, "Help me find whatever we can to stuff under the crack in the door."

Immediately, Jasper grabbed some of the pillows off the window seat and brought them to her. Harlow stuffed as many of the pillows under the door as she could, hoping the stuffing would more effectively stop the smoke than if she stripped them and just used the covers. The pillows stopped most of the smoke, but she could see that it was still coming in from the cracks around the edges of the door.

Spinning, she ran to the window and unlocked it. Praying harder than she'd ever prayed in her life, she shoved at the pane with all her strength. Thank God, it moved. She pushed it up as high as it could go and leaned out.

She didn't see any people wandering around the back alley. Wanting to cry, she estimated how far it was to the ground below.

Too far.

They were three floors up, and there was absolutely nothing to break their fall. They couldn't jump. No way.

Coughing, she took a deep breath of the fresh air, then turned and climbed off the window seat. "Come here," she said, wiggling her fingers at the kids. They came toward her as a group, and she helped them sit as close to the window as possible. "The air is better here," she told them, even though she knew the open window would eventually draw more smoke into the room, making it harder to breathe. "Milo and Jasper, hold on to Sammie and Jody. Make sure they don't lean too far out."

"What are we going to do?" Jasper asked. "How are we going to get out?"

Harlow didn't have an answer for him. Instead she tried to give him a reassuring smile. "The firefighters will come and get us. Don't worry."

But she didn't believe her own words. She'd seen how fast the fire had spread. Whatever had started the fire had to have been fast and traumatic, not giving the women time to warn them or get to the kitchen to help the kids.

Suddenly, Harlow remembered that she'd put her phone in her pocket after she'd texted Lowell earlier.

Sobbing in relief, she pulled it out and coughed as she clicked on his name. The others had surely called 911 by now. Lowell would come for her. Of that she had no doubt.

She just wasn't sure he'd make it in time.

Chapter Twenty-Three

Black drove faster than he normally would, Rex's words echoing in his head. "She's fine," he muttered as he rolled through a stop sign.

His phone rang on the seat next to him. Normally, he would've ignored it because he was driving, but he reached for it without hesitation. He saw it was Harlow and breathed out a sigh of relief.

"Hey, baby," he said.

"Lowell!"

Every muscle in his body stiffened at the sound of her voice. Something was wrong. *Really* wrong. "I'm here."

"I need you!"

"I'm on my way. Probably about five minutes out. What's going on?"

"I don't know. But there's a fire."

Black's heart stopped. "Are you out?"

"No," she said, and he heard the panic in her tone. "We couldn't get out in time. I was in the kitchen with the kids and a fire started right outside the door. I got Lacie out the window, but Jody ran up the stairs and Jasper went after her, and I couldn't leave them!"

"Slow down, baby. Where are you, and who's with you?"

He heard her take a big breath, then she immediately started coughing.

Black pressed his foot harder on the gas pedal.

"I'm upstairs in Loretta's office. Jasper, Sammie, Milo, and Jody are with me. I put stuff under the door to try to keep the smoke out, but it's coming in around the doorframe."

"You did good, Harl."

"We can't jump, it's too high," she told him.

Black's blood froze in his veins at the thought of any of them trying to jump out of the three-story building. "No, you can't. Hang tight, baby. Have you called 911?"

"No. I called you."

Her words made his throat close up. "Did the women get out?" he asked.

"I think so. I didn't stop to do a head count, but I saw a lot of them out front when I handed Lacie out the window."

"Okay, I'm sure they're fine. They've probably already called the fire department. Stay calm, Harley."

"Okay. Lowell?"

"Yeah?"

"I just want to say that the last month has been the happiest I've ever had. Even though I didn't know we were dating, I loved every second."

"Don't," Black ordered harshly. "Do *not* say goodbye. I won't have it. I haven't gone through all the trouble to sneak in some amazing dates to have you give up now."

He heard her chuckle, as he'd hoped she would.

"I'm not giving up," she said softly.

"Good. Because I'm coming for you," Black told her. "I'm gonna move heaven and earth to get you and those kids out of there. Hear me?"

"Yeah, Lowell, I hear you."

"Good. I'm coming for you, Harlow. I'll always come for you."

"Okay. I . . . I need to go." He heard her voice break.

"Okay. Be brave, baby."

The line went dead.

"Fuck!" Black swore and floored it. He was going sixty miles an hour in a thirty-five-mile-an-hour zone, but he didn't care. Every second counted. The building was old. He didn't even think it had a sprinkler system, or if it did, it was probably years out of date and not up to code.

The thought of Harlow, or any of the kids with her, dying of smoke inhalation while waiting for rescue made his skin crawl.

Not gonna happen on his watch.

Black didn't take the time to call the rest of the team or Rex. He was using all his concentration to get to Harlow safely. If he crashed, she'd die for sure. Somehow he knew he was her only hope.

Three and a half minutes later, Black slammed on his brakes when he was a block away. Traffic was backed up, and no one was moving. Throwing his car in park, he leaped out, not caring if someone stole the damn thing or not. His eyes were glued to the black smoke rising into the air in front of him.

He sprinted toward the buildings but stopped when he saw Loretta and the other women who lived in the shelter. Lacie was standing in her mom's arms, and everyone else was huddled together, staring up at the building in horror. They were all crying, and the parents of the kids with Harlow were hysterical.

"Black!" Loretta cried when she saw him.

"Are you okay?" he asked.

"Yes, but Harlow and the other kids are still inside! She told us to call 911 and said she was going up the kitchen staircase after the kids who'd panicked and ran to their rooms."

"I know. She called me. Is everyone else out?"

Loretta nodded. "Yes. Someone threw a brick through the front window, and before we could really do anything, a bomb or something came through next. It rolled in front of the kitchen door and caught the rug on fire. It went up with a big whoosh. There was nothing we could do! Then a second bomb flew in, and we had to get out."

"You did the right thing," Black reassured her, mentally assessing the building as he listened. His eyes went from the black smoke rolling out of the crevasses of the building to the flames he could see coming from a few windows on the second floor. He knew Harlow and the kids didn't have much time.

"When the fire department gets here, send them around back," he ordered, then rushed off before she could ask for more information.

Black ran down the block, nearly slamming into people who were standing around staring at the fire. He ran through the parking lot and swore when he almost ran into a big white delivery truck parked around the corner. He caught himself before he went sprawling on the ground and ignored the driver's yelled warning to watch out.

He stared upward as he ran, and knew exactly which room Harlow and the kids were at. Four little heads were sticking out the window at the far end of Loretta's building, the room farthest away from the fire.

Thanking his lucky stars that Harlow had been smart enough to choose that room to hole up in, he stopped directly under the window.

"Harlow!" he bellowed.

"Lowell!" she yelled back.

He held up his arms. "You've got to help them out. One at a time. I'll catch them!"

Harlow stared down at Lowell in horror. Jump? They couldn't jump! It was too high. "It's too high!" she yelled. The fire was extremely loud. She hadn't thought it would be so darn loud.

"You have to!" he yelled back. "Stop arguing and do it!"

She was coughing almost nonstop now, as were the kids. Their eyes were bloodshot, and they were absolutely terrified. So was she. But she was the adult. She had to be the strong one.

"Okay, guys, here's what we're going to have to do. Lowell is here. He's going to catch you."

Jasper's eyes got wide, and he opened his mouth to protest, but Harlow shook her head at him in warning.

"It's high, but you guys can do it. Look, I'll hold on to your hands and lean out the window as far as I can. I'm almost six feet tall. You guys are what, three to four feet or more? And Lowell is my height too. When you add all that together, it'll be almost like you're jumping out the kitchen window like Lacie did."

The kids didn't look convinced, but unfortunately, Harlow didn't have time to cajole them. "Jody, you're first," she said.

The little girl was absolutely terrified, but she didn't balk when Harlow picked her up. "Scoot back, guys," she told the others, and they immediately made room for her at the window. "Jasper, hold my legs," she ordered.

The teenager immediately kneeled on the window seat and sat on her calves. Harlow nodded her approval. Then she took Jody's face in hers. "Close your eyes, baby. Before you know it, you'll be on the ground and with your mommy, okay?"

"Okay," she said, and Harlow almost broke down at the complete trust she saw in the girl's eyes. Taking a deep breath and trying not to cough, she turned Jody until she was sitting on the ledge facing out. She took her wrists in her hands and slowly lowered her out the window.

Harlow then leaned out as far as she could without falling herself. She felt Jasper's weight on her legs and knew if he weren't there, she would've tumbled out.

"That's it!" Lowell called from below. From way too far below. "I've got her. Trust me."

She did. She trusted Lowell with her life. And with the life of the child in her arms.

Catching Lowell's gaze, she nodded at him and, without warning the little girl, she let go of Jody's wrists.

She wanted to squeeze her eyes closed, so she wouldn't see what happened next, but she didn't. Jody fell downward like a rag doll, and like a superhero from the movies that were so popular nowadays, Lowell caught her in midair. He fell backward on his ass, but he cradled Jody close to his chest, keeping her safe. Within seconds, he was standing. He put Jody down and said something to her as he pointed toward the parking lot at the end of the alley. She took off running.

"Next!" Lowell demanded.

Crying nonstop now, Harlow eased herself back inside the room. She turned to Sammie. "Your turn."

Sammie shook her head frantically. "No! I don't wanna!"

"You have to," Harlow said, trying to keep her voice calm.

"No!"

Harlow was ready to simply grab her, but Milo thankfully interrupted. "You can do this, Sammie. I believe in you."

And just like that, Sammie sniffled and turned to Harlow.

More thankful than she'd ever been in her life, she sat Sammie on the edge of the window just as she had Jody. She wasn't much heavier than the five-year-old, but she was taller. Harlow grabbed her wrists and slowly lowered her out the window. "Ready?" she asked.

Sammie bit her lip and shook her head. "No, don't! I changed my mind. I don't wanna—"

Without letting her finish the sentence, Harlow let go.

It killed her. Everything inside her balked at dropping a kid out a three-story building, but the alternative was death—and that wasn't acceptable.

Sammie screamed all the way down, which was only for around two seconds before she landed in Lowell's arms. Once again, he stumbled and fell but popped right back up, and soon Sammie was running down the alley just as Jody had.

"My turn now, right?" Milo asked.

Harlow pulled herself back inside the window and nodded. But already she was having second thoughts. She'd seen how bad the impact was on Lowell when he'd caught the other two. And they were smaller and lighter than Milo. She had a bad feeling that there was no way he'd be able to catch either her or Jasper without hurting himself.

Looking out the window, first one way, then the other, she listened. But she couldn't hear anything over the crackling and popping of the fire.

She had no idea if the fire department was on their way, or even there already, out front spraying water on the fire.

"Okay, Milo. Your turn."

Without a word, the nine-year-old climbed onto the windowsill. He was coughing, and tears were streaming down his face, but he didn't hesitate. He held up his arms. Harlow took hold of his wrists and carefully leaned out the window once more. She couldn't lean out quite as far because Milo was heavier than the girls had been. She felt her center of gravity tipping dangerously.

"I'm ready!" Milo said, and Harlow let go.

She watched as he fell, but this time she gasped when Lowell crumpled to the ground with Milo in his arms. It took several seconds for him to move, but eventually, Milo climbed off him and headed for the end of the alley.

The second Lowell looked up at her, she knew he wasn't going to be able to help her and Jasper.

It was exactly as she'd thought. They were too heavy, and the drop was too high. If he tried to catch them, he'd be severely injured.

She wiped her running nose and coughed. Turning away from Lowell, she held out an arm to Jasper. "Come closer to the window," she told him.

The teenager did as she asked, and they clung to the side of the window and leaned out as far as they could. Black smoke had filled the office and was rushing out the window as if it too wanted the fresh air.

Something she'd seen on television a while ago flashed through her brain. She'd been watching a documentary on the September 11 tragedy in New York City. She'd watched in horror as the program rolled footage of people jumping out of the top floors of the Trade Center towers.

She hadn't understood it then. Didn't know how someone could jump from that high, knowing they'd die when they landed.

But she got it now.

The heat coming from the room behind her was almost unbearable. She was leaning as far out of the window as she could, and she still couldn't get enough air in her lungs. Her brain was telling her to lean out farther, to get more fresh air. The idea of suffocating was terrifying, as was burning to death. She had the sudden thought that if she knew for certain she'd die quickly if she jumped out the window, she'd do it. But she wasn't high enough. If she jumped, she'd hurt herself. Badly. But she might not die. She might be paralyzed. She'd cause more pain for herself and for her family.

But if she were one hundred floors up right now? Jumping absolutely would seem the better way to die.

Tears streamed down both her and Jasper's faces, and Harlow knew this was it. She tried to console herself that at least she'd gotten four of the kids out.

She looked down at Lowell.

He was staring up at her as if he could use mental force to lift her out the window to safety. She was coughing nonstop now. She brought her hand up to her mouth and blew him a kiss.

Instead of responding in kind, Lowell spun and jogged down the alley in the direction he'd sent the children. He was limping badly, and Harlow hated that he'd been hurt even the smallest bit when he'd caught the others.

"He's leaving?" Jasper choked out.

"No."

"He *is*," he insisted. "He's leaving us here to die!"

"He can't catch us," Harlow explained. "We're too big. We'd probably kill him."

Jasper's eyes were huge in his face, which was streaked with soot. "I thought he was different. But he's just like my old man! No one's reliable. No one! Not even Loretta. She's kicking us out too!"

Harlow didn't know how Jasper had found out about the shelter closing, but she had to do damage control. Even if they only had minutes to live, she didn't want this boy who'd already been through way too much in his young life to think that so many people were unreliable. "Lowell is *not* leaving us," she said sternly. "Look at me, Jasper."

He did, and she saw his anger had turned to sorrow. More tears ran down his cheeks, and not because of the smoke in the air.

"He's not leaving. He'd never leave me."

"You don't know that."

"I do. I believe in him. He's going to do everything in his power to get us out of here. He'll die trying. Do you believe me?" Her voice was husky from smoke damage, but she had to make Jasper understand.

It took a few seconds, but finally he nodded.

"I love him. But more importantly, I *trust* him. With my life. And yours."

"Okay," Jasper croaked.

"And if there was any way Loretta could keep the shelter operating, she would. But it's expensive. It's not about you. I hate to say this, but everything isn't about you, Jasper." She smiled to ease the rebuke.

He looked down for a second, as if embarrassed, but then quickly rebounded. "It's not? Well, it should be," he said.

Harlow smiled and coughed. Then something caught her eye, and she looked past the teenager toward the end of the alley.

And breathed a sigh of relief.

Black knew he'd fucked up his knee. He'd felt something pop when he caught Milo, but he ignored the pain. The second he fell that last time, he knew he wouldn't be able to catch Jasper or Harlow. He needed to come up with a solution, and fast. He looked up and saw both of them leaning dangerously far out the window. Black smoke rolled out from behind them.

He watched as Harlow blew him a kiss—and he snapped.

No.

No fucking way was he going to watch the woman he loved burn or choke to death.

Something clicked in his brain, and he abruptly turned and headed back down the alley the way he'd come. Limping badly, he forced himself to endure the pain and keep going. He turned the corner and headed for the white delivery truck that was, thank God, still sitting in the parking lot. He wrenched open the passenger-side door and jumped in. "Drive," he barked, pointing toward the alley.

"Dude! You can't just get in my truck."

"I just did. Now, fucking *drive*," he said again.

The man lifted his hands off the steering wheel as if surrendering to Black. "I don't want no trouble."

Knowing Harlow's and Jasper's lives were literally hanging in the balance, Black pleaded, "My woman needs help. She's in that burning building. I need you to *drive*! For the love of God, please! I'm begging you."

The older man behind the wheel must've seen something in Black's eyes, because he nodded and turned the key in the ignition.

He followed Black's directions and listened as he told him the plan. He jumped the curb in the parking lot and drove as fast as he dared down the alley.

Black looked up and was relieved to see both Harlow and Jasper still hanging out the window. "There!" he said, pointing. "Get as close as you can."

"The building's on fire," the driver said stupidly.

"I realize that," Black said impatiently. "As soon as you hear the second thump, drive like hell away from here. Got it?"

"Oh yeah, man. *That* I can do."

Black waited until the truck had stopped directly under the window. He quickly pulled himself out the side window and climbed on top of the truck. The height of the truck put Black less than a story and a half below the window, rather than the three stories he had been.

He stood, looked up at Harlow, and lifted his arms once more. "Come on, baby," he whispered, knowing she couldn't hear him. "Jump."

The second Harlow saw the truck coming down the alley, she knew what Lowell had planned. The big white delivery truck would give them something to jump onto. They could do this. They were saved.

"See?" she choked out. "Told you he'd be back."

Jasper was beyond talking. He was coughing so hard he was dry heaving, and Harlow grew increasingly alarmed.

She watched Lowell haul himself out of the passenger-side window and climb onto the top of the truck. He held up his arms, and she saw his mouth moving.

Knowing they were out of time, she scooted closer to Jasper and grabbed hold of his arm. She pointed to Lowell and the truck. Jasper nodded. She inched backward, feeling the heat of the fire on her legs, and knelt up on the window seat once more. She couldn't lean over like she had with the other children, but she took Jasper's wrists in her hands and helped him slide over the edge of the windowsill. She looked down at Lowell, saw him nod, then let go.

Jasper fell right into Lowell's arms. Once again, Lowell fell backward, but it didn't look quite as painful as it had when he'd fallen with Milo.

Without hesitation, Harlow threw one leg over the sill and balanced there for a moment. She looked back at the doorway.

It was gone. Flames were shooting upward and crawling across the ceiling toward her. The heat was intense, and she knew if she didn't go now, she wouldn't get the chance.

Lowering herself over the edge, she tried to hold on until she could make a controlled drop, but her hands wouldn't corporate. The second she swung her second leg over the edge of the windowsill and started to lower herself, the strength in her hands gave out, and she was falling.

She felt Lowell's hands grab her around the waist painfully—then she was lying on her back.

She gulped in the fresh air, but couldn't seem to get it into her lungs.

Harlow felt Lowell move out from under her, but she couldn't open her eyes long enough to see him. She certainly couldn't talk. Couldn't ask him if he was all right.

The truck began to move under them—and not a second too soon. She managed to pry her eyes open long enough to see a shower of sparks and debris fall from the top of the building she'd just been in as it collapsed in on itself.

Closing her eyes again and concentrating on the feel of Lowell's hand on her forehead, trying to get oxygen into her lungs, Harlow let every muscle in her body go lax.

She didn't have to be strong anymore. Lowell was there. He'd take care of her. He'd make sure she was safe.

Chapter Twenty-Four

"I'm sorry I can't come and laugh at you for getting hurt," Lance told Black over the phone a few days after the fire.

He'd just had a visit from his parents, and Harlow had been taken back to her room by *her* parents. He hadn't been by himself since the fire, except at night when he was sleeping.

"It's okay," Black told his little brother. "You all right?"

"Yeah. I'm headed down to Peru for a shoot in the morning."

"Cool." And it was. Lance was a very good photographer who traveled around the world. His specialty was going into the bowels of a city and taking pictures of the residents' daily lives. From the homeless communities who lived in the drainage tunnels under Las Vegas to life in Siberia in the middle of winter, to the African plains and the slums of Mexico City, he'd seen and experienced it firsthand. Bringing the plight of those less fortunate into the limelight was his mission in life. "When are you going to be back?"

"Not sure," Lance said. "I'm actually accompanying a film crew on this one. They're doing a story on prostitution and how women are exploited in lower economic countries and cities."

"You'll be careful?" Black asked. "Believe me when I say the guys who own the prostitutes don't take kindly to being on film or having their operations exposed."

"Of course. It's not like I'll be on this job by myself. We've got a shitload of cameramen and others with us."

Black still didn't like it, but he'd learned to keep his mouth shut. Lance was an adult, and it wasn't like *he* could really talk, considering what he did for the Mountain Mercenaries. "When you get back, I want you to come visit. I want to introduce you to Harlow."

Lance paused a moment before he asked, "You really like her, huh?"

"Yeah. I'm going to marry her someday," Black told his brother.

"No shit?"

"No shit."

"She meet Mom and Dad yet?"

"Yeah, although she's been kinda out of it recently. But they're going to stick around."

"She okay?" Lance asked, concern easy to hear in his voice.

"Yeah. Terrible case of smoke inhalation. She was lucky she didn't burn her lungs or throat. She's on oxygen and bronchodilators, and the doctors say she'll be able to be weaned off them soon. She's still coughing a lot, but we're both just thankful she's alive."

"Thank God."

"Yup."

"Hey, Lowell?"

"Yeah, bro?"

"I'm proud of you."

Black's throat closed up. Finally, he choked out, "Thanks."

"But don't think getting hurt will make you Mom and Dad's favorite son. That'll always be me. So just suck it up."

Black burst out laughing. Leave it to Lance to say something mushy, then turn around and give him shit. "Whatever, asshole. Travel safe, okay?"

"Will do. I'll be in touch when I'm back in the States."

"You'd better be."

"Later."

"Bye, Lance."

Black clicked off the phone and closed his eyes. He'd been extremely lucky. Lucky he'd left for the shelter when he had. Lucky that the white van had been parked at the end of the alley. Lucky that, considering he and the team hadn't discovered what was going on before Woolf made his move, all the women and children had gotten out of the building alive.

They'd learned a valuable lesson with this case. Their handler might be extremely smart, but he was also very human. They couldn't rely on him for every scrap of information in the future. Teamwork was vital in their line of work, and their team included Rex. He wasn't just a voice on the phone. If they were going to be successful, they needed him as much as he needed the rest of the team.

Black had no idea if Arrow had talked to Rex yet about his missing wife and the team's offer to look into her case, but without a doubt it had to be done. Rex couldn't go on the way he was, and the team couldn't continue with their rescues knowing their handler didn't trust them with the most important case of his life.

Shifting on the bed, Lowell winced when he moved his leg the wrong way. His knee hurt like a son of a bitch. But he'd heal. As would Harlow. They'd move on with their lives, and he'd be able to take her on many more dates in the future. At the moment, that was all that mattered.

He fell asleep thinking of all the different things he could do with Harlow, and how much fun they were going to have for the rest of their lives.

A couple of weeks later, Harlow sat next to Lowell in The Pit and watched as their friends played pool. She rested her head on his shoulder and felt his hand tighten on her thigh, where it'd been resting.

"You okay?" he asked quietly.

Harlow nodded. "Perfect."

"Your parents get off all right?" Morgan asked as she stood to the side of the pool table, waiting for her turn.

"Yeah," Harlow said. "I love them, but it was time. They were driving me crazy." Her parents had rushed to Colorado Springs when they'd heard about the fire and had stayed until they were satisfied she was all right.

"They just wanted to make sure you were one hundred percent healed before they left," Lowell told her.

She sat up and faced him. "I know, but honestly, I was fine not too long after the fire. It was *you* who wasn't okay."

And he hadn't been. Catching Milo had torn a bunch of ligaments in his knee, and running on it, climbing onto the top of the truck, and subsequently catching both her and Jasper hadn't done him any favors. He'd had surgery and was currently seeing a therapist, but it still obviously hurt him.

Jasper had fared about the same as her, suffering from severe smoke inhalation, but she was happy to hear that he was doing well. As a kid, his body had bounced back faster than hers had. The other children were also fine. The entire community had rallied around all the residents, and every single one of them had new apartments to live in. Some were even in the same complex, so they could continue to see each other on a daily basis.

"I'm fine," Lowell said.

Harlow rolled her eyes. He was *such* a guy. He was sitting there wearing a knee brace and wincing when he moved the wrong way and still insisting he was fine. Whatever.

"It was nice to meet *your* parents too," Allye said. "I thought maybe you were hatched out of an egg or something."

"Watch it," Lowell growled, reaching for her, but she laughed and jumped out of range.

"So . . . did all the parents get along?" Gray asked, wrapping an arm around Allye's shoulders and pulling her into his side.

"They did," Lowell told his friends. "I think Harl's folks are even planning a visit to Orlando in the near future."

"Wow. That's great!" Chloe exclaimed.

Harlow nodded. "Yup. Although I'm not surprised. My parents are very easy to get along with. And it doesn't hurt that the Lockards lived in Topeka for a while. They even know some of the same people. So are you guys ready to take my sample cooking class next week?" she asked.

Chloe, Allye, and Morgan all nodded at the same time.

"I can't wait to get cooking lessons from *the* Chef Reese." Chloe grinned.

Harlow rolled her eyes. "I just want to make sure I'm not doing anything too hard for my first class. I want the women who take the classes to feel comfortable making healthy gourmet meals, but not feel intimidated."

"I'm sure you've picked the perfect meal," Allye said.

"And we're happy to serve as your guinea pigs," Morgan threw in.

Just then, Ball entered the back hall, carrying a trayful of drinks. He was walking extremely carefully so he didn't spill anything. He placed the tray on a nearby table and sighed in relief.

"Jesus, I don't know how waitresses do that shit," he said.

Ball handed out the drinks, beers for the guys—except Black, who got a glass of water on account of the meds he was still taking—a bottle of water for Allye, and margaritas for Chloe, Morgan, and Harlow.

Then he nodded at Gray and stepped back.

Gray cleared his throat and put his beer on the table. Then he faced Allye and took the bottle of water from her.

"Oh my God," Allye said quietly, as if she knew what was coming.

"I was going to do this when we went up to Denver, but obviously that didn't happen. So, I figure the second best way to do it is while surrounded by our friends. Allye Martin, you are the most important person in my life. I can't imagine not spending the rest of my days with you by my side. I love you more than anything. Will you marry me?"

As far as proposals went, it was short and sweet, but everyone heard the sincerity and love in Gray's voice.

"Of course I will," Allye said. "I love you so much!"

They embraced and kissed until Meat called out, "Enough already!"

Everyone chuckled and congratulated the newly engaged couple.

Then Dave walked through the door to the back room, carrying a large cake with candles. "Congratulations!" he boomed in his deep southern accent.

He placed the cake down on a pool table, and everyone laughed at the inscription.

2 DOWN, 4 TO GO

Dave turned to look at Morgan and Arrow with one eyebrow raised.

Arrow held up his hands in his defense. "Hey, don't look at me. I'd marry Morgan tomorrow if I had my way."

"Yes," Morgan said softly.

Arrow's head whipped around to stare at the woman by his side. "*What?*"

"If that was a proposal, my answer is yes," she said calmly.

"Oh, but . . . I don't have a ring yet . . ." Arrow stammered.

Morgan stood up on tiptoe and wrapped her arms around Arrow's neck. He bent over and picked her up off her feet.

"I love you," Morgan said.

Arrow's grin was almost blinding as he looked down at the woman in his arms. "Did you seriously just agree to marry me?"

"Did you ask me?"

"Well, kind of."

"Why don't you try again then?"

"Morgan Byrd, will you marry me and make me the happiest man alive?"

"Um, I don't think that's true," Gray mumbled. "Can't be when *I'm* the happiest man alive."

"Yes. Yes! I'll marry you," Morgan told Arrow.

Dave had slipped out while Morgan and Arrow were having their moment, but he returned with a knife in one hand and a small squeeze bottle in the other. He immediately scraped off the *2* and the *4* on the cake, then leaned over and replaced both with *3*s.

"There," he said, standing up—then he turned to look at Harlow and Black questioningly.

Harlow looked at Lowell and burst out laughing. He joined her, and they chuckled until they could hardly breathe.

"What's so funny?" Ball asked when they had themselves under control once more.

"I just got accustomed to the fact that Lowell and I are *dating*. I think we need to wait awhile before we agree to tie the knot."

"Don't wait too long," Dave said. "Life's too short to have regrets." Then he turned to the rest of the group and said, "Drinks are on the house tonight."

Everyone cheered, but Harlow only had eyes for Lowell. He was staring at her intently.

"What?" she asked.

"When I was standing in that alley, looking up at you hanging out that fucking window, one of the things I was feeling was regret. Regret that I hadn't told you how I felt about you. I've been thinking about this a lot over the last month. Even though you were the one who went through the ordeal, even though you were the one who was suffering from smoke inhalation and having nightmares, you got ahold of my parents and told them what happened. You kept in touch with Loretta and even helped her figure out some of the insurance stuff. You went and visited Lacie, Jody, Milo, Jasper, and Sammie. You've been everything to everybody, and you haven't asked for anything for yourself."

"Lowell—" she began, but he brought her hand up to his mouth, kissed the palm, and continued.

"Before you, I couldn't imagine spending the rest of my life with one person. Couldn't fathom how I wouldn't get bored waking up to her morning after morning. But I can honestly say that, after spending the last month with you, the reason I couldn't imagine being with someone forever was because I hadn't met *you* yet. I've realized that no other relationship had worked out because she wasn't you.

"I'm not asking you to marry me right this second, because neither of us is quite ready for that, but I can see it happening. I'll spend the rest of my life trying to make up for the bad dates you've had. I'll do everything in my power to make sure you like surprises again, at least the ones that I arrange for you."

"When Jasper and I were hanging out that window, and you turned your back on us and ran away, Jasper lost it. He thought you'd abandoned us, just like his father had." Harlow was crying now, and having a hard time getting the words out, but she forged on. "But I knew you hadn't. I knew you'd be back for me. From the bottom of my soul, I knew that. And the second I saw that truck come around the corner, I knew it was you. You don't have to make up for any bad dates I might've had—you do that every day, just by being yourself. I . . . I love you, Lowell."

She saw his eyes get misty before he hauled her out of her chair and into his lap. Making sure to keep her weight on his good leg, Harlow buried her face between his neck and shoulder and simply held on.

Since Lowell had been released from the hospital, she'd been living with him in his apartment. Her parents had stayed in her apartment while they'd been in Colorado Springs, and his parents were in a nearby hotel. She'd taken care of him, even when he hadn't wanted to be taken care of. She'd bullied and babied him, vowing to do whatever it took to get him back on his feet and working with his team again.

He wasn't ready yet, and she knew it was eating at him, but he'd been working with Meat behind the scenes, learning some of the tricks the other man used to find information online.

"Here, you guys," Harlow heard from in front of them. She picked up her head to see Ball standing there with two plates in his hands. "Can't let good cake go to waste."

She smiled and took them from him. "Thank you." Looking at Lowell, she smiled wider. "Cake?"

"I'd rather eat something else," he said, once Ball had turned his back to get more cake for himself.

"Lowell!" Harlow protested.

He chuckled and tightened his hold around her waist. "I can't help it that you're way too fucking sexy, and I can't keep my hands—or mouth—off you."

"Well, you can certainly help talking about it when we're hanging out with our friends," she told him haughtily.

He laughed again. "Look at them, baby. What do you think Gray, Ro, and Arrow will be doing the second they get home tonight?"

She refused to blush. "It's not polite to talk about."

Lowell shook his head. "Fine. Sorry. But you should know, as much as I love having you on top, the second I get the all clear from the doc, you're going to be flat on your back for hours."

"Jeez, Lowell," Harlow said, knowing she was probably beet red.

"I love you," he said solemnly. "Dave was right. Life *is* too short to have regrets. I was so fucking scared that day. I was afraid I was going to have to stand there and watch you die or jump out that window."

"I'm fine," Harlow told him.

"I know you are. And I plan on keeping you that way."

Loving how sweet he was being, but needing him to get back to the Lowell she was used to, she asked, "Any news on Nolan Woolf?"

It took him a second to process the change of subject, but finally he smiled. "I can't believe I forgot to tell you. The Denver cops found him."

"They did? Where? What happened?"

"He was hiding out in one of his apartment complexes up in the city. Unfortunately for him, though, some of his tenants figured out who he was. They weren't happy he'd been ignoring their maintenance requests. Apparently there's mold in the building, the elevators don't work, the stairways are crumbling, and there's only intermittent hot water. They beat the shit out of him. Then they called the cops and let them know where they could find him. The fact that his face was all over the news, along with what he did, made it all the easier for the tenants to turn him in."

"I honestly don't think he meant for us to be trapped," Harlow said quietly.

"You think I care? The asshole threw two Molotov cocktails into an occupied building. I don't know what he thought would happen, but that's attempted murder in my eyes. And the DA agrees."

"So it's over?" she asked.

"It's over, baby," Lowell told her. "We've got him on video throwing the bombs into the building. He kept his head down, but that mole on the side of his neck is a dead giveaway. Not to mention the rock-bottom offer Loretta received from him the next day. He hasn't confessed yet, but I have no doubt he will."

Harlow gave him the side eye. "Why?"

Lowell smirked. "Because I've been invited to sit in on the interrogation."

"And you always get your confession, don't you?"

"Yup. Especially when it concerns the woman I love."

Harlow felt goose bumps break out on her arms when he brought his hand up and palmed the side of her neck. "Just don't do something crazy. I can't stand the thought of you getting in trouble and having to go to jail."

"I'm not going to go to jail, baby," he reassured her.

"Because how am I going to get more awesome dates if you're behind bars?" she asked, ignoring him. "I mean, if I have to visit my baby-daddy behind bars and hope for conjugal visits, that's entering bad-date territory again."

"You want my baby, Harl?" he asked, leaning in until it felt like it was just the two of them.

Swallowing hard, she forced herself to look into his eyes. "Not right this second. But if you continue to not be a douche, I'm thinking . . . yes."

A laugh burst out of him. "I'll see what I can do about continuing to not be a douche."

"You do that," she said.

Resting his forehead on hers, he asked, "You gonna officially move into my apartment?"

"I'll think about it," she teased.

"I like having you there," he told her seriously. "I like waking up with you. I like showering with you, although I'll like it more when I can stand up properly. I like cooking for you, and watching you putter around my kitchen while you make *me* something to eat. I like helping you figure out what you want to do next, and I like knowing at the end of the day, I don't have to watch you walk out the door to go to your own place. I pretty much like everything about you."

"Funny. I feel the same about you," Harlow told him. She felt as if she were glowing. She still hadn't figured out where she was going to work, but being with Lowell, helping him out while he was recovering, was the happiest she'd been in a long time.

"Did you talk to Loretta today?" Lowell asked.

Harlow nodded. She'd been talking to the older woman almost every day since the fire. "Yeah. She and Edward went to the courthouse this past weekend and got married. She sold the building—well, what's left of it—to a developer who wants to restore it to its original historical charm. The people who owned the other buildings have come forward and claimed that Woolf basically threatened them and forced them to sell, so those purchases might be made null and void as well, leaving the buildings to be purchased by developers who will all work together to make the area beautiful and prosperous again. Loretta still feels guilty about selling, but I think she's finally moving on."

"Good."

Just then, Gray whistled loud and long.

Everyone stopped talking and turned to see what the noise was all about.

He held up his cell and gestured to the large table off to the side of the room.

Harlow knew what that meant—the Mountain Mercenaries had business to discuss.

She got off Lowell's lap and helped him stand. She couldn't keep her eyes off his ass as he made his way to the table, following his buddies.

"I have to admit, he's got a nice ass," Chloe commented.

Harlow giggled. She wasn't concerned in the least that the other woman would horn in on her man. She had her own. And a ring on her finger showing how much Ro loved her.

"Well, girls," Allye said, linking her elbows with Morgan and Harlow. "I have a feeling the night's almost over. I know Gray was already itching to get out of here to celebrate our engagement. If that"—she nodded at the table—"is any indication, I'm guessing they'll be heading out on a mission soon."

"Shit," Harlow said under her breath. She wasn't ready for this yet. She had been spoiled and hadn't yet had to watch Lowell head off to what would surely be something dangerous. She didn't think he'd be going on this mission either, not with his knee still healing, but it was simply a matter of time. She couldn't see Lowell retiring from the Mountain Mercenaries. He was good at what he did, and besides that, he *needed* to do it. Needed to help women and children escape their tormentors and captors.

No. She'd never tell him how much she hated him leaving. She'd just make sure he knew how much she loved having him home.

"Come on," Morgan said. "I need to finish my cake and drink. Then I need to take my fiancé home and give him a damn good reason to come back to me in one piece."

"I'll drink to that," Chloe said.

"Me too, even though I'm only drinking water," Allye agreed.

Shrugging, Harlow picked up her margarita off the nearby table. "Me three. Although I don't think Lowell will be going anywhere."

"Who's that?" Allye asked, gesturing to a woman standing in the doorway, looking around at the pool tables and patrons.

"No clue," Chloe said.

Harlow glanced over. The woman was tall and had beautiful, long, red hair. She had freckles on her nose and cheeks, and if Harlow had to guess, she would say her eyes were probably green. She wore scuffed and dirty jeans, a pair of black combat boots on her feet, and a long-sleeve black T-shirt.

She wasn't someone Harlow would want to get into a tiff with. She looked like she could wipe the floor with anyone, man or woman.

All four women watched as the newcomer noticed their men sitting at the table in the corner—and immediately headed in that direction.

"She looks like she can definitely take care of herself," Harlow muttered.

"You think?" Morgan asked. "Sometimes the women who look the most competent from the outside are the ones who are the most broken inside."

Everyone was silent as they watched the unknown woman stop about five feet away from the table where the Mountain Mercenaries were talking.

~

"Got a text from Rex," Gray said.

"When do we leave?" Ball asked.

Gray shook his head. "Not quite yet. He said something about more research being needed before we head out. Oh . . . and it looks like we might have a civilian tagging along on this one."

"What? No. Fuck no!" Ball exclaimed.

"What's crawled up your ass and died?" Arrow asked. "We've been on missions with civilians."

"It's bad enough that we'll be a man down because of Black's knee. But to have to babysit some soldier wannabe sucks. You all know it. We've done it before."

"You haven't even heard what the case is yet," Meat said. "Why don't you just chill?"

Ball sighed and ran a hand through his hair. He knew he was being an asshole, but . . . seeing all his friends paired up, knowing they were happy and content, was killing him.

Once upon a time, he'd thought he'd found a woman to spend the rest of his life with as well. But it had all been a lie. She'd cared more about her job and covering up her mistakes than owning up to them. And ultimately, her mistakes had gotten him discharged from the Coast Guard, a job he loved. She hadn't cared, had only been worried about her *own* ass.

He'd learned a lot about what love was and wasn't from her.

"Fine. I'll bite," he grumbled. "What's the case?"

Gray cleared his throat. "I don't know all the details, but in a nutshell, a fifteen-year-old girl disappeared from her home in Los Angeles. She was living with her grandparents because her parents are druggies, and she didn't want anything to do with them anymore. Her older sister was worried when the grandparents called and told her they hadn't seen her sister in a couple of days. They'd already contacted the police, who assumed she was a typical runaway and hadn't been immediately worried. The sister dropped everything and went to Los Angeles to try to find her."

"Where's the sister live?" Meat asked.

"Here, actually. Colorado Springs," Gray said.

"How old is she?" Ro asked.

"Thirty-four."

"Why didn't the teenager come and live with the sister?" Arrow asked.

"Don't know," Gray admitted. "But anyway, the sister found out enough to make her extremely nervous, and apparently she knows of Rex. She got in touch with him, and he promised to help her."

"This doesn't make sense," Ball complained. "We don't have nearly enough detail to be able to do anything at this point. Why didn't the sister take the kid? I don't like this. Not one bit. Is this Rex being too distracted again to get us all the intel we need?"

"Ball, you—"

"No, seriously. And let me guess, this middle-aged sister, who's probably some rich housewife, sweet-talked Rex into letting her tag along? I mean, Rex wouldn't normally do that to us, but after what happened recently, I'm just not sure anymore. Unless we're going to head to the mall to pick up this teenager, there's no way a civilian isn't going to be in the way."

Ball was on a roll, and he ignored the way his friends were looking at him with their eyes all big and shit. They'd always said exactly what they thought, and just because some of them were now pussy-whipped didn't mean *he* was going to change.

"You know I have no problem doing what it takes to rescue women and kids in danger. Hell, we've all made it our life's mission. But I've already been in a situation where a woman fucked up both the mission *and* my life. I'm not keen on doing it again."

"Maybe you should stop talking now," Ro said with a small smirk on his face.

"No. Get Rex on the phone, Gray," Ball ordered. "We need more details. And I'm telling him there's no way in hell I'm letting a chick who didn't care enough to let her little sister live with her when she needed help tag along like a lost fucking puppy."

Silence met his outburst.

Ball knew he'd gone too far, but the night had been tough for him.

When no one said a word, but Black widened his eyes comically and nodded, as if pointing with his head toward something behind him, Ball swallowed hard.

"She's standing behind me, isn't she?" he asked his friends.

"Yup," Gray said with a smirk.

"Fuck," Ball muttered his breath.

"Hi. My name is Everly Adams. I'm the not-so-rich, middle-aged sister your friend was so eloquently talking about. My half sister, Elise McLane, is deaf. She wasn't living with me because she was already attending one of the best schools for the deaf out in Los Angeles. I currently work for the Colorado Springs Police Department as an investigator and SWAT officer. I can hold my own in the city, the middle of a jungle, and anywhere else you can think of. And I'm coming with you because Rex said none of you yahoos know sign language and can't actually talk to Elise when you find her."

Ball clenched his teeth together, hard, and turned to apologize. He still didn't want the woman going with them on a mission, no matter that she was a cop.

He opened his mouth to tell her that—but his words got stuck in his throat when he saw Everly Adams for the first time.

She was fucking beautiful. Red hair that seemed to go on for miles. Adorable freckles on her face. Jeans that molded to her well-defined, muscular legs.

But it was her dark-green eyes that rendered Ball completely speechless. They were shooting fire—at *him*. She was definitely pissed. But that wasn't what made him immediately change his mind about having her accompany them to find her sister.

It was the level of pain in those eyes.

This was a woman who hadn't led an easy life. She'd had to fight and claw for everything she wanted.

How he knew that, Ball had no idea, but the emotion in her eyes made him sorry he'd said all the horrible things he had. He'd never met her before, didn't know her story.

But he would.

Pushing back his chair slowly, Ball stood. He was taller than her by around half a foot, but then again, he was taller than most people. He estimated she was around five-ten or so. Tall for a woman, a perfect height for him. He held out his hand.

"I'm Kannon Black. My friends call me Ball."

She looked down at his hand with disinterest and crossed her arms over her chest, refusing to take it.

Ball sighed. He'd fucked up. And he knew he had a lot of groveling to do to make it up to her. He had a feeling working with Everly was going to be a challenge. It had been a long time since a woman had forced him to use his brain, not just his body.

Why he was looking forward to that idea, he had no clue.

Acknowledgments

Thank you to all of my readers in my Facebook group, Susan Stoker's Stalkers, for sharing all of your awful dates—and for letting me use them in this book. I hope you've all found your Prince Charmings, and if you haven't—don't give up! Your "Lowell" is out there!

About the Author

Photo © 2015 A&C Photography

Susan Stoker is a *New York Times*, *USA Today*, and *Wall Street Journal* bestselling author whose series include Mountain Mercenaries, Badge of Honor: Texas Heroes, SEAL of Protection, and Delta Force Heroes. Married to a retired Army noncommissioned officer, Stoker has lived all over the country—from Missouri and California to Colorado and Texas—and currently lives under the big skies of Tennessee. A true believer in happily ever after, Stoker enjoys writing novels in which romance turns to love. To learn more about the author and her work, visit her website, www.stokeraces.com, or find her on Facebook at www.facebook.com/authorsusanstoker.

Connect with Susan Online

Susan's Facebook Profile and Page

www.facebook.com/authorsstoker

www.facebook.com/authorsusanstoker

Follow Susan on Twitter

www.twitter.com/Susan_Stoker

Find Susan's Books on Goodreads

www.goodreads.com/SusanStoker

Email

Susan@StokerAces.com

Website

www.StokerAces.com